DATE			

HEIRS OF THE FIRE

ALSO BY ROBERT CULLEN

FICTION:

Soviet Sources

Cover Story

Dispatch from a Cold Country

NONFICTION:

Twilight of Empire

The Killer Department

HEIRS OF THE FIRE

ROBERT CULLEN

FAWCETT COLUMBINE

THE BALLANTINE PUBLISHING GROUP • NEW YORK

A Fawcett Columbine Book
Published by The Ballantine Publishing Group

Published in the United States by The Ballantine Publishing Group, a division of Random House, Inc., New York, and simultaneously in Canada by Random House of Canada Limited, Toronto.

http://www.randomhouse.com

Library of Congress Cataloging-in-Publication Data
Cullen, Robert, 1949–
Heirs of the fire / Robert Cullen.
p. cm.
ISBN 0-449-00025-7
I. Title.
PS3553.U297H45 1997
813'.54—dc21 97-15070

Manufactured in the United States of America

First Edition: November 1997
10 9 8 7 6 5 4 3 2 1

FOR JEAN AND HEYWARD,
WITH GRATITUDE

HEIRS OF THE FIRE

CHAPTER 1

A loudspeaker crackled, sounding like pebbles dumped on a tin roof: "Briefing in two minutes." Burke remembered yet again why he hated filling in at the White House.

He heard a muted chorus of creaks and groans creaks as the press-room regulars stirred in their chairs and groans as they realized there would be no early lid this evening.

White House reporters trod a wavy line between journalism and stenography. They recorded and transmitted whatever the president's aides deemed the message of the day. If they disliked the message, or didn't believe it, they might add a dollop of dyspeptic "analysis." But they rarely uncovered, as opposed to being fed, anything that could be defined as news. And their knowledge that they were being used added a faint, constant, and miasmic air of resentment to the room in which they worked.

In return for doing this dirty job, they got to filch an occasional pen from Air Force One and tell people at cocktail parties that they covered the White House.

Burke had given up cocktail parties and needed no pens. He was substituting for the *Tribune*'s regular reporter on the beat, a woman named Susanne Braithwaite. Braithwaite had taken three weeks off to have a baby. Subbing for her would give him only the satisfaction of helping someone else enjoy a newborn.

He got up and grabbed the wrinkled khaki suit coat off the back of his chair. A button from the right sleeve snagged on the backrest and popped off, rolling under the cubicle wall and into the adjoining territory of *The Washington Post*. He scowled as it disappeared and decided against pursuing it. The left sleeve was already missing a button. Now they would match.

He put the jacket on and slipped his tie up until it was snug against his neck. The collar felt tight. He promised himself to run on both mornings during the coming weekend.

The phone in the cubicle rang and he picked it up.

"Colin," the voice on the other end said. It was Ken Graves, his boss. "Got a request from the Living section."

"Sorry," Burke said, looking at his coat cuffs. "I'm not modeling for any fashion pictures. No matter how much they offer."

"Ralph Lauren will be crushed," Graves said, sounding less than amused. "Anyway, the Living desk got a call from a lady in Bethesda. She was shopping at Montgomery Mall last night, at Nordstrom's."

"And?"

"And half an hour before closing time, they cleared the store. Booted all the customers. She says she heard it was because Prince Qabos, the Saudi defense minister, wanted to take his family shopping."

"It's a good thing Saudi princes can only have four wives," Burke said. "Otherwise, they'd have had to close the whole mall."

"Yeah. Well, Living wants to run a little story. But they can't confirm it. Called the store, and they're not saying anything. Called the Saudi embassy, and they're not saying anything, either. Called the hotels. No trace of him. Can you ask Walters, see if the White House has anything on it? Maybe he's staying at Blair House."

Burke looked at his watch and suppressed a sigh. It was 5:45. Desdemona McCoy was due for dinner at eight.

"Maybe," he said to Graves. "They've called a briefing here in a few minutes. But you should check Georgetown Hospital. Remember he had prostate surgery there a couple of years ago."

"Oh, yeah," Graves said.

"And he's still buying gifts for his wives," Burke added. "Those surgeons at Georgetown must've done a good job."

"Briefing," the loudspeaker announced.

"Gotta go, Ken," Burke said, and hung up.

He walked in a small, docile crowd moving three abreast, down a short corridor that was broken by a Palladian window that looked out onto the North Lawn, where television correspondents did their standups. The opposite wall held a bulletin board that contained old pool reports and sign-up sheets for upcoming presidential trips. A rack offered press releases announcing the routine minutiae of the executive branch. Someone had been nominated to the bench in Louisiana. The president had signed a proclamation naming July National Breast Cancer Awareness Month.

"Whatever happened to getting an early lid on Fridays?" grumbled someone a few yards ahead of him.

"Baa," someone else said, and Burke could not tell whether the comment was meant to convey disgust or the idea that they were all sheep.

They emerged into a room that resembled a small theater, except that in place of a silver screen there was a stage with a blue curtain backdrop, a White House seal, and a lectern.

Burke slid into the third-row seat that bore a small brass plaque designating it for the use of the *Tribune*. In the old days, in the Watergate era, fights had erupted over seats at critical briefings. The brass plaques had been the solution.

The press corps waited expectantly, chattering and telling jokes, like children at a school assembly. Burke looked at his watch: 5:52. If they were going to call a briefing, they ought at least to start it on time.

At that moment Maynard Walters strode through a door at the front of the room, a door that led into the West Wing offices of the president and his staff. He was a tall, sepulchrally thin and pallid man with a shining, bald dome and a nose like a hawk's beak. He wore a baggy gray suit and dull black, wing-tipped shoes. He was the physical opposite of conventionally telegenic, which seemed perversely to explain his success as White House press secretary. Viewers felt instinctively that anyone as homely as Maynard Walters must be telling the truth.

He stepped to the lectern and opened his briefing book, a loose-leaf binder covered in black plastic. It contained all the answers the bureaucracy had prepared for him to give to anticipated questions. Part of Walters's talent lay in his ability to appear as if he were disgorging them spontaneously.

"The president," he intoned, "had a few minor changes in his afternoon schedule. At three o'clock, he met with the secretary of transportation to review the needs of the nation's air-traffic-control system in light of last week's crash in Chicago. We are considering a supplemental appropriation request and will be consulting with the congressional leadership. At 6:15 he'll be visiting with the NCAA women's basketball champions from the University of Southern California in the Rose Garden. Open coverage."

A few reporters groaned softly. That was why they'd be working late—so Detwiler could get his face on the West Coast evening newscasts.

"Detwiler's going to advise them to have safe sex—only with Trojans." The reporter next to Burke snickered softly.

Burke grimaced. He'd heard better Trojan jokes when he was a sophomore at Berkeley.

"Questions," said Walters.

Eleanora Richardson of International Press Service stood up. Had she been carrying a few shopping bags, she could have changed places with one of the homeless women who slept across the street in Lafayette Park. But she was the doyenne of the White House press corps.

"There's a report," she said, declining to enter the name of the Associated Press into the White House record, "that the attorney general is going to ask for a special prosecutor to investigate whether Secretary Johnstone's friends were illegally favored in the awarding—"

Flustered, she stopped for a second, reached into her purse, and pulled out the AP copy.

"—of contracts for labor retraining programs," she concluded. "Is that true?"

Walters nodded briefly and paused, as if pondering his response.

"We've seen that report, Elena," he said. "You'd have to ask the Justice Department about it. The president has not been involved in that question."

A reporter from one of the local Washington television stations popped up.

"Maynard, does the president still have confidence in Secretary Johnstone?" he demanded.

"Of course," Walters said mildly.

There were four more questions about Secretary Johnstone and his future in the government. Walters declined to fire him on the spot.

Burke waited until that vein had been exhausted. Then there was a round of questioning about the president's plans to spend the last week of July in Pebble Beach, playing golf.

Once that had been settled, Burke raised his hand.

"Mr. Walters," he said. "Is Prince Qabos of Saudi Arabia in town, and has the president seen him?"

Walters looked, for a fleeting moment, as if he'd bitten into something furry in a carton of Chinese food. Then he recovered his bland aplomb.

"I'll take that question," he said.

Burke blinked. Walters's response, technically, meant that he had no information about Prince Qabos. "Taking" the question meant that he would endeavor to find some.

But Walters, Burke knew, had access to the president's private schedule. If Qabos hadn't been on it, Walters would simply have said so.

That meant there was at least a strong likelihood that Qabos had met the president, that the White House hadn't announced it, and that Walters wanted to check with his superiors before deciding what to say about it.

He could, of course, simply have lied and said there had been no meeting. But Walters was immensely proud of his ability to deceive the press without actually lying to them. He considered himself the master of the verbal hip fake. He would flat lie only if someone at a higher pay grade ordered him to.

Walters no-commented a question from Reuters about plans to sell more of the Strategic Petroleum Reserve and Burke glanced at his watch again. Nearly six.

He pushed as unobtrusively as he could to the aisle, and headed back toward the *Tribune* cubicle. Behind him, he heard an NBC reporter ask whether the president would veto a bill that was poised for passage in the Senate, restoring a federal speed limit of seventy miles an hour. The bill was a reaction to the proliferation of racing on Interstate 90 in Montana, where the state legislature had abolished the speed limit.

"The president hasn't decided on that," Walters said.

Washington's clearinghouse for gossip and information on the Middle East was a think tank called the American Institute for Arab-Israeli Studies. It was a front for the Israel lobby, but a relatively honest front. It was influential because it tried to provide a pound of information with every ounce of propaganda. Burke picked up the phone in his cubicle, punched in the number, and asked for Steve Katz.

"Qabos?" Katz said when Burke had asked his question. "I'm not surprised."

"Why not?"

"The PAC-3."

"The antimissile missile?"

"Yeah. Like the Patriot. Only it works, unlike the Patriot. The Saudis have been desperate for it ever since the Chinese sold IRBMs to Iran."

Burke didn't follow weapons procurement very closely; that was the Pentagon reporter's job. But he knew enough to know that the PAC-3 was not supposed to be exported.

"I thought it was too new for foreign sales," he said.

"That's the policy," Katz said. "Even the Israelis haven't been able to buy it."

"But you think the Saudis might be able to get it? To protect the oil fields?"

"Why else would Qabos be in town?"

"Medical treatment?"

"Oh, horseshit," Katz said. "He's been deflowering sixteen-year-olds for the past year."

"But if they were going to sell it to the Saudis, why keep it a secret? Don't they have to let the Hill know when they sell something that expensive?"

"They can't keep it secret forever," Katz said. "But that sale is going to piss off a lot of people. It destroys Israel's qualitative edge. It neutralizes the Jericho missile. And you can bet if the Saudis get it, the Egyptians will be next. Peace treaties are fine, but Israel needs a deterrent."

"But still, why keep it secret?"

"Because they want Lockheed to have time to subcontract enough of the PAC-3 components to spread the wealth to key states and congressional districts. Once that's done, there won't be enough votes on the Hill to stop it."

"But none of your friends have actually seen Qabos."

"Nope," Katz said. "But keep looking. You'll find someone who has."

The other phone in the cubicle started to ring. Burke said good-bye to Katz and picked it up. It was Maynard Walters.

Burke looked at his watch: 6:07. Walters was certainly being prompt.

"So, Colin, how'd you hear about Qabos?"

Burke saw no reason to prevaricate. He told Walters the truth.

"I have something for you on background," Walters said.

"Okay," Burke agreed.

It meant that whatever Walters said would be attributed not to him but to a White House source.

"Well, your lady in Bethesda was right. Qabos is in town for a couple of days. He's here for medical reasons. You know that story. It's a sensitive subject; that's why we're not on the record and why the visit is private. This morning, he did pay a courtesy call on the president."

That much, Burke figured, Walters had decided the *Tribune* would have found out anyway. So he might as well tell them and get credit for candor.

"How long'd they meet?"

"I don't know precisely. Not too long."

"What'd they talk about?"

"I haven't got any details on that. The usual rundown of the U.S.–Saudi relationship."

"PAC-3 missiles?"

There was a slight hesitation on the other end.

"I haven't got anything on that," Walters said.

"Are you selling them the PAC-3?"

"We haven't sold the PAC-3 to anyone," Walters said.

"I know you haven't; the question is, will you? Saying you haven't could just mean that the check hasn't cleared yet," Burke responded.

He was irritated. He accepted the fact that Walters's job, on occasion, was to mislead him. He wanted Walters to know that he ought to be trying to do it a little more imaginatively.

"You know our policy," Walters said, with a note of ritual determination in his voice. "We haven't sold the PAC-3 to anyone."

That was clearly all he was going to say. Burke thanked him and hung up. He looked at his watch again: 6:10. Somehow, he needed to nail down this story and get out of the White House by seven o'clock. That would give him time to buy some food, get home, shovel the debris into a closet, and cook a respectable meal by eight. It was going to be tight.

He told himself it didn't matter whether he created the proper ambience this evening, that their relationship was more substantial than that. Then he told himself he would be foolish to be complacent about her. He sighed.

Burke thought, almost involuntarily, of calling McCoy. It would be the most natural thing in the world. Say something sweet. Confirm their date. Tell her he might be running a little late. Tell her it was because of this late-breaking story he was chasing. See what she said. It would be, he thought, in her interests to help him. And besides, he loved the sound of her voice on the phone—low and alluring and rich in knowing undertones.

He pushed the thought out of his mind. Doing that would violate the first rule of their relationship: he had to act at all times as if he didn't know what she did for a living.

"This is the last call for coverage of the president's meeting with the University of Southern California women's basketball champions," the loudspeaker said.

Henry Hoffman, Burke remembered, had done his graduate work at Southern Cal. He would no doubt attend part of this ceremony. Hoffman, unlike some of his predecessors, believed that the national security adviser should keep his name out of the papers. He let the State Department handle most interviews and briefings. But maybe, Burke thought, he could get a wink or a nod from him.

He got up and joined the gaggle of photographers and wire-service reporters who had no choice but to attend any Rose Garden ceremony. Eleanora Richardson looked at him suspiciously.

"The *Tribune*'s covering this?" she asked from under a glowering brow that had long since been plucked clean of any human hair.

"Just want to admire the flowers, Eleanora," Burke said cheerily.

A pert young woman whose father owned half the chickens in Mississippi had been detailed from Walters's office to escort the journalists. She led them through a corridor carpeted in thick, beige pile and lined with paintings of naval vessels under fire. A couple of Secret Service agents in tight blue suits looked mildly bored and mildly contemptuous as the rabble passed by, bristling with strobe lights, microphone booms, and telephoto lenses. Most White House cameramen spent none of their income on clothes or haircuts; they saved it for fishing cabins in West Virginia. As a result, the press corps for lesser Rose Garden photo ops like this one looked like a crowd of homeless men looting an electronics store.

The girl from Mississippi pushed open a French door and led them out into an evening soft as a baby's breath. The heat of the day had eased. The sun was slowly settling in the sky to their right, somewhere over the Old Executive Office Building. A pair of enormous elm trees filtered the light and gave it a dappled, golden quality. The roses, pink, white, and red, seemed to glow from within. For Washington in early July, this was rare, bearable weather.

Much of the Rose Garden was a grassy rectangle, the western border of which was a colonnade. Beyond the colonnade were the thick, blurry, bulletproof windows of the Oval Office. At the opposite end was a platform for the television cameras and an enclosure, bounded by velvet ropes, for the press.

Before the garden became a backdrop for photo events, Burke thought, it must have been pleasant for presidents to sit here on evenings like this one. Maybe Truman had been the last to do so.

He looked at his watch: 6:16.

The basketball players were clustered in the far corner of the garden and they peered curiously at the photographers filing in. They wore what Burke imagined would be their job-interview clothes, coordinated skirts and jackets and, in a few cases, pantsuits that looked as if they had been sewn at home by mothers who had long despaired of finding off-the-rack clothes for their long-legged daughters. The white girls had their hair uniformly pulled back in a bunch and secured with rubber bands. The black girls had short, straightened hair except for one, a tall, slender woman with a mop of curls that softly framed her head, and Burke thought again about McCoy.

He wondered if she would be here. She loved basketball, at least the NBA version. She'd watched from her father's knee on the night Willis Reed hobbled onto the court to defeat the Lakers in the seventh game of the '73 finals, and she had been devoted to the Knicks ever since.

But she was not, he could see, in the thin line of White House aides that straggled out of the West Wing office area and onto the grass, awaiting the president. Henry Hoffman was.

"Ladies and gentlemen," an unseen announcer said, "the President of the United States."

Peter Scott Detwiler emerged from the West Wing and stepped into the sunlight, smiling and tanned in a sharply creased blue suit. Burke wished, momentarily, that White House jock-greeting ceremonies had the same protocol status as diplomatic receptions, because at diplomatic receptions the Marine Band played "Hail to the Chief." Burke was a sucker for ruffles and flourishes. They reminded him of his childhood, when he would watch Kennedy on television and hear the band and think that the White House must be the noblest seat of government on Earth.

Detwiler walked slowly past the basketball players, shaking the hand of each and saying something personal to several of them.

Then he stepped behind a small lectern, facing the cameras.

"Until today," he said, "this White House has been graced by only one representative of the University of Southern California. That's my very capable national security adviser, Dr. Henry Hoffman, who took his Ph.D. from Southern Cal.

"However, I have reliable scouting reports that Henry can't shoot the trey, can't tell the pick-and-roll from a jelly roll, and can only go to his right."

There were some titters. Burke watched Hoffman. The adviser's thin lips curled into a smile.

"So I'm mighty glad the Women of Troy are here!"

Detwiler grinned his shockingly handsome, white grin. The basketball team and the rest of the Southern Cal delegation broke into applause, and one of the players, a short, towheaded girl, stepped out of line with an Instamatic camera and took a snapshot.

Burke sidled over to the edge of the reporters' pen closest to Hoffman while the president was trying on his burgundy-and-gold Southern Cal basketball shirt with the numeral one on the back. He waited until Hoffman's eyes wandered over the crowd. He waved circumspectly. When he had Hoffman's eye, he pulled out his notebook and pantomimed asking a question and writing down the answer. Hoffman looked the other way.

Burke looked at his watch: 6:24.

He waited impatiently while Detwiler milked the event for all the sound bites he could. As the president left, Hoffman broke from the line of aides and walked back toward the West Wing. He moved, as always, with a stiff-legged gait that gave him the appearance of a penguin heading toward the edge of an ice floe. He was not fat, just slightly pear-shaped, but endowed with almost no physical grace. He was smiling slightly. Hoffman had thin lips and puffy, florid jowls. He combed his sandy hair loosely to the side of his head and wore horn-rim glasses, bow ties, and baggy suits—tweed in the winter, seersucker in summer. The bow tie of the day was madras plaid. He looked studiously donnish, and the smile was a little incongruous.

Burke, risking the wrath of a Secret Service agent, leaned over the velvet rope and called to him. Hoffman was faced with a choice between ignoring him and being civil. Civility seemed to win out. He stopped and offered his hand. Burke took it. Hoffman, he noted, was still biting his fingernails.

"Can't keep anything a secret from you, can we?" Hoffman said affably.

I wish, Burke thought.

"Some lady just happened to call us," he said.

"Yes, but you're on top of things," Hoffman said. He seemed determined to be complimentary.

"So what about the PAC-3? Are you going to sell it to the Saudis?"

Hoffman's smile stayed fixed on his face. "Maynard mentioned you were asking about that. I'm not surprised. A lot of people around town are a bit obsessed with it."

He meant, Burke assumed, the Israelis.

"So are you going to sell it to them?"

Hoffman's eyes narrowed behind his glasses, but the lower half of his face remained friendly.

"We have no plans to."

"That's not really telling me anything."

Hoffman reached out and put his hand on Burke's elbow.

"Look, Colin, I really can't say any more about this. You understand."

"But—" Burke started to try to pose the question another way.

"Nice to see you," Hoffman said. And he was gone, striding briskly into the colonnade.

Burke watched him go for a second. He looked a bit less graceless from the rear.

He looked at his watch again: 6:28. Fifteen minutes spent on Henry Hoffman. All he had was the growing suspicion that there would be a missile sale. He had nothing to back it up. Hoffman, to the best of his knowledge, had never flatly lied to him. His refusal to answer the question, to deny that there would be a sale, could be read as an oblique confirmation. But it was nothing solid.

He went back to his cubicle in the press room. "The lid is on," the loudspeaker said, meaning there would be no more news events at the White House that day. Cameramen began stowing their equipment.

The wire-service writers banged out the brief stories they would send on Detwiler's meeting with the Women of Troy.

If the PAC-3 sale was happening, he knew, there would be an assistant secretary of something sitting somewhere in Washington and fuming about it. Burke's job was to get to that man before he went home, had a gin and tonic, and decided that this was yet another instance where the wise option was quietly to go along with a bad policy and try to effect change from within.

He looked at his watch: 6:31.

He made a rapid succession of calls, all to bureaucrats high enough on the information chain to know what was going on and low enough to be frustrated by their inability to affect it. The assistant secretary of defense for international affairs was in a meeting. Would he care to leave a message? No. The assistant secretary of the navy was gone for the day. He could call back Monday. The chairman of the Senate subcommittee on the Middle East was making a speech in Chicago, but his press secretary would be glad to call back. The press secretary for the National Security Council was handling all reporters' calls to staff members. Would Burke care to be transferred? No.

It was 6:35.

He tried the undersecretary of state, Maury Pavilecki, a man whose tenure as ambassador to Russia had overlapped with Burke's stint in Moscow. Pavilecki was not a friend, not really a source. He was at best a nodding acquaintance, a cautious foreign-service officer who considered reporters to be flies buzzing around the banquet table of diplomacy. He returned about one in four of Burke's phone calls, usually when the State Department had ordered all hands to push a particular line-of-the-day with the media. But he knew enough about Burke to know that Burke protected his sources. And he had been working mightily for the last year to keep the Israeli withdrawal from the Golan Heights on schedule. The sale would not make that Sisyphean job any easier. He might be angry.

Pavilecki got on the phone. His voice was a little gravelly. Burke told him he wanted to ask about the meeting with Qabos.

"What are the ground rules?" Pavilecki asked.

Burke discarded his normal practice of asking for on the record. The last time Pavilecki had talked on the record was probably his wedding.

"What makes you comfortable?" he replied.

"No attribution to State, or to diplomatic sources."

"Informed sources?"

"Only that."

"Okay," Burke said.

He opened a notebook and scrawled *DBG* at the top of a blank page, for "deep background."

"I'm told the administration is getting ready to sell PAC-3s to the Saudis and Qabos was in town to close the deal," Burke said.

Pavilecki was silent for a moment.

"Who tells you that?" he said.

"If I told you that, then you wouldn't really believe that I'd keep you on deep background, would you?"

Pavilecki's grunt conceded the point.

"I'm told the announcement is being delayed so that Lockheed can subcontract a few components to the right districts."

"Not entirely true," Pavilecki said.

"What is true?"

"Use your head," Pavilecki rasped. "No administration that wants to be reelected would piss off the Israelis that way."

"So why was Qabos here, then?"

"I can't tell you that."

"What can you tell me?"

Pavilecki exhaled loudly into the phone.

"What's the biggest concern you think the United States would have about selling these things?"

"That they won't work?"

"They work," Pavilecki said flatly. "At least they'll work against anything Iran or Iraq has got."

"Leak of technology?"

"I always thought you were fairly smart."

"But with the Saudis, that's not a problem? Because they hire whomever you tell 'em to to handle the missiles?"

"Right again."

"But the Israelis want to control it themselves, take it apart, and figure out how it works and how to beat it?"

"They've been known to do that in the past."

"So let me guess. Hoffman is figuring that Qabos will go back home, tell all his brothers he's got this deal. The Israelis will get wind of it. They'll decide they have to have it, but they'll agree to let U.S. contractors handle it, just like the Saudis?"

"You're a good guesser. Sounds like the kind of plan they'd hatch over there, doesn't it?" Pavilecki's contempt was clear in his voice. By "over there," Burke assumed Pavilecki meant the White House.

"But it won't work because the Israelis won't play the game," Burke said, finishing the hypothesis.

"Of course it won't work," Pavilecki snorted. "Nixon and his crowd couldn't manipulate the Israelis while Sadat was crossing the Suez Canal. And they knew something about manipulation! What makes these guys think they can do it is beyond me."

"And if the Israelis don't buy?"

"One of two things. Either the Saudi sale is blocked in Congress, or Congress forces the administration to sell the damn things to the Israelis on the Israelis' terms. No one's happy."

"So it's a firm commitment to the Saudis?"

"Supposedly," Pavilecki said. "If you write a story, maybe we'll find out."

Burke looked over his notes. Pavilecki had obviously decided that getting the story out now would alert Congress and perhaps force the administration to abort its plan. He was hardly a disinterested source. But he had never factually misled Burke before. Burke looked at his watch: 6:50. He had enough to run with.

He opened a file on the computer:

PAC-3
Ex Burke
WASHINGTON—The Detwiler administration has offered to sell PAC-3 missiles, among the most sophisticated weapons in the American arsenal, to Saudi Arabia, informed sources said Friday.

White House sources confirmed that the president met Friday with the Saudi defense minister, Prince Qabos.

The rest of the piece wrote itself. He checked out of the White House compound at 7:01.

Shrimp. She had ordered shrimp the last time they had eaten dinner together. She liked shrimp.

Burke elbowed his way next to an old man staring dubiously at a tray of mullet in the display case of the Chesapeake Seafood Company.

"Pound of the jumbos," he said, raising his voice, to a man with a dirty white smock, a crew cut, and a tattooed Harley-Davidson logo on his forearm. "Better make it a pound and a half."

She might, he thought, be hungry. One of the things he liked about her was that when she was hungry, she ate, unabashedly. It was the way she was about a lot of things. She liked her appetites. She liked satisfying them.

He paid for the shrimp and strode outside, feeling the coolness of the air as darkness fell. The setting sun left just a crescent of light atop the blank brick wall of Capitol Hill Junior High. He thought he could smell wisteria from one of the gardens tucked behind the row houses, and his body felt light and agile. He looked at the darkening sky and smiled. It was an evening full of promise.

An old black man in a plaid flannel shirt and a greasy fedora, his ankles bulging over his shoes, pushing a cart with a trash can and a broom, bent over near the curb and picked up a stray red carnation that had fallen from the table an equally old woman had set up to sell flowers.

Burke knew that the bankrupt city had no money to pay street sweepers. He imagined that the old man swept out of habit, or kindness.

"Thank you," the woman said, replacing the carnation amid the wares she was selling.

"Thank Jesus I could help," the old man said in a voice that sounded like dry paper rustling.

"Oh, I always thank Jesus," the woman replied.

Burke bought five dollars' worth of gladioli.

His part of Capitol Hill was an amalgam. A hundred years ago, it had been a neighborhood of immigrant Irish, living in row houses. Fifty years ago, it had turned into a black neighborhood as the Irish moved out. Twenty-five years ago, gentrification occurred. Whites moved back in, fixed up the old houses, and waited confidently for the neighborhood to turn into a second Georgetown and reward them with massive real-estate appreciation. Ten years ago, gentrification had run out of steam, and now the neighborhood was shared, not always amicably, by a combination of blacks and whites, congressmen and clockers, coffee bars with decaf mocha java and corner liquor stores with heavy steel mesh around their windows. It was a neighborhood where no one was quite at home, where everyone had a neighbor he could look on as someone alien. Burke liked it.

He checked his watch: 7:20. He picked up the pace, dodging cars as he crossed Pennsylvania Avenue against the light, cutting across the paved lot of an Exxon station, and into an alley. It was strewn with rubbish—old tires, a mattress, rustling brown leaves. One garage door was open, and inside, stagehands from the Shakespeare Theater downtown were spray-painting tree branches for scenery. The rest of the alley garages were shut tight, double-locked, and wreathed in concertina wire, gleaming silver in the last rays of the sun.

He emerged onto G Street between St. Henry's Episcopal Church and a restored row house with a plaque on the front wall that said John Philip Sousa had been born there in 1854. His house was across the street, a flat-faced, two-story row house with a bit of wooden filigree across the roofline, like the other row houses except that he had recently had it painted, light gray with black shutters. Burke had bought the house a dozen years ago, purchasing it from some impatient gentrifiers, and kept it all the years he was abroad.

A black man lounged on the stoop of the house next to Burke's, his Raiders cap on backward, his long legs dangling over the wrought-iron banister that separated the two houses, intruding on Burke's space. His name, Burke knew, was Rodney. His mother owned the house, and from time to time he lived there.

"Hey, man," Rodney said. "Bringing home flowers. Got a date with that sister tonight?"

Burke hesitated. He had thought no one knew of his relationship with McCoy, at least no one in his neighborhood. He felt exposed. And he wondered, for a second, if he had heard hostility in the question. Then he decided he had not.

He managed a tight smile. "Yeah," he said. "I do."

"Fine-lookin' woman," Rodney said, a small leer displaying a chipped tooth. "Fine."

"She is," Burke agreed, wondering when this man had seen her, wondering whether everyone in the neighborhood had seen her. She had been there only three times, arriving after dark and leaving at dawn. He put the key in the lock and turned it.

"I bet she be nice in bed," Rodney said.

Your lips to God's ear, Burke thought. He said nothing.

The telephone inside began to ring, and he fumbled with his keys until he had the one that opened the front door. He got to the phone on the third ring.

"Burke," he said.

"Colin." Her voice was smooth and had little bell tones in its upper register.

He could guess what she was going to say before she said it.

"I'm still stuck here," she told him.

"I'm sorry," he said, trying not to let her hear too much disappointment.

"I'm not sure when I can get away," she continued.

"Well," he said, "will there be time for me to take some other girl out for a drink before you get here?"

"Go ahead. Break my heart," she said.

"Actually," he said, "that's the farthest thing from my mind."

"That's better," she said.

"Just don't cancel," he said, stifling the urge to add the word *again* to the sentence. "I've got something special planned for tonight."

"What?"

"A surprise."

"Tell me."

"Then it won't be a surprise."

"Does it involve scented candles?"

"No, just a little Jell-O and some shackles. Disappointed?"

"Relieved. I can't stand scented candles."

He laughed. "That's what I like about you, Des. You're so romantic."

"Next to you, Burke," she said, "Henry Kissinger is romantic. I'll be there as soon as I can."

He went into the kitchen and peeled the shrimp, then boiled them and coated them in a mix of bread crumbs, butter, garlic, and red peppers. He turned on the oven and put the shrimp aside, then refilled the pot with water and started to heat it. When she arrived, he would use that water to cook some ziti to go with the shrimp.

For company, he turned on the radio. On "Fresh Air," Terry Gross was interviewing a woman who worked with refugees and AIDS patients in Zaire. He listened for ten minutes, until the conversation started to depress him, and turned it off. He wanted to maintain the buoyancy he had felt walking home, the result of the evening air, the good story he'd gotten, and the pleasant tickle of nervous anticipation. Doing it without her was like dancing alone.

He draped a cloth over the table in the dining room and arranged the gladioli on top. He added a candle, making certain it was unscented.

There would be time, he decided, to do more than throw the old newspapers and magazines into a closet, and he went to the stairs.

He paused in the stairwell. The wall was lined with snapshots in little wooden frames, pictures he had taken in Moscow during the summers when his son had visited. There was Sam, nine and slightly chubby, in front of St. Basil's. Sam, fourteen, with braces on his teeth, in front of the Lenin Mausoleum. Sam, at eighteen, taller than his father, just before his freshman year at Colorado, in front of the Russian White House. Now he was a senior, and this summer there would be no visit. He had invited Burke to fly out to San Francisco, where he had a summer internship, and spend a weekend. Burke thought that he probably would.

McCoy, on her first visit to this house, had walked up these stairs, her hand around his waist and his around hers. Then she had stopped on the stairs and studied the pictures. He remembered that he had let his hand fall to his side, as if looking at the pictures had placed a distance between them.

Burke had said, by way of identification, "my son," and she had nodded and smiled and said there was a resemblance, and they had gone upstairs to his bed. But that was the one night that he had been distracted and anxious with her.

He walked upstairs and changed the sheets on the double bed. This room, like the rest of the house, was sparely furnished: the bed, a dresser he had picked up at a yard sale, a Kazakh rug in the empty space on the floor, a couple of bookshelves for the overflow from the study downstairs, and a night table with a telephone, in case the office needed to reach him. He had lived much of his adult life in apartments that came furnished, and he was not the type to accumulate possessions.

He pulled the little jeweler's box from the corner of the sock drawer and put it in his pocket.

It was now dark outside, and he checked his watch: 8:15.

Downstairs, the water in the pot had boiled half away, and he refilled it.

The phone rang, and he strode into the study and grabbed it.

"Burke."

"Stay on the line," a machine said, "for an important call from—"

He hung up.

He felt annoyed with himself, annoyed for being frustrated. Being alone was at least tolerable when he expected to be alone. Waiting for someone was difficult.

He pulled a book from the desk against the window facing G Street. *War and Peace.* He was trying to read it in Russian, trying to keep his memory of the place and the language fresh.

Monsieur Pierre did not know whom to answer, looked all around, and smiled. His smile was not that of the other people. . . . he read, laboriously, and then tossed the book aside.

The bell rang, and he opened the door, and he forgot about Tolstoy.

Desdemona McCoy was tall, only an inch or so shy of his own height, and her body was taut, edging on thin, and energetic. She was wearing a gray suit appropriate for the Old Executive Office Building, but she managed to wear it well. It might have been the way her ivory blouse sat against her smooth, cocoa-colored skin. She had tightly curled black hair and brown eyes set wide apart. The ceiling light cast slight shadows under her cheekbones and put a golden glow in her eyes. She had a way of looking at people she did not know or did not care for, her eyes slightly closed and her mouth set, that suggested coolness and a certain disdain. But when she smiled, she was the best-looking woman in any room she was in.

He grinned at the sight of her, without having to remind himself to do it. She stepped over the threshold and into his arms, and he was content to let her be there, feeling her against him, smelling the perfume in her hair, until he remembered that the neighbors might be watching and closed the door.

"Missed you, love," she said, and he believed it. "Thanks for waiting."

"It's okay," he replied. "Delayed gratification is the cornerstone of civilization."

Smiling, she put her arm around his waist as they walked into the house. "Is it?"

"Well," he said, "that and the infield fly rule."

She smiled and stopped at the CD player he kept tucked on the lower level of an end table near the fireplace. She pressed the power and play buttons without looking at the disk inside.

Ella Fitzgerald whispered the opening bars of "Embraceable You," her voice edged in sweet melancholy. Humming, her feet moving without leaving the floor, McCoy turned to him and opened her arms.

They danced, after a fashion, her arms draped over both of his shoulders. He relished the sensation of her legs brushing against his. He leaned forward and smelled her hair, then kissed her on the neck where her hair was fine and downy, running his hands up and down her back.

She tilted her head back and kissed him, slowly and languidly, while they turned. He felt himself getting hard and dizzy, like a seventeen-year-old.

Then she pulled her head back.

"When are you going to get some music that was written after 1970?" she asked him.

He grinned. "When you stop dancing so nicely to the stuff I've got."

"I hate to be the one to break this to you, Burke," she said. "But what you do is not dancing. Copping a free feel, maybe. But not dancing."

He sighed theatrically. "I was hoping you wouldn't notice."

She kissed him again, and then said, "Not that I'm objecting."

They swayed together some more, and then she said, "That shrimp I smell?"

He smiled. "I was beginning to hope you wouldn't notice that, either."

She caressed his cheek. "Delayed gratification," she said, "is the cornerstone of civilization."

He seated her and poured her a glass of Pouilly-Fumé, her favorite wine. Though she was a light drinker, she usually had a glass at dinner and he liked to watch her drink it. It reminded him pleasantly of his own drinking days without, somehow, making him antsy for them.

He went into the kitchen, cooked the pasta, the sauce, and heated the shrimp while she contentedly watched and sipped wine, sitting on a stool behind him. They took the food to the dining room.

She ate with zest, saying little that didn't pertain directly to the shrimp.

He stopped halfway through his own shrimp, feeling the silence beginning to be palpable. Usually, she carried their conversations.

"You have a good day?"

She shook her head. "Rough day," she said.

"Sorry," he replied.

He did not press her, because this was the closest they could allow themselves to come to a discussion of her work. Desdemona McCoy was special assistant to the president for intelligence programs—the National Security Council's liaison to the CIA, the DIA, the NSA, and other agencies whose initials were more obscure. If she had told her superiors that she was involved with a reporter, they would have told her to stop. She hadn't told them. She had worked in intelligence long enough to be a realist about the counterespionage bureaucracy. They were great at writing petty rules to control the lives of loyal employees and lousy at catching the real security risks. So she made up her own rule. She would see whomever she wanted outside the office, and use her own good judgment. And her good judgment, she had made clear to Burke, required that he respect a barrier between him and what she did for a living.

"I had a good day," he said, knowing as the words left his mouth that they might be unwise, but unable to stop himself. "Got a good story."

She nodded, but the ease was gone from her face.

"That's one of the reasons I had a rough day."

"Oh," he said. "Sorry. Didn't think it would involve you."

McCoy, he had found, had a healthy disrespect for the tendency of her colleagues to stamp *secret* anything they were afraid might embarrass them. Occasionally, she had seemed to be rooting for him to pry something loose from the bureaucracy and publish it. Evidently, though, this wasn't one of those times.

"Colin," she asked, the tone of her voice rising a little and hardening. "I respect your ability to cut through the crap and get to a story. I sometimes even admire it. But I also sometimes wish you thought a little more about the consequences of what you write. I mean beyond the fact that you'll have your name on the front page tomorrow."

"I do," he said, hurt.

"Well then, how do you suggest we handle the Israelis and the Hill when they read what you're going to say about the Saudis?"

"Tell 'em the truth," he said, feeling irritated. "I think they might like it."

"We've tried that in the past," she said. "You know it doesn't work."

He slumped a little in his chair. This was an argument he had occasionally conducted at embassy dinner parties. Once in a while he even enjoyed it. But he did not want to debate it this evening.

"Let's not talk about this," he said.

She nodded, but the stiff posture of her body told him that her mood had changed. "All right. What do you want to talk about?"

"Maybe this isn't the right time," he said.

"No," she said. "What is it?"

He inhaled, groping for words. There was a formula for writing a newspaper story, a pyramidal exposition of the facts. He liked that. Under deadline pressure, unable to figure out a creative way to tell a story, he could always fall back on the formula, and often had. But there was no formula for this, at least not that he knew.

"I wanted," he said, "to talk about you and me."

She raised her eyebrows, a silent question.

Through the fabric of his pants, his right hand twitched over the bulge of the jeweler's box in his pocket. It was like a touchstone, reminding him of where he was going.

"About you and me," he repeated. "I—" He stopped. "I'm not very good at this."

He tried to read her face, but he could not. His own, he could feel, was flushed and hot.

He reached out with his left hand and took hers. He squeezed.

He might as well, he thought, just blurt it out.

"I haven't ever met anyone like you, Des. I'm happy when I'm with you."

Her eyes, which had been open and warm, got wider and stiffer.

"And I'm tired of keeping things secret. I want to be able to take you out to dinner and not worry about who sees us. I think I have to, anyway," he said, "because I've about run out of recipes."

She smiled.

"Basically," he said, taking a deep breath and pulling the little box from his pocket, "I love you, and I want you to—"

He stopped. Her eyes were plainly fearful. Then they started to glisten.

"Oh," she said. The sound came out of her mouth in a little ripple of descending tones, like the pained low notes of a good blues saxophone.

"Don't," she finally said.

Chapter 2

Burke lay in bed alone. The glow from the streetlight outside seemed harsh, and he got up to pull down the shade. The street was deserted, desolate. A few shards from a broken bottle glittered in the gutter. A low, nearly full moon cast the shadow of St. Henry's stubby spire across the street. He checked his watch: 12:30. He got back into bed and resumed berating himself.

"It's ironic," she had said, meaning that it wasn't. "A few minutes ago, I was thinking that you and I were so lucky to have each other, and . . . " She held out her hands, palms up.

He remembered a feeling of numbness settling over him, a sense of detachment, as if this were a play and he was watching someone else perform in it.

"And what?" he had managed to say, stuffing the jeweler's box back in his pocket like incriminating evidence.

"This is so sad," she'd replied. He'd withdrawn his hand, but she had reached out to take it back.

"I love you, Colin," she'd said. "And I'm flattered—flabbergasted. I didn't think you were the sort to get serious."

"Oh, no," he'd said. "I tell women I love them all the time. It's sort of a hobby."

He didn't know why he always got sarcastic when he was uncomfortable. He wished he didn't.

The hum of the air conditioner, fending off the humidity, had been the only sound for a moment. He'd smelled the butter and bread crumbs and the garlic he'd cooked with the shrimp, growing cold and slowly congealing.

"We may love each other, but it's not enough," she'd said gently.

"Be realistic. Look at today. Whom do you think Hoffman would blame for leaking your story if he knew we were together? I could get in trouble just because I haven't told them I've been seeing you."

He had thought that out and he had an answer ready.

"You could quit the Agency," he'd said.

"*I* could quit," she'd said, but it was not an affirmation. From the tone of her voice he realized that he had stepped ankle-deep in trouble.

But he'd kept going.

"Why not?" he'd said. "You wouldn't have any trouble finding a good job somewhere."

"Colin, don't you see?" she'd said. "This *is* my good job. If I use it right, yes, it can be a springboard to even better things. But not if I quit after six months."

"I think you could walk out onto the street tomorrow and get ten job offers," he'd said.

Her brown eyes had narrowed, and her lips had compressed to a thin line. "I'm flattered. But why don't *you* quit?"

"And do what?" he'd said. "Reporting is what I do. And you don't know how much trouble I had getting this job after I left *America Weekly*."

She had started to say something, paused, and then shook her head.

"What?"

"I almost said you could get a job in some department as a press spokesman. But you wouldn't, would you?"

He had shaken his head. "Not that they'd have me. I'm not exactly the spokesman type."

She had smiled, but only with her lips. Her eyes remained sad.

"Colin, it's just—there's another thing. I've never told you this; there hasn't been a reason, you know? But my mother left college before she got her degree. She married my father. He was the big football hero."

"You mentioned that he played for the Jets for a couple of years."

"Got the bonus and then blew out his knee. Well, my father—he screws around. I think he always has. I found out about it when I was fourteen. I saw him driving down the main street in Iselin with another woman in his car.

"And then I'd start noticing that he'd be gone a lot on weeknights, maybe all weekend to a 'convention.' My mother was miserable and angry, but what could she do? She didn't have much to fall back on. She had to go back to school and get her teaching degree. And I made up my mind that I would be independent before I got married. That I would never depend on any man."

"But you have a degree and a job—" he'd said.

"But in another couple of years, with this NSC experience, I can leave and walk into something really good."

"And then you'll consider a husband," he said.

"That's the plan," she'd said.

"Plan?"

She'd smiled ruefully.

"The plan is that in a few years I'll be set, and then I can look for the right man to marry."

"And until then, you just mess around with Mr. Wrong?"

Her eyes had started to spill over.

"Damn you!" she'd said, but without anger in her voice. "Remember you told me, back in St. Petersburg, that you had never lasted more than six months with the same woman since your divorce?"

"Yeah," he'd said grudgingly.

"Well, after I got transferred back to Washington, I thought that within a year or so, you'd get tired of me, and you'd move on. I wasn't planning on a long-term relationship. I didn't want one."

"But you love me." He'd said it wondering if she would retract it.

She bit her lip and nodded. The first tear rolled down her left cheek, catching the candlelight.

"Well, if you love me . . . "

"Oh, Colin," she'd said, almost moaning. "I won't let love run my life. There's got to be more than that."

He thought it might have been easier if she'd said she didn't love him.

"What? Younger? More money?"

"Those things don't matter," she'd said. He had seen her jaw harden as she said it, but he'd plunged ahead.

"Not so divorced? Not so white?"

The pain in her eyes had intensified.

"Well," she'd said, "since you mention it, maybe so. I don't really care that you're divorced. But I think you're naive if you don't expect that race would be a problem."

"I don't think it would be," he'd said stubbornly.

"Not a problem for you, not for me. But we haven't even gotten to the meet-the-parents stage. What do you think your relatives will say when you introduce them to this black chick who's joining the family?"

"I don't know, and I don't really care."

"You don't know," she'd exploded. "Look, it was fine when we met in Russia. Strangers in a strange land. Being American trumped being black and white. But here it's different. You just don't know because we've kept this thing secret. We're separate tribes."

She had started to cry in earnest. Her shoulders had quivered and in another second she was sobbing.

For a moment he had sat there, paralyzed. He had never known quite what to do with a woman in tears.

He'd stood up and awkwardly reached out to her, ending up in a half embrace.

"Damn," he'd said. "I'm the one who should be crying."

She had giggled a little at that, the laughter mixing with the tears for a moment, and then she'd wiped her tears. "Why couldn't you have been the person you seemed to be?" she'd asked him.

"What do you mean?"

"You know. Mr. Six-months-and-gone."

"I'm beginning to remember why I was that way," he'd said.

She wiped her eyes again, and as she did, her hand had brushed against the bulge in his pants made by the jeweler's box.

"God," she'd said, almost shuddering. "That is what I think it is, isn't it?"

"Well, considering the circumstances, it's not likely to be that I'm just glad to see you," he'd replied.

She had pushed away. "Don't show it to me," she'd said. "I couldn't stand it."

She'd stood up, taken his face in her hands, and said, "Please believe me. I never expected this from you."

Then she'd kissed him, quickly, briefly, with finality.

"I'm going," she'd said, "while I can still think with my head. I'm so, so sorry, Colin."

That was the time, he thought, when he should have said something charming and persuasive.

But he hadn't. He had stood there, shoulders slumped, silently telling himself he would not beg. He had watched her let herself out the door, then moved to the window and almost furtively watched to make sure she got to her car. She drove a Mercedes sports convertible and he worried about the kind of attention the car might attract from people who didn't know she'd bought it used.

Then he'd walked back to the dining room, taken her glass and the open wine bottle, and poured their contents deliberately down the sink. The smell of alcohol had wafted up from the disposer, mixed with the smell of rotting shrimp shells.

He'd gone into his study and picked up a book, reading intently until his eyes started to hurt. Then he'd gone to bed. He had not slept.

He tried to remember the name of the book, and couldn't.

He dozed.

The phone beside his bed jerked him awake. He thought it must be McCoy, and the thought of talking to her sent adrenaline gushing through his system. He grabbed, spastically, for the phone and knocked it off the night table. Cursing, he groped on the floor with one hand and found the cord. He pulled on the cord until he had the receiver in hand, and he jerked it to his mouth, hoping she was still on the line.

"Des?" he said.

He heard only a low, crackling hum.

"Shit," he muttered.

"Mr. Burke?" a man's voice said, just before Burke could hang up.

Burke blinked and exhaled. It was a male voice, and though the connection was bad, he could tell it was not a voice that had spoken its first words in English. He gave his *r*'s a guttural roll, and he pronounced Burke's name as if it were spelled *Boork*.

"Yeah. Who's this?"

"My name is Habib. I would like to meet with you."

"What's it about?"

"I cannot speak of it over the telephone."

Burke wished he had a nickel for every anonymous caller who wanted to speak to him about a matter that was too sensitive to discuss over the phone. Almost invariably, their stories turned out to be too trivial to interest anyone with the wherewithal to tap Burke's phone.

He pressed his head back into the pillow.

"Why don't you try the *Post*? They've got a lot of reporters with time on their hands."

"I am a friend of Janet Kane."

Burke sat up in bed.

"Now, there's a name to conjure with," he said.

"She hoped you would remember her."

"She was always modest," Burke replied. "Where is she? How is she?"

"She needs your help, Mr. Burke," the man said. His accent, Burke could now tell, was Middle Eastern, probably Arabic. He spoke in a constantly rising inflection, emphasizing the last word in every sentence, clipping off his *l*'s.

"How?"

"I cannot discuss that over the telephone," Habib repeated.

"Oh, yeah. I forgot. Well, where are you? Where should we get together?"

"I am in Toronto," the man said. "I will be arriving at Dulles at eight-fifteen this morning on Air Canada flight 735. You can meet this flight?"

"I can."

"Please be at the customs exit," Habib said. "I will recognize you."

The connection was severed.

He hung up the phone and lay flat on his back, staring at the ceiling cracks, thinking about Janet Kane and Desdemona McCoy and ruptured relationships.

He had a lot of experience with them. Most of the time he was able to forget the women who passed out of his life. But there were a few he could not get over easily. Their images periodically came to him, unbidden, and he would find himself thinking about them, wondering where they were and what their lives had become. On rare occasions, he would go so far as to track one of them down, find out where she was living and with whom and what she was doing, and think for a while about sending her a letter. Then he would think better of it and the moment would pass.

Janet Kane, whom he had not seen in more than twenty years,

was one of the women whose faces came back to him. Desdemona McCoy, he suspected, would be another. But her image would be stronger and come more often. He was tired of living his life that way, in the past.

Then he wondered how Habib knew what he looked like.

It was a long time before he closed his eyes.

CHAPTER 3

The phone rang in McCoy's apartment, and Burke silently counted. Three rings. Four. Her answering machine clicked on, but he put the phone down. He disliked talking to machines and he couldn't risk it in this situation, even though he was calling from a pay phone.

He looked at his watch: 8:10. Either she was not answering the phone, or she had gone to work already. Nine chances out of ten, it was work. Like everyone he had ever known who was employed by the White House, McCoy seemed to believe that the fate of the world depended directly on the number of hours she put in.

He stuck another quarter in the phone and dialed her office number, hoping he could catch her there before her secretary arrived. But the secretary answered. He identified himself.

"Is this the Colin Burke who works for the *Tribune*?" the secretary asked. Her voice had the warmth of a loan officer's.

No, he thought, it's the Colin Burke who got shot down by your boss.

"Yes," he said.

"Well, then let me connect you to the press office," she replied.

This was the White House rule. Calls from reporters were supposed to be routed through the press office. If the press office deemed it prudent to answer, a call might be switched back. The press office, Burke knew, almost never deemed it appropriate to connect reporters to NSC staff members who dealt with intelligence.

"That's okay," he said, and hung up. Calling her had probably been a bad idea anyway. He walked down the concourse to the customs-area exit.

* * *

Burke spotted Habib before Habib spotted him. In a throng of fair-haired, clean-shaven Canadians, he was the only man with black hair and a trim goatee.

He was short and double-chinned, perhaps fat, but his body looked almost sleek in a navy blue, double-breasted, pin-striped suit that bore the crisp lines of London tailoring. He carried a matching garment bag and briefcase of tooled brown leather; they looked Italian, privately made. Habib limped, favoring his right leg. And he was holding a torn piece of glossy magazine paper in his right hand, peering alternately at the paper and into the cluster of people standing outside the door to the customs area.

Burke stepped forward.

"Mr. Habib?" he said.

The man's pensive face relaxed slightly. "Habib," he said. "Habib is my given name."

He set his bags down and offered his left hand. Burke looked down and saw that the middle three fingers of his right hand were missing, giving him a hand like a prehensile claw. Habib was holding the paper between his fifth finger and his thumb.

Burke shook the left hand, feeling the awkwardness that always attended a first encounter with a physical deformity. As always, he tried unsuccessfully to pretend he hadn't noticed.

"You are more handsome than your picture, Mr. Burke," Habib said.

"Picture?"

Habib extended the piece of glossy paper in his right hand, and Burke saw that it was a clipping from an old issue of *America Weekly*. It was the column the editor wrote on one of the first pages with a flattering little profile of one of the magazine's staffers. In this case, the staffer was Burke. The clipping was six years old. It contained his picture, taken in front of St. Basil's in Moscow, and it was about the cover story he had written on the failed *putsch* of August 1991.

But Burke did not reread the encomiums to his resourcefulness the blurb contained. A handwritten note in blue ink, flowing through the margin, arrested his attention:

Colin,
I trust you can help me.
Janet

He recognized the handwriting. It hadn't changed since high school, and he realized that she must have clipped the article when it appeared and saved it.

"You know her?" he asked Habib.

Habib smiled. "Yes. She is the wife of a close friend of mine."

Burke smiled wryly. He was formally pleased that she was married and he formally hoped it was a happy marriage. But the image of Janet as someone's wife was not quite as soothing to his sore ego as the fleeting thought of a lonely woman saving his picture and regretting what might have been if she had only been wise enough.

"How long has she been married?"

Habib paused and reflected. "Eighteen years, I believe."

"Where is she?"

Habib gestured with his good hand, taking in the surroundings. "We must go somewhere a little more . . ."

"Don't tell me," Burke said. "Private."

An expression of sincere bewilderment passed over Habib's pudgy face.

"Why, yes. How did you know what I intended to say?"

"That's what they all say," Burke replied. "Come on. We'll take my car."

Habib's face registered slight shock when Burke stopped at his Mercury and opened the trunk.

"Don't worry," he said. "It runs. Just needs washing."

Habib nodded, but he still seemed dubious.

"The '85 Grand Marquis is the perfect Washington town car," Burke said. "No one would want to steal it and one more dent won't make any difference."

Silently, Habib nodded and got in on the passenger side. The door creaked as he closed it. Burke pulled out of the parking space and paid the four dollars at the exit, wondering if Habib would reach for his own wallet. He did not.

Habib's attention was directed out the back window. He had turned in his seat and was watching the traffic carefully as Burke drove onto the highway into the city.

"Don't tell me," Burke said. "You're afraid you're being followed."

"No," Habib replied. "I know I am not. I was wondering if you were."

"I doubt it," Burke snorted. "I think I paid all my bills this month."

But at Habib's request, he drove twice around the airport Hyatt before he parked.

"Coffee shop okay?"

"Yes," Habib replied.

They found an empty table with a view of the lobby. Burke ordered coffee and melon. Habib asked for a bit of tea and sounded vaguely British doing so. The waitress left.

"Okay," Burke said as soon as she was gone. "What's the matter with Janet and why all this B-movie crap?"

Habib's eyes flickered angrily.

"I'm sorry you regard it as crap, Mr. Burke. Believe me, it's not."

He pulled from the pocket of his jacket a set of worn, glossy ivory beads on a string and started running them through the fingers that remained on his right hand.

Burke no longer saw a reason to pretend to be polite.

"How'd you lose those fingers?"

Habib smiled thinly. "I didn't lose them," he said. "They were taken from me. One at a time."

"Police?"

Habib nodded.

"Sorry," Burke said. The apology covered both the loss of the fingers and his disdain for Habib's nerves.

"To answer your last question at the airport, Mr. Burke, Janet lives in Saudi Arabia. In Riyadh."

"Who's she married to?"

"To a cousin of mine and a close friend. His name is Abdulrahman Massoud."

Burke blinked. "A Saudi?"

"Of course," Habib said.

"Janet wears an *abaya*?"

Habib nodded.

"That's a little hard to imagine. The last time I saw her, she was in jeans. And she liked to drive."

"Her husband is a physician. They met while they both were studying at Columbia."

"Kids?"

"They have two. A son and a daughter."

Burke nodded and smiled. "I'll bet she's a great mother. She was—"

He stopped, unwilling to go farther in the presence of a stranger.

Janet Kane had moved into Santa Rosaria when she was sixteen and he was fifteen. A teacher had assigned her to be his lab partner in chemistry class and he had been intrigued. She seemed not to care about the things that her peers cared about. Rather than The Beatles, she hummed snatches of Cole Porter songs he had never heard. She wore her hair short and curly instead of long and straight. She had never been inside a Papagallo store.

When he was sixteen, and finally had his driver's license, he asked her out and she accepted. She had expected that he do things properly—drive up to her house, hands damp, and meet her parents. Her mother was from Bahrain and the source of Janet's dark hair and eyes. Her father was a Brit, a petroleum engineer who worked for Chevron. They lived in one of the big new houses that had replaced a walnut farm he remembered from his boyhood. The movie was Antonioni's *Blow-Up*, and she had held his hand and suggested a plausible explanation for the pantomime scene on the tennis court, and when he kissed her good night, he was thoroughly smitten.

She was at once more and less worldly than he. She had lived, for a time, in Paris, she spoke fluent French, and she preferred Degas to Monet and knew why. She could rationally analyze the causes of the Six-Day War. But she did not know which stores in Daly City sold beer to minors or how to go pool-hopping, which were things that he taught her. He was, she told him much later, the first boy she had ever kissed, and he believed her, because she had gone to a girls' school in Paris for four years before Chevron transferred her father to California. And her mother, whose name was Hadeyah, was very strict.

He took her to football games and she took him to see *Carmen* at the opera in San Francisco on a night when her parents couldn't use their tickets. He took her on picnics and she cooked a soufflé for his birthday. But she was, in the end, her mother's child, and her interpretation of her mother's rules, albeit much relaxed, still required him to keep his hands above her waist and his mouth above her collar at all times, and after a while he could not stand that. So although he was the first boy she had ever kissed and she was the first girl he had ever loved, they had broken up, and now he thought it had been his loss.

She had gone to Smith when he went to Berkeley, and the next year the Kanes moved again and she was gone from his life, if not from his mind. Twenty years had gone by since he had last heard from her—six months since he had last thought of her.

He realized he had stopped talking in the middle of a sentence, leaving his mouth open and Habib slightly puzzled. He jerked his mind back to the present.

"So why's she need my help? She in trouble?"

"No. He is."

"What kind of trouble?"

"He was arrested six days ago and charged with spying for the United States."

Burke blinked. "Was he?"

"Not really."

Burke scratched his chin.

"So why doesn't the U.S. embassy help?"

"So far, she has seen no evidence that they want to. She is afraid to approach the embassy herself because it would be used as evidence that her husband worked for the Americans."

He began to understand.

"So she wants me to write a story about it to put pressure on our government to do something."

"Yes. Abdulrahman Massoud did not sell out his country. He is a democrat. He helped the CIA because he believed that when the time came, the CIA would help us to set aside the Saud family and establish a democracy."

"Sounds pretty naive to me."

Habib almost imperceptibly shrugged. "Perhaps."

"And who is 'us'? Whom do you represent?"

The waitress arrived with a carafe of coffee, a pot of tea, and Burke's melon.

Habib slowly and deliberately poured his tea, then added enough cream to make it the color of caramel and enough sugar to make it taste like it.

"Do I," Burke asked, "detect a hint of Brit in you?"

Habib smiled. "I live in Kent, Mr. Burke. I have my degree in politics from Cambridge."

"But you called from Toronto."

"Because there was a reasonable chance my call wouldn't be monitored from there."

Burke nodded. He looked at his melon. It had the semiglazed look of fruit left several days past ripeness. He poured some coffee and left it black. He tried to pick up the thread of his questioning.

"And the name?"

"We are a group that has no name, Mr. Burke. You have been to Saudi Arabia?"

"A couple of times, when I was covering the State Department. Flew in with the secretary of state. Saw the king. Went to a banquet. Flew out."

Habib nodded and sipped his tea. He added still more sugar. "You saw the veneer."

"Of course," Burke said.

"Under that veneer, Saudi Arabia is not a happy country," Habib went on.

The women were covered from head to toe in black, it was 110 degrees outside, and beer was prohibited, Burke thought. Who expected happy?

"So I've heard," he said. "Why doesn't your group have a name?"

"It might attract attention we cannot afford," Habib replied. "We are a group of people who would like to see change. Radical change. Some of us have been exiled. Some of us are working inside the kingdom."

"Fundamentalists?" He didn't imagine Janet Kane as a fundamentalist. But then, he hadn't imagined her married to a Saudi and living in Riyadh.

Habib looked pained. "Now that there are no communists," he said, "you Americans demonize Muslims."

"Some of them do a pretty good job of demonizing themselves," Burke responded.

"We are Muslims," Habib said. "But we are not the Ikhwan, if that's what you mean."

"The Ikhwan?"

"The Wahhabi warriors who rode with King Abdul-Aziz years ago. They are fundamentalists."

"And they still exist?"

Habib shrugged. "Their sons and grandsons. We are against them."

Burke did not want to get into a detailed discussion of Saudi internal politics.

"I'd like to help Janet," he said. "But I'm not sure I can. It could be very hard to get anyone in Washington to confirm that this man Massoud has been arrested, let alone that he was working for the CIA."

He left unspoken the fact that he could not simply take Habib's word on such a story.

"Of course. You must come to Saudi Arabia. Witness the trial," Habib said.

Burke scratched his head. "And I assume you have a way of getting me into the country and into the courtroom?"

Habib nodded. "Of course."

"The last I checked, the Saudis didn't give out journalists' visas unless you came in with the secretary of state. Or the U.S. Army. Let alone courtroom passes."

Habib, for the first time, looked pleased with himself. "We can take care of all that. You will have a visa as a business consultant. A company that belongs to a brother of mine in Riyadh."

"And if they catch me reporting instead of consulting, what? The judge is your cousin?"

Habib's face flashed annoyance, then settled back into its slightly pudgy, slightly worried state of equilibrium.

"Probably," he said, "they will expel you."

"Probably," Burke said.

He mulled it over for a few minutes, toying with his melon.

"When does the trial start?"

"We are not sure. Perhaps in two days."

"So I'd have to leave right away?"

"Tonight, if possible."

Burke set his elbows on the table and propped his chin in his hands. He thought about McCoy. He thought about Janet Kane. He thought about the story he might get. He thought about McCoy again.

"It's just not a good time," he said. "There's a personal situation I need to take care of. It's not a good time to leave town."

"You would be back in a few days."

Burke thought about McCoy. What would she think if he left town for a few days?

"If nothing is done," Habib quietly prodded him, "Janet's husband could be sentenced to death. Her family will be destroyed."

Burke decided he was right. And going to Riyadh would put off the necessity of deciding what to say to McCoy.

"If I can get my editor to approve it, I'll do it," he said.

"I will check into this hotel," Habib said. "I will await your call."

Habib permitted himself a small, satisfied smile that puffed his pudgy cheeks into the shape of macadamia nuts.

"You know, Janet said you would agree."

"Oh? What else did she say?"

Habib looked intently for a second at the little glass of sugar packets on the table in front of him.

"She said you would probably make some rude comments about Saudi Arabia, but that I should ignore them. I am glad you did not."

"Maybe," Burke said, "that means I'm a little smarter now than I was in high school."

"It sounds like horseshit to me," Ken Graves said.

"That's a relief," Burke replied. "For a moment there I was afraid you'd be skeptical."

They were sitting in the office of Lyle Nelson, the *Tribune*'s executive editor. Through a glass wall, they could see the early-shift reporters and editors slowly scrolling through their computer files, sipping coffee, and gazing vacantly at the newsroom ceiling.

"I mean, how do you know this is for real?" Graves went on. "Just because it comes from the girl who kissed you in the moonlight?" He grinned derisively. "I never thought you'd go romantic."

"I'm hearing that a lot, lately," Burke responded. Graves did not ask him to elaborate. "But it's a good story, regardless of the fact that I knew her—"

"In the biblical sense," Graves snorted.

Burke shook his head but ignored Graves's interjection. He could correct the record, but Graves would think what he chose to think anyway.

"The point is that if a senior Saudi is arrested and accused of working for the CIA, we ought to cover it if we can," Burke said.

Graves sighed. "I know. But dammit, we just gave early retirement to twenty-five people out there. Morale is crap. How's it going to look if we turn around and send you to Saudi Arabia—if you can actually get in?"

Burke looked at Nelson. Like everyone else in the *Tribune* newsroom, he had learned to gauge the trends in management thinking at the paper by the trends in Nelson's wardrobe.

In years when Nelson affected a professorial look, with tweed jackets and button-down shirts, *Tribune* editors tried to fill their columns with thoughtful, analytical pieces. There had been a year not long ago when Nelson had stopped wearing ties altogether, and the paper had made an awkward attempt to write stories that would appeal to people who watched MTV. For the past six months he had favored dark suits and white shirts with starched collars—the accountant look. Like the rising population of homeless men sleeping on Washington's heating grates, this was a barometer of hard times.

So Burke expected Nelson to back Graves. But Nelson surprised him.

"What do you think the story is going to say?" Nelson asked him.

I don't know what the story is going to be, Burke wanted to say. It hasn't happened yet. That's the definition of news.

Burke loathed editors who wanted to know in advance what a story would be. He could remember when editors sent reporters out and asked them that question only when they came back.

He also loathed unemployment.

"I think it'll have a lot of facets," he said, hoping that Nelson would give him a hint about a facet that might interest him.

"You know," Nelson obligingly said to Graves, "I was looking at the front page today and there was not one story where a woman was the central character."

Graves nodded defensively.

"We had the Bosnia story, as usual. We had a piece on the budget deficit. We had your PAC-3 missile story. We even had an inside-baseball piece on Russian politics! What's a woman reader supposed to find of interest there?"

Graves started to respond that women had an equal right to be interested in Bosnia, but Nelson silenced him with a wave of his hand.

"This piece Burke wants to do reminds me of a flick I saw a few years ago—*I'm Coming Out with My Children*, I think it was called. An American woman in Iran. Wore a veil. Couldn't get her kid out. Good film."

He turned to Burke.

"So do this piece," he said, "but do it as a piece on an American woman confronting an alien, sexist culture. Okay?"

"Works for me," Burke said. He saw no reason to inform Nelson that Janet was half-British and half-Bahraini.

Graves stonily nodded assent. They got up and left Nelson's office.

"Goddamn diversity consultants," Graves muttered when they had heard Nelson's door close.

"Wave of the future, Ken," Burke said. He smiled for the first time that day.

He sat at his desk and a red light was blinking. There was a message from someone named Klempfer in Senator Higgins's office who wanted to offer his boss's views for any follow-up Burke might do on the PAC-3 story. Burke could guess what they would be, and they did not much interest him. But he wrote the name and number down. Higgins was running for president.

He punched the button for his second message.

"Colin," the recording said. "It's Des. Sorry I missed you."

There was the faint recorded sound of a click. Her voice, he thought, had sounded flat and depressed.

He thought about dialing McCoy's office number and trying to bluff his way past the secretary. He decided against it. Let her keep trying to call him.

He hung up and stared at a hole in the ceiling where the *Tribune* intended to install new computer wiring. She was fading out of his life. He knew it, and he could think of nothing he could do to bring her back in.

Chapter 4

Seven hours out of Dulles and an hour from Riyadh, the man in the seat next to Burke stood up and politely pardoned himself before stepping into the aisle. He was dressed in a blue Fila warm-up suit with red trim, and when he stretched to open the overhead bin, the fabric of the jacket rode up and exposed a hairy sliver of skin. He pulled a traveling bag from the bin and walked up the aisle to the lavatory.

Burke watched him go and drowsily closed his eyes. He had been trying to sleep, with mixed success, for four hours. He squirmed and shifted in his seat, seeking a posture that would not feel cramped and dully painful. Every year, transcontinental flights seemed to take longer. He licked his lips. They were dry, and he realized he had forgotten to keep sipping water.

A strong whiff of sandalwood wafted past him. He opened his eyes and saw the backside of a woman walking up the aisle toward the other lavatory. She wore Guess jeans; he estimated that they were two sizes too small for her. Her wavy, crow-black hair hung straight down her back, almost obscuring a silk blouse with puffy sleeves and red and blue stripes. She was shod in heels so high that she teetered from side to side as she walked, and when the plane yawed slightly to the left, she had to grab the seats on either side of her for support. The bag she was carrying thudded softly in the face of the American sitting in front of Burke. She leaned down toward the man and murmured an apology. Her lips were painted a thick carmine red.

Burke dozed off for a few minutes, and when he awakened again, he thought he was dreaming. An apparition in white seemed to hover before him. It was McCoy, in a long, white gown, and he opened his mouth and started to ask her if she'd changed her mind.

He blinked his eyes, and looked again. It was his seatmate, but his attire had changed. Instead of the blue Fila warm-up suit, he was garbed in white: a long-sleeved white robe that hung down to the floor and a white *ghotra* over his head. Two plain black bands encircled his head and held the *ghotra* in place. Silently, Burke swung his knees to the left and allowed the man to pass. The man sat down and began to work at the folds of the *ghotra*, pushing and prodding, until he was satisfied with the way it framed his face.

Then the door to the other lavatory opened, and the woman emerged; or, at least, it seemed probable that it was the woman Burke had seen wobbling up the aisle in her high heels. He could not tell with certainty because every inch of the woman was obscured by a black *abaya* and a slightly thinner black veil. She looked only vaguely human, like a mannequin draped in mourning. Even her hands were hidden somewhere in the black folds. She passed slowly down the aisle, evidently peering through a sheer patch in the veil.

More Arabs were lined up in the aisle, awaiting their own turns in the lavatories. The clothing they would put on bulged out of shopping bags that dangled from their hands.

Burke looked down at his blue paisley necktie and khaki poplin suit. "Drat," he said to the Saudi next to him. "It's so hard these days to know when to wear a tie."

The man did not smile.

Ahead of him, a Saudi customs guard in an olive uniform with large, dark green epaulets and shiny, silvery buttons, pawed slowly through the baggage of a short dark man wearing a knit skullcap and a dirty brown-and-red striped smock that hung nearly to the floor. The man's bags were red vinyl, and the clothes inside were, if anything, more ragged than the clothes on his back. But the guard indolently picked through it all. He held up a pair of linen underpants to the light. He turned smocks inside out. Then he tossed them onto a pile of clothing at the end of his stainless-steel inspection bench. He said something in Arabic to the man, and the man slowly removed the sandal from his right foot. He handed it over. The guard glanced at it, holding it in his fingertips, then tossed it atop the pile of clothing. The man shuffled, hopped, keeping his bare foot off the floor, down to the end of the bench and began trying to stuff his clothes back into the valise.

The guard gestured for Burke to come forward. Burke was carrying a folding suit bag with a few clean shirts and some fresh socks and underwear on one shoulder. The other arm held a bag with his laptop computer, a couple of books, and a few yellow legal pads. He had an aluminum suitcase. Burke had spent a half hour on the airplane, carefully purging the computer's hard disk of old stories and anything else he thought might identify him as a journalist. He had left his tape recorder and his usual narrow notebooks at the office.

None of that seemed to interest the guard. "Videotapes?" he said after taking a quick initial look.

Burke shook his head. No.

The guard picked up the books Burke was carrying: *War and Peace* and Wilfred Thesiger's *Arabian Sands*. As soon as he saw that neither was printed in Arabic, he tossed them down the bench. Then he grabbed the current issue of *America Weekly*. He flipped through it, back to front, and stopped when he came to the film-review page. He held the page up to Burke's face with a stubby index finger pointing to a photo of an actress and an actor in bed. The man's body dominated the picture, and he was wearing a shirt. The woman lay behind him. Only her face and a bare arm, draped over the actor's chest, were visible.

"Harram," the guard said to Burke. He did not know what that meant, but he suspected it was not a term of approbation.

The guard ripped the page out of the magazine, crumpled it up, and tossed it into a trash can behind him.

Then he continued his examination of the magazine, but apparently found nothing else subversive in it, because he handed it back to Burke and waved him on.

"Don't feel bad," Burke said to him. "I'd read that page."

The guard looked at Burke. His eyebrows came together underneath his hat and his eyes narrowed from the shape of almonds to the shape of almond slivers. But he said nothing and waved an indifferent hand over the rest of the luggage.

Burke stuffed the books back in his shoulder bag and made his way out of the customs area, looking for the man that Habib had promised would meet him. He found himself in a terminal hall roughly the size of an airplane hangar, with a domed roof. People swirled around him, and he involuntarily began to sort them by dress and skin color: the Saudis, in their white *ghotras* and robes, their skin tinged with olive, almost always with neatly trimmed goatees and mustaches; the foreign laborers, darker-skinned, their heads covered by various kinds of caps and turbans, their dress an assortment of T-shirts and smocks and jeans and sandals; and the Westerners, pale-skinned, dressed in business suits, with, he imagined, a tinge of greed on their faces, like the greed he imagined had been on the faces of prospectors disembarking in San Francisco during the Gold Rush. People talked to one another at a decibel level midway between conversational and shouting. He thought he smelled burning frankincense in the air.

Ahead of him stood a cluster of chauffeurs, each holding a sign with someone's name on it. He saw his own name on a piece of stationery with the logo of a company called Arabian Global Communications, the same company whose name appeared on his visa. The stationery was in the hands of a short man, no more than five feet tall, in a *ghotra* that seemed to have yellowed after many washings. He wore the garment folded up in such a way that his ears and a fringe of gray hair showed.

Burke stuck out his hand and introduced himself.

The little man did not take it. Instead, he bowed, nervously and jerkily, three times and smiled, showing a few mottled brown teeth.

"Salaam alaykum," he said. "Kamal," he added, pointing to himself.

"Salaam alaykum," Burke replied, thereby exhausting about a third of his Arabic vocabulary. He also knew the words for thank you and let's go. He and Kamal, he suspected, would have brief conversations.

Kamal took his bag and they stepped out of the terminal building. The desert air was cooler than he had anticipated, perhaps seventy degrees, and he reminded himself that it was not yet dawn. But a wind was blowing, and he could feel fine bits of sand swirling around his face, coating his teeth when he opened his mouth.

Kamal scuttled off toward a row of parking spaces and produced a key from somewhere within his white robe. He opened the trunk of a blue Mercedes and then hustled in front of Burke and opened the back door.

Burke got in. The Mercedes, somewhat to his surprise, did not smell new. The upholstery was worn and wrinkled and he could see a Snickers wrapper protruding from under the driver's seat. Burke was accustomed to new cars in Saudi Arabia. Whenever the secretary of state had visited, the Saudis transported him and his delegation, and even the reporters from the back of the plane, in bright new Cadillacs.

Kamal found the entrance ramp to the airport highway and gunned the engine. The Mercedes powered up smoothly, and the desert flashed by. In the east, dawn was just arriving. Burke could see a band of golden-orange light against the flat horizon, overlaid by a white-yellow glow that extended another fifteen degrees into the night sky before it petered out from magenta, into indigo, and finally into blackness, punctuated by a few strong stars. The sky, he thought, was the only beautiful part of the desert. The rest of the landscape, still in darkness and silhouette, was lunar and alien in its harsh ugliness.

He wondered what Janet Kane looked like now, and what she would think of him. He thought about the flecks of gray in the hair around his ears, and then about how long his hair had been when he had known her. He sought out and caught a glimpse of his face in the driver's rearview mirror and he was struck by how deep the lines around his eyes had become.

What the hell, he thought. She hadn't stayed seventeen, either.

Then he shook his head, surprised yet again at the folly that he was capable of when women were involved. He had a lover, or more likely an ex-lover, at home. He didn't know how to deal with her. But he could still find time to wonder whether he would look good to a married woman whom he hadn't seen in twenty years.

Kamal jerked the Mercedes off the airport highway as they entered the outskirts of the city, and Burke's attention returned to his surroundings.

A sliver of the sun had risen above the horizon, casting a pale, gray light on the streets and buildings.

It was, he was reminded, a brown country. Brown soil, the color and texture of cinnamon, barren and dusty. Jagged brown rocks that reminded him of the rocks he had seen on broadcasts from the moon. Brown buildings, made from that same stone and soil. The surroundings, he recalled, had made the alabaster princes' palaces look garish and alien when the secretary of state had visited.

The quarter they were passing through had something the secretary's motorcades had never seen—shanties. They were hovels, jammed together on odd lots and built of whatever was available—blocks of concrete, swatches of canvas, bits of plywood scavenged from construction sites, even an occasional highway sign. They reminded him of the miserable Palestinian refugee camps of Damascus—which the Syrians, of course, had made certain every visiting

American had to pass by. In the alleys between the shanties, he could see women, completely veiled, carrying buckets and jugs of water from communal taps, already at work on their morning chores.

They crossed an intersection without slowing down and the shanty quarter ended. The leaves of palm trees protruding above thick, high brown walls signaled a different sort of neighborhood. The houses in this quarter were hidden, but he could imagine their size by the dimensions of the walls that enclosed them. They were not palaces. But they were close. If Riyadh had had a Georgetown, he thought, this would be it. The street was lined with parked cars. He had counted two Bentleys and three Land Rovers when Kamal stopped the Mercedes.

Before the chauffeur could come around and open the door, Burke was out of the car. Slowly, he turned and began taking in the details of the neighborhood. But before he could see much, Kamal was at his sleeve, half nudging and half dragging him toward a gate. Burke stepped through it, hearing the driver close it quickly behind him. He had the impression that Kamal's instructions had been to get him off the street and behind this wall as quickly as possible.

He stood in a small car park. To his left was a playground, with a soccer goal, a basketball hoop, and a swing set. A few palms and cedars grew from carefully delineated beds, and in the center of the open space was a fountain covered in ceramic tiles of iridescent aquamarine, half-full of still water. To the right stood houses, six of them, facing one another across a median of sidewalk and flower beds and lampposts. It looked like a very small village square. He heard a drone, and recognized the sound of air-conditioning condensers, one of which he could see around the side of the first house to his right.

The houses seemed to be of different ages. The two closest to him were built of gypsum and cement, with recessed, wooden doorways and protruding second stories. The windows of the upper stories were made, he guessed, of cedar. Farther up the path, the houses were clearly newer, with big glass windows and louvered shades. He saw a little boy in pajamas standing in front of the farthest house, looking at him, curious and silent.

Behind him, Kamal pulled the Mercedes into the car park, setting it under a tin-roofed canopy that seemed designed to shelter it from the sun. Then he plucked at Burke's sleeve, leading him toward the door of one of the older houses. He opened it without a key and they stepped into a large, open room that Burke at first glance thought was totally unfurnished. Then his eyes adjusted to the light that was still filtering only dimly through the gauzy white curtains on the opposite wall. The floors of the room were covered with carpets, carpets the color of rubies and sapphires, deep rich reds and blues. There were a few low tables, and there were pillows scattered around the room's perimeter.

Kamal gestured toward Burke's feet and said something Burke could not understand. Burke looked down. He didn't seem to be standing on anything but a marble floor in an open antechamber to the big room, where the floors were rough white marble.

Then Kamal pantomimed removing his sandals, and Burke understood. He slipped out of his shoes. Kamal smiled, satisfied, and led him forward over the carpet to one of the low tables, where a silver pot stood next to a single china cup and saucer.

Kamal gestured for Burke to sit down, and Burke looked around. There were no chairs. He piled a few pillows atop one another and perched, uneasily.

The little man wrapped his hands around the silver pot for a moment. Then he took it by the handle and, holding it eighteen inches over the table, directed a steaming stream of brown liquid into the cup. Not a drop was spilled. Burke picked up the cup and sipped. It tasted of cardamom.

He held the cup close to his face and the smell of the spice enveloped him. He thought, suddenly, of the women in the plane, changing into their *abayas* as they neared Riyadh, and he wondered how Janet Kane could live in such a society.

He heard the sound of footsteps from the end of the room and he turned.

Janet Kane walked toward him, smiling. She looked thinner than the girl he remembered, almost haggard, and the lines around her eyes were new. But her hair was still black and tightly curled, and her eyes were dark and bright, as they had been, and she still had an air of self-possession about her, something that said she was just a little detached from whatever company she found herself in and very self-assured.

She was wearing a severe gray business suit with a high-necked, ivory blouse and plain black pumps. He was relieved that it was not an *abaya*. In the background, hanging back by the door, he could see two teenagers, a boy in a Saudi *thobe* and *ghotra* and a girl in a long-sleeved dress.

In a moment she was in front of him, and he stood there, uncertain, until she stepped into his arms and hugged him, then pulled her head back, eyes shining now, and kissed him on both cheeks.

"It's so good to see you," she said after the second kiss. Her voice had lost its faint British accent and was now completely cosmopolitan, oddly placeless. "I'm so grateful you've come."

Despite his fatigue and despite the circumstances, he found himself smiling. "You look just like I thought you would," he said. "As pretty as ever."

He stopped, thinking that the words would sound stupid under the present circumstances.

But she smiled, tightly. "Thank you, Colin."

He let her go.

"I hear you're in a bit of a jam."

She didn't reply directly. Instead, she beckoned to the children, who came forward.

"This is Mr. Burke," she said to them. "One of my oldest friends in the world. My son, Rahman. My daughter, Sarah."

Rahman had a seventeen-year-old's wispy goatee. He shook hands gravely. Sarah did not proffer her hand. She looked like her mother, only taller. She was a year or two away from growing into her height, and he guessed she was sixteen. She nodded to him and smiled shyly.

Janet took his arm and led him back toward the coffee table. She gestured toward the pillows.

"I'm sorry I can't offer you a chair to sit on," she said. "This is not my house. It belongs to my husband's late uncle. This is his family's compound."

"They all live together?"

"Parents, brothers, sisters, and their wives and husbands. The nuclear family is a very broad concept here."

She smiled slightly. "I bet you never thought I'd be the one to end up living in a commune."

He thought of his own house in Washington and it seemed to him that it would be nice to walk outside in the morning and see people you knew, perhaps even loved.

"I envy you," he said, "if you live in a compound like this."

Her face turned serious again. "I do. But I couldn't have you come there. It's being watched."

She poured more coffee for him, but he left the cup untouched and the pillows unused.

"Watched?"

"They've been out there ever since the arrest," she said. "They're quite obvious about it. They're outside this house now. But they didn't see you come in."

"Tell me in a few sentences," he said. "How'd you get from undergraduate at Smith to under surveillance in Riyadh?"

She looked away from him, toward the gauzy windows. The light from outside was getting stronger, harsher.

"I'm sorry if that's too . . ." Burke said, groping for a word.

"No, I realize it must seem bizarre to you. Sometimes it does to me," she replied. She turned around and looked at him.

"I met my husband in New York, at Columbia. I was working on my M.A. in Middle East Studies. He was in medical school. We fell in love. After he graduated, we got married and moved to Cambridge. He did his internship and residency in cardiology at Mass General. I worked on my Ph.D.

"Then we moved to London. The children were born there. He had a good practice and I was just starting to teach when he got the summons."

"Summons?"

She smiled wryly. "The call. The royal family wanted him to return and head the cardiology department at King Khaled Hospital."

"Did he have a choice?"

She shrugged. "Not really. The royal family had paid for his education. If he had refused, it would have been hard for his father and brothers to stay in business. They are importers. They depend on the royal family's good graces."

"And how did you feel about it?"

Again, the wry smile. "Ambivalent. I was very happy in London. But we visited here frequently. His parents live in Jedda and sometimes we would go see my mother's family in Bahrain. I was—I am—part of this world. I knew that conditions here were repressive. But I thought they were changing. I thought I might help them change. I teach, you know, in a school for girls. I don't teach them what the *ulama* wants them to hear."

"The *ulama*?"

"The clerics."

"And did your husband become a spy?"

She sighed. "Not really."

"How 'not really'?"

"After he had worked for a while at the hospital, we started to get invitations from people at the American embassy. It was a normal thing. A couple of them were people I had known in graduate school. But some of them, we could surmise, were CIA."

"Surmise?"

"Well, you know, the embassy is not so large. It's not hard to tell if you meet, say, a cultural attaché who has an intense interest in politics, or oil production. Everyone pretty much knows who they are."

"But you talked to them."

She nodded. "But you have to understand, my husband never took a penny. He did it because he believed it would be useful, in the future."

"How?"

"If you spend any time here, look around. This country is on the edge of an explosion. The royal family is corrupt beyond belief. It's not just that they siphon off half the money. There's money to go around. But they're personally, morally corrupt. They drink. A lot of them are alcoholics. But they'll cut the hands off some poor Korean guest worker they catch brewing beer. They import pornographic films by the planeload for themselves, but they let the *ulama* censor our television. They subsidize half the whores in Europe, but they insist that Saudi women cannot even drive automobiles."

Her voice was rising in intensity, and Burke could sense the disgust in her.

"Those aren't secrets," he said.

"No. But the idiots in Washington ignore it all and keep propping them up because they can't figure out a way to get along without Saudi oil."

"Okay, but I still don't get why this made your husband play ball with the CIA."

"He believes in the ultimate rationality and pragmatism of the U.S. government. He wanted them to know how badly the corruption had rotted the royal family. And that the Ikhwan isn't the only alternative."

He wanted to ask more about the political situation, but he needed to know other things more urgently.

"When does the trial start?"

"This morning." She looked at her watch. "In about ninety minutes."

"You know I'm going to have to see it, or at least see court documents or something so I know exactly what the charges are."

She nodded. "We have a way to get you in."

"How? Even if they buy the idea that I'm a communications consultant and not a reporter, they're not going to just let me sit in at an espionage trial, are they?"

She shook her head. "No. You're going as a member of the family."

"What?"

"You're going as my daughter."

He thought he had misunderstood her.

"Pardon me?"

She repeated it.

"And you were such a serious person in high school," he said.

"I am serious, Colin. It will work. Women are not allowed in the courtroom. They are not allowed anywhere where men gather. But there is a small room off the courtroom where female family members may watch a trial. Sarah and I are expected there."

He began to comprehend.

"And you think I can get in there? How?"

"Because you'll be veiled. You will wear the *abaya*. Like any good Saudi woman."

"You never take that stuff off?"

"Only in our homes. Or in special places that are reserved for women. We would be forbidden to take it off anywhere in the courthouse."

"But I'm taller than she is."

"By a couple of inches. Coming over here, she wore heels. When we leave, I'll wear the heels. The proportion will be the same."

"They don't ask for identification?"

She reached into her purse and pulled out a laminated card. It appeared to be identification of some kind, in Arabic. In the upper-right-hand corner was a picture of a veiled woman. Not even her eyes were visible.

"That's incredible," he said.

"When it comes to women, this is an incredibly backward society," she replied.

"Damn," he said, and shook his head.

"What?"

"I was thinking about my obit. The last paragraph's going to read, 'Just before his execution, he became a transvestite.' "

He turned in the backseat of the car, conscious of the way the black silk folds of the *abaya* felt against his clothing, of the way they bunched between his pants and the slippery leather of the car seat. He peered through the black cheesecloth that covered his face at the equally shrouded figure of Janet Kane sitting next to him.

"I have to tell you," he said, "that it's hard to understand how the Janet Kane I knew could wear this every time she goes out." He pushed his arm outside the shroud. "What happened to you?"

"Keep your hands in the pocket inside the *abaya*," she reprimanded him. "They give you away."

He stuffed them back under the silk. And then she answered the question.

"Life happened to me."

"It would drive me nuts," Burke said.

"There is one advantage," she told him. "It makes you invisible. If the typical Saudi male sees a woman veiled, he ignores her. If he sees a woman unveiled, he thinks she is a whore. He approaches her and treats her like a whore. If he is an ordinary man, he demands sex. If he is a *mutawa* he beats her and orders her to put the *abaya* on."

"A *mutawa*?"

"The religious police."

He glanced backward, to the red Cadillac with four Saudi men inside that had pulled quickly into a trailing position when they left the house.

"Not those guys."

He could see that she was shaking her head by the horizontal rustling of the veil.

"No, those are the political police."

"Well," he said, "I'm glad it's not the religious police. It's been a long time since I've been to church. But what do you mean, life happened to you?"

"I mean that you meet someone, you fall in love, you start a family, and then you do the best you can with the choices life gives you. Not everything turns out the way you want it to, but—well, I could have said to my husband, no, I won't go to Saudi Arabia. But it would have hurt so many people. Him. His family. It would have hurt me. When I married him, I became part of all their lives.

"Compared to that, wearing this"—her hand emerged and plucked at the fabric, holding it toward him—"this is a trivial thing."

Rahman, who was driving, jumped on the brakes and the car came to a sudden stop. Ahead, Burke could see traffic converging on an intersection from four directions. There was no stoplight, and nothing was moving. Two red pickup trucks, a Bentley, and a Nissan had all entered the intersection at the same time, and no one was prepared to back off.

"Traffic," Janet said. "It takes forever to get anywhere."

But her mind was on the conversation that had been interrupted, and she resumed it.

"Surely you would understand that," she said. "Didn't your wife move to Moscow with you?"

The question surprised him. "You knew I got married?"

"A friend sent me a newspaper clipping."

Behind the veil, his lips turned upward for a moment. "God, I guess my mother had one published. I never saw it."

"She looked very pretty," Janet ventured.

"Yeah, well, I guess my mother didn't ask them to publish a divorce announcement," he said. "Came about five years later."

"I'm sorry," she said.

"Long time ago," he replied.

"What happened?"

He sighed. "I don't know. I lived with her the last year or so I was at Berkeley. She was the first woman I really liked since you."

The voice from inside the veil opposite him said, "I'm flattered."

"We had a very easy relationship then. Go hiking. Make love in the woods. That kind of thing. After college, she was teaching at an alternative school. I was working for the *Berkeley Barb*. We were happy. Then she got pregnant. She said it was accidental. But anyway, she wanted to keep the baby, and we got married.

"Then, you know, Sam was born and we needed more money. I went to work for *The Oakland Tribune*. I had to work nights, and we saw a lot less of each other. She started going to law school. We started arguing a lot. Then I got offered a transfer to Washington. I wanted to go. She didn't, and the marriage by that time didn't seem worth compromising for. So we split up. She lives in Marin County today, she's married to a judge, and they have two BMWs and a condo at Lake Tahoe. I've got a nifty collection of canceled checks for child support and tuition payments."

"I'm sorry," she said again.

"That's life," he said.

"No, no, it isn't," she remonstrated. "And I wasn't sorry for your canceled checks. I was sorry because I don't remember ever hearing you sound bitter about anything."

"I'm not bitter," he said. "Just experienced."

The words rang false, even to him. She let it go.

"And you never married again?"

He shook his head, then remembered that she couldn't see his head. "No."

"But I'm sure there have been lots of women."

"Not as many as I wanted," he said. "More than I should have had." There was something oddly confessional about the veil, he thought.

"Is there someone now?"

He thought of McCoy.

"Yeah," he said. "There is. But it's not exactly working out."

"Do you love her?"

"I guess so. I almost asked her to marry me."

The cloth rustled across from him and he could vaguely see her veil tilt, and he could imagine her head cocking to one side the way it once had done when they sat in his car, talking, and she was about to ask something more of him than he was able to give.

"And what stopped you?"

"Tribal differences."

"I beg your pardon."

"Just irreconcilable differences," he said. He found himself reluctant to tell her what they were.

"Really?"

Her voice had always possessed a devastating clarity. It was at once warm and sympathetic, detached and observant, and yet wiser and more mature than he could ever aspire to be. It had been that way when she was seventeen.

"I guess so," he said. The words sounded callow.

"Poor Colin. It's hard to imagine a woman resisting you."

He hated the notion that a woman with as much trouble as Janet had could feel sorry for him, even a little.

"You did," he said.

"Well, I was young and foolish," she responded, and he could almost hear laughter in her voice.

The car lurched forward, and he turned and peered through the windshield. The near collision at the intersection ahead of them had somehow resolved itself, and Rahman was pressing forward, nearly running up the trunk of the car in front of him. Though there was no skyline of skyscrapers, Burke could tell by the rising height of the buildings and the increasing density of stores and pedestrians that they were approaching downtown.

"What happens," he said to her, "if this doesn't work?"

"It will work."

"What if they ask me to take the veil off to be checked?"

"It could not happen. In this society, it is unthinkable for a man to ask a woman who belongs to another family to take her veil off."

"That's a comfort. But what if I trip and fall and expose my big, hairy hands?"

"You'll probably be detained and expelled," Janet said.

"What happens to you?"

"I would be detained."

"But not expelled."

"No."

"That's a lot to risk."

"My husband," she said, "would risk it for me."

Chapter 5

It was, Burke thought, ridiculously easy to get into the courthouse.

Rahman, the seventeen-year-old, took the lead as soon as they parked the car. Burke and Janet shuffled along behind him, every inch of their bodies covered in black. He copied her pace.

He resisted the impulse to look around. He could see that they were in a square of some sort, and that the interior of the square was filled with parked cars. Beyond the cars, he could see the base of a tower, with a clock and the shield of the Saudis, palm trees and crossed scimitars on a green field, but he did not dare look up to see how high the tower rose. They stopped as a street sweeper in orange coveralls, trundling a tin cart laden with brooms, moved slowly across their path.

They resumed walking. He could tell that the sun had risen over their heads, and that it was becoming quite warm. He could see that the pavement they were walking over seemed to be made of crushed brown stone. But he could also see that Janet was walking steadily, looking at nothing but what was straight ahead, and he copied that as well. He could hear the hem of his *abaya* brushing against the pavement stones as he walked.

They entered an alley, and it was darker and cooler, because the sun had not yet risen high enough to cast light into it. It smelled of dust and, faintly, of tea. He could hear Rahman talking to someone in Arabic, and then he saw the boy hand over the documents, three ID cards and a letter that she had told him amounted to a trial ticket.

True to Janet's prediction, the guard barely looked at Burke. It was, Burke thought, as if Rahman, the male, were getting permission to bring two dogs into the building. The identity of the dogs didn't matter.

The guard and Rahman engaged in a brief give-and-take in Arabic. Burke imagined that he was asking directions.

The guard opened the door and they entered. Burke carefully walking two feet behind Janet, slightly hunched over, keeping his eyes focused on the small of her back. His garments induced him to adopt a slow, subservient stride. He could hear the footfalls of another guard walking behind him, and he wondered if something—the way he walked, or smelled, or the beads of perspiration that had started to form on his forehead—would give him away. But nothing happened. They seemed to be the only ones in the corridor.

Janet stopped, and he stopped, and ahead of them, the guard produced a ring of heavy brass keys. He opened a door, and Rahman led the way in. Burke entered, and he could hear the door shut behind him.

They were in a small room, barely larger than a closet, lit from overhead by a bare, fluorescent bulb. The walls were painted a pale, institutional green, and the paint was flaking from the corners. The room held four battered folding chairs, and there was a window on one side, covered with a curtain.

Janet pulled a chair up beside the curtain and beckoned silently for him to do the same. He sat beside her and he could feel Rahman come up and stand close behind them.

Her hand emerged from her *abaya* and slowly, carefully, parted the curtain.

They were looking at the back side of a heavy, carved wooden grille of some kind, not unlike the ones he had seen covering the windows on the upper stories of the homes in the compound where he had met Janet. He could not tell precisely what the carving was supposed to represent, if anything. Perhaps, he thought, a growth of vines and flowers. It made sense that a desert people would prize representations of foliage.

Through the crevices in the design, he could see a broad slice of the courtroom.

To his left was a riser of some kind, and a wooden judge's tribune with three chairs trimmed in red, separated from the rest of the room by a rail. There were two counsel's tables in front of the tribune. A man with his *ghotra* tucked up so his ears showed sat up on the tribune, to the right of the judge's position, writing something in a pink folder. A clerk, Burke thought. A man in a military uniform with braids hanging from the epaulets stood stiffly at the counsel's table on the right. The prosecutor.

A color photo of the king, solemn and stern, hung in a gilded frame behind the central judge's chair.

Directly across, where a jury box would have been in an American courtroom, stood half a dozen armed soldiers. But Burke's eyes were arrested by the table closer to him, where two men sat, each dressed in white *ghotras* and *thobes*. One of them, in addition, wore manacles and shackles.

The manacled man was tall and sallow, clean-shaven, with hollowed cheeks. Burke thought he saw a bruise along his left cheekbone. The man's brown eyes were focused on the grille that hid the women's viewing room, and Burke imagined that he could see the barest hint of two black outlines behind it.

There was a stirring in the courtroom and the defendant swiveled his head back toward the judge's bench. An elderly man, his goatee and mustache a yellowish gray, had quietly emerged and taken his seat in the middle. Two younger men took the seats flanking him.

"Just judges? No jury?" he whispered to Janet.

She clenched his arm and he could see her head bob up and down under the veil.

The presiding judge began orating in Arabic. Burke could pick out the word *Allah* in the first sentence. The rest sounded like something midway between a prayer and a stump speech.

Janet leaned very close to him.

"He is announcing the case and the charges and telling the prosecutor to call his first witness," she whispered.

He heard doors open at the back of the courtroom, beyond the range of his vision. In a moment a short, dumpy Saudi man strode toward the bench and stood before the judge. His *thobe* was snowy white and he wore an outer cloak of gauzy black trimmed ostentatiously in gold thread. A gold Cross pen was clipped to the lapel and gold cuff links shone dully under the *thobe*'s sleeve. The shoes under the robe were buffed a bright oxblood. He had a wall eye, which gave his round face a slightly grotesque, skewed tilt.

"He is the deputy minister of the interior," Janet told him. "Rafik al-Fauzi."

"Obviously, the golden boy of the police bureaucracy," Burke whispered back.

Somewhat obsequiously, the prosecutor said something to al-Fauzi. Curtly, the little man nodded, turned to the judge, and began to speak. After a second Janet began providing a translation.

"He says that about a year ago they began to suspect that someone close to the royal family was supplying intelligence to the Americans. They decided to test this. They began planting false information with people they suspected might be the spy."

The judge interrupted al-Fauzi with a question.

"He wants to know how they compiled this list of suspects," Janet said.

Al-Fauzi replied.

"He said they were people who were observed associating with CIA agents on the staff of the American embassy," Janet translated.

Al-Fauzi resumed his narrative.

"They, um, recruited Prince Turki. During his annual physical, he told my husband that there had been a big argument within the royal family that was causing him stress and lack of sleep. It was about the Al-Musara oil field near Dhahran. According to this story, it was ready to come into production a year ahead of schedule. The king wanted to begin production. Prince Faisal and Prince Turki wanted to wait until some other field was depleted so overall production would not rise. The king, according to the story, had prevailed."

Al-Fauzi answered one more question. Yes, he told the judge, Dr. Massoud was the only one who had received this false intelligence leak.

"They're setting something up," Burke said to Janet.

The judge asked the defense lawyer, a short, bulky man with a drooping mustache, if he had any questions. He did not.

"Who's your husband's lawyer?" Burke asked.

"I don't know," Janet whispered. "A public defender. Probably a Palestinian or an Egyptian. Appointed by the court. We tried to hire someone good, but no one would take the case. They were afraid."

After a moment al-Fauzi left the dock and the prosecutor called another witness.

Burke jerked to attention when the man came into view. Unlike everyone else in the courtroom, his head was bare, showing off a head full of wavy, silver hair and an aquiline nose. He was wearing a gray, pin-striped suit of lightweight wool.

"I know that guy," Burke whispered to Janet. "It's Stokes Burnham. He's the Saudi lobbyist in Washington."

Burnham, like al-Fauzi, faced the judge. An interpreter stood between him and the prosecutor, translating the questions. Burnham began answering questions.

"I am Stokes Burnham," he said, in a baritone that Burke could remember occasionally hearing during congressional testimony. The voice was smooth and polished. It suggested to Burke that this was the sort of man whose mother had made him practice public speaking. "I am with the firm of Burnham, Maxwell and Curran in Washington, D.C."

Briefly, Burnham recounted his past: an aide to Richard Nixon and Gerald Ford. Assistant attorney general under Ronald Reagan. Deputy secretary of state under George Bush. He left out, Burke knew, his spectacularly expensive and unsuccessful candidacy for the Senate in Texas and the annual retainer that, according to rumor, he received from the Saudis: $750,000 per year.

Burnham's voice got lower and softer as the questioning went on, and Burke strained against the wooden screen. He took out a sheet of yellow paper and began to take notes.

Did he, the prosecutor asked, know a woman named Candace Ross?

"Yes. We employed her as a lobbyist. For several of the firm's clients."

And had Candace Ross received some information about Saudi oil production?

"Yes, she did. She was told that Saudi production was going to go up. She was advised to buy call options on oil futures in anticipation of a decline in oil prices."

"And who gave her this information?"

Now Burnham's voice sank to a level less audible.

"It was, uh, a senior official in the government."

Now the judge broke in, asking who the senior official was.

Al-Fauzi replied instead of Burnham. He asked to approach the bench. He and Burnham conferred with the judge in whispers.

"Can you hear anything?" Janet asked Burke.

"No. But obviously, Burnham must have some arrangement where he doesn't have to name the official. Al-Fauzi is breaking the news to the judge," Burke whispered.

"Could it be the president?" she asked.

The same thought had occurred to Burke. Detwiler had been dogged by rumors of a zipper problem. Nothing had ever been proven.

"Could be," Burke said.

It more than could be, Burke thought. It was just the sort of thing everyone in Washington suspected Detwiler was capable of.

Burnham and al-Fauzi stepped back from the bench.

This Ross woman, the judge wanted to know, was she a whore?

"No, Your Honor," Burnham answered gallantly.

The judge peered down from the bench, leaning forward.

"Then why did she sleep with a married man and accept this gift from him?"

A look of acute distaste flashed over Burnham's face, as if a rat had crossed his path some night on K Street.

"Your Honor, is this really relevant?" he responded.

The prosecutor and the judge began a long colloquy in Arabic.

"They're arguing about whether the question is relevant," Janet explained.

"You think this is all they have on your husband?" Burke asked.

"I don't know," she said. "Probably."

"It's all hearsay and circumstantial," Burke said. "Can they convict him on that?"

"This is not Los Angeles."

"They don't even have this Candace Ross to testify," Burke said.

"Women don't testify," Janet told him. "Whatever they said wouldn't be worth anything in the judge's mind."

"Well," he said, trying to sound encouraging, "that's good in this instance. It makes their case weaker."

"It doesn't matter," she replied. For the first time that morning, her voice quavered, and he was glad he could not directly see her face.

In the courtroom, the judge appeared to win the relevancy argument, because he said something to the translator and the translator asked Burnham to answer the question.

"I don't know why," he said stiffly. "I considered it her personal business."

The judge listened to the translation, glowered at Burnham, but didn't pursue the question.

The prosecutor asked Burnham what he had done with the information.

"The next time I saw the ambassador, I mentioned it to him," Burnham said. The Saudi ambassador in Washington was Prince Mishaal, a nephew of the king—and the son of Prince Turki.

That was all for Burnham. The prosecutor said something brief to the judge, and Janet hesitated before translating it.

"I believe he said the prosecution rests," she finally told him. Her voice rose slightly. "That's all they have! They're going to convict him on just those witnesses!"

"They shouldn't," he told her.

But he had covered enough Soviet dissident trials to know that an effort this perfunctory by the prosecution meant that the result was preordained. The prosecution didn't have to try hard.

The judge finished shuffling a few papers and said something to the defense.

Massoud's lawyer rose and leaned over his client, whispering for a moment. Massoud nodded. The lawyer put a hand under his elbow and helped him rise to his feet. Slowly, the two men moved back from the table and made their way toward the bench. Massoud dragged his right leg behind him.

Janet's hands, still shrouded, grabbed Burke's arm and squeezed. "He's been hurt," she hissed.

Massoud and the lawyer took their position in front of the judge. The lawyer asked Massoud a question.

"He asks, 'Have you ever betrayed the people of Saudi Arabia?' " she translated.

Massoud straightened up and began to speak. His voice was low, gravelly, and weak.

"I love the people of Arabia and I love the country. I would never betray them. I—" he began.

The judge, his own voice rising, interrupted.

"Did you tell the CIA what you heard from Prince Turki about the Al-Musara oil field?"

Massoud's voice rose and began to sound forceful. Burke waited impatiently for Janet to translate.

"I have spoken honestly to many Americans. None of them told me they were CIA agents. None of them paid me. I wanted them to know the truth about conditions in this country. Because I believe that the

Arab people deserve better than the corrupt tyrants of the House of Saud. I believe they deserve a democracy. And I believe that someday soon they will demand it. And I do not want the Americans to interfere when they do. I want the—"

As Janet translated Burke realized that Massoud had no hope of an acquittal, or even a jail sentence. He knew as well as Burke that the result of the trial was preordained, and he was speaking, Burke imagined, for the benefit of his children, so that they would know what their father had died for.

The judge's complexion had gone from nutty brown to pallid yellow and now to purplish red in the space of about fifteen seconds. His mouth opened, and his lips moved, but no words came out for a while. Finally, he found his voice.

"Silence!" he bellowed.

Massoud kept on speaking and Janet kept on translating. "I want the Americans to know that there are democrats in Arabia—"

The judge screeched something at the soldiers on the side of the courtroom and three of them leaped forward and grabbed Massoud. One clapped a hand over his mouth and the other two seized his arms. All four sank to the ground in a tangle of arms and legs, punctuated by moans and muffled oaths.

Janet stiffened and then started to tremble. Burke kept taking notes, losing himself in the details of his work, detaching himself.

It was like watching a news video of police beating up a suspect, not knowing they were on camera. He patted Janet's arm in a feeble attempt to comfort her.

When the melee stopped, the soldiers stepped back from around Massoud. Blood flowed copiously from a wound in his left cheekbone. His eyes were swelling and about to shut. He was gagged with a piece of white cloth, tied behind his head. The edge of the cloth was turning red from the dripping blood. The soldiers propped him up by the elbows.

The judge gazed down at this scene for a moment, his face still pale with shock and anger. Then he began to speak.

"In the name of God, the merciful—" Janet started to translate. Then she stopped, and he could hear her weeping.

The judge continued to speak for perhaps another minute. Janet gasped. The boy behind them groaned.

Burke could imagine what was being said. He had heard guilty sentences pronounced before.

Massoud shook his head slowly, apparently in answer to a question from the judge. They led him away and the courtroom emptied.

After a while the sobbing stopped.

"He finds him guilty of treason," Janet said.

"The sentence?" he asked. He felt ghoulish, but for the story he would have to know.

She started to sob again.

"It is execution," said a voice behind him.

The boy stepped around, knelt down beside his mother, and wrapped her in his arms. She appeared to gain strength from this, for in a moment she stopped sobbing and stood up.

Wordlessly, the boy led his mother out of the small room and back through the corridor. Burke followed behind, conscious of the fact that the guards this time were not looking at them, were staring studiously elsewhere as they passed by.

They walked through the same alley toward the car, and this time, stepping outside was like walking into a furnace. The sun had risen high in the sky and the dust was thick in the air. He could feel it seeping through the black cheesecloth that covered his face, coating his teeth with a fine, foul grit.

There was a big crowd this time in the square, people standing five and six deep, watching something. Rahman turned his head away from the general direction of the crowd's attention and picked up his pace, pushing his mother along. Burke lengthened his stride to keep up.

Then he heard a howl of pain and anguish that pierced directly to his brain, and he turned around. In the crevice between two shoulders, he could see a man, stripped to his waist, held firmly by two soldiers. His body and head glistened with sweat. A wide leather belt was wrapped firmly around the biceps of his right arm, like a tourniquet.

The man's right hand was pinned by the more burly of the two soldiers to a wooden block. A third man, armed with a gleaming butcher's cleaver, was hacking it off, alternately sawing and chopping.

The screams of the man grew higher in pitch and intensity until they sounded like a buzz saw in Burke's ears.

The man with the cleaver completed his task. The victim, his face chalky white beneath the sweat and grime caked on it, went limp and silent, his eyes rolling toward the top of their sockets. The burly soldier pulled the stump of the arm, dripping only slightly with bright red blood, toward a fourth man, who held a brass bucket full of a steaming liquid. He plunged the stump of the man's hand into the liquid, and the shock revived the man. He screamed again.

Burke, transfixed, felt a tug on his sleeve. It was Rahman.

"We must go," the boy hissed in his ear.

He turned and stumbled after Rahman and Janet, saying nothing until they reached the car.

"What . . . ?" he blurted.

"A thief," the boy answered.

Rahman opened the back door for him, and Burke was about to get in. The sight of Janet slumped in the corner of the seat stopped him. She seemed to need comfort that he could not provide.

"You ride with your mother," he said to Rahman. "I'll drive."

"Colin, you can't," Janet hissed from the backseat. "The police would stop us in a minute."

Burke remembered how he was dressed and remembered that women were forbidden to drive in Saudi Arabia. He got in the backseat. His *abaya* was starting to feel like a cage.

"Now you see why we need your help," Janet said when they were under way. "You'll write a story?"

"Of course," he told her. "The embassy hasn't helped you?"

"Friends call and call," she said, and he could hear the bitterness in her voice. "It's always, 'He's not in. May I take your number and have him call you?' "

"I know the drill," he said. "For me, it's an occupational hazard. The bureaucrat's first line of defense is not taking calls."

"Do you think it's because of this senior official Burnham spoke of?" she asked.

"You remember what we used to say in California about wild bears?"

"And, 'Is the Pope Catholic?' " she said.

"Still is, last time I checked."

"You don't seem surprised."

"No."

"So how will you handle it in the story you write?"

"I won't," he said.

"Why not?"

"It's too vague. It's conceivable Burnham could be making it up because the Saudis are paying him to do it. If I just write what he said, I may be amplifying a lie. And the White House would have an easy time denying it. When I write it, I want to know who the guy is and I don't want to leave him room to wriggle out of it. So this story is just going to be about your husband. I'll work on the senior-official part of it when I get back to Washington."

She shifted on her seat and he could tell by the way the folds of her *abaya* rearranged themselves that she was facing him.

"Colin, there's one thing I haven't told you," she said.

"What's that?"

"Well, we got you a room at the Inter-Continental. But if you file your story from there, you'll have to check out right away. Because—"

"Because the *mutawa* monitor telephone calls?"

She shook her head. "Not the *mutawa*. The political police."

"It's all right," he said.

"No!" Her voice rose in urgency. "They'll arrest you. I wanted to find an office somewhere that you could use, but I haven't so far, and the only thing I can think of is for you to—"

"It's all right," he repeated.

"How?"

"I brought a little something with me. Latest technology. Direct satellite link from anywhere. All I'll need is a car."

Her hand came out from the folds of her *abaya* and covered his.

"Colin," she said, "I'm so glad you're here."

"So am I," he said. "Where else would I have gotten to wear an *abaya*?"

Getting out of the *abaya* was like getting out of a cell. He walked around the room for a moment, flexing his arms, rolling his neck and nearly strutting.

"I have to leave you now," Janet said. She handed him some keys. "Kamal was not happy when I told him you would drive the car yourself."

"The less he knows, the better off he is," he replied.

She leaned forward and kissed him on both cheeks. "One of my friends will call you at the hotel tonight," she said. "And you have my number if there's an emergency."

He watched her put on the *abaya* again and leave with her two children, and he pondered for a moment the strength that had brought her to this place and was bearing her through this calamity.

Then he put those thoughts out of his mind and sat down on a chair she had provided. His laptop lay open in front of him on a small table. He felt the familiar, reassuring succor he always felt when he sat down to write a good story. He had seen things happen. He could organize and recount them. His work would mean something. This kind of moment came as close as any in his life to putting him at ease.

In an hour the story was done. He left out the senior-official angle in Burnham's testimony. He allowed himself to be graphic in describing the way the soldiers had gagged Massoud and how he looked when they dragged him to his feet. He thought of the thief in the square.

He put his byline on the story and closed the file. Then he reconsidered, opened the file, and took the byline off. No need to make it easy for the Saudis to find him. He took the piece of aluminum luggage from the corner where Kamal had left it.

The temperature outside had climbed, he guessed, well above one hundred, and he loosened his tie and took off his jacket. He glanced up long enough to see that the sun, burning white in a clear blue sky, was over his right shoulder. That would be southwest. He pointed the car north and drove.

It was the reverse of driving in from the airport. The community of high-walled villas gave way to shanties and then to desert, sere and brown, strewn with rocks. The road narrowed until it was two lanes, paved, but without a median stripe, and traffic was light. Occasionally, he passed an irrigated farm, with an improbably green field of wheat or grass. He couldn't tell. He wasn't much at picking out crops.

Ten miles out of the city, he found what he was looking for. It was a low, brown ridge that ran parallel to the road about a quarter of a mile distant. He turned off on what seemed to be a path of some kind and drove slowly to its base. He got out of the car and began to climb.

The sun was like a burden on his back, weighing him down. He thought, having lived in Washington, that he was used to heat, and even worse, to humid heat. This air was dry, but it seemed that he was standing a lot closer to the sun. He could feel the skin on the back of his neck start to burn even before a sweat broke out on his forehead, and he hoped the equipment he was carrying would work properly the first time.

The rock and sand underfoot had the consistency of gravel, and he was slogging with every step as he reached the top of the low ridge and scrambled down. He looked around. No one on the road could see him. There was nothing but open desert before him. It was an ideal spot.

He crouched down and opened the aluminum suitcase. The machinery was in two parts. On his left were folded leaves of a polished, silvery metal—he had no idea what metal it was. He released a catch and pulled the leaves out from the bed of the luggage. Then he opened them up like a fan unfurling, until they had taken the shape of a small parabolic dish—his transmitter and receiver.

On the other side there was a telephone receiver and number pad and an array of dials and switches, one of them a compass. He checked it to make certain that east was to his right, and he pointed the dish in that direction. The satellite he was looking for was over the Indian Ocean.

He flicked on the power switch, heard an answering hum, and then checked the window marked LOCATOR. A flickering green bar, the same kind that measured volume on an amplifier, told him that the link with the satellite was strong enough for transmission. He plugged his laptop into the jack under the telephone receiver.

Now he turned his attention to the display screen on the computer. He typed in the number and his personal access code for the *Tribune*'s computer.

He could hear the disk honking and clicking inside the computer for a moment, and then the number being dialed. The transmission took about two minutes. He waited until the machine told him "message received." Then he packed the equipment up and started the hike back to the car.

Burke turned back at the top of the ridge and looked once again at the site of his transmission.

He looked at his watch. It would be about nine in the morning in Washington. He thought about calling McCoy. She would be finishing her morning meetings now.

But the ever-efficient NSC secretarial staff would be certain to deflect his call to the press office. And God knew what he would give them for a number to call back.

It was better, he thought, for her to wonder where he was until he got back.

He watched the faint breeze flick little curls of sand over his shoes for a moment. Then he headed back to the car, contemplating the pleasure of his own company for the rest of the day and the night ahead.

Chapter 6

The tiles in the fourth-floor corridor of the Old Executive Office Building had always reminded Desdemona McCoy of a chessboard. They were squares of black and white marble, worn and scarred beneath the veneer of polish applied to them each night by the maids and janitors. She and her sister had had a black-and-white board one summer when she was eight and Juliet was ten. Most boards then were red and black, but this was an old one, passed down to the two girls from a cousin in North Carolina, and that was what they had used. Now sometimes when she walked down that corridor she thought about that summer and the concentration she had had to muster to finally beat her older sister. That had been among the first times she had felt aware of her adult self.

She got to the elevator and pushed the down button. Doors slid open to her right, and she stepped inside. As the doors closed a hand was thrust between them. They opened again, and Brian Barrett stepped inside.

Barrett was the youngest old man she had ever known. He was something like thirty-two, almost her own age. But his body would not have looked misplaced in a nursing home. He had a wispy halo of red hair, rheumy blue eyes behind rimless spectacles, appendages like pipe cleaners, a little potbelly, and a bit of a stoop. If he had worn old cardigans, people might have called him Pops.

When he got to be an old man, she thought, he would be a dirty one. Brian Barrett was the kind of man who could not ride in an elevator without ogling the women in it. Reflexively, she checked to make sure her blouse was buttoned nearly to her throat. Barrett liked to look for cleavage.

He was also, by reputation, the best Arabist Harvard had produced in twenty years.

He looked at her, and she could tell what he was thinking: *McCoy. The meeting must be about intelligence,* just as she was thinking, *Barrett. The meeting must be about the Middle East. Maybe Iraq, but probably Massoud.* But neither would discuss such assumptions in an open elevator.

He got in and she focused her eyes on the illuminated numbers above the door. She could almost feel him scanning her body.

"Think Henry's going to be in a good mood?" he asked her.

"I don't know," she said carefully.

"I heard that he was for a little while," Barrett said.

"When?"

"Christmas 1967," he said. "His brother didn't get a BB gun."

McCoy smiled just enough to be polite.

"The foundations of his arms-control policy," Barrett went on. This time, McCoy didn't bother to smile.

The elevator stopped and the doors opened onto a lobby with a guard desk that controlled admission to the building and the exit through the east doors toward the White House. The guard was a bony, graying black man whose name tag said SIMMONS, MICHIGAN. Barrett walked past, flashing his White House ID, otherwise oblivious.

"Hello, Mr. Simmons," McCoy said, and the guard smiled broadly at her. She had used to wonder when, if ever, she would stop noticing little things like the different ways she and Barrett related to a black security guard. Then she had decided that she never would.

She had never spoken with Simmons beyond exchanging pleasantries, but she imagined that the older blacks on the White House staff, the ones who opened the doors and swept the floors, were fond of her. She was taking advantage of the opportunities their generation had suffered to create. Their smiles carried messages of approval, and on the occasions when she faced a trip across the street to the White House with trepidation, she took comfort from them.

The West Wing of the White House loomed through the door in front of her, pale and radiant in the afternoon sun. The flag above it hung languidly. After the brief cool spell of two days ago, the air had returned to its July norm—hot, humid, and oppressive. She hoped she would not start sweating before they reached the West Wing.

They walked briskly across West Executive Avenue, once a public street that divided the White House from the Old EOB. Now it was sealed from traffic, partly for security reasons, and partly to provide parking spaces that were among the perks that separated the mid-ranks of power from the drones on the White House staff.

McCoy had felt a quick flush of pride and pleasure when she got the right to park her car there. Then she had felt embarrassed and guilty for caring about it. But she had kept the spot. That was the way the White House worked, she thought. It seduced people with its trappings and its grandeur. They were smart enough to know they were being seduced. And then they made conscious decisions to let it happen anyway.

To forgo nearly everything else in their lives, she started to think, then caught herself.

"Bet you a lunch it's the Massoud case," Barrett said, confident that the drone of traffic on Seventeenth Street would make his voice inaudible to anyone but her.

"That would be a sucker bet," she said.

"All right, then I bet a lunch we have to talk someone out of sending the marines in after him," Barrett persisted.

McCoy smiled tightly. "You must really be hungry, Brian," she said. She would starve before she'd go to lunch with Brian Barrett.

Another white-shirted guard, recognizing them both, snapped to attention and passed them through the gate into the White House grounds. The grass of the North Lawn was littered with tripods left by television cameramen who, later that afternoon, would be using the building as a backdrop when they taped their reports for the evening news.

They entered the West Wing and walked across a little lobby dominated by a portrait of Andrew Jackson. McCoy had never gotten used to the portraits of slave owners she saw in the White House. She always noticed them. They didn't make her angry anymore, and she would not have taken them down had she the power to do so. She simply noticed them.

In the anteroom of Hoffman's office, clerks were sitting nearly haunch to haunch, typing at computers fitted with yellow shields so that visitors could not read over the clerks' shoulders. The screens cast a faint, yellowish glow on their faces. One of the clerks jumped up and opened the door to Hoffman's office.

The shining, bald pate of the man sitting in the chair opposite

Hoffman was the first thing she noticed, and it mildly surprised her. It was Maynard Walters, the press secretary, and he did not normally sit in on Hoffman's staff meetings.

Hoffman, in shirtsleeves but with his bow tie still knotted with studied imprecision, was reading something and making marginal notes, an intent scowl on his slightly doughy face.

McCoy settled into a vacant chair that was drawn up close to Hoffman's desk, making her part of a semicircle with Walters and Barrett.

Her eyes fell on a lump of gray concrete encased in Lucite that adorned Hoffman's desk, serving as a paperweight. It was a chunk of the old Berlin Wall, and seeing it there always annoyed her. Hoffman had been the NSC's Soviet-affairs expert in 1989, but in her judgment, he deserved about as much credit for the fall of the Wall as the mayor of Chicago did for the triumphs of the Bulls. Yet there it was, like a trophy.

Hoffman finished reading whatever it was, scratched something at the bottom of the last page, and looked directly at McCoy.

"Have your people in Riyadh reported in on the Massoud trial yet?"

She had suspected it was going to be a long afternoon when she saw the scowl on Hoffman's face. As soon as she heard the words *your people*, she knew it.

"No, Dr. Hoffman, not as far as I know. The station reports that Prince Turki has promised we'll be kept informed—"

"Well, the *Washington Tribune* knows what happened." Hoffman's voice was cold. He slammed a desk drawer shut.

"Are we paying the damn Agency thirty billion dollars a year so that Prince Turki and the *Washington*-damn-*Tribune* can decide what we know about Saudi Arabia?"

He was almost shouting. His face reddened. Wrinkles twitched around his eyes. McCoy said nothing. She knew better than to waste her time defending a poor performance.

She declined to be cowed.

"Of course not," she said evenly.

Hoffman, having failed to intimidate her, looked at Walters, giving him his cue.

"The *Tribune* foreign desk called me half an hour ago," Walters said. "They want some comments on a story they'll be running tomorrow about how our agent was gagged, convicted, and sentenced to death in a matter of about two hours, and what we're doing about it."

"About ten minutes ago I got a call from the Senate Intelligence Committee. Senator Higgins has also been asked to comment, and he wants to know what the hell is going on," Hoffman added.

McCoy stiffened at the mention of the *Tribune*. She could feel heat in her face. Not trusting herself to say exactly the right thing, she said nothing. She had weathered Hoffman's tantrums in the past. They were like storms. They always ended.

"How did they get the story?" Barrett asked.

"They're not saying," Walters replied.

An air force officer whom McCoy did not know spoke up from the back of the room.

"Uh, sir, forgive me for coming in late, but I just got a callback from Fort Meade on that. The *Tribune* received a satellite transmission of the story at 0730 Washington time. It had no byline. But the transmitter's internal identification number corresponds to the one used out of Moscow for a number of years by a correspondent named Burke."

McCoy took a deep breath and struggled to maintain a blank face. She felt a rush of guilt and desire and frustration. How had Colin gotten to Saudi Arabia?

"That bastard," Barrett said.

"Yeah," Walters concurred. "One of the Urawans."

Urawan, McCoy knew, was part of the jargon in Walters's office, an acronym picked up from the Secret Service. It stood for "ugly, rude asshole with a notebook."

"Well, I don't know that he's—" she began, speaking before she really thought about what she would say.

Hoffman's purplish rage faded slightly to an angry scowl. "He had that PAC-3 story. Now this. Obviously, someone is leaking to him."

His eyes jerked around to McCoy.

"Don't you know him? Didn't you run across him during that business in Russia at the Hermitage?"

McCoy forced her face into the best simulation she could manage of nonchalance.

"Yes, Dr. Hoffman, I did. We got to know each other. He seemed very capable. Spoke very good Russian."

She stopped, her mind in control of her mouth again, too politic to go further and unwilling to lie.

"Any idea how he got wind of this story?"

She realized how pointed the question was, and she was suddenly glad, for the first time, that their phone calls had missed one another over the past two days.

"No, Dr. Hoffman, no idea," she said, relieved that it was the truth.

Her stomach knotted again, and she struggled to control it.

"He close to Senator Higgins?" Hoffman asked Walters.

Walters shrugged. "Wouldn't surprise me."

Hoffman glowered. "The whole press corps thinks Higgins would make such a great president. Can't they see he's just pandering to them?"

"That's what they want," Walters said.

"Well, Higgins is sure going to run with this one. He's going to make it look like the king has us on a leash."

"The first thing he'll go after is the PAC-3 deal," Walters said. "The Israelis and their friends are just desperate for a good reason to use to block it. This'll give it to them."

One of the clerks from the anteroom opened the door and two men entered the room. One was Delvin Crandall, the assistant secretary of state for the Middle East. The other was Thaddeus Hirsch, the silver-haired director of central intelligence. A few minutes passed as Walters filled them in on the calls from the *Tribune* and Higgins.

Hoffman impatiently tapped a pencil on the blotter on his desk.

"Thad," he said, "I'd like a report on why we find out about this from the newspapers."

Hirsch flushed and scowled.

"Brian," Hoffman said, turning to Barrett. "How could we get the king to exile this Massoud instead of executing him?"

Barrett's freckled face turned redder.

"Well, I'm not sure we can, Henry. Not sure we want to."

"Well, pretend we do for a second," Hoffman said, sarcastically.

"Look," Barrett persisted. "The guy may not have been on our payroll, but he did give us information. They have a case against him. If we pressure the king to let him off, there won't be any question who's holding the leash."

"Mm, I believe we second Brian's opinion," said Crandall. "It would be a terrible blow to the king's prestige, even his legitimacy. It could have destabilizing—"

Hoffman peered at them over the rims of his eyeglasses like a schoolmaster staring at unruly boys.

"Let's keep in mind whose prestige we're being paid to look out for," he interrupted.

"Well, of course," Barrett said, "but a friendly Saudi Arabia is in our interests. Don't forget that what we're seeing here is an opening skirmish in the succession battle. The king is seventy-seven years old and at least that many pounds overweight. He's got diabetes and severe heart problems. This Dr. Massoud has done a hell of a job keeping him upright this long."

"So?" Hoffman asked, a slight note of impatience in his voice. He hated wasting time at meetings going over things people were supposed to know.

Barrett flushed. "Well, of course," he said, "the struggle to succeed him is on between Ahmed and Faisal. Ahmed and the king are both sons of old Abdul-Aziz's eleventh and favorite wife, Hussara. So is Qabos. So is Rashid, who oversees the ministry of health. So the Hussara brothers are probably seen as responsible for Massoud. Faisal is a full brother of Turki, the interior minister. They're both sons of Jamila, Abdul-Aziz's, um, tenth wife, I believe it was."

Hoffman smiled thinly.

"Well, it's nice to know that we're not the only country where political leaders have zipper problems."

"Turki's the one who had Massoud arrested," Hirsch offered.

"We know that," Hoffman said, with a cold glance. "Tell us something we don't know."

Hirsch glared back. He was in over his head as CIA director, and everyone in the room knew it, beginning with him. He had been an automobile executive, then governor of Michigan. The president had appointed him to oversee an administrative reorganization of the intelligence community, but Hirsch had found the baronies of the Pentagon, the Congress, and State Department more resistant to reform than Oldsmobile, Pontiac, and Cadillac. And his ignorance of foreign affairs was not helped by the time he insisted on carving out of his schedule for fly-fishing and tennis.

"Des, what do you think?" Hoffman asked.

It was a calculated question, designed not so much to elicit her views as to insult Hirsch, who would normally have been the one to state the position of the intelligence community.

McCoy was, in fact, ambivalent. Her head agreed with Barrett. But she had spent seven years in the field, in Russia. Most of the sources she had run were venal men, out for money or vengeance. She had grown to appreciate the courage and the vulnerability of the people who chose to become sources because of principle, and she suspected Massoud was one of them. Her heart was with him.

Moreover, she was still flustered by Burke's connection to Massoud.

"It's a very difficult call—" she began. A muted ring from Hoffman's desk interrupted her.

Hoffman picked up the phone, listened briefly, and then said, "Yes, sir." He hung up.

"The president," he said, pausing evanescently to let the two words sink in a little, "wants us to continue this conversation in his office."

There was a moment of quiet as the participants in the meeting ingested that information. McCoy had found that no matter how often a person walked into the Oval Office, crossing its threshold always caused a certain dryness of the mouth, a desire to be right, a desire to be impressive.

Then Hoffman got up and led the way out of the room. They walked down the short, beige-walled corridor that linked Hoffman's office to the president's. Two phlegmatic Secret Service guards stood at either side of the open door. Billy Parker, the president's personal assistant, smiled at them from his gatekeeper's desk in the anteroom.

The heavyweights in the meeting had already arranged themselves in the conversation area of the Oval Office. Peter Scott Detwiler, in a precisely creased navy blue suit and brilliantly polished black shoes that were a Massachusetts-made copy of Guccis, was in one of the wing chairs that flanked the fireplace. Hoffman had the other. Hirsch and Walters had the facing couch. McCoy looked for a chair behind the couch and found one, along with Barrett, Crandall, and the other middleweights.

As Hoffman explained how news of Massoud's trial had reached the White House, McCoy watched a red flush spread from Thaddeus Hirsch's neck to his ears. She thought of Burke and wondered how he had managed to get himself into Saudi Arabia, much less get the news out. She wondered if he was all right. Then she reminded herself to focus on the business at hand.

Hirsch spoke up as soon as Hoffman had finished his summation.

"Mr. President, I'm not sure it's so damn important who gets the news first, although we're going to find out why it happened this way. The main thing is, what do we do about it? Henry and Maynard can tell you all the political reasons why we ought to do what we can for this guy Massoud. But there's another reason to think about."

Hirsch paused. He seemed to have the president's attention.

"We can't run an intelligence service if we get a reputation for leaving casualties in the field, just like the marines can't run the marines without doing everything they can to recover their wounded. Our officers get demoralized. We can't recruit agents. Now that this has become a high-profile case, especially, we need to make sure everyone knows we take care of our own."

Detwiler looked quizzically at Hirsch.

"But until it became high profile, we were ready to let Massoud take his chances?"

Hoffman coughed. "Well, sir, there was a feeling that we ought to wait and see what the Saudis did before we reacted."

Detwiler grimaced and nodded.

Maybe now he'll decide to pay a little more attention to his intelligence briefings, McCoy thought. She waited to see whether anyone else would support Hirsch.

Leila Atherton, the only other woman in the room, spoke up. She was the White House lobbyist in Congress.

"I don't know about the Agency," she said, "but you can forget about the PAC-3 sale if this man hangs. Higgins will stomp all over it."

"It might not be unrealistic, then," Hoffman said, "to tell the king he can forget the PAC-3 unless he extends clemency to Massoud and, say, exiles him."

In the right corner of her eye, McCoy caught Barrett looking at her. If there was a time to speak up, it was now, his look said. If anyone was going to do it, she was.

McCoy cleared her throat.

Detwiler looked at her. "You have something to add, Des?"

She never ceased to be impressed by Detwiler's use of her first name, even though she had long since learned that it was a skill he used indiscriminately, on virtually everyone with whom he came into contact.

More important, she had noticed that Detwiler liked hearing argument at his meetings. He liked to think he had heard all sides before he made a decision. Her guess was that he valued staff members who dissented—until, of course, he'd made up his mind.

So she plunged ahead, effortlessly dredging up details from reports and briefing papers she had consumed weeks and months ago.

"I don't think, sir, that we should do anything without considering its impact on *al-aqd wal hal*, as the Saudis say."

"In English?" Detwiler asked.

"It means 'those who tie and untie.' It's the informal Saudi version of the old Soviet politburo. The princes with clout," she said.

"It seems likely that Faisal and Turki are using this against Ahmed and the rest of the Hussara brothers. I think the king had no choice but to order Massoud's arrest and trial once they presented him with whatever evidence they had."

McCoy stopped. Detwiler seemed to pause for reflection.

"The Saudis," he said, shaking his head as if pondering the misdeeds of a twelve-year-old. "You'd think that after the Gulf War and now that I'm about to stick my neck out to sell them the PAC-3, they'd cut us a little slack. If it weren't for us, the king and all the little princes would be shining Saddam Hussein's shoes right now. But Qabos didn't mention a word about this to me."

McCoy turned toward Barrett, wondering if he would have the nerve to rebut the president. Barrett was carefully studying the open file on his lap. But he raised his head, face mottled.

"Maybe," Barrett said timidly, "Qabos didn't know what was going to happen. Maybe he thought the king would be able to handle the pressure from Faisal and Turki. Certainly it's fair to say no one planned on publicity."

Barrett looked around the room for support and, hearing none, lapsed into silence.

McCoy realized it was again up to her.

"There is, sir, a kind of perverse backlash factor," she said, addressing the president. "When we sell them something like the PAC-3 system, or defend them against the Iraqis for that matter, it only underscores for a lot of Saudis that this king, unlike old Abdul-Aziz, isn't able to defend the country on his own. Worse, he gets help from infidels—us."

The expression that crossed Detwiler's face might have greeted the entry of a process server with a subpoena.

"Frankly," the president said, "I'm getting tired of their sensitivities."

That silenced the room for a moment.

"Well, you can never tell for certain," McCoy began. "But I don't think we want to see the throne slip out of the Hussara brothers' control, and it very well might if we humiliate them. Faisal has a Syrian wife. We're told he's fairly close to Hafez el-Assad. He's been seen at Arab summit meetings conversing amiably with Qaddafi. According to what we hear, he thinks production should be cut and prices raised.

"The Hussara brothers, on the other hand, have kept Saudi oil production over eight million barrels a day for more than ten years now. They've broken OPEC for us."

She paused. "I would say there's reason to believe that our interests would be better served by not embarrassing the Hussara brothers until the succession is assured."

"Presumably to the trusty Ahmed?" the president asked.

"Yes, sir."

"Ahmed or Faisal," Hirsch growled, "it doesn't matter to Massoud. We still ought to be picking up our wounded."

McCoy had had enough of amateurs like Hirsch trying to run an intelligence agency.

"Sir, I've been in the field needing support, so I know what Massoud feels like," she said, trying to keep from being stentorian.

"I recruited an agent and then lost him. He was a chemistry professor in St. Petersburg, and he helped us pin down the remnants of the old Soviet nerve-gas program. He used an old contact code one day, the ministry of security caught him, and he disappeared. And I grieved for months. But we didn't try to force the Russians to let him go. We knew that would do more harm than good. We knew that sometimes you have to accept a loss and move on. This may be one of those times."

Hirsch's outrage grew more evident with every word McCoy spoke. His frown deepened into a scowl and the angry flush spread from his neck to his cheeks. She realized that if Hirsch survived as CIA director, her career at the Agency would be over the minute she finished her NSC assignment. She was betting he wouldn't survive. The face she was focused on was Detwiler's. He seemed interested in what she had to say.

Hoffman, too, was reading Detwiler's face.

"Those are good points," he said to McCoy. From the way he said it, she knew what side he was going to come down on. It was not hers.

"But," Hoffman went on, "I think we also need to keep in mind what Leila said. The hard fact is that if the Saudis go ahead and execute this man, we can forget about the PAC-3 sale. We might then expect a strategic shift in the Gulf region as the Saudis look for more accommodating ways to deal with Iraq and Iran.

"It seems," he continued, "that there are two basic choices. We can let the Saudis do what they will with this man and perhaps do no damage to the Hussara side in the succession struggle. Or we can tell the king that if he allows the execution, we'll have no choice but to withdraw the offer to sell the PAC-3 and urge him to commute the sentence to exile."

"The first way," Detwiler said, "we lose the PAC-3 sale. The other way, we might save it."

"That's true, sir," Hoffman said.

The way Hoffman had presented the choices, she thought, distorted them. It minimized the risk of destabilizing the Saudi government and exaggerated the importance of the PAC-3 sale. But she sensed that it would be counterproductive for her to argue further. She had done her job. Now it was up to Detwiler to do his.

"There's one other thing I want," Detwiler said. "To stop these goddamn leaks."

Barrett spoke up.

"I think I might have a word with Mishaal. Just let him know who the *Tribune*'s anonymous correspondent is. Might help."

Prince Mishaal, a nephew of the king, was the Saudi ambassador to Washington.

Detwiler said nothing, his silence signaling assent.

McCoy felt an instant of vertigo, and she closed her eyes. A crisscross pattern of yellow lines seemed to appear and waver on the inside of her eyelids.

She would have to warn him, she thought, and she wondered how she could do it. A call to his editor? No. An anonymous call. From a pay phone. Would they take it seriously? Perhaps they would.

She could see herself skulking out of the EOB and walking up Pennsylvania Avenue to a pay phone, trying to look over her shoulder.

She bit her lip. She had miscalculated badly with Burke, and she was not used to miscalculating. For a moment she allowed herself to imagine what would happen if she were to say yes. To what? Her feelings for him? Her fear of being old and alone?

What if she did marry him?

She could imagine her family's reaction. Her parents would probably accept him with formal, guarded politeness. Her sister would be openly angry.

She thought for an instant about children, then pushed the thought from her mind.

Then she thought of an evening they had spent together two weeks ago, the simplest of evenings. She'd cooked spaghetti. They'd talked about Viktor Yerofeyev's new novel. They'd watched the Bullets' playoff game on television. They'd made love. She had been happy that evening, so happy that she had caught herself noticing it.

She had been happy until he got up an hour before dawn and left before anyone would see him and then she had been surprised at how strongly she wanted him to stay.

Did she love him? Yes, she did, she thought. But she had been in love before and things had always ended badly, and she had learned not to be one of those women who let love, or the pursuit of love, run their lives. Yet maybe it was time to stop being so hardheaded, to go with what she felt rather than what she thought.

Almost imperceptibly, she shook her head. That choice no longer existed. If she knew Burke, she knew that he would not forgive her for rejecting him.

She had gotten over love in the past, and she knew that she would again, but she sensed that in this case it would take a long time, and it would be painful, and she did not want to think too much of the way she would be when she finally stopped missing him.

" . . . quietly," the president was saying.

McCoy jerked her attention back to the conversation around her, dismayed that she had been so easily distracted again.

"Of course," Hirsch responded, and Hoffman nodded assent.

"I think everyone understands that," Hoffman said, and this time McCoy thought he was looking directly at her and she wondered again what he knew. Then she realized he was looking in turn at each of the underlings around the room, silently but ostentatiously warning them not to leak.

It was a joke, of course. Except for the Botanical Gardens, the White House leaked more than any building in Washington. If and when it suited Detwiler's or Walters's purpose, the *Post* or the *Times* or the *Tribune* would carry a story exculpating the president and his inner circle in the Massoud case, putting the blame, most likely, on Hirsch.

That thought reminded her of how vulnerable her affair with Burke had made her. Her mouth tasted dry.

"What are the chances that the king will spring Massoud if I put it to him that way?" Detwiler directed the question at the room in general.

"Hard to say," Barrett offered.

"He'd let him go," Crandall predicted. "He wouldn't be happy about it. But the Saudis feel very vulnerable to Iran's Scuds and Israel's Jericho. The PAC-3 is the only way the king has to protect against them."

"Plus he has to think of all the commissions his sons and nephews are going to make on the sale," Hirsch said. There was a general titter around the room.

"Well, then, I think it's worth a try," Detwiler decided. "I'll make the call."

"Very good, Mr. President," Hoffman said. "We'll arrange it for later this afternoon."

One by one, the participants filed from the room. But before McCoy could leave, Hoffman touched her elbow and silently gestured for her to remain behind.

She gulped, wondering what Hoffman could want, trying to think of something she could say that would deflect attention from her if Hoffman seriously pursued the leaks to Burke.

But Hoffman, after everyone else was gone, addressed the president. "One other thing, sir."

"Yes?"

"We've had a serious breakdown by the Riyadh station. I think we need to crack a few heads down there. The Agency won't do it on its own. I think we need to send a personal presidential representative to sort things out and make recommendations. Be on the scene."

"All right," Detwiler said. "Who?"

"I was thinking of Ms. McCoy," Hoffman said.

McCoy blinked, thinking instantly of Burke.

Detwiler smiled that magical smile. "Can you clear your schedule for a few days, Des?"

"I work for you, sir," she said automatically. "Of course."

Chapter 7

Burke arose before the sun, unable to sleep. He opened the sliding-glass door to the small balcony outside his room and stepped into the desert air.

It was warm, but not yet hot. The air was still. Below him, the city lay dark and unimposing, except for the spires of the minarets, floodlit and phallic against the starry sky, encircled, in a few lavish cases, by white lights that gleamed like pearls.

He wondered, suddenly, what McCoy was doing and what it would be like to awaken with her and share this view and what spin she would put on the Freudian interpretation of Islamic architecture. He glanced at his watch. He imagined that she was in her bedroom at this hour, flipping through one of her gallery catalogs. It seemed like a nice place to be.

He walked back inside the room, sliding the door closed behind him to keep the sand out. He switched on the television, an enormous Sony, looking for CNN, but didn't find it. All channels were blank.

Undeterred, he rummaged in his luggage until he found the little black portable radio he carried on overseas trips. He fiddled with the antenna and the tuning dial until he heard some English amid the whistles and squawks. It was the BBC.

He waited while a woman announcer read the overnight domestic news. There was a strike in Glasgow by software programmers, believed to be the first strike in history by people who worked in their homes; tickets for the summer's Open at Carnoustie had sold out on the first day of offering; and traffic through the Channel tunnel to France had fallen 15 percent in the previous year, apparently because of the rising price of Bordeaux.

"In Washington, the White House have announced that President Detwiler, in consultation with King Khalil ibn-Abdul-Aziz of Saudi Arabia, has secured the release of a Saudi physician convicted of spying for the United States," the announcer said.

Burke smiled into the darkness and turned up the volume.

"According to a report from Riyadh in the *Washington Tribune*, the physician, Abdulrahman Massoud, was convicted and sentenced to death yesterday by a Saudi court. The White House says, however, that the Saudi monarch has agreed to send Massoud, who was educated in the United States, into exile."

He started looking for the piece of paper on which he had written her address. Before he could find it, his phone rang.

"Have you heard?" she said, without using his name.

"Yeah, I'm happy for you," he said.

"I'm so grateful to you for—" she started to say.

"No," he interrupted. He sensed the relief in her voice. She sounded almost giddy, and for a few seconds he felt that way, too.

"It's the least I could do for the woman who introduced me to Bizet."

"Colin," she said, with a hint of a lilt in her voice. "Do you still go to the opera?"

"Nope," Burke replied. "But if not for you, I wouldn't know what I was missing."

She giggled. "You can still make me laugh," she said.

"Not too hard to do this morning, I suspect."

"No. I, we—well, you've helped us keep our family together when we thought we might lose it."

"Glad to be of service," he said.

The silence suggested she was slightly overwhelmed.

"I'm trying very hard not to cry," she eventually said.

"A good idea. What are you going to do next?"

"Rahman and I will go to the jail as soon as morning prayers are over," she replied. "I hope they will release him by then."

"Pick me up on the way."

He was standing in the lobby, dressed in khaki slacks and a blue polo shirt, when the call to dawn prayer started to sound from amplifiers in the minarets of the city.

For some reason, he had not expected amplifiers. He had thought the voices of the *muezzin* would waft through the desert air unaided and natural. The amplifiers reminded him of Russia, in the communist days. At parades there had always been amplified voices, leading the assembled workers in cheers for the Party.

On the street outside, he could see a few people scurrying toward a mosque at the end of the block. Virtually all activity in the hotel lobby stopped. The clerks and cashiers, using small rugs, knelt and bowed, foreheads to the floor.

He felt alien and alone as the population prayed. Then he noticed a few other foreigners, sitting quietly in chairs in odd corners of the lobby. This, apparently, was the appropriate behavior. He copied it, feeling afresh the meaning of the word *infidel.*

The prayers lasted for ten minutes. Ten minutes after that, the Massouds' Mercedes, Rahman at the wheel, pulled up under the hotel's porte cochere.

He glanced back at the hotel driveway. If the police were still following Janet's car, they were being less ostentatious about it.

He got into the backseat. She was dressed in the black *abaya* again, but her arms shot out of it and she gave him a hug. She smelled of silk and a faint trace of perfumed soap.

He could feel the tension in her arms and back, and he imagined that her giddiness had given way to fear again, fear that something would go wrong. He let her remain silent as Rahman drove perhaps three miles north on an expressway called the Mecca Road, skirting the central district where the courthouse and the government ministries were. They turned right near a factory that appeared to bottle Pepsi-Cola and parked on a side street adjacent to the prison building.

He saw a squat, thick wall of badly whitewashed concrete, shaped like a wedge, so that the facade slanted up and away from the street. Every twenty feet or so there was a small, square window covered with thick iron bars that bowed outward like the bars of a catcher's mask. Streaks of rust bearded the windows. Each corner was marked by a guard tower, and there was a gate of what looked like cast iron, studded with rivets.

"It's called Al-Malaz," Janet said. She shuddered.

"What's that mean?"

"Nothing. Just the name of this quarter of the city."

He nodded, thinking of the Lubyanka in Moscow, which was named after an insurance company. The worst prisons had the most prosaic names.

Rahman got out, walked up to the gate, and knocked. In a moment a door within the gate opened, and he stepped inside. In another moment he came out again and walked back to the car.

He spoke to his mother in Arabic.

"They say we have to wait five minutes," Janet said to Burke.

They waited for a minute that seemed like ten. Then he asked, "What will you do after he's released? Where will you go?"

"Well, we have a house in Marbella," she said.

"Not a bad place to be exiled to."

"We won't stay there long. There are exile groups in London, other cities. Probably we'll go there. My husband will practice medicine and we will continue our work."

"Good," he said.

"And you? What will you do?"

"Go back to Washington," he answered.

"And what," she said, sounding slightly arch, "about this poor, misguided woman who doesn't appreciate you?"

He guessed that she wanted to be distracted again, but he found the possibility of discussing his own life too painful to encourage.

"I'm afraid that's over," he said.

"Over? You were ready to propose to her and now you think it's over?"

He shrugged, uncomfortable. "It's very complicated, Janet."

"Oh. Does she love you and do you love her?"

He felt himself blush.

"Yes, but that's not enough."

"Why not? Tribal differences? What did you mean by that?"

He was surprised she remembered.

"Well, to start off with, I'm a, uh, civilian, and she's not. She's not supposed to socialize with me."

"I don't understand."

"Well, she's with the government. The Agency."

"Oh," she said, drawing the word out. Then she chuckled, but it sounded mirthless. "Those people do get around."

"Yeah."

"What else?"

"She's black."

"What else?"

"Well, she says she has this plan. She wants to get her career to a very high level, then marry. She's not quite there yet. She needs a couple of years where she is, and where she is, she can't publicly be involved with me."

Janet's reaction to that was hidden by her veil.

"So how old is this woman?"

"Thirty-one."

"Didn't she read the *Newsweek* article about the prospects for single women over thirty?"

"I guess she subscribes to *Time*," Burke said.

"I assume you carefully laid the groundwork for this proposal and introduced it to her gradually?"

Burke scowled, embarrassed. "Yeah, right. I basically sprang it on her."

"Why am I not surprised?"

He laughed. "I always thought I was patient and sensitive with you."

She laughed with him, but there was an edge under it. "Only you would think so."

He said nothing.

"So you're going to just walk away." She took it up again.

"What else can I do? Beg?"

"I don't know what else you can do," and her voice turned softer. "But I remember you walking away from another relationship when you didn't get what you wanted, on the terms you wanted it."

He had to strain to hear her. Then he wished he hadn't.

"It's not the same thing, Janet," he said. "We were kids."

"Oh," she said. "I see."

He turned away from her and stared out the window.

"Rahman," Janet said. "Go see if it is time."

They watched the boy walk back to the gate and step inside the small door. In a moment he emerged.

He came back to the car, opened the back door this time, and spoke to Janet in Arabic. She started to scramble out of the car, gathering the folds of her *abaya* around her.

"They're ready!" she turned and said to him. "Wait here!"

He watched as they both disappeared into the jail. He moved into the front seat of the car so that Janet could ride with her husband in the back. He waited.

Minutes passed and it seemed to him that he could almost see the shadow of the jail's outer wall receding over the dusty pavement as the sun rose higher overhead. He rolled the window down to get some air and heard the sounds of the city around them, the rumble of trucks, the beeping of horns, and murmur of voices. He began to fear that something had happened.

Just as he had formulated a hypothesis that Henry Hoffman had duped the BBC in order to lure the rest of Massoud's family into captivity, the door opened. Rahman emerged first, followed by his father, who was leaning heavily on the boy's shoulder. Then Janet came out, supporting her husband's right side. Slowly, the trio made its way toward the car. Two prison guards sauntered out of the gate behind them and watched.

Burke wanted to get out of the car and open a door or something, but the sight of the guards deterred him. He pressed his back into the seat behind him, trying to stay unobtrusive. Rahman opened the door and helped his parents get in.

Abdulrahman Massoud winced as he folded his body sufficiently to pass into the car. He was wearing what Burke took to be prison garb—a plain brown caftan that stopped below his knees, and a knit skullcap.

His face looked like it had just come through a windshield. It was cut over the eyes and under the cheekbones, and one eye, his right, was almost swollen shut.

When she was inside, and Rahman had started the car and pulled away from the jail, Janet introduced them.

"Thank you for being here, Mr. Burke," Massoud said in English that had only a hint of an accent. "It's nice to have a representative of the free press."

"In these circumstances, it's nice to *be* a representative of the free press," Burke said. That reminded him that he would have to write a story.

"Tell me why you think the regime agreed to let you out," he said to Massoud.

"It's because . . . " Massoud began.

His voice trailed off.

A chanting mob of perhaps a thousand people had suddenly filled the street ahead of them. All of its members were men. They wore the standard dress of Saudi society, some in white *ghotras* and some in red-and-white checks, but their clothes were coarser than those Burke had seen in the airplane and in the courtroom.

On the sides of the crowd, he could tell, the chants were being led. An individual would yell a phrase in Arabic, and the crowd would roar an answering phrase.

He heard a sharp intake of breath from Janet.

"What are they yelling?" he asked.

Her voice was taut, like a wire.

" 'Death to the traitor,' " she said. " 'God is great.' "

Rahman jammed the gear lever into reverse and started looking for a way to back up. But a big Volvo truck blocked the street behind them.

"They're probably going to the jail, Rahman," Burke said sharply. "They won't recognize your father. Sit still."

The boy looked desperately around the car. His father said something to him in Arabic, and he shifted the transmission back to neutral.

The front line of the marchers moved rapidly closer to the car. The windshield through which Burke watched them gave an air of unreality to the mob, making it seem as if they were sitting in a movie theater, watching a western with a stampede scene, frightened and yet knowing that the thundering herd was only an illusion of sound and light. But these were real people, and he had no illusion about what they would do if Massoud were recognized.

The marchers reached the car. They parted and moved around it like minnows making way for a bigger fish. Their pace slowed as they squeezed between the car, the truck behind it, and the surrounding buildings. Some of them pounded on the fender, yelling and chanting, but they were intent on their goal, and after a few minutes the last of them had passed by.

"Dear God," Janet said.

Burke could smell urine in the car, apparently from the driver's seat. He couldn't blame the boy for being afraid. His own forehead was dripping with fearful sweat.

"Get going, Rahman," he said to the boy. "Now!"

Rahman put the car in gear and it lurched forward, tires squealing.

He made it out to a boulevard of some kind and turned right, where traffic again halted.

An even larger band of marchers, coming from the eastern side of the city, was crossing the boulevard. Burke heard the same yells and chants he had heard before. He gauged the size of the crowd at perhaps three thousand people.

Across the boulevard, in an olive-colored truck coming from the south, he saw a squad of National Guardsmen, rifles at their shoulders, red-and-white *ghotras* flapping gently in the warming breeze. The truck was not moving, and though the men stared intently at the marchers, they did not look as if they were about to intervene.

He made a decision.

"Janet, I've got to get out and see what's going on," he said. "I wouldn't go to your house. Find someplace where people won't expect you to be. Then call my room at the Inter-Con and leave a message from Miss Kane, telling me the phone number. As soon as I get back, I'll get in touch with the embassy and see what they're doing to get you out of here. Okay?"

She nodded.

"Miss Kane," he repeated. "Call me at the Inter-Con."

She nodded again.

He hopped out of the car and watched as the last of the second group of protesters finally made their way across the boulevard. He watched the Mercedes drive off and was thankful that the mob had no idea what Massoud looked like, or what car he drove.

He crossed the street and jogged around the block, eager to pick up the tail of the protesters before they made another turn. He felt the sun on his head and realized he should have been wearing a hat. Drops of sweat dribbled down his forehead.

He was in a street of small shops and apartments, and he noticed that most of them had drawn down the metal shutters that they used to close their stores at night. They did not seem to be anticipating a peaceful protest.

He felt, suddenly, quite conspicuous with his bare head and his polo shirt, like a cardinal in a flock of sparrows. Once he had the demonstrators back in sight, he slowed down and tried, without much success, to look as if he happened to be walking down the same street they had chosen.

In a few moments he was back in the same block with the jail, the one they had parked in just half an hour ago. The street was filling rapidly with people, and a thin pall of dust hung in the air between the buildings.

Another column of angry Arabs marched in from the south. That made three groups that he had seen, and the crowd had swollen to ten thousand men, converging the way iron filings cluster around a magnet.

Someone at the front, near the prison gate, was shouting over a bullhorn, but he could not make out the words. Even if he had been able to, he would have understood nothing.

But at the rear of the third group of protesters, he saw something that almost made him smile, with his lips if not with his eyes.

A moving cluster of demonstrators, attended by two Arabs with video cameras, carried signs in English.

DEATH TO THE TRAITER MASSOUD, said one.

CIA, ISRAYEL OUT OF ARABIA, said another.

Their awareness of the power of television exceeded their grasp of spelling, he thought. He wondered how long it would take for a copy of the videotape to make its way out of the country and into a CNN bureau. Probably no longer than twenty-four hours.

Because he could not understand what they were saying, he paid particular attention to the faces in the crowd. The eyes of the protesters belied their numbers and their action. They were hesitant, wary.

A chant arose, rhythmic and repetitious. As they chanted, the men began to raise their right hands in fists above their heads and thrust them forward in time with the dactyls of the chant until ten thousand arms and fists were swaying in unison, like sheaves of wheat in a capricious breeze.

But even as they flexed their power he saw men looking furtively over their shoulders.

Behind him he heard the muffled throb of engines, barely audible over the sound of the mob. He turned to look. A dozen trucks, filled with soldiers, like the one he had seen on the boulevard, were taking up positions. They wore brown camouflage fatigues under their *ghotras*, and they carried M-16 rifles.

Gauging quickly where the lines of fire might be, Burke sidled back toward the trucks, took shelter in the shaded doorway of a "cold store" under a sign that promised ALWAYS COCA-COLA, and watched.

A moment later a piece of the mob detached itself and started moving toward the trucks, led by a tall, gaunt man in a dirty white *thobe*, clutching a bullhorn.

Ten yards from the lead truck, the man with the bullhorn stopped and began talking, apparently at the soldiers. His voice had an oddly soothing quality, even as it rose in pitch and strength.

Burke watched the faces of the soldiers. They looked quite young—draftees, probably, in their late teens or early twenties.

As the man with the bullhorn talked on, Burke could see a change come over their faces. At first, they had been cocky and bland with the look of cultivated nonchalance and latent danger affected by young men under arms in all the countries he had worked in. But soon their shoulders slumped a little, and he could see some of them start to study their shoes. Others looked up and he thought he could spot fear in their eyes, fear and indecision.

Finally, an officer stepped out of the cab of the truck and stepped toward the man with the bullhorn. The man fell silent. The captain, ostentatiously, raised his rifle toward the sky. Burke held his breath.

With an audible click, the captain slipped a catch and removed the magazine from his rifle. Grinning, the other soldiers in the truck did the same.

These soldiers were not going to fire their weapons.

A cheer erupted from the crowd of protesters and the man with the bullhorn gleefully turned toward the main body of the crowd.

"Allah akbar!" he yelled.

The crowd answered in kind.

They surged back toward the entrance to the jail, chanting something with Massoud's name attached to the end of it. Burke imagined that it was, "Give us Massoud."

A cluster of perhaps a hundred men, arriving from some other sector of the city, swarmed into the space in front of him. These were not Saudis, at least not Saudis as he had come to know them in spotless, well-tailored robes and precisely arranged *ghotras*. These were poorer men, their beards scraggly and unkempt, their clothing soiled. The fact that they all wore head coverings of some kind suggested they were Muslim, but their dress said they were guest laborers from one of the desperately poor countries in the Saudi neighborhood—Palestinians, or Yemenis, perhaps, or Egyptians. No matter. They joined in the chants. A couple of them looked around at Burke, staring.

Burke scanned what he could see of the prison, wondering whether any armed force was going to intervene to stop this mob, which was still swelling. He saw no sign of authority beyond the soldiers in the trucks with the empty magazines in their rifles.

He had witnessed a couple of revolutions, in Romania in 1989 and in Russia in 1991. Each of them had turned on an incident like the one he had just seen, when a crowd realized that the forces of authority were impotent. But in those cases, the people in the streets had seemed benevolent and their cause just. They had been thrilled to know that correspondents from the West were watching. There was a sense that the reporters and the revolutionaries were, if not working together, tacit allies.

But this crowd frightened him. It was, perhaps, due to the mechanical way they responded to the men with the megaphones. Perhaps it was the hostility he thought he saw in the eyes of those closest to him. He had the sense they could turn on him. He started to sweat copiously.

He felt the need to move, to get away from the staring eyes before there could be a confrontation. Besides, he could no longer see the jail entrance. The crowd was too big.

He stepped out of the shadows and into the sun, keeping his back to the shops behind him, pressing against the buildings, feeling the texture of rough, dried-mud bricks, doorknobs, and corrugated steel shutters through the thin cloth of his shirt.

The sun was dazzling bright now, and he squinted. The dust in the air was thick, rising from the soles of thousands of shoes pounding on the cobblestones of the square.

Stepping sideways, he made his way steadily toward the corner formed by the west and north ends of the jailhouse.

He could see, at the entrance to the jail, a conversation under way between a man in uniform and an elderly, bearded Saudi. The man in uniform, he guessed, represented the jail garrison. The old man represented the crowd.

He could smell the crowd now, smell the sweat on their bodies and the sweet coffee on their breath; the air in the square was getting thick with dust and adrenaline.

And he could hear the crowd, hear the chants, the voices now sounding stronger and more confident.

But he could not understand it. He looked around behind him as he crossed the street.

He saw a squat little man with curly blond hair, dressed in a khaki business suit and wire-rim glasses, standing by the driver's side of a little English Ford, taking notes on a pad. He had ears like Brillo pads and his legs seemed too short for the rest of his body.

Burke stepped back to him.

"Speak English?" he asked quietly.

The man stopped writing and gave Burke a long look.

"Yes."

"What are they saying?"

The man smiled just a little, the corners of his thin lips turning upward.

"They're saying, 'Massoud is a traitor. Death to Massoud.' Occasionally, they're saying, 'Down with America.' "

His accent was vaguely British, but not quite. Australian, maybe.

"Oh," Burke said.

"You're an American, I take it?"

Burke nodded.

The little man's eyes twinkled.

"I wouldn't advertise it right now."

He extended his hand. "George Ferguson, New Zealand embassy."

Burke shook it.

"Colin Burke," he said. He did not volunteer his professional association.

In front of them, the conversation between the man with the bullhorn and the man in uniform ended. The man with the bullhorn turned to address the crowd. He said something about Allah, the same words Burke had heard the judge use the day before.

Slowly, like an engine coming to a gradual halt, the noise in the street subsided.

The man with the bullhorn spoke about two sentences. An angry roar erupted from the square.

"He says that the jailer swears Massoud has been released."

"The jailer's right," Burke said.

Ferguson's eyes opened a little wider.

"How do you know?" he asked.

"I know," Burke said.

"Are you the reporter from the *Trib*—"

Burke cut him off with a quick nod and a question.

"What's he saying now?"

"He's denouncing the king for caving in to pressure from the Americans . . ." Ferguson's voice trailed off as he strained to hear the amplified sound over the underlying din of angry murmurs from the crowd. ". . . And he's saying they must force the state television station to let them broadcast their message to the entire country."

The crowd, prompted by its shepherds, took up a new chant.

" 'To the television station,' they're yelling," Ferguson said.

Burke nodded. "You know where it is?"

"As a matter of fact, I do," Ferguson replied.

"Going that way?"

"Perhaps."

"Taking riders?"

"If you'll tell me how you came to be here and got that story," Ferguson bargained.

Burke nodded. "Let's go."

Ferguson quickly opened the door on his side, got in, and reached over to unlock the door on Burke's. Burke squeezed in, jamming his knees under the dashboard. The car smelled of stale candy and diaper ointment. There were a couple of child seats in the rear, along with a battered copy of *Horton Hatches the Egg*.

"You can push the seat back if you want to," Ferguson said. "My wife's a good bit shorter than you."

The car's little engine whirred at a pitch that seemed tiny and high to Burke after a couple of days of traveling in a Mercedes. Ferguson executed a deft three-point turn and got the car going.

Burke felt something hard under his right thigh and pulled it out. It looked like a set of ear protectors, with white plastic cups and a few dangling straps.

"You a wrestler?" he asked as he stashed the device on the dashboard.

"Rugby player," Ferguson answered. "Started wearing those too late."

He grinned and Burke thought that one of his front teeth looked porcelain.

"You play here?'

Ferguson nodded. "Just casual Sunday stuff, with some of the chaps from Australia, South Africa."

"What do you do at the embassy?"

"Political officer."

"And what do you think is going to happen here?"

Ferguson turned a corner, the car swaying slightly on weak springs. They were on a broad boulevard, headed south. Burke could tell by the sun. The median of this road was lined with palm trees and precisely clipped green hedges.

"I don't know what's going to happen," Ferguson said. "This country is like an old wooden house on a seacoast. Termites have eaten away the foundations. It's rotten. Every time a typhoon comes along, you think the house is going to blow into the sea. Year after year it somehow doesn't. And then one morning, after a storm that didn't even wake you up, it's gone."

Ferguson stopped at a red light, watching over his shoulder as a truck full of soldiers pulled up behind and to the right of them, blew its horn, and barged through the intersection against the light.

"Is this the morning?" Burke asked, watching the sun glint on the barrels of the soldiers' rifles.

"Wish I knew," Ferguson muttered, looking for an opening to run the light and stay behind the troop truck.

The sidewalks around them were nearly empty. Burke couldn't tell whether people were staying inside because word had spread about the demonstration at the jail, or because people in Riyadh, like people in Southern California, traveled everywhere by car.

Ferguson gave up on the troop truck, made a quick right, and got back onto the highway Rahman had used, the Mecca Road. But instead of stopping, he turned in front of the Inter-Continental and headed toward the clocktower square where the trial had occurred.

A few blocks short of that, he turned, and Burke could see a spindly transmitter rising above a cluster of low government buildings. In the predawn darkness, from his hotel room, he had taken it for a minaret. In the light, he could see what it was. It towered over a barren preserve, dry and rocky, hatched with new roads that linked a series of low, ugly government buildings.

Ferguson parked about three hundred yards from the tower and shut off the engine.

Now Burke could see people walking again, protesters like the ones in front of the jail, carrying placards and proceeding in the company of men with bullhorns. But he knew they were not the same people. They couldn't have beaten a car to the television station. These were new demonstrators, responding, he guessed, to some kind of intra-mosque communications network.

"I imagine the show will be starting in about ten minutes," Ferguson said pleasantly. "You were going to tell me how you came to be here and break this Massoud story."

Burke bit his lip. He disliked being on the answering side of a question. He didn't know this man, although he liked him. He didn't want to compromise himself or anyone else.

"How are we talking? Off the record?"

"Well, I won't publish anything, if that's what you mean," Ferguson said.

"I don't want the Saudis to know about it."

"That's no problem."

"Or the Americans."

"No problem again. Don't see much of your blokes."

"Massoud has a wife who grew up partly in the U.S. I knew her in high school. When her husband was arrested, she contacted me. Indirectly. A visa was arranged. They got me into the courtroom for the trial."

Ferguson blinked.

"Nice work. How'd you get into the court?"

Burke grinned. "I'm too embarrassed to tell you."

"The American embassy wasn't helping her?"

"No."

"Was he, in fact, spying?"

"He says he wasn't a paid agent. But he passed along some information to people he knew in the embassy."

"How'd they get wind of him?"

Burke hesitated. "I'd rather not say. I'm still working on that part of the story."

"But we're off the record."

Burke grinned at the man. "You'd make a good reporter. But I really can't say. I don't have any verified information."

"Fair enough," Ferguson said.

The sun beating down on the car started to heat it up, and Burke rolled down the window. It didn't make much difference. The temperature outside, he guessed, was well over ninety.

"Too bad we can't park in the shade," Burke said.

"I would if there were any," Ferguson replied.

Dust was rising into the air as protesting men moved into the area in front of the television station, first in twos and threes, and then in larger groups, until the numbers, Burke gauged, had swollen into hundreds and then well over a thousand.

Ferguson pointed to his left, and he could see troop trucks, more this time, entering the area in orderly lines. He counted them—four, six, nine, a dozen. The trucks lined up in a phalanx a few hundred yards from the front entrance to the television station. The red-and-white checked *ghotras* of the soldiers shone in the sun against the dull green of the trucks.

"Army?" Burke asked Ferguson.

"By the uniforms, yes," the New Zealander replied.

"What do you mean, 'by the uniforms'?"

"There are all kinds of special units in this country with all kinds of missions," Ferguson said.

Flashing blue lights caught their eye, and they watched as a convoy of police cars, traveling at high speed, screeched around a corner and up the drive in front of the television station. The cars started parking in such a way as to form a barricade between the pavement and the door.

"Looks like Prince Turki, or someone, wants to handle this without soldiers," Ferguson observed.

The cops getting out of the cars wore blue helmets and carried riot shields. They looked like they had been equipped in the United States.

The dust got thicker as the crowd continued to grow.

Now a man with a bullhorn had taken up a position at the front of the crowd, perhaps ten yards away from the line of police cars, chanting. The protesters from in front on the prison, Burke thought, had not yet arrived, but when they did, the crowd would be formidable. It was already, he guessed, about five thousand strong.

The protesters looked like an organic mass of brown, black, and white, oozing toward the entrance, growing, shifting, sprouting signs and placards like fibrils that waved slowly back and forth. He saw the gap between them and the police narrow.

The shots, when they came, sounded at first like the backfire of trucks—*pop, pop, pop*. It was only when he saw bodies start to crumple in front of the television station, and heard more and more rapid popping, that Burke realized someone was firing automatic weapons.

He panicked, ducking as far under the dashboard as his legs would allow, wishing he had bothered to move the seat backward, fumbling for his seat belt and trying to unbuckle it, for reasons he could not have specified. Fresh sweat poured off his forehead and the palms of his hands, and he started to pant, waiting for the sound of bullets hitting the windshield. But there was no sound, except for the pop of the rifle shots, which seemed louder now, and the muted screams and muffled shouts of the crowd.

He raised his head, cautiously, above dashboard level. The mass of protesters had splintered and become frightened individuals, running for their lives, dozens of them halting, twisting, and falling. The sound of rifle fire filled the air above him now, and he could smell the burned charges.

He felt an urge to duck again, but he told himself that was foolish and forced his eyes upward, beyond the crowd. Another hundred yards away, on the flat roof of a brown, four-story building, he spotted the source of the fire—three men in red-and-white *ghotras* and brown camouflage fatigues. They were standing, not bothering to conceal or shield themselves, their rifles at their shoulders, raking the crowd with fire. A thin cloud of oily white smoke was rising over their heads.

As he watched they moved in unison, dropping their weapons to their waists, turning, and jogging off to the opposite end of their rooftop. In a moment they disappeared. He imagined that they had a ladder or a staircase at the opposite end of the building.

In front of him, the carnage started to sort itself out. Maybe a hundred bodies, their white robes looking like shrouds, lay in the street in front of the television station. Most were still. A few were twitching. Thousands more demonstrators were fleeing in panic in all directions save one—the direction of the troop trucks and their armed soldiers. Burke took a quick look at the soldiers.

They were crouched in their trucks now, rifles ready, but he saw no evidence that they were firing.

He looked back at the police in front of the station. They were still crouched behind their riot shields. He heard the *twock, thwock* sound of shells being launched from canisters. Within seconds clouds of tear gas started to spread through the square.

Burke opened the car door, but before he could get out, he felt Ferguson's strong hand on his forearm.

"I wouldn't," Ferguson said. "You'd make a good target."

He hated being restrained, but he realized Ferguson was right. He took out his notepaper and started counting the bodies. When he was finished, he wrote the number down: ninety-three. He looked at his watch and jotted down the time: 8:12 A.M.

CHAPTER 8

Ferguson looked carefully through the windows of his car, twisting his body around in his seat to get a look at all sides around them. He started the engine.

Outside, there was a sudden and noticeable loss of sound, as if someone had turned the volume down. The shouts and the wailing had ceased, as had the sound of shots. The only noise was the scuffling of feet along the pavement and the dusty earth next to it as people fled. Burke saw one man hobble past clutching his leg, a bright red stain spreading slowly under his hand, glistening against the background of a white *thobe*.

"What are you doing?" he said, startled by the sound of the starter turning over.

"I'm getting us out of here," Ferguson replied.

"Why?"

"Because no police cars are coming. This is the best time to get away."

"Why get away?"

Ferguson looked at him as if he had asked why get in out of the rain.

"Bad enough I saw this. But you?"

"So?"

"Well, if *I* were to be found here after this, I imagine I'd be in trouble enough. And *I* have diplomatic immunity. But you, friend. You're in a terrible position. Do you understand?"

He did, but he wanted to hear it. "Spell it out for me."

"They'll want to suppress any news that this ever happened. You've probably violated at least a dozen Saudi laws already. Now, how do you think they'll treat you?"

He said nothing as Ferguson pushed the car through a three-point turn and began to retrace their route toward the Inter-Continental.

They passed a building with some English lettering on a plaque by the door. SAUDI NEWS AGENCY, it said.

This event, Burke thought, could not be suppressed. Too many people had died. Too many people had seen it. Somewhere down the road, he would be asked about it. And then he would have to acknowledge that he had left the scene before the story was over.

He was a coward, but he could not stand being thought of as a coward.

"Shit," Burke said. "Stop the car."

The car was gathering speed, up to forty miles an hour now.

"What?"

"Stop. I'm getting out."

Ferguson tapped the brakes, but not enough to stop the car.

"You sure?"

Burke nodded.

Ferguson pulled over next to the curb. Burke opened the door.

"Well, I admire your nerve if not your good sense," Ferguson said. "Should I ring your embassy and tell them I saw you here?"

Burke leaned in the doorway to hear him better.

"Their phones bugged?"

Ferguson nodded. "Most likely."

"Think you could drop by there and just let someone know?"

"Sure. Can do. It's in the infidels' compound with us."

"Thanks." He shut the door and watched as Ferguson pulled away. Then he turned in a full circle, looking for a vantage point.

There was nothing—no shrubbery, no trees, nothing to stand behind. There was only bare, dusty brown earth, interspersed with buildings garlanded by carefully tended wreaths of grass bordered by rows of pansies. He felt naked and vulnerable.

On the road leading down from the direction of the prison, he could see a cloud of dust rising, which he imagined to be the main body of protesters. In front of the television station, the riot police were slowly recovering from their shock, standing, changing formation. In the dusty patch of earth where the shooting victims lay, a couple of men were crawling away, hoping to miss the next fusillade. The rest of the demonstrators had dispersed. Burke thought he could sniff the scent of blood in the hot air.

Then he heard sirens, and he could see two distinct convoys of police cars, blue lights flashing, heading at speed toward the scene of the carnage. The second convoy, he realized, was heading toward him, and would be on him in a minute. He remembered Ferguson's warning and wondered why he had been so foolish as to stay.

He could see only one potential source of cover—the Saudi News Agency building about a hundred yards to the south. He would have to take his chances there.

He sprinted, breaking again into a sweat that soaked through his shirt and stuck it to his back like a damp paper towel.

Under the portico of the building, he found he was not the only one to see it as a possible sanctuary. About a dozen erstwhile protesters had clustered in the shade. Two of them were slightly wounded. They lay on the polished marble staircase as friends improvised bandages from strips of cloth. Men were muttering angrily, their Arabic vowels sounding harsh and guttural. Burke could only imagine what they were saying. He did not want to linger long enough for them to start saying it to him.

In such situations, he had learned, the best thing was to act as if he knew what he was doing and had every right to do it. So he pushed through roughly, opened the door to the lobby, and stepped through quickly. He expected to see a security guard inside, but there was only an empty desk, surrounded by blown-up photos of the king, opening a hospital, holding a racehorse's bridle, and sitting with some elderly men at what appeared to be some kind of council. A few more protesters sat, wounded or exhausted, against the walls near the door. But otherwise, the lobby was empty. The guard, he imagined, had sought his own shelter when the shooting started.

The guard would be back. What Burke needed was a place on the floor above, perhaps a bathroom, with a window overlooking the television station. Failing that, he might try to go to the roof.

There were a couple of elevators at the end of the lobby, but he walked past them until he saw a sign with a zigzag line that he took to mean staircase. It did.

The staircase, like the lobby, was deserted. He walked up a flight, conscious of the way his footfalls resonated. At the second floor, he stopped. The staircase went on, presumably to the roof. But perhaps the roof was reserved for snipers. If so, better to stay off it.

He pushed open the door and emerged into a wide, roomy corridor, carpeted in gray, with half a dozen wooden doors on each side, all closed. Each door had a brass plaque over it, with writing in Arabic. A large bottle of water, turned on its head, stood at the far end on a kind of platform. It might have been the offices of an insurance company after hours. He heard nothing.

Cautiously, he tried a door on the north side of the corridor. It was locked. He tried the next one, and the one after that. Both locked. He pushed a little harder on the last one. The door and lock seemed sturdy.

He looked at his watch. It was almost 8:30. He wondered when people came to work in this building. And where they went when they had to urinate.

He tried three more doors, all locked. Outside, he could hear a slowly rising sound, a kind of keening, and he guessed that the protesters from the jail had arrived and found the bodies in front of the television station.

He tried to peer through the window at the end of the hallway, but it afforded only a look at a bleak, empty parking lot. He needed to be in one of these offices.

Carelessly, he shoved at the final door in the corridor. Unexpectedly, it yielded. The momentum of his thrust carried him into the room before he could look around. He saw a figure at the window turning toward him.

Before he could bolt in the other direction, the figure revealed itself as a tall, thin man with a precisely trimmed, black mustache and a face lined with deep wrinkles around the eyes and mouth. He wore a pair of pin-striped navy trousers and a white shirt, open at the collar. Burke could see a patch of gray hair beginning to spread from the man's temples. The top of his head was bald. His hand was at his chest. He looked like a shoe salesman in shock.

The man said something in Arabic. He had a deep, gravelly voice.

"Salaam alaykum," Burke replied.

The man looked carefully, nervously at Burke and considered the accent he had just heard.

"You are American?" he asked in English.

Burke nodded.

"By God, you gave me a start," the man said.

"Careful," Burke said. "I hear they're pretty tough on blasphemers around here."

The man peered at him for a moment, then got the joke. He smiled briefly. Then he fingered the phone, and Burke could almost hear him pondering whether to call the building's security office and report the presence of an unknown foreigner. Then the man put the phone down.

"My name is Sarawi," he said, extending a hand.

Burke took it and gave the man his name.

"You are doing what here?"

Burke answered the question as narrowly as he thought he could get away with.

"I thought I ought to come in out of the bullets."

Sarawi pulled a cigarette from a package of Marlboros on his desk and lit it. He took a deep drag and exhaled slowly.

America's contribution to world health, Burke thought.

"Well, so far, we are out of the line of fire," Sarawi finally said. "Please be seated."

Burke took a chair and pulled it to the edge of the window. He sat and peered out. The square was still a scene of latent chaos. The bodies lay crumpled on the pavement in front of the television station. The police cars were making an effort to form a perimeter around the area. The next wave of demonstrators, the one from the prison, was about a block away. He could measure their progress by the advancing cloud of dust and the growing audibility of their chants.

Sarawi sat at the desk on the other side of the window. It was covered with papers that Burke could see were wire-service dispatches. There was a computer on one side of the desk, some kind of story on the screen. In a frame, there was a color photo, made in a studio, of this man seated at the forefront of a family that included a wife and four children.

He had the sensation that Sarawi was staring at him.

"You are with one of the oil companies?" the man asked.

"No," Burke said.

"The military?"

Burke had no wish to deceive Sarawi, but no interest in telling him something that would only jeopardize both of them. He had Sarawi pegged: the overnight editor, the man who drew the scut-work shift.

There were dozens of people like him in wire services and newsrooms all over the world, putting out night scores and late-breaking murders.

"No," Burke said. "I'm here as a consultant."

"Oh." Sarawi nodded, his bushy eyebrows flickering nervously.

Burke realized the man thought *consultant* was a euphemism for spy. It made him feel uncomfortable, but not as uncomfortable as he would have felt if the man had known he was a reporter. Sarawi probably would have felt obliged to turn a journalist in to the police. Consultants were another matter; they didn't publish their reports.

But he didn't want Sarawi to keep asking questions. So he asked some himself.

"How many bodies do you figure?"

"I've counted ninety-three," Sarawi said, still peering out the window.

"You're a good reporter," Burke told him. "How'd you wind up here?"

"If one has four children to educate, one cannot do it on what a journalist earns in Jordan," Sarawi replied.

"That's where you're from?"

Sarawi nodded. "I was the managing editor of the *Jordan Times*."

It was the English-language paper in Amman, and though it reflected the views of King Hussein, it was not toadyish about it.

"I've seen it," Burke said. "Good paper. What's your job here?"

"I read the wires from around the world," Sarawi said. "I translate the important stories into Arabic. A lot of it is financial—gold fixings and spot oil prices in Tokyo and Singapore and such. Then the day editors come in and decide how to distribute it."

"When do the editors get here?"

"Oh, a couple of British expatriates toddle in at nine or so. The Saudis show up at ten to put their chop on things."

"Nice hours."

"They seem to think so."

In the streets below, the police finished their formation of a light perimeter around the television station.

"How do they distribute it?"

"The financial news goes straight out to the Saudi papers. The political material has two channels. One for the papers, after it has been vetted. The other for the ministries—foreign ministry, oil ministry, that sort of thing."

It reminded Burke of TASS in the old days, but he kept his opinion to himself.

He saw the first ranks of the marchers from the prison, finally arriving. Their numbers had swollen, it seemed to him, until there were at least fifteen thousand of them. Their column stretched back up the road from the north until it disappeared behind the facades of intervening buildings. The sound of their chants was like the dull roar of the ocean in the distance. The lead marchers, he saw, had stopped, apparently surveying the bodies and the scene in front of them.

"So what have you filed on what happened outside a few minutes ago?"

"Right," Sarawi snorted, rolling the *r*. "A good way to find yourself wandering in the desert without your ticket home."

"See who did the shooting?"

"Yes. National Guard."

"That's what I thought. I saw three on that roof over there."

"So did I."

"Any others?"

"No. I did not notice. But I was not extending my head out the window to have a good look, you know." Sarawi smiled at this.

"Odd that those three fired and none of the others did."

"There have been many odd things in this country," Sarawi agreed. Burke wondered what he meant.

Before he could ask, Burke saw below them the front ranks of the protesters surging forward. A cluster of two dozen men picked up and overturned a police car, leaving it on its roof, wheels spinning in the air. The police, he saw, backed away, letting the crowd have its way.

The chanting of the protesters became a disorganized, angry roar as more and more of them saw the bodies lying on the ground. Then the roar changed tone as the police continued to retreat. He could hear individual voices, screaming.

Two more police cars went upside down as the perimeter they had constructed disintegrated.

Burke waited for the sound of shots. But he heard none. The troops in the area, like the troops in the street outside the prison, were not firing. They sat in their trucks, watching a riot develop in front of them.

He could not tell whether they had orders not to fire or whether they had simply refused.

From a distance, the wave of demonstrators seemed to gather itself and then break, washing over the line of police cars like the incoming tide washing over a sand castle. It was inevitable, irresistible.

Police fled from in front of the television station. He heard a couple of shots—*pop, pop*—but they sounded tentative. No one fell, and he imagined that someone had fired into the air.

Sensing triumph, the crowd began to run, routing the police before it, covering the remaining ground to the television station in a matter of a few minutes.

He could see the leaders enter the station and faintly hear the sound of glass breaking.

"Praise God," Sarawi said. "The police will not fire." There were elements of fear and exultation mixed in his voice.

Burke looked around the office. There was a television set, a small, red Hitachi, on a bookshelf that covered the wall opposite the window. A portrait of King Khalil, in a gilded frame, sat on the shelf above it. Burke reflected, not for the first time, that in any country, freedom and democracy were likely to be in inverse proportion to the ubiquity of pictures of the head of state.

"Might be interesting to turn that on," he suggested to Sarawi.

"They will have only morning prayers and educational lectures on now," Sarawi said, but he sidestepped gingerly over to the set, turned it on, and churned through the channels, extending his arm so as not to step in front of the window.

The screen showed gray static on all channels.

"It looks as if they've gone off the air," Sarawi said.

Burke nodded and resumed watching the crowd below. The front of the television station was completely enveloped now.

He took out his notepaper and jotted down a few observations, feeling increasingly frustrated and inadequate. He knew little of Saudi history, nothing of the language, little or nothing of the culture. How could he understand what was happening in front of him? He had, by chance, become a parachute artist, dropping in on a strange country to report a big event. In Russia, he had at least known the language and some of the history, and he had disdained the reporters who flew into Moscow and had to ask people to fill them in on things they should have known. Now he was one of them.

Sarawi, he realized, was staring at the notes he was writing. What the hell, he thought. He had a sense he could trust this man.

"Ever seen anything like this?" he asked.

"Never," Sarawi said, emphatically. "The authorities here are always very quick to crack down on the first signs of dissent. I suspect we will see that here soon."

Burke nodded, but he was skeptical. The Soviets had been quick to crack down on dissent. So had the Romanians under Ceausescu. And then, one day, they hadn't been able to do it anymore, and their regimes fell apart almost instantly. Sometimes, authoritarian governments rotted from the inside out, and the facade of power was the last part to crumble.

He frowned. It would be the worst sort of mistake to transpose what he knew of Russia to this country. He would have to write very carefully, sticking closely to what he observed, staying clear of interpretation.

"Here they come now," Sarawi said. He pointed.

Two dozen military trucks had started moving, conveying perhaps six hundred soldiers toward the entrance to the television station. The trucks looked large and purposeful.

"Dear God," Sarawi whispered. "This is going to be bloody awful."

He must, Burke thought, have learned his English at a British Council school.

Burke slipped off his chair to be able to poke his head out the window and get a more panoramic view. He saw a column of APCs trundling slowly down the Mecca Road about three miles away.

"Or awfully bloody," he said.

Below, Burke could see a man with a bullhorn step out in front of the crowd and face the lead truck. It might have been the same man he had watched at the prison a couple of hours earlier—he was too far away to be certain.

For perhaps ten minutes they watched some kind of dialogue take place. It was like watching mime theater. The body language suggested that the man with the bullhorn was exhorting the troops.

Suddenly the trucks started moving again. But this time, they turned outward, forming a perimeter surrounding the crowd.

"What is happening?" Sarawi wondered.

"I'm not certain," Burke said. "But I believe the soldiers have changed teams."

"Alhamdulillah," Sarawi said.

The buzz of the crowd slowly rose and grew into a triumphant roar as the same opinion spread among them. The sound floated up and washed through the window.

At the same time Burke heard the background of television crackle cease. He turned around.

The camera work was a little cockeyed, but the screen showed a man in brown robes and a red-and-white checked *ghotra*. Judging by the wrinkles around his eyes and the streaks of gray in his full beard, he was middle-aged. He had one brown eye and one blind one. The blind eye was a milky-gray eyeball floating in its socket, without an iris. Someone to his right, off camera, held a microphone up toward the man's mouth.

"In the name of God, the merciful," he began, and then Burke lost the Arabic. Sarawi began a condensed translation.

"He says the nation has witnessed one, um, sacrilege, I guess, or big sin, after another since the death of King Abdul-Aziz forty-four years ago. King Saud was a drunk and a lecher. That is so! King Faisal invited the Americans to enter the kingdom and betrayed the Palestinians by ending the oil embargo. King Fahd turned the country over to the infidels and let them wage war against a fellow Arab. King Khalil has betrayed Islam. He does not allow believers under the age of fifty to make the *hajj*, which is their duty before God."

The man on the screen spoke in a tightly controlled, melodic voice. His bad eye gave him the look of a medium, of someone transmitting another's thoughts.

"Now he says they have completed the humiliation of the country by allowing the American president to tell them what to do with a traitor to Islam and the Arab nation. They are not a genuine Islamic government. They are drunkards and thieves who chase after whores and deserve to have their right hands cut off. And then, he says, the king . . ."

The man on the screen paused, and so did Sarawi.

"He says of the king and his family that as God told the Prophet, 'Neither their riches nor their children shall in the least protect them from God's scourge. They are the heirs of the fire.' "

"Does that mean what I think it means?"

Sarawi nodded, still engrossed in the television screen. "They are condemned," he said, his voice slightly tremulous. "They deserve to die."

"Do you know who's talking?" Burke asked, finishing the notes he was jotting.

"I'm not sure," Sarawi said. "But I think I believe it is Sheikh al-Jubail."

There was a flicker, a moment of empty air, and then an image of the sky showed up on the screen. The image changed as a camera panned, and a slightly grainy image of the area in front of the television station emerged. But instead of the big crowd that was still roaring down below, the screen showed only a few hundred protesters. They were yelling, but the camera was not equipped to pick up sound.

Burke looked out the window and then back at the screen. Then it came to him.

"It's a tape," he said. "Made maybe fifteen minutes ago."

Sarawi nodded, fumbled with the cigarette that had burned itself out in the ashtray, and lit another.

"How are they doing this?" he asked.

"They've got friends inside, or they're pretty sophisticated about broadcasting," Burke guessed.

The image on the screen wiggled and jumped. It remained silent, but Burke could tell from the jagged panning that the photographer had taken cover behind a corner of the TV station, which blocked the right side of his field of vision, then trained the camera back on the crowd as bodies started to twitch and fall.

Then the scene changed as the photographer panned toward the building where the firing had originated. The screen showed the same image Burke had seen—three men in National Guard uniforms, spraying the crowd with bullets, standing up in plain sight, and then moving in orderly fashion off the roof and out of sight.

The tape stopped, there was another thirty seconds of dead air, and the one-eyed man reappeared on the screen. He was looking not into the camera, but off to one side. Then he apparently received a signal, because he turned back to the camera and resumed talking.

"All of this has happened because the rightful line of succession was . . . usurped?" Sarawi said, uncertain of the translation.

There was no chance for a clarification.

There was a kind of general sigh as electric power ceased flowing to the Saudi News Agency building. Burke could hear the absence of sound as air conditioners stopped running. The picture on the television screen dissolved into a white dot and then faded to black. The lights overhead went out, though there was still plenty of sunlight coming in the window.

"I suspect someone's cut off the power," he said to Sarawi.

"To the whole area," Sarawi replied.

Burke looked out the window. The line of APCs was perhaps a mile away, traveling very slowly. He imagined that whoever commanded them had to be wondering now about the loyalty of his troops.

More police cars, sirens wailing, entered the area from behind the Saudi News Agency building, reinforcing the detachment of officers that had retreated in the face of the mob a few moments earlier. As Burke watched, groups of eight officers, swathed in riot gear, started to enter each of the buildings in the neighborhood, presumably to secure them.

They would, he calculated, be in this building in five minutes.

Sarawi noticed, too.

"If you are a journalist, this is not a good place for you," he said.

"People keep telling me that," Burke replied.

CHAPTER 9

From the lobby of the Saudi News Agency, Burke watched as five police cars pulled up, tires screeching. Through the window glass, he could see that these policemen had heavy riot gear—helmets, shields, and shotguns.

The demonstrators who, fifteen minutes ago, had taken shelter in the lobby had evidently fled. He was the only one left.

It was a time, Burke decided, for a display of outraged innocence. He pulled his blue passport out of his pocket and held it up in front of his face like a battle flag. Then he sprinted out of the lobby, leaving the door ajar in his wake, directly to the first of the police cars. He crouched down and pounded with an open palm on the car's window.

"I'm an American," he yelled, pushing the passport up against the glass. "Open up and get me out of here!"

Nothing happened.

"American! Help!" he yelled, still pounding, still holding the passport against the glass.

It took, he calculated, nearly thirty seconds for the police inside to react.

Two of them emerged from the backseat of the car, one of them ducking low as he sprinted around to Burke's side, the other nearly falling on his head as he tried to come out the door without offering anyone a target to shoot at.

"I'm an American," Burke yelled again. "I need help!"

He let each of the policemen get a hand around one of his elbows. They began pushing him toward the door of the news-agency building. Once he understood that, he began sprinting, grabbing one of the policemen by the sleeve of his camouflage jacket and pulling him along faster.

They reached the lobby. Burke sized up the two policemen. One had a single stripe on his sleeve and the other had corporal's chevrons. They each had wispy black goatees. They looked young, confused, and frightened.

He pushed the passport again into the face of the corporal.

"I'm an American," he said in a lower, calmer voice. "I need help. People are shooting at me."

The corporal looked at Burke, uncomprehending.

Burke did as American tourists do when confronted with a foreigner who has somehow failed to master English. He spoke louder.

"I'm an American," he said, nearly shouting into the policeman's helmet. "I need help. People are shooting at me."

Again, the policeman failed to react.

Burke put his hands on his hips. "Find me someone who speaks English." He waited for a response. "English!" he yelled.

Finally, the corporal spoke, saying something in Arabic to the private. He ducked out the door and headed toward the last car in the queue that had formed in the driveway.

"English," the private said, smiling and showing a splayed front tooth. He nodded vigorously. "English."

Through the glass doors, Burke could see the crowd in front of the television station, still swelling. A dozen more APCs appeared on the horizon, trundling slowly toward them. Even if the National Guardsmen who had turned their trucks around and faced outward had indeed changed sides, they were relatively lightly armed. The government would soon have an overwhelming edge in firepower—if its soldiers and police could be trusted to use it.

The corporal jogged into view, followed by a policeman in neatly pressed fatigues and mirrored sunglasses. His epaulets had a couple of stars on them and he carried only a pistol. He walked rather than ran.

The man looked older and more certain of his place than the underlings. Silently, Burke reminded himself of his own role—the frightened, aggrieved innocent.

Projecting fear would require no acting. His palms were clammy and his mind was flitting like a crazed water bug from one thing to another, from Janet Kane and her family to the Al-Malaz prison, to the three snipers to how angry he should pretend to be, to Desdemona McCoy and what she would think if he got arrested and never returned and back to the snipers. He thought that he had never been able to stay calm and deliberate in the face of hostile authority. He swallowed. His throat was dry.

He tore himself free of the private's grasp and ran straight at the officer, meeting him just as he stepped inside the lobby.

"You speak English?" he yelled. He waved his passport again. "You've gotta get me out of here! Speak English?"

The officer took a step backward.

"Documents," he said. His accent sounded reasonably well schooled.

Burke thrust his passport into the man's hands. He spoke a little faster than he expected the man in front of him could understand.

"I was taking a walk. They started shooting. I'm staying at the Inter-Continental. Can you get me out of here? I want to go back there."

A dozen more policemen entered the lobby, shotguns at the ready. The officer gave them a command in Arabic. They loped in pairs toward the staircase. Burke presumed they would secure the building.

The officer leafed through Burke's passport until he found the Saudi visa, stamped in green ink and embellished with the royal seal, the date palm over crossed scimitars.

Then he looked at Burke's photo. He looked at Burke.

"I don't want to be here when the shooting starts again," Burke said, putting what he hoped sounded like a plaintive whine into his voice. "I'm just a public-relations consultant. I don't want any trouble."

The officer handed the passport back to Burke. He looked around.

"Go," he said. "Go back to Inter-Continental. Stay there."

"You going to give me a ride?" Burke asked. "I don't want to take a chance on getting shot."

The officer grimaced.

He nodded.

He gave a command to the corporal, who grabbed Burke's arm again. The corporal half dragged, half pushed Burke into the backseat of the black-and-white lead car, a converted Chevy Caprice.

Burke waited as the corporal turned on the siren. Once it was wailing, and the lights were flashing, the man thrust the transmission lever into gear and drove off, tires squealing.

Burke sighed deeply and grabbed for some support as the car careened out of the driveway and headed toward the Mecca Road and the Inter-Con.

He turned to the corporal, who he knew would understand nothing. "That was a close one," he said, and smiled.

The corporal smiled back.

There were two messages from Miss Kane, one at 8:45 and the other at nine. Both left the same number. He looked at his watch. It was 9:10.

He picked up the phone and dialed the number.

Someone answered in Arabic.

"Miss Kane, please," he said.

He heard the receiver hit something wooden, like a tabletop. For thirty seconds the phone conveyed the sounds of feet moving across a floor and muffled voices.

"Colin?" Her voice sounded as taut and uncertain as he had ever heard it.

"Hey, kid." He tried to sound chipper, but he knew he had never been the chipper type.

"Colin, we're at"—she paused—"where we met yesterday. But we can't stay here. My relatives—"

"Don't explain," he said. He didn't want her to say anything over the phone that would identify her—or him.

"What should we do? We have to leave."

He had no idea what they should do.

"You'll have to come here," he said.

"And then?"

"Tell you later," he replied. "Don't worry."

"All right," she said. "I won't. We'll be there in fifteen minutes."

He did not want to place the call from his own phone. One line or the other—his or the embassy's—would be tapped, and the call would be traced. He put on a suit, the khaki Haspel that was the closest he had to what he assumed an American businessman would wear in Riyadh. He knotted his tie. Then he opened his door, shut it quietly, and stepped out into the hall, carrying the bag that he used for his computer and papers in one hand and the attaché case that contained the satellite phone in the other.

He looked down the hall for the maid's cart. It was ten doors away. He walked down there, holding his key card in his hand.

The maid was a man, a Filipino in a red uniform. He was stripping the linens off the bed. Burke walked in, making sure the man could see the key card.

"Sorry," he said. "I went to breakfast but I forgot about a call I have to make. Can you come back in about five minutes?"

He looked carefully as the man surveyed his suit, his tie, his black bag, and his attaché case, and the key card in his hand. He saw no suspicion in his eyes. He was squat and homely, and when he nodded and smiled, Burke saw a gap where one of his front incisors should have been.

As soon as he had gone, Burke dialed the American embassy.

"This is Jim Davenport from San Francisco," he told the operator. "I was at a party last night and I met one of your first secretaries. He used to be at the embassy in Moscow. And he told me he might be able to help me with a project I'm working on. But for the life of me, I can't quite remember his name. Started with an . . ."

He let his voice trail off. The American embassy in Moscow had a big staff. Its alumni were in most major capitals. He hoped they would be here.

"Mr. Laird?" the operator said. "He just came in from Moscow."

"That's it," he said. "Begins with an L, just like I told you."

"I'll connect you, Mr. Davenport."

Burke thought that he vaguely remembered a guy named Laird, someone whose stringy hair fell over his forehead, someone who still wore Barry Goldwater autograph-model black plastic eyeglasses. He'd worked in the commercial section.

"Laird," a voice said. "Mr. Davenport?"

"Nyet," Burke said. *"Vas byespokoit gazeta* Washingtonski Tribun. *Zvonyu iz goroda."*

He had given him the name of the paper and told him he was calling from Riyadh. Russian was a clumsy subterfuge, but he figured it would take whoever monitored this phone a few hours to find a translator and figure out what had been said. The Saudis didn't do much business in Russian.

He got Laird's attention. "Good God," the man said.

"I have a message I want you to convey to someone who's in a position to do something about it," he said, still speaking in Russian. "I have four friends, a couple and their two children. The man in question was the subject of an article today in our paper."

"Yes," Laird said, also in Russian. "Go on."

"I want to bring them to you in a little while—maybe half an hour. I want you to get them out of the country. I'm going to know whether you do it or whether you stiff them for some damned reason, and I'll write what I learn."

"You don't have to threaten," Laird said. Though his Russian was lame and rusty, he managed to sound icily shocked that anyone would question the integrity of the United States government. "Where can we contact you?"

"You can't. Let the marines know we're coming, okay?"

"We'll do our best," Laird said.

"That's very reassuring," Burke said. He hung up.

He swallowed, checked the knot in his tie, and wiped a little sweat from his eyebrow. He walked into the hall and turned toward his own room.

He stopped. Two dark-haired men in blue suits were standing in front of his door. As he watched they knocked. Burke stopped in his tracks.

The men knocked again. "Open up, Mr. Burke," one of them said.

Burke turned and walked, as calmly as he could, to the opposite end of the hall, where the fire exit was.

He opened the door and started down. As he did he could hear the knocks on his own door getting louder and more insistent. He heard the word *police*.

He was on the seventh floor, on a stairwell that was not intended for guests to use except in emergencies. The pile carpet gave way to rough, concrete flooring and the recessed lighting of the guest areas yielded to fluorescent fixtures in the ceiling.

He began to descend, moving as quickly as he could with the two bags and the imperative to make as little noise as possible.

On the third floor, he heard the door to the stairwell open four floors above him. He froze. He heard a voice in Arabic, then the rough static of a police walkie-talkie answering back. The door shut again.

He was, he realized, uncertain of where the staircase ended. But if it came out in the lobby, it might be dangerous. There was, he remembered, a covey of hotel security officers in gray Inter-Con blazers stationed down there. They had walkie-talkies like the ones the police were using. And it was altogether likely that they were working together. Even if they were not, it was likely that there would be a third cop covering the lobby.

He had to find another way out. He glanced at his watch. He had ten minutes until Janet and her family were supposed to arrive. He had perhaps less time than that before someone proposed a thorough search of the stairwell.

He swiveled his head and looked around. There was a window, and it looked out over a low pavilion attached to the main tower of the hotel. The pavilion, he remembered, contained banquet rooms and a shopping arcade. Its roof was only a few feet below the window sash.

But there was nowhere to open the window.

It was a single sheet of glass, designed to hold the refrigerated air of the hotel in and to keep the hot, desert air outside.

That left the bottom of the staircase. Maybe it would open onto some kind of service corridor and a back entrance.

He padded quickly down to the first floor and opened the door a crack.

He was looking at the center of the lobby. The men in gray blazers, he noticed, seemed to be in a heightened state of alert. Rather than clustered near the front door, they were dispersed throughout the lobby, looking carefully at each person who walked through.

Quickly, he closed the door.

It was, he realized, a big, heavy fire door. Maybe it would muffle sound.

He climbed back to the second floor, aware that he was sweating liberally despite the air-conditioning. He stopped at the window.

He swung the black nylon bag tentatively against the glass. Nothing happened. He swung harder. There was a thunk, and a crack, but still nothing.

The third time, he wound up and slammed the bag into the window, unwinding like a discus thrower.

The glass cracked, and a hole appeared, but the entire pane did not shatter. It was some kind of shatterproof, insulated glass, he reckoned. Whoever had built the hotel had bought excellent materials.

He kicked this time, and kept kicking until he had made a hole big enough to squeeze through, conscious each time of the noise he was making. The glass fell in small, powdery shards to the roof.

He stepped to the sill and squeezed through, holding a bag in each hand. The air outside was truly hot now, and he stood on the roof for a moment, panting.

Squinting, he looked over the roof. It was the size of a couple of tennis courts, punctuated by a low glass bubble that enclosed an atrium.

He would, he realized, be visible from half the windows in the hotel as soon as he stepped into the middle of the roof. So he stuck close to the wall and sidestepped, trying to stay out of sight.

He looked at his watch. Only five minutes had gone by since he had seen the police at his door. It felt longer.

The sun was high in the south now, casting sharp black shadows on the roof, which was coated in gravel and tar. The footing was spongy as the tar heated up in the sun.

He needed a way down now, a way that would avoid the front of the hotel. He looked for any sign of a fire escape. There was none.

Whoever found the broken window, he knew, would understand that someone had left via the roof. He had to move quickly. He scuttled to the edge of the wall and the open end of the pavilion building.

He wanted to see a ladder, but there was none. Failing that, he would have been pleased to see a tree. No luck.

He glanced back at the broken window. He thought he heard voices in the stairwell.

He looked out over the edge of the roof. It was about fifteen feet down, he estimated. He could see a back parking lot, half-full of cars. Around the corner, he knew, were the hotel's swimming pool and tennis court.

The ground between the parking lot and the edge of the pavilion was landscaped, with the soil turned over and a hedge of scraggly bushes that looked like boxwoods. He had no other choice.

Stretching prone on the roof, he extended first his right arm and then his left, dropping his two cases into the bushes. Their fall seemed to be cushioned. They hung up in the branches.

He swung his own legs over the side, dimly aware that his suit was going to be covered with tar. He hung by his hands for an instant, but he had nothing to grip. He could feel the skin on his palms scraping away as he lost his purchase and dropped toward the ground.

The bushes, he immediately learned, were not boxwoods.

They were something else, something close to a cactus, with thorns that tore at his clothes and his flesh as he plunged into them. He felt his knees jam together, and an ankle turned. He bit down on the tip of his tongue and tasted blood.

"Shit!" he yelped, then forced his mouth closed. He listened as the oath seemed to echo for a moment in the air. If someone had heard him, if someone was coming, he could not detect it.

Gingerly, he stepped clear of the bush, trying to do no more damage to himself. He took a quick inventory. His pants were torn in half a dozen places, and they were stained with a dozen or more spots of blood. The wounds from the thorns were starting to sting. His jacket sleeves were covered with tar. His right ankle was tender, but his legs seemed still operative.

He wondered, for a moment, whether he could persuade the editorial accountants to approve a request for a new suit.

He looked at his watch. Janet and her family would be coming by in about eight minutes, if they were not delayed. He needed, he realized, a vantage point, someplace from which he could watch the road without being seen and intercept their car before they drove up to the hotel entrance and into the purview of the police.

Burke picked up the two bags and cautiously walked to the edge of the building. He peered around the corner.

The swimming pool lay before him. At this hour, no guests were out there. An attendant, wearing a brown smock of some sort and a flat black cap, was hosing down the deck. In the shrubs by the edge of the hotel, another worker, someone from one of the less prosperous Arab countries to judge by his dress, slowly pulled weeds.

At the rear of the pool area was a cabana of red-and-white striped canvas. From there, he thought, he might be able to see the road.

Burke smiled at the pool attendant, trying to look as if he walked into cabanas in suits stained with blood and tar every morning of his life.

The attendant's hose stopped moving. He watched as Burke walked past. From the corner of his eye, Burke could see the man's head swivel, and then he thought he could feel the man's eyes on his back as he walked through the canvas flap into the shade of the cabana.

It was set up in three sections. In the middle was a small bar, but a bar devoid of alcohol. The shelves behind it held only juices. The men's changing room was to his right and the women's to his left. This was a place for foreigners only, one of the only public places in Saudi Arabia where the sexes could mingle in this way.

In the men's changing area, there was a low bench and a row of plastic lockers. No window. Burke opened the bag that contained the computer and rummaged in it until he found his penknife. With it, he cut a four-inch slit in the canvas at eye level.

The slit afforded a limited view of the western grounds of the hotel and the drive leading into it. He could survey a small part of the road.

Traffic was light, much lighter than it had been the day before, and he imagined that word of the riot at the television station had spread. People were staying home.

He was worried about the pool attendant, and he weighed the risks of missing the arrival of Janet's car against the risks of staying where he was. If the attendant had gone to notify the management of the strange American with the bloody clothing who was in the cabana, he was in trouble. He decided to check, and he walked quickly to the front entrance.

The man was hosing down the deck again. Burke breathed a little easier and went back to the changing room.

Now he had to wait, and waiting was always hard for him. He was the sort of person who would pass up a movie rather than stand in line, the sort who fidgeted and muttered under his breath when nothing happened.

He did both of those things now, checking his watch frequently. It seemed to him that the sweep hand, whenever he looked at it, was caught motionless. Only when he watched it did it start to move.

He imagined that the police, if they were normal police, would extend their search by looking through the common rooms of the hotel, on the theory that he was eating breakfast or had gone downstairs to read the newspaper. That should consume at least ten minutes.

But what if they wanted him urgently, and began immediately to comb the hotel and question the staff?

Then he would have less time.

A blue Mercedes came along the road and he started to tear at the slit in the cabana, ready to sprint directly for the car. But it sped past the hotel, and now he had to worry whether the slit had become so large that someone might notice it from the front of the hotel and investigate. He pinched it closed with his fingers.

He looked at his watch again. She was due. But there could be a hundred reasons for a delay, beginning with the prospect of police checkpoints set up to keep traffic away from the site of the riot.

Or, perhaps, she had come in early, during the brief interval when he was checking on the pool attendant, and they were sitting there near the porte cochere, engine idling, nervously wondering where he was.

No, he thought. She couldn't have done that; there hadn't been enough time. But the thought nagged at him. There was nothing else to occupy his mind as he waited, and the idea grew that doing something, doing anything would be better than waiting in a cabana until the police decided to conduct a thorough search.

He wondered why the police had come for him, and he turned over in his mind the things that he had done and the traces he had left. Maybe, he thought, the appearance of a story in a Washington newspaper had led them to check the list of Americans arriving recently from Washington. His name had been on it. Maybe someone had matched his name with a file of the bylines of journalists who had written something about Saudi Arabia. Or maybe it had rung a bell because of the PAC-3 story. Whatever the reason, his time in Saudi Arabia was probably going to be limited.

He looked again toward the porte cochere and wondered about going out to check. Then, on the road, he saw another blue Mercedes, this one badly in need of washing, and he recognized the desert dust he had kicked up onto the fenders. The car was moving slowly, almost tentatively, toward the Inter-Con's entrance drive.

He tore through the slit in the cabana and found that his right ankle had stiffened. Sprained, he thought, when he dropped from the roof. As quickly as he could, he hobbled toward the car, hoping to intercept it before it got to the hotel and into the purview of the security staff in the lobby.

There was no cover, and he realized that running would only attract the attention of anyone watching this area of the hotel grounds. So he forced himself to slow down and walk. He waved, as discreetly as he could manage, and saw the car stop.

It was fifty yards away, and he imagined as he walked to it that the security guards had noticed him and that they were notifying the police and that at any moment he would hear someone tell him to stop, and he would have to decide what to do.

Now the car was twenty yards away and he could make out the outlines of the people inside. He counted to make sure there were four—Abdulrahman Massoud at the wheel, dressed now in the standard Saudi white *thobe* and *khafiyeh*, his son beside him, and the two women shrouded in black in the backseat.

Then, to his great relief, he was at the car, and the back door opened, and arms draped in black stretched out to welcome him inside.

The coolness of the car's interior struck him immediately and he realized that he had sweated through his suit.

"I always did try to look my best when I had a date with you," he said to Janet, but there was no answering laughter from anyone in the car. He squeezed in.

Abdulrahman Massoud, his face still puffy and distended from the beatings he had taken, turned around expectantly.

"They're waiting for us?" he asked.

"So they say," Burke said. "You know how to get there?"

Massoud permitted himself the slightest hint of a smile. "Unfortunately, yes," he said.

He turned the car around and slowly headed off to the south, toward the infidels' compound.

"What happened to you?" Janet asked him.

"Couple of guys were knocking on my door," Burke said. "Might've been bill collectors. Had to go out a window and over the roof."

"Oh, Colin, I'm so sorry I got you mixed up in this," she said, and he heard a taut edge in her voice. She was, he imagined, close to breaking.

He looked at her. "I'm not sorry," he said.

He heard sirens behind them, and he stiffened. He turned around.

Three police cars were bearing down on them at a terrific clip, blue lights flashing. The sun glinted off their windshields.

In the front seat, Massoud moaned softly.

"Just keep driving. In the slow lane," Burke said. "Maybe they're not looking for us."

Massoud obeyed, edging over to the right until the car was riding on the shoulder and about to veer off into the soft sand beyond it.

The cars overtook them in a matter of seconds, growing large in the rearview mirror and then speeding past with an audible *whoosh*.

"Good job," Burke encouraged Massoud, though he knew that nothing Massoud had done had anything to do with it.

Ahead, the police cars turned left on a street that was marked in both English and Arabic and that he could therefore tell was called Al-Nasiriyah.

"That's the road to the television station?" Burke asked, but it was more a statement than a question. He knew that was where the police would be headed.

"It is one of them," Massoud said.

"We're going in another direction?" Burke asked hopefully.

"Yes."

They drove slowly past Al-Nasiriyah and then turned southwest, onto an arterial road that headed off to the city's suburbs.

"Oh, no," Massoud moaned softly.

The Saudi police had established a roadblock a few hundred yards ahead of them. Two police cars with lights flashing had parked astride the pavement. Half a dozen civilian cars were lined up on the shoulder.

"Don't worry," Burke said. "They're making everyone pull over. It's not aimed at you."

As they pulled in at the back of the line, a Saudi in a gold Mercedes 600, as long as any car Burke had ever seen, roared past them on the inside lane and pulled up to the police car, blowing his horn.

"Didn't know they made that one in gold," Burke said.

"They'll make anything if you can pay for it," Janet replied.

Immediately behind him came a caravan of expensive automobiles—a couple of Lexuses, two more Mercedes, and a small, gull-winged sports car that Burke thought was a Lamborghini. He didn't know. He didn't see many Lamborghinis in his neighborhood on Capitol Hill. They wouldn't last long there.

A short, rotund man in a silky white *thobe* trimmed with gold thread jumped out of the lead Mercedes and strode up to the police car.

"It's Prince Zaki," Janet said.

"Who's he?"

"The king's nephew," she replied quietly, as if afraid of being overheard.

"Roll down the window," Burke asked. "See if you can hear what he's saying."

Janet obliged. The air from outside was stifling, but the breeze was blowing in their direction, and the conversation ahead of them carried easily to their ears.

The king's nephew was yelling.

"He says he doesn't care what has to pass through here, he is taking his family out to their country house," Janet translated.

"Odd, considering that it's Monday," Burke said.

"Yes," she said. "I wonder why?"

"Maybe that scent in the air is the smell of rats sweating as the ship starts to take on water."

"I think you're right. I think maybe we shouldn't go," Massoud said. His voice conveyed more sense of duty than enthusiasm.

"No," Burke said. "You have to."

Massoud did not object.

Prince Zaki seemed to win his argument. The policeman to whom he was talking saluted smartly and pulled the lead car off to the side. Another cop took up a position in front of the first in the line of plebeian cars, making sure that none would move. The big gold Mercedes roared off, followed by the Lexuses, the other Mercedes, and the Lamborghini.

Burke peered down the road after them and saw headlights approaching, their light pale in the competition with the desert sun.

"Now we know why they've stopped traffic," he said.

It was a convoy of flatbed military trucks, rumbling along at about twenty miles per hour. On the back of each truck was a tank, painted in brown desert camouflage, guns pointed toward the rear.

The road trembled slightly as the lead truck pulled past the roadblock and moved toward the center of the city, straddling the yellow line that divided the pavement.

Burke started counting as the fourth truck rolled past. When the thirtieth had rolled by, the procession ended.

In the front seat, the boy broke the silence, saying something in Arabic to his father.

Burke cocked an eyebrow toward Janet.

"He said he counted thirty tanks," she translated.

"Same as I did," Burke said. "Lot of firepower."

She shuddered. "I know Abdulrahman wants to stay," she said. "That is his character. But I am glad we're leaving."

He noticed that under stress, her speech got more controlled, more formal. He wanted to reach under the *abaya* and take her hand, but he reminded himself that her husband was in the seat ahead of them and might mistake the gesture.

The police started dismantling the roadblock, moving their cars to the shoulder. The cop on the pavement, his eyes shielded by sunglasses, waved the lead car along. Burke felt himself involuntarily stiffen as they passed under the man's scrutiny. When he did nothing to restrain them, he exhaled.

"How far is it to the embassy?" he asked Janet.

"Not far," she replied. "Perhaps two miles."

They were entering the outskirts of the city, where vacant, rocky brown land started to appear along the roadside. Massoud pushed the car up to about fifty miles an hour, keeping up with the traffic.

They crossed another road on an overpass, and almost immediately encountered a high wall with a gate.

"The infidels' compound," Janet said, and he suspected she was smiling wryly under the veil.

It was a site designed to cut the foreigners off from the rest of the city, segregated by open land, walls, and the concrete barrier of the highway: a ghetto, albeit a luxurious ghetto.

The road through the compound wound past a number of green, carefully watered traffic circles and a park where he could see a soccer field. There was virtually no traffic.

The embassies were set behind inner walls, their names mounted on raised copper plaques, their flags hanging limp in the windless air.

The American embassy was toward the back of the compound, and when he saw the flag, he felt, somewhat to his surprise, a sense of relief.

Four marines stood guard at the wrought-iron gate to the American property. They wore combat fatigues rather than the blue dress uniforms Burke had become accustomed to seeing at embassies.

They motioned to Massoud to stop, and he did. Burke got out.

He showed his passport to the marine with the most stripes on his sleeve.

"Mr. Laird," he said, "is expecting us."

The marine did not confirm or deny this.

"Have everyone get out of the car, and open the trunk and hood," he said to Burke.

The trunk and hood popped open and the Massouds got out of the car.

One of the marines started poking carefully through the trunk. Another inspected the engine. A third rolled a contraption that looked like a mirror mounted on a mechanic's jack under the car. After a minute Burke realized the marine was inspecting the underside of the chassis, looking for bombs.

"Don't worry," he whispered to Janet. "I'm sure this is just routine. Ever since Iran in 1979, it's been like this."

A woman's voice from behind the gate interrupted them before Janet could reply.

"That won't be necessary," the woman said. He knew the voice. "These people have been through enough."

Burke felt the hair on the back of his neck stand up. He turned around.

Desdemona McCoy, dressed in a white pantsuit and a black T-shirt, stepped through the gate and extended her slender hand.

"Mr. Burke," she said. "What a pleasant surprise."

He took her hand and shook it, robotically. It seemed implausibly cool.

"Saudi Arabia is full of surprises," he said. "Sometimes I'm not sure if it's a country or a Cracker Jack box."

CHAPTER 10

The room was bland and quintessentially governmental, a white box with a window, beige curtains, brown furniture, and a color photo of President Peter Scott Detwiler hanging on one wall. There was a coffee percolator in one corner.

But it was cool, blessedly cool, after the heat of the sun in front of the embassy gate, and Burke welcomed it. He could feel the perspiration start to dry on his forehead.

Janet Kane and her family sat down in chairs designated for them by Desdemona McCoy and the American ambassador in Riyadh, a man named Thorne. Janet and her daughter removed their veils, but kept their *abayas* on, as if they needed to maintain some separation between themselves and the Americans. Burke remained standing in the corner.

Thorne cleared his throat.

"Mr. Burke. There are some things we need to say privately to the Massouds. Would you excuse us?"

"No," Janet said, quietly and firmly. "We prefer that he stays. We trust him."

The implication that she did not trust Thorne was obvious, and the ambassador reddened.

"I'm afraid that's impossible, Mrs. Massoud." He paused, groping for an explanation. "He's a journalist," he finally said, with the same tone he might have used in saying he was an idiot.

"That's why we want him to stay," Abdulrahman Massoud joined in.

Thorne swallowed and looked around. Desdemona McCoy assumed control.

"Mr. Burke," she said, "would you agree to consider what you hear here off the record?"

Burke thought it over for a second, struggling to focus his attention on what McCoy was saying rather than on her. But images of her flashed through his mind, images of her dancing slowly in his living room, images of her in the snow next to the Neva River shortly after they met, and then the image she had presented outside the embassy, an image of cool control. He blinked. He reminded himself why he was there.

"If it ends with the Massouds getting safely out of this country, yes," he said. "But if this is about why you can't do that for them, then no."

Thorne got positively red, a color that matched one of the stripes in the regimental tie he was wearing. But, Burke observed, he was deferring, not altogether graciously, to McCoy.

"Well, we are going to get them out," McCoy said. "You can take that to the bank. So we're agreed."

"Ms. McCoy—" Thorne began, but McCoy cut him off.

"I know Mr. Burke's reputation," she said. "When he says something will be off the record, it is."

Burke noticed that Janet Kane was looking inquisitively at him, one eyebrow tilted up, and he realized she had connected the black lover Burke had described to her with the black woman sitting in front of her. It was not a great feat of deduction, given the number of black females occupying positions of power in American foreign policy.

In reply, he nodded slightly to Janet, confirming her analysis. Then he turned to the government's end of the table.

"Thanks, Ms. McCoy," he said. "I'll consider that a compliment."

"Oh, it is," McCoy said, letting a hint of a smile sit for a moment on her lips. Then she turned to the Massouds and her face became again businesslike.

"On behalf of the president, I wish to apologize to you, Mr. Massoud. And to your family," she said. "We made mistakes. You should have been offered American assistance before this time. You weren't. I'm sorry."

Ambassador Thorne was starting to show white blotches around his hairline, and Burke immediately understood what had prompted the little *pas de deux* over his presence. Thorne had known McCoy intended to apologize. He had not wanted Burke to hear it.

The apology made clear that when fingers were pointed over this affair, as they no doubt would be, the White House intended that they be pointing at Thorne. It would be, in the White House version, a case of State Department clientitis, a case where the Arabists on station in Riyadh had confused the interests of their own government with the interests of a Saudi royal family upon whose hospitality and good graces they depended for a wide range of things, from information about oil production to tacit permission to make wine in their basements.

The White House version might even be partially right, Burke thought. It wouldn't be the first time.

He resented being manipulated, though, and particularly by McCoy. Going off the record, in this case, was a sham. It would mean that Burke couldn't report her apology. But it didn't mean he would forget it. And when he wrote his postmortem, he would not be able to ignore the White House spin she had just put on the case.

But he kept all these thoughts to himself and concentrated on McCoy. He had seen her operate in the field, in St. Petersburg. But this was the first time he had seen her operate as a diplomat. She was deft, and he admired deftness. She could apologize because she honestly felt sorry for the way the embassy had failed to help the Massouds, and because she wanted the blame fixed away from her boss, the president. She had, in any situation, an ability to see how she could simultaneously do good and do well. It was a kind of grace, and he envied it.

It made it all the more frustrating to be rejected by her.

He barely registered the details of the Massouds' evacuation as McCoy laid them out. A helicopter would take them to Amman. It was on its way to the embassy; she did not say from where. The Massouds would have to sign some documents, which the embassy staff was preparing. In the meantime they would make themselves comfortable, have a meal in the embassy cafeteria, have coffee, whatever they wished.

"We would just like to be alone," Abdulrahman Massoud said. "It is a difficult thing, to leave your country. Especially at a time of crisis."

"I understand," McCoy said. "Is this room adequate?"

"Yes," Massoud agreed. There was a heavy sadness in his voice.

"We'll leave you, then," McCoy said. She turned to Burke.

"Mr. Burke," she said. "There are a few questions I'd like to ask you. Would you mind taking a walk with me in the ambassador's garden?"

Ambassador Thorne, beyond apoplexy now, looked simply pale and wilted, as if the starch had been removed from his shirt. He said nothing.

"As long as you promise not to lead me down the garden path," Burke said.

They walked into the adjoining office, which was Thorne's, and out through some French doors into the garden.

It was an oasis, planted in imported soil, irrigated every day with enough water to see a Bedouin clan through a summer. Date palms planted in clusters towered overhead, providing shade. But the garden itself was vaguely Japanese, with precise paths covered in white gravel, lots of ferns, the occasional low, craggy rock, and a couple of fountains where water gurgled. It was enclosed by a wall of whitewashed cement, maybe seven feet high.

"The ambassador thinks," McCoy said when they were sufficiently removed from the building, "that I've taken you out here so he won't hear me telling you slanderous lies that will destroy his career. I'm the bitch from hell as far as he's concerned."

"Not a nice way to describe Washington," Burke said.

She laughed lightly and her shoulder brushed against his. He was intensely conscious of her physical presence. He could smell her over the scent of the green plants baking in the sun.

"I want to thank you for being discreet in there," she said.

"Discreet about what?" He wanted to wound her, to provoke her, he realized, and he struggled against that desire.

"About . . . you know."

"Well," he said, "I don't know. But I'll continue to be discreet about it."

"I wish we could have a long talk," she said.

"But this isn't the time or place, is it?"

She stopped and sat on a low, concrete bench. He declined the tacit invitation to join her.

She looked up at him. "Please sit down."

He sat.

She ran a finger over a tar stain in his jacket lapel. "You're going to have to get this cleaned," she said.

She had always cared about the way he dressed, cared much more than he had. He had thought about it once, and decided that it came from her childhood as a member of one of the few black families in a white suburb on Long Island. He had not met her parents, but she had talked about them, especially about her mother, and they sounded like ferociously respectable people, the kind of people who would tell their daughter that she could not afford to go to school looking anything but neat and properly put together, because whites would never make allowances for dirty clothes on the back of a black child.

It had been too long since anyone cared about things like the condition of his clothes.

"I'll throw it out," he said. "I'll buy a new suit."

"Colin," she said, and hesitated. She looked at a spot somewhere between his knee and hers. "I just want you to know that I'm sorry if I hurt you. It was the last thing—"

"Forget it," he cut her off. "It comes with the territory."

Then she looked at him directly and he thought he could see pain in her eyes.

"You're angry, I know," she said. "But you're right. This isn't the time or place to talk about it."

He said nothing.

"Colin, just out of curiosity, how did you find out about this story?"

He considered refusing to tell her. Had he found out from a source in the government, he would have refused. But he could see nothing that would be compromised if he gave her the truth.

"Massoud's wife," he said, "is an old—"

He was going to say flame, but her eyes widened and she interrupted him. "An old lover?"

"Not exactly," he said. "I dated her in high school. The first girl I ever loved, actually. But not a lover."

McCoy shook her head ruefully and almost smiled. "And, of course, after all these years she hadn't forgotten you."

Burke shrugged. "Maybe you'll find it easier."

He regretted it instantly. She looked pained again.

"Don't," she said, so softly that he could barely hear her.

"Sorry," he said, and he was. He believed her. She hadn't meant to hurt him. He was the one who had pushed her to it.

She sat up straighter and a distance seemed to open between them, though neither had moved on the bench.

"Colin," she said, "I want to ask you to go out on the helicopter with the Massouds to Amman."

He was only slightly surprised.

"Why?"

"Please believe it's not because I don't want you reporting here, though God knows there are people back in Washington who don't."

"Well, I'm glad to hear that," he said.

"It's because you're not safe here."

He understood everything, he thought, but he wanted to drag it out of her, to shame her.

"Why not?"

"You know I can't tell you that," she said.

"You mean that the police here know who I am and where I'm staying?"

For the first time she looked startled and off balance.

"They came by the hotel this morning," he said. "Wonder who tipped them off?"

She closed her eyes for a second and seemed to be groping for strength.

"I can't tell you that, either," she said.

"But you know."

Now her face showed signs of distress, and she folded her arms in front of her chest as if to protect herself.

"Stop, Colin," she said. "Please."

Suddenly ashamed of himself, he stopped. He had broken their basic agreement. He had pressed her for information.

"I'm sorry," he said.

She nodded. "Anyway," she went on, "it doesn't matter how they know. They know. They'll arrest you. It won't be easy to get out."

"I know," he said.

She leaned toward him.

"Colin, it's a chaotic situation out there. People are dying in the streets. They might not just pick you up. They might do worse."

"I've seen what they can do," he said. "I was at the television station."

She blinked, and then shook her head.

"You do get around."

"Not as much, maybe, as you think."

She leaned closer as if to touch him, looking into his eyes again, and this time her eyes were bright, even in the shade of the date palms.

"This makes it even more dangerous for you, Colin," she said. "They'll do whatever they can to prevent your story from being published. It's dangerous to them."

He shrugged. That was not his concern.

She tried again.

"You've done what you came here to do. You've helped your friend and her family."

"Sorry, Des. The story's too good to quit on now. Too important."

"Even if I asked you to do it for me?"

She made him believe it. Something in her eyes and the tilt of her body persuaded him that she was asking because she cared about him, not because his departure would suit the interests of her employers.

But he couldn't agree. He rubbed the toe of his shoe in the gravel for a minute, digging a small trench.

"Des, that's not fair," he finally said.

Her expression got a little less warm. "But it was fair a few days ago when you asked me to give up my work for you."

She had a point, and he smiled a little in acknowledgment.

"And as I recall, your answer was that you couldn't."

She swallowed hard and then gave it up.

"You're an exasperating man, Burke," she said, but he sensed no anger behind the words.

"That may be the lead in my obit," Burke said. " 'He was an exasperating man.' "

He wanted to hug her, but he knew that was something she would not allow in the presence of others; she would only pull away.

In the distance, they heard the rhythmic *thwack-thwack-thwack* of an approaching helicopter. He turned to look.

It was larger than he expected, painted in brown desert camouflage that matched the camouflage of the tanks that had passed them on the road to the embassy. The paint reminded him of the close relations between the American military and the Saudis. The noise grew louder, until it drowned out all other sound. Behind the glass of the cockpit he could see a pilot and copilot in plain green overalls, wearing sunglasses.

The helicopter settled onto the ground beyond the garden wall where he imagined there must be a landing pad. Wind from the rotors blew fronds off the date palms and set off a small dust storm. The pilots left the engine on.

He leaned closer to McCoy.

"I want to say good-bye to Janet and her family," he said, in a voice that stopped just short of yelling.

McCoy nodded affirmatively.

He followed her back through the French doors, through the ambassador's office, and into the conference room.

Abdulrahman Massoud and his son were at the room's lone window, watching the helicopter.

"Ours?" Massoud said.

McCoy nodded. "Have you filled out the forms?"

"Yes."

"I'm afraid there's always paperwork," McCoy said, and smiled reassuringly at them.

Massoud spoke to his family in Arabic. They lined up to go, stepping from the conference room into a corridor. McCoy and Burke followed them.

In the hallway, Janet Kane said something to her husband, also in Arabic, and then turned to Burke.

"There are some things I need to say to you," she said. She turned to McCoy. "May we use this room for a moment?"

"Of course," McCoy said.

They stepped inside and she closed the door. Burke was mildly surprised. Janet was not a conventional Saudi woman. But seeking privacy with another man, a nonrelative, grossly violated all Saudi norms. Even her husband, liberal that he was, would be wondering.

Her hands came out from inside the *abaya*, and took both of his.

"I owe you so much," she said. "From a long time and a long distance you came and saved my family."

"Not at all," Burke said. "I owe you for a good story. If this were Washington, I'd have to take you someplace fancy for lunch."

She shook her head. "No."

He was egotistical enough to stop arguing.

"That woman, Miss McCoy," Janet said. "She's the one, isn't she?"

He nodded.

"From what little I've seen of her, I like her. And I can tell that she cares for you."

"Now you're being romantic."

"Body language doesn't lie," she said. "I can see the way she reacts to you."

"Well, her body may be saying 'yes, yes,' to you, but her mouth is saying 'no, no,' to me," Burke said.

Janet smiled. "You always could be remarkably obtuse."

"Thanks," he said.

"No," she said. "I mean it. You have to understand who she is. If you're a minority, and you get involved with someone from outside your community, you must be extremely cautious." She paused. "The way I was with you."

"You were?"

"Of course! Don't you think I felt like a minority then? A girl who was half-Arab? In white-bread Santa Rosaria?"

"Well, I don't think—"

"No. You didn't think then and you're not thinking now. You just make up your mind what you want and you pursue it. And if you don't get it right away, you sulk."

"But—"

"Hush and listen, dear old friend. I think she loves you. But I know she cannot give up her job, everything she has built for herself just because you've been having an affair for a while and you say you'd like to make it permanent."

"Why—"

"She needs to trust you. She needs to trust you as she has trusted no one else. You have to build that trust."

"Well—"

Again she interrupted him.

"If you love her, don't do what you did with me. Don't sulk. You were seventeen then. It was excusable. You're too old to be that way now. And too smart."

"But she says—"

She squeezed his hands.

"I know what she says. I'm telling you what I think she feels. Don't push her. But don't give her up. I think she's worth it. And I want you to be happy."

He shook his head, too bemused to argue.

She kissed him, first on the right cheek, then on the left. Then she opened the door and stepped into the hallway.

Abdulrahman Massoud was standing there. Behind him stood the two children. Massoud's lip was twitching—whether from anger or humiliation or sadness, Burke could not tell. He could only imagine what was going on in the man's mind.

"You know," Burke said to him, "I covered Andrei Sakharov in the old Soviet Union. I remember when he was sent into exile in Gorky. The apparatchiks thought they had defeated him. But his exile only increased the love and respect his people had for him. When he returned to Moscow, there was no one with his moral authority."

He kept to himself his opinion that Sakharov, saintly though he was, had been a political naif whose achievements were being rapidly eroded in the new Russia.

"I think the same thing may happen with you," Burke continued. "When you return."

Massoud drew himself up straight, and the quivering chin grew firm. "If God wills it," he said.

He took Burke's hand.

"Thank you."

"Take care of Janet," Burke said. He almost added that he envied him.

Massoud nodded, turned, and walked out toward the helicopter. Janet and her daughter fixed their veils back over their faces and followed him. The boy brought up the rear. McCoy and Thorne walked beside the family.

Burke watched as the copilot, in his anonymous green fatigues, helped them up a small ladder that dropped down from the passenger cabin. The door shut. McCoy and Thorne, their hair blowing wildly in the wash from the rotors, walked briskly back to the building. The helicopter's engine noise intensified, and it slowly rose from the ground, hovered for a second, then wheeled away from the sun and headed north, toward Jordan. The last Burke saw of the Massoud family was the two dark shrouds of the women silhouetted against the glass of the window.

For a moment the three of them—McCoy, Thorne, and Burke—watched the helicopter get smaller in the blue sky. McCoy patted her head a few times and Burke watched her hair immediately and artfully resume the slightly tousled look she favored.

Thorne, scowling and saying nothing, opened the door and went back inside. McCoy hung back a half a second.

Burke put his hand on the door and shoved it shut. She looked at him expectantly. He remembered what Janet had told him.

"Two things," he said. "One, thanks for caring enough to try to talk me into leaving."

She started to say something, but he didn't wait for her.

"Two," he said, struggling to get the words out before he changed his mind. "I'm sorry if I pushed you to go farther and faster than you were ready to go. I won't do it again."

Her mouth opened slightly and hung open, and for the first time since he had known her, she appeared to be at a loss for words.

He grinned at her. "But that doesn't mean," he said, "that I don't expect to get you there someday."

He opened the door. Thorne was waiting for her, and he could only guess what she would have said in response.

Chapter 11

He felt the cannon fire before he heard it. Loose change in the ashtray of the Massouds' Mercedes started sporadically to jingle. Over the thrumming of the tires on the highway, he sensed a series of tickling pulses that vibrated in the ground. He rolled down the window and he heard it—dull thuds coming from over the horizon. It was almost like being around a thunderstorm on the Blue Ridge over the Shenandoah on a summer afternoon, seeing lightning and then, a moment later, hearing the thunder.

Rounding a corner, he peered at the horizon. He saw columns of smoke begin to rise, and he guessed that somewhere in the city, demonstrators were being shelled.

He pondered his options. The information he already had—the deaths in front of the television station and the flight of the Massouds from the American embassy—was enough to lead the paper. But it was just dawn in Washington, long hours before the deadline for the next paper. He had time to collect more.

If he were caught at it, he risked losing what he already had. And he knew the chances were rising that he would be caught. The warning from McCoy had only confirmed it. Because of the rioting, there could be roadblocks, security sweeps on the streets. If the police caught him, the least they would do would be to take his computer and his telephone.

Not if, but when they caught him, he thought.

He saw a road branching right, to the east and out of the city, and he jammed on the brakes. There was no one behind him. All of the traffic seemed to be headed the other way—an assortment of limousines and pickup trucks, buses and vans. Drivers of fast cars pulled right onto the shoulder and passed slower traffic, spewing rooster tails of sand before they regained the road.

Burke took the right turn. The road was a washboard, jouncing even the Mercedes like a buckboard on a rocky road. He kept one eye in the rearview mirror until the road disappeared from sight. Then he stopped the car.

It was not a perfect spot for a transmission. It was too close to the road and there was not enough natural cover. It was just a flat, rust-colored spot in the Saudi desert, punctuated by enormous, craggy sandstone rocks.

He parked and kept the motor running so the air-conditioning stayed on. He typed a quick, five-hundred-word story on his laptop, outlining what he had seen that morning, writing it as a wire-service man might, putting the facts in pyramidal order and refraining from embellishing them.

At the end he typed: *More TK*. It let Graves know he intended to file a longer, updated story later in the day.

He stepped out of the car and set the telephone and transmitter up in the thin patch of shadow it cast. The sun was almost directly overhead, and he had trouble orienting himself until he remembered that he had been heading north when he'd turned off the road. Then he found east, and the transmitter located the satellite on his second attempt. The story was gone in ten seconds.

Sweat dripped from his forehead into the leaves of the little transmitter dish as he packed it away, and he realized that the heat of the day had come. He couldn't gauge it precisely, but it seemed to him to be at least one hundred degrees. He could feel the skin on the back of his neck heat up and start to burn. He was intensely thirsty, and he wished he had taken the time to find and buy a bottle of water at the embassy commissary before he left. But all he had wanted to do was get away, before Thorne or someone figured out a good excuse for keeping him there.

He got back in the car and drove on toward the center of the city, keeping one eye in the rearview mirror, half expecting to see blue lights flashing. But nothing came. The only traffic he encountered was from the other side of the road, when drivers desperate to get out of town pulled into his lane to pass. A group of helicopters flew overhead, and he counted them—eight. There was more traffic in the air than on his side of the road.

He was back in the city now, and there was little open space. The cannon fire seemed to have stopped. Dust hung in the air like fog. He wondered where to go, where he could see what he needed to see without getting caught.

He was feeling very hungry and his thirst had grown, and he wished he had taken time to have more than some toast and fruit juice in the morning at the hotel. The thought of the hotel, with its cool rooms and crisp sheets, was very attractive. It would be calm, and it would be safe. The restaurant would be serving from an enormous buffet. He wished for a moment he could go back there.

To the right, he saw a shopping center. It looked as if it had been transported from New Jersey by an enormous blimp and plopped down in the desert, complete with a Safeway and a Sears. It was made of white brick and surrounded by parking spaces.

Impulsively, he pulled into the lot and found an empty spot toward the rear. As he walked toward the Safeway he saw a steady stream of women in black veils coming out. Their drivers walked in front of them, pushing grocery carts laden with food.

Water, he thought. Water and something packaged that he could keep in the trunk.

Inside the store, he heard the sounds of shouting and glass breaking. He stepped onto the ramp that activated the doors and looked inside.

A small riot had broken out. Only one of the ten cash registers was manned. A long line of women in black stretched from that register into an aisle of canned vegetables with bright green labels. A man in a white apron and a knit skullcap, perhaps an Egyptian, was standing near the exit, trying to block shoppers who, despairing of the long line, had bolted for the door with their provisions. He was, Burke figured, the manager. As Burke watched, the man in the knit cap pushed a shrouded figure in black, shoving her away from the door and toward the rear of the line. A penetrating shriek came from within the veils.

A man in a dirty *thobe*—Burke imagined he was the woman's driver—leaped into the face of the man in the apron and knit cap. Both tumbled to the floor, punching, kicking, and gouging.

That started a stampede. In seconds Burke was pinned to the plate-glass window at the front of the store by a mass of frightened, desperate Saudis, shouting and moaning, clutching their food to their chests, cursing as their grocery carts got stuck in the melee.

In two more minutes the store had emptied. Burke walked down an empty aisle. Most of the stock was gone, but he was able to find a few cans of corn and a couple of six-packs of Perrier. He walked back to the register. The checkout clerk was helping the manager to his feet. They seemed not to notice Burke, and he dropped a ten-dollar bill on the counter and walked out.

In the car, the Perrier seemed to have to cleave its way through the dust that had accumulated on the roof of his mouth. He could feel the bubbles exploding on his tongue. He savored it, draining two bottles before telling himself to stop.

He thought he knew what he had seen—the flight of frightened people from a war zone. But it was still hard to reconcile that image with the tightly controlled monarchy he had entered two days before.

Cautiously, he slipped the car into gear and set off toward the center of the city, in the general direction of the cannon fire.

He kept looking for roadblocks. In Bucharest in '89 and in Moscow in '91, there had been roadblocks everywhere. If the regime hadn't set them up, the rebels had. But here the streets were empty, save for the occasional pedestrian hurrying toward shelter or the big sedan heading out of the city.

He rolled down the window again. He heard no cannon fire, but he could hear the sound of rifles. Slowly, he drove toward it.

Finally, he began to see people—Saudi men in white *thobes*, laborers in grimy smocks and knit caps like the one worn by the manager in the grocery store. They were all moving in the same direction. Some shouted and brandished fists. He saw one man waving a dagger. Burke pointed the car in their direction and began picking his way through the streets, following.

He had just crossed under a six-lane highway when he saw a crowd of men, several hundred strong, reminiscent of the crowds of protesters he had seen that morning. Plain green banners flapped in the hot breeze above them. They were marching toward the center of the city. In contrast to the crowd this morning, he thought, this one looked defiant and unafraid.

Burke looked around. He was next to a new, glassy, high-rise building, perhaps twenty stories high. A sign, in English and in Arabic, identified it as the Directorate-General of Traffic. It would not, he thought, be hard to find again.

The parking area next to it was nearly empty. He wheeled the Mercedes into it and parked. He stuffed a notebook and a pen into his pocket and set off on foot.

The sound of rifle fire intensified. Somewhere up ahead, perhaps only a few hundred yards, there was a firefight. He could smell the scent of powder in the air.

He had entered the old *souk*, the marketplace. It was a warren of narrow, alley-sized streets and small shops. Swatches of canvas stretched overhead shaded the alleys and gave it the feeling of an enclosure. Normally, at this hour, it would have been thronged with shoppers, with merchants standing in their shop doors, with delivery boys on bicycles. But it was deserted.

Burke took shelter in the shade of a goldsmith's doorway. The store was locked, but no grates secured the door or window. Rows of gold bangles hung on a rod in the window like beads on an abacus.

Burke waited for a moment, trying to get his bearings. Somewhere in front of him he heard the sounds of rifle fire, strung together like firecrackers. A machine gun, he thought.

He did not, he reminded himself, have to be a hero. He only had to get close enough to see what was happening.

He edged his way along the storefronts until he came to an intersection. He crouched down under the window of a women's-wear shop. A row of plastic knees, shins, and ankles, mannequins' lower legs, was arrayed in the window like a chorus line, modeling a variety of sheer black stockings. He wondered for an instant how the shopkeeper had evaded the ire of the *mutawa* over the display. He peered around the corner.

It was indeed a battleground, but the battle was almost over. In the center of the intersection lay three buses, overturned. A few hundred men crouched behind them, rising occasionally to fire a few rounds from their rifles at the upper floors of a ten-story building that bore the unmistakable look of a government bureaucracy. They wore knee-length smocks and turbans instead of the standard *ghotra*.

The building's windows were nearly all shot out, and in a couple of them he could see small fires burning. But it was the sight in front of the building that transfixed Burke.

It was an armored personnel carrier, a machine gun mounted on its turret. It was pointed not at the men laying siege to the building from the street below. It was pointed at the building itself. A ragtag green flag fluttered from its radio antenna—not the Saudi flag, but a revolutionary banner.

As he watched, a fighter in a stained turban rose from the turret of the APC and fired a burst from the machine gun. He could see the bullets shatter glass and raise pockmarks on the concrete around the fourth floor. The burst continued for perhaps thirty seconds. A slug ricocheted off a wall and hit the front of a spice shop across the alley from him, rupturing a burlap bag full of cardamom. The scent floated through the air, mixing with the acrid smell of burned gunpowder.

There was no answering fire.

Shouting something Burke could not understand, a group of perhaps six men, bandoliers crossed on their backs, stormed the entrance to the building, firing wildly as they ran. The fighters in front of Burke watched for a minute. When the first six entered the building, the rest began to yell. Scores more ran across the broad street, firing their rifles in the air. Then all of them followed, and Burke could hear the sound of more glass breaking in the building.

He peered across the street. There was a sign in Arabic and English in front of the building: CONTROL AND INVESTIGATION BOARD.

Burke ducked back behind the corner of the building. Had he heard in Washington that the Saudi monarchy had so abjectly failed to squelch a riot, he would have regarded it skeptically, as a rumor. The regime was, if not popular, rich. He would have thought that it had the means to buy the loyalty of soldiers, if not to buy popularity. But he had just seen one of the kingdom's armored vehicles, flying a flag of revolt, fire on one of the kingdom's ministries. He had seen the building fall.

Trembling, he leaned against the window of the stocking shop. If he could stay alive and out of jail, he was going to have a hell of a story. He was going to have it alone. It would be read and reread and thoroughly parsed by everyone in the world whose opinion mattered to him.

He would have to make it good.

The first thing he would have to do was find out whether what he had just seen was an isolated event or part of a pattern of crumbling Saudi authority.

A bullet, apparently fired at random from the Control and Investigation Board building, whined through the air above him and hit the facade of the spice shop, maybe ten feet off the ground. A small puff of pulverized concrete floated into the air and fell on an open sack of yellow saffron.

He amended his plan. The first thing he would have to do was keep his head down.

Squatting, he turned toward the core of the city and looked for a landmark. He saw a water tower, like a great, galvanized mushroom, gleaming in the sun. He had seen it before. It was a couple of blocks from the clocktower square where Massoud's trial had been held.

Cautiously, he made his way down a narrow street lined with apartment buildings, with mud walls and balconies screened by carved wood.

A pack of shouting boys, no older than twelve, burst like racehorses from a starting gate out of an inner courtyard and into the street. They seemed to Burke fearless, and he followed them, picking up his pace to keep up.

The streets were filling up with people as if a signal of safety had been given. And they were all streaming in one direction. He could hear shouts and cheers in the distance, mixed with random rifle shots.

They made a right turn and he saw the two towers of the city's central mosque, Al-Jumea, the source of the noise.

The streets were clogging with people now, some on foot and some driving slowly in cars, leaning out the windows and blowing the horns as if the country had just won an international football game. They seemed to come from all layers of Saudi society, from pudgy, wealthy Arabs in snowy *thobes* to dark little Yemeni in sweat-stained smocks and tattered knit caps.

Before he could get within a hundred yards of the mosque, the crowd thickened and became impassable. The dust in the air was thick, and he could see bullet marks in the walls of a building on the other side of the street.

What he saw in the midst of the crowd, up ahead, quickened his pulse. Four tanks, like the ones he had seen on the road that morning, stood idly in the street leading up to the mosque. Small boys and men were climbing over them like ants on an apple, waving fists in the air. He could see soldiers, their heads in helmets, standing up in the tank turrets.

So much, he thought, for the Saudi army. He could imagine, suddenly, a frantic king, or one of the king's subalterns, phoning base after base, searching for units ready to shed their countrymen's blood to put down this revolt.

Then he thought he heard his name being called. He turned in the direction of the sound.

"Mr. Burke!"

At the edge of the crowd, in a patch of shade provided by an awning, he saw Sarawi, the overnight editor from the Saudi News Agency. His white shirt was wrinkled, stained with the reddish dirt of the city, and half soaked through with sweat. His bald head gleamed. He had a cigarette cupped in one hand. For a moment Burke wondered if Sarawi had been following him. In some contexts, it would make sense. Sarawi was an employee of an agency that no doubt was subservient to the Saudi police. But the sweat and the dirt suggested otherwise. Sarawi looked like someone who had been swept up in a crowd and spent a hot, dusty day in the streets.

Sarawi waved him over; in the midst of the fervor and danger of the crowd, his thin face was cracked by a smile.

Burke, grateful to see anyone familiar and friendly, grateful to see some shade, responded by pushing through to his side. They were in a small pocket of calm as the crowd continued to swell. He heard a voice, in Arabic, shouting something through a loudspeaker system.

"Quite a day, Mr. Sarawi," Burke said.

Sarawi's smile grew wider. "It is a day we have long been praying for. And my name is Marwan, my friend."

"Mine's Colin," Burke said.

They shook hands and watched and listened for a moment to the chanting crowd.

"You've been praying for this, Marwan?" Burke asked him.

"Yes." Sarawi nodded. "For years."

"Why?"

"The al-Saud are hypocrites. God promised that the hypocrites shall be cast down into the lowest depths of the fire, where there shall be none to help them."

Sarawi said this with the beatific confidence of a believer. Burke had the sense he was hearing the Koran paraphrased, if not quoted.

Two small boys, pushing to get closer to the mosque, jammed Sarawi closer to Burke, until their shoulders and legs were pressed together.

Burke fought for a breath of air.

"And who do you think will replace them once they're down there?"

Sarawi looked at him as if the question were both naive and absurd. "An Islamic government."

"You could have fooled me. When I saw the prayer police and the women in *abayas*, I thought this was already an Islamic government."

Sarawi shook his head. "Hypocrites. They profess faith, but they subvert it. Drunkards and whoremongers."

Burke listened to the chanted prayers around him for a second and said nothing.

Sarawi poked him in the shoulder.

"You are an American, so you think an Islamic revolution is bad."

"Well," Burke said, "we do have a tendency to let the seizure of our embassies cloud our judgment."

Sarawi shook his head. "That was not Islam. That was the work of apostates. Islam is a charitable faith, a faith of peace. The world has not yet seen a true Islamic government."

Burke did not want to argue with the man.

"What have you seen today?" he said.

"It has been much like what we saw this morning," Sarawi said. "The army troops come in. The holy men appeal to their consciences. They do not fire."

"Does the king have any reliable troops?"

"The National Guard, he thinks."

"What's the difference between the National Guard and the army?"

"The National Guard are elite troops. They are designed to be a counterweight to the army. All Bedouin tribesmen, under the command of Prince Turki. My guess is that Turki has been holding them back until his half brothers in the Hussara clan have been thoroughly humiliated. He thinks that will make clear his brother Faisal's path to the throne."

"Risky," Burke said.

"It will not work," Sarawi said. "This"—he gestured toward the mass of people, filling side streets now—"is the will of God."

"Who's leading them?"

"The Ikhwan," Sarawi replied.

"I've heard of them. What does the word mean, exactly?"

"It means 'the brotherhood.' They are warriors for Islam. Two generations ago they helped Abdul-Aziz conquer Arabia and consolidate the Saudi kingdom. Then he turned on them. He thought they had been destroyed. But they have been waiting for their opportunity."

"The guy who spoke on television, with the blind eye, he's a part of the Ikhwan?"

"Sheikh al-Jubail? He is their spiritual leader. He was arrested two or three years ago. I thought he was still in jail."

"Apparently not. In fact," Burke observed, "that sounds like his voice now, coming over the speakers."

They listened.

The man's voice rose and fell in a regular cadence. It seemed, even with the scratchy amplification, that he was almost singing. Looking over the crowd, Burke could gauge the power of the rhetoric. The men in front of him seemed to sway in time to his words, leaning forward as the voice fell and straightening up as it rose in pitch and volume.

"He's saying that there must be a monument to the martyrs who fell in front of the television station this morning," Sarawi said.

"He's saying it should be built at Al-Nasiriyah . . . on the site . . . of the blasphemous pink palace . . . that they should go and liberate this site . . . now."

A chant arose in the crowd, growing louder, more staccato and more insistent with each moment. Fists rose in the air, punctuating the rhythm of the chant.

Burke could understand only the words Al-Nasiriyah, repeated again and again in the middle of the incantation. He spat on the ground.

"Not to your taste?" Sarawi asked.

"I've never been a fan of mass hysteria," Burke said. "What's Al-Nasiriyah?"

"It's a district just south of here, where the pink palace is."

"And what's the pink palace?"

"It's an enormous place that King Saud built in the fifties, after he succeeded his father and before he was deposed. Cost tens of millions of pounds even back then. Nearly bankrupted the country. It's been empty since he went into exile."

Burke had heard of Saud. "Saud's the one who drank himself to death?"

Sarawi nodded.

"And almost ruined the kingdom. His brothers finally got together and told him that Feisal was taking over in 1964."

"And it's been empty since then?" Burke found it hard to believe that no one would claim such a place.

"It's got a lot of bad spirits associated with it," Sarawi said. "But to tear it down would be a sign of . . . well, it would be like urinating on his grave."

The crowd in the square seemed to have gotten some order, because people started to move. In clusters of several hundred, they started seeping out of the square and headed west, into a warren of narrow streets and alleys.

From one of the streets in that direction, Burke could hear an amplified voice, resonating from the facades of the buildings, echoed by the crowd.

"Feel like a stroll?" he asked.

"Nice day for it," Sarawi replied.

They set off, keeping to the bits of shadow, hugging walls, trying to be inconspicuous. Despite himself, Burke began to feel excited. It was in the air.

In the street nearest them, two boys were painting something in white on the brown facade of an office building. As they worked, protesters stopped to read and cheer their work.

"It says, 'Down with the tyrants,' " Sarawi translated.

"And up with one-eyed sheikhs?"

Sarawi shook his head. "Please don't let yourself be prejudiced, Mr. Burke," he said.

Burke flushed. "Okay. You're right," he said.

Ahead of them, he could see an enormous gate and a wall of stone, fifteen feet high, that reminded him of the rocks he had sometimes seen in the desert in Arizona, a kind of mauve that could be called pink.

He heard shots being fired again, wildly and sporadically, two here, three there, and then a burst from another direction.

Burke glanced around over his shoulder, sweating now. The men in the streets were starting to run, headed in the same direction, but less festively.

They emerged into a broad street bounded on one side by the pink wall. Burke looked for any sign that the regime was prepared to defend itself. There was none—no policemen, no soldiers. The wall itself had a faintly derelict air to it.

"Pretty smart, picking this place to go after," he said to Sarawi. "It sticks it in the eye of the royal family without risking a direct confrontation. Someone's done some planning."

They heard a rumbling two blocks down and looked that way. A tank, painted in the now familiar brown camouflage, entered the street, churning up bits of hot asphalt underneath its treads.

"Maybe you spoke too soon about a confrontation," Sarawi said.

"Nope," Burke responded. "This tank's on their side. Look at the little kids running alongside it."

The tank had an escort, like a shark with its pilot fish.

It stopped, and he could see a soldier pop up from the turret, gesturing and shouting until the boys had backed off about fifteen yards. Then the turret swung around until it pointed directly at the black iron gate in the walls of the palace.

The tank's cannon belched fire and a roar split the air. Burke could feel the echo bounce off the building next to him and wash over him. A cloud of smoke appeared in the street and hung there. He looked at the gate. It had all but evaporated.

Within seconds a horde of screaming men and boys had pushed through the remains of the gate and into the palace complex. Burke and Sarawi cautiously mixed with the crowd and followed.

He had anticipated one large building. He had not anticipated a complex of them. But there they were—the enormous pink palace, so big that it looked like an ocean liner in a lake, dwarfing its surroundings. Pinkish stone glinted dully in the sun, and he decided it was marble.

But there was more—an array of outbuildings, each one the size of a mansion. A small, elegant mosque of white marble. Some distant buildings that looked like barracks. And surrounding it all were the remnants of flower gardens and fountains of lapis. The gardens were brown and withered. Only sand filled the fountains. They suggested the complex's desolation. It was uninhabited.

The first tank lumbered through the gate, followed shortly by another, each ringed by a running, almost dancing crowd of cheering men and boys. Slowly and awkwardly, the two tanks took positions facing the front facade of the palace, fifty meters away.

With a boom, the first tank opened fire. A blackened hole opened in the second story of the palace a few feet to the right of center. The crowd, swelling now as more and more men poured through the gap where the gate had been, cheered ecstatically. Allah, they said, was great. The acrid scent of spent explosive wafted in the air.

The second tank opened fire, evoking an identical reaction from the mob.

Then the first tank fired again, and soon there was an orgasmic rhythm established, with the delirium of the crowd punctuated by cannon blasts from the two tanks. Slowly and grudgingly, the second story of the pink palace began to crumble and flames licked out of several windows.

Burke's eardrums began to throb with the noise of the cannon fire and he felt, for a moment, light-headed. He took some scant refuge in the intermittent shade of a spindly date palm by the wall.

Someone with a torch ran toward the side of the palace and set some withered shrubbery afire; rosebushes, Burke thought as he watched the flames spread. A shroud of smoke hung over the complex.

Shouting to make himself heard, he asked Sarawi why the complex had so many buildings.

"Well, there was the barracks for the personal guard. The family mosque. And those mansions, I imagine, were for divorced wives."

"How many did he have?"

Sarawi grimaced. "Who could count? No more than four at a time, of course. But the pattern for Saudi kings was to have one or two favorite wives. The other two spots were rotated. A lot of what you Americans call one-night stands. They would marry and divorce them the next day. Partly they wanted to knit the tribes into an alliance with the royal family. The king would take a chief's daughter as a wife. She would produce a prince. Her father the chief gets a stake in seeing the monarchy survive. In some cases, the king undertook to maintain the divorced wives in suitable fashion. That's what those homes were for, I assume. Or perhaps for adult children."

"How many children did Saud have?"

"Fifty-five sons. I don't know how many daughters."

The cannon boomed again, and Burke waited until the reverberations died away.

"Fifty-five sons?"

Sarawi nodded. "The only way in which he outdid his father, Abdul-Aziz. Abdul-Aziz had only forty-five or so."

Burke watched the cannon fire again and wondered at the frustrations that must build in a society where one man could own not just so much wealth but so much flesh, so many souls.

Whoever was guiding this revolt—and he was convinced that someone was—was doing it in well-conceived stages. First, seize the media. Then, government ministries. Now an oblique attack on the royal family itself. He wondered when the monarchy would fight back. Or whether it could.

Chapter 12

The desert sun, as it fell toward the west, played beautiful games with the smoke that hung over Riyadh. In open places, it seemed to color the top layer of the smoke a delicate, pale yellow. In the shadows of buildings, it turned the smoke blue, a darker, roiling reflection of the sky itself. And in places where the smoke was still patchy, great shafts of light broke through to the ground and stayed there, like cockeyed pillars of illumination.

There were, Burke thought, fewer and fewer places in the city where the smoke was patchy. After six hours of fighting and burning, it lay like thick clouds over most of the town, touching the small clouds of sand, tear gas, and burned cordite that rose to meet it and creating a haze that burned his eyes and throat. He occasionally wished he had a *ghotra* so that he could tie it around his mouth and nose the way most of the men in the crowd were doing. His ears rang, and he had noticed that even shots and explosions that he could see now sounded muffled.

He had long since stopped worrying about being seen by the Saudi police. They had more pressing matters on their minds. He moved through the streets with notebook in hand, ducking into doorways when he heard new firing. He tried always to orient himself to the water tower.

As he walked he jotted notes and composed story leads in his mind. Some of the notes would make interesting details for the story—how the shooting and rioting had stopped twice for prayers, the shattering sound as the giant chandelier in the entrance hall of the pink palace had crashed to the marble floor.

But the lead, he thought, would have to be the apparent collapse of

Saudi authority. No matter where he had gone that afternoon, he had found rioting men in white *thobes* with rifles in their hands, taking over buildings without encountering resistance. The uniformed soldiers he had seen had gone over openly to the rebel side. In the space of twelve hours, since the crowd first assembled outside the prison just after dawn, riot had reached the brink of revolution.

He looked at his watch. It was seven o'clock, and he had to start thinking about filing what he had witnessed. But he hung back, unwilling to believe that the al-Saud family would let the day end with rebels holding the streets of Riyadh.

Marwan Sarawi heard a snatch of conversation from three dark-skinned men in patched brown smocks hurrying past them in the opposite direction.

He grabbed one of them by the arm, and a tortured exchange in Arabic followed, the three men all shouting in Sarawi's ears. Then the men detached themselves, moving off at a near trot.

"They are Yemeni laborers," Sarawi filled Burke in. "Their accents are terrible and they are upset, so it was hard to understand them. But they said they have seen tank columns heading toward the king's palace. They hear there will be an attack there."

"Whose tanks?" Burke asked.

Sarawi shook his head. "They do not know."

"How can I get there?" Burke asked.

Sarawi looked at him speculatively. "You are the journalist who wrote the story about Massoud, correct?"

Burke hesitated. He had started to like Sarawi. He did not want to lie to him. But the truth might get one or both of them in trouble.

"Don't ask the question if you're not sure you want to know," he replied.

Sarawi looked at him directly, his brown eyes unblinking.

"I want to know," he said.

"Yes," Burke said. "I am. And I need to see what happens in this attack, if there's going to be an attack—assuming I can find a rock or something to duck behind."

Sarawi nodded.

"We can go there. But tell me. Your government is allied with the king. Will it permit your newspaper to publish such a story?"

"My government," Burke said, "won't have anything to say about it."

A gust of wind blew up. A corrosive mix of sand and CS gas stung his eyes. Burke lowered his head and tried to shield his face with his hand. Coughs racked his body for a minute. He could stop them only by leaning down, hands on his knees, and spitting until he was panting for breath.

"When I was in college," he finally said, "I could sing six choruses of 'Give Peace a Chance' in gas thicker than this. My lungs were tougher then."

Sarawi, his own eyes watering, nodded sympathetically.

"The ravages of time," he said.

"I doubt it," Burke replied. "I think it's because I gave up all that illegal stuff I used to smoke."

Had Marwan Sarawi not known the road to the king's palace, the helicopters would have shown the way. Burke counted six different groups of them, converging from several directions on an area south of Al-Nasiriyah. Sarawi, driving a red Toyota, followed the choppers.

So did a swelling, motley army of rebels, many in cars and pickup trucks, openly defying authority now, brandishing rifles and, in a few cases, machine guns.

Burke played with the radio. He got nothing but shrieks and static. Broadcasting in Saudi Arabia appeared to be suspended, or jammed.

The land around them became flat and barren as the city converged on the desert. Little or nothing grew naturally. The soil was gritty and rocks littered the open spaces. But the roadway itself was lush with foliage. Clipped green grass grew at its sides. Acacia trees and palms grew in the median between lanes. Flower beds flanked the grassy area.

They appeared to be in a royal suburb. The houses were enormous and set well off the road, each behind its own high walls. Their roofs and second stories were the only parts visible, and in the slanting light from the setting sun, they glowed softly. Marble, Burke guessed.

"If this revolution succeeds," Sarawi said, "we will finally have a press that prints the truth. Like yours."

Burke doubted that, but he refrained from saying so. "I hope you're right," he said.

Sarawi took his eyes off the road for a second.

"You do not believe me," he said. His eyes reflected hurt.

"No," Burke said. "I don't."

"Islam loves truth," Sarawi said. "Islam calls down the curse of God on every liar."

"Keeps God busy," Burke said.

He peered through the windshield at a circling helicopter that was dropping gas grenades on a concentration of rebels about a mile ahead of them. He heard firing. Suddenly the helicopter lurched to one side and dropped like a stone. He could not see it hit the ground, but a column of smoke rose quickly over the spot where it had disappeared. He watched as the other helicopters in the area immediately rose from less than a thousand feet to several thousand, high enough for their own machine guns to be ineffective against the crowds.

Burke scribbled some notes.

"Soon, Khalil will start fighting back," Sarawi said.

"He may have to grab a gun and go out on the roof himself," Burke replied. "I haven't seen many soldiers willing to do it for him."

"You are right," Sarawi said. "But perhaps he just has not wanted to create any martyrs."

Traffic ahead of them slowed and stopped. Suddenly the air filled with the sound of gunfire, so much so that individual shots were no longer distinguishable. It was a general roar.

"This is as far as it is safe to go," Sarawi said.

A half mile ahead, Burke could see an enormous wall of beige stone. It stretched for what seemed to be a mile in each direction. Behind it stood two rows of towering palm trees.

He heard a boom, a whine, and a hundred meters in front of them, the road exploded. A pickup truck was tossed six feet in the air and turned over. Three bodies flew from its cargo bay and landed, inert, on the shoulder of the pavement. Another car swerved and ran head-on into a wall that enclosed one of the last houses neighboring the palace grounds.

"Good God," Sarawi said.

"Looks like the king's decided he'd rather create martyrs than be one," Burke said. "I think we better find some cover."

There was another boom, another whine, and Burke shoved the door open, sprinted out of the car, and spread-eagled himself on the ground. This shell struck the center of the road about fifty meters behind them. He felt the earth tremble underneath him. A quick shower of dirt and pebbles fell on his neck. He spat the dust from his mouth.

Now he desperately wanted shelter. Ahead of him, through the haze, he saw the gate of one of the lesser palaces in the king's neighborhood. Gingerly, he got up. His knees were scraped and bleeding. He saw Sarawi sprinting toward the gate.

Bending over to stay as low as possible, he ran in the same direction. The gate was made of heavy wrought iron, about eight feet high. Inside, there was a watchman's post. But the post was deserted. Beyond that was a long, massive house that appeared to have been inspired by *Gone With the Wind*. It was Tara, executed in marble, with faux-Palladian windows and a red tile roof. No lights burned inside.

It looked like a smarter place to be than in the road.

Sarawi leaped for the top of the gate and got a hand on it. Burke cupped his hands and boosted him over. He wedged his own foot into the pattern of the wrought iron, grabbed hold of the top, and slowly pulled himself up. He felt Sarawi's hand under his knee, and he used it for leverage. He got his right foot up over the top, and pulled again. He had not scaled a wall this high since he was a boy, and his mind told him he was not in condition to do it now. But fear was a great stimulant. He pulled himself up, felt a sharp stab of pain as his groin rolled over the top, and dropped to the ground inside the gate.

The impact caused him to bite down hard, taking a scrap off the tip of his tongue. He tasted his own blood, spat, and looked around.

Like the pink palace, this was a compound, though much newer. There were several buildings, all seemingly empty. The grounds around the perimeter were in deep shadow, almost dark. They were gardens, well watered, covered in rose and lilac bushes, interspersed with palm and orange trees. A grassy rectangle covered the middle of the area.

He took a second to consider his situation. If the king had finally ordered the troops to open fire, to crush this revolt, then they would surely start by killing everyone in the vicinity of the palace and on the road leading to it. As if to confirm this, he heard another whine, another explosion on the road outside.

They would not, he realized, be likely to make distinctions between rebels and bystanders, including reporters. He felt like a swimmer who lets himself drift with a current, then suddenly realizes that he is too far from shore in water way over his head. He felt panic. He wondered for an instant about the journalists who wrote nostalgically about feeling the adrenaline rush of witnessing battle at close quarters. He felt more likely to wet his pants.

Sarawi looked as if he were feeling much the same.

"Maybe through a window and into the house?" he panted.

"No," Burke said. "First place they'll look."

He sprinted for the tallest orange tree he could find and reached it. Sarawi followed. They sat in the dark shade of the wall for a minute, listening to the battle outside. Burke heard more artillery fire and the cacophony of the small arms seemed, if anything, louder and denser. Somehow, in the course of a day, the rebels had armed themselves.

The noise of brakes squealing diverted their attention back to the gate. A truck, apparently a delivery truck of some kind, had pulled abreast of the gate, and a half-dozen armed men were piling quickly out the back of it. The lead man scurried to the front of the truck and mounted the hood. Then he hopped over the windshield, onto the roof, and prepared to climb over the gate.

They wore the same turbans and short robes as the men he had seen fighting in the streets.

"Ikhwan?" he whispered to Sarawi. Sarawi nodded.

He wanted to hide. He looked upward. The branches of the orange tree were thick with leaves. There was no other sanctuary around.

"Up a tree," he whispered to Sarawi.

Sarawi shook his head and remained where he was. Burke started to climb, conscious that every move rustled the leaves, every step might cause a branch to crack.

He wedged his foot into the first crook in the tree's trunk and hauled himself up. The branches above him looked sturdy enough for about four more feet. He looked down. That should be enough to cloak him in the tree's leaves, especially now, as the sun was going down.

Cautiously, he peered back over his shoulder. The armed men from the truck had deployed in an orderly line with an established field of fire in front of them. They worked their way at a steady, deliberate trot up to the house, as if waiting for defensive fire.

There was none. The lead man stopped near the front door and aimed his rifle at the lock. He fired off a burst of half a dozen shots, then walked up to the ruined lock and kicked the door open.

The men, still in formation, sprinted through the door, covering one another. In a moment he heard them break their silence and begin shouting jubilantly at one another.

Another palace liberated for the revolution, Burke thought.

He saw the top of the compound wall at head height ahead of him and he risked a step upward. He felt the branch bend under his weight, and he slid his foot close to the trunk, so close that his ankle scraped against the bark. Another shell exploded in the road, perhaps forty meters away. He felt the tree shake, and he hugged the trunk with his left hand.

His head emerged slightly over the line of the wall, and he was able to see, for the first time, the battle raging at the gates of the king's palace.

Troops in helmets, gas masks strapped to their faces, were holding down the entrance area. This time, they were showing no compunctions about firing at civilians.

The Ikhwan forces were firing back from behind makeshift fortifications of overturned cars and trucks. He counted at least a hundred bodies in the plaza in front of the gate.

From somewhere on the wall above the palace gate, someone started operating an antitank gun. He heard the whoosh of rocket acceleration, and then one of the trucks the rebels were using for shelter exploded as its gas tank was hit. An enormous ball of black-and-orange flame blossomed from the truck's midsection, and he could hear the screams of men caught in the blast and heat. In another second the truck was a blackened hulk, burning brightly, its tires rolling slowly in the air. A dozen scorched, still bodies lay behind it. Burke blinked and ducked his head as the wave of heat and gasoline fumes washed over him.

More antitank rockets whooshed from the palace's improvised ramparts and more cars and trucks burst into flame. The sun, settling close to the western horizon, was eclipsed by the brightness of the lights. The steady chatter of machine-gun fire played counterpoint. The dust blossoms kicked up by the bullets looked like raindrops exploding on a pond during a thunderstorm. Clinging to his tree, Burke watched the bodies pile up behind the charred vehicles.

To his surprise, though, the dead fighters were replaced by live ones and the charred vehicles by new ones arriving from the center of the city, driven by men in dirty brown-and-white *thobes* with their *ghotras* pulled over their faces. A few of them had their own machine guns, and they were firing them to good effect. Bodies fell behind the palace wall, though not as often as they piled up in front of it.

He heard the sound of rifle fire behind him, and he turned, jerkily, almost losing his hold on the tree. On the veranda beside the house, two of the rebel fighters had dragged a white statue, tilted at a forty-five-degree angle against the balustrade. It looked, he thought, like a nude woman. He could see the swell of one white marble breast. It looked old—Greek, or Roman, he imagined.

They fired at it for a minute, sending chips of stone flying into the air. Finally, the statue's head fell off and rolled into the garden below. Then they ran back into the house.

So much for idols, Burke thought.

Over the din of the battle, he heard the creaking rumble of tank treads on the road outside the walls. Two tanks, flying the green rebel flag with the hole where the Saudi seal used to be, appeared in the plaza. Almost simultaneously, two of the helicopters circling overhead dropped down low over the palace grounds. He saw two missiles underneath the fuselages of each ignite and take off. They streaked toward the tanks.

But the pilots firing them must not have taken time to aim them properly, because all four missed. He watched them flash by the tanks and heard explosions toward the rear. His tree shook in the backwash.

That gave the tanks time to fire, and each got off several shots at the palace gates.

But these gates were sturdier than the ones on old King Saud's pink palace. When the smoke partially cleared, he could see that they were still standing.

A new wave of antitank rockets whooshed off the top of the palace walls and one of the tanks took a direct hit. Its armor pierced, it started to flame. The heads of two screaming soldiers emerged from the turret at the same time. Wedged into the small opening, they could not move, and Burke could only imagine what was happening inside the tank as their bodies burned. In seconds, their cries died down and he could no longer hear them over the throbbing engines of the remaining tanks, the helicopter, and the machine guns.

In the courtyard behind him, he heard voices again. He turned his head slowly and carefully and saw the Ikhwan guerrillas emerging onto the wide veranda of the house, still in their defensive formation. They looked carefully around the grounds.

He heard a rustling in the dead leaves below him and he looked down onto the bald pate of Marwan Sarawi. Sarawi's arms were up and he had a wallet of some kind open in his right hand. He was striding toward the Ikhwan fighters. But his walk was not the walk of a man giving himself up. It was too confident for that. More like a stride.

The fighters saw him. Two of them instantly turned their rifles on him. The remaining four, from wary crouches, surveyed the grounds, the barrels of their guns turning slowly.

Sarawi said something to them in Arabic. The second man in line stepped forward, rifle aimed at Sarawi's head. Sarawi kept talking in Arabic, his voice louder now, and higher.

The guerrilla reached Sarawi midway across the grass, pointed the rifle between his eyes, and screamed something. Sarawi stopped, standing stock-still, arms still raised above his head.

Burke felt his knees start to tremble involuntarily. The tree started to shake. He willed the trembling to stop, but it did not.

The guerrilla screamed again, and Sarawi slowly got to his knees and then leaned forward until he was prostrate on the ground, face-down. Keeping the rifle aimed at the back of Sarawi's head, the guerrilla grabbed the wallet from his hands and tossed it toward his comrades. The lead man stopped to pick it up. Sarawi raised his head slightly and kept repeating something in Arabic.

For perhaps five seconds the lead man examined whatever was in the wallet. Then he gave a curt, lone phrase of command.

Burke saw Sarawi's head jerk an instant before he heard the shot. Blood and brain cells, pale pink in the dying light, erupted from the other side of the bald pate. The body twitched spasmodically for a second, then went limp.

Burke felt vertiginous, and he clung desperately to the thickest branch he could find in his orange tree. The trembling in his legs spread to his arms and teeth and it felt to him as if the tree must be shaking violently, swaying and bending, and that the Ikhwan men would surely notice it.

He told himself that with the battle going on beyond the walls, with shells going off, machine guns firing, and the drum of helicopter rotors in the skies, he was camouflaged.

But he could not tell himself that he had not contributed to Marwan Sarawi's death. He had done it unintentionally, with his offhand remarks about how his own government couldn't stop him from printing what he chose, about his doubts that an Islamic government could respect free speech. He had goaded Sarawi to come to the palace to cover the battle. He had goaded him, perhaps, to demonstrate that the Ikhwan guerrillas would respect a reporter.

What he had said to Sarawi had combined arrogance and carelessness. It was almost worse than if he had shot the man himself. Burke's mind flashed to the photo on Sarawi's desk, the photo of his family.

He could not bear the thought for very long, and he found his mind detaching itself, fleeing backward to Washington, to McCoy, to Janet Kane, to the embassy that morning, to a kaleidoscope of shifting images, and then the movement of the Ikhwan guerrillas below him arrested his attention.

They stepped carelessly around the prostrate body of Marwan Sarawi and headed for the gate. This time, one of the soldiers found a switch in the guardhouse and flipped it. The twin doors swung slowly open, and they were gone. From the top of the tree, Burke watched them jog down the road toward the palace.

He felt dizzily grateful that they had not seen him, and then shamed by his own survival.

A cascade of cannon fire distracted him. The artillery pieces inside the palace walls were going off like a string of firecrackers, the booms with each shell melding into a single cacophonous noise, and soon the roads around the palace were trembling with explosions. Then, suddenly, they stopped.

He heard the sound of rotors and he looked up. There were no helicopters visible in the sky. Then he heard the whine of jet engines and a half a dozen fighter jets, F-15s by the look of their twin tail rudders, hove into view from the north. Within seconds they were over the palace, flying at about five hundred feet. He thought he could feel the tree around him shudder in the backwash as they flashed by.

Then, about half a mile away, he saw a bright green helicopter rise slowly from behind the roof of the main building in King Khalil's compound. He peered at it carefully. It bore the royal seal, but no armaments that he could see.

The fighter jets, banking sharply against the setting sun, returned and flew by again as more identical green choppers rose from what must have been a pad behind the palace. There were five in all. One by one, the choppers gained an altitude of about a thousand feet and then flew northwest, at an oblique angle to the sun, escorted by the F-15s.

He heard a triumphant shout from below, where the Ikhwan guerrillas were clustered, beyond the wall. The shout was taken up by others and then hundreds of voices were roaring and cheering.

And he understood. Those were the king's personal helicopters. The king was fleeing. He watched until the helicopters had dwindled to specks in the sky, and he checked his watch: 8:12.

The shelling from within the palace stopped, and a fusillade of fire began from the ranks of the Ikhwan in the streets. He could not distinguish single shots—it was a celebratory, jubilant crackling noise that filled the air with the smell of cordite.

He heard again the creaking treads and throaty diesel grumble of tanks, and this time there was no answering whoosh of antitank rockets. In that patch of ground within the palace walls that he could see well, he saw soldiers moving quickly—away from the gates.

The tank cannons roared simultaneously, and repeatedly, for nearly two minutes and finally the gates to the palace yielded.

Screaming triumphantly, the men of the Ikhwan bolted through the smoke and gathering darkness, across the road and through the gate. No resistance met them, and Burke wondered how the palace's defenders could have fled so quickly. But they were gone.

Now, in darkness, he saw the shadows of hundreds of the Ikhwan scattering over the palace grounds. He could imagine them entering the king's dwelling itself, and he thought for a moment of how much a description of that scene would add to his story. He could imagine their feet spreading grime on pristine rugs and their rifle bullets gouging chips in marble fountains, like the Bolsheviks entering the Winter Palace in 1917. Then he remembered what had happened to Marwan Sarawi.

Slowly and carefully, keeping one eye trained on the gate, he made his way down from his perch in the tree. At the bottom, it was completely dark, and he stayed there for a moment, feeling that the shadows were his cloak and shield and unwilling to give them up.

He peered out at the road beyond the gate. The traffic was thick, with headlights flashing past and horns blaring. But there was no sign that anyone was paying attention to this courtyard, not when the king's palace was open for inspection.

He trotted across the lawn to Sarawi's body. The leather wallet he had shown to the Ikhwan lay in the grass an inch from his fingers. Burke picked it up. It was open to some kind of identity card, written in Arabic. A color photo of Sarawi was pasted into the upper-right-hand corner. He put the ID card in his pocket and, feeling ghoulish, patted the area of Sarawi's pockets. He found no keys.

Cautiously, feeling exposed, he walked to the edge of the gate and peered outside. As he did, a pickup truck full of turbaned Ikhwan fighters came by and one of them fired a burst from an automatic rifle. Burke cringed behind the wall of the compound until he realized the man was firing in the air.

Hugging the wall, he stepped out into the road. He saw the silhouettes of half a dozen vehicles along the sides of the pavement. Closest to him was the charred, bent chassis of a truck. He assumed it had been hit by one of the shells from the palace's defenders. Across the street and back some fifty yards was a compact car, and he thought at first that it could not be Sarawi's Toyota, because he did not remember running that far when the shelling had started.

But it was the only compact car he could see, and he went to it, staying close to the wall until he was directly across from it, and then sprinting across the road, hoping no one would see him, or care if they did.

It was Sarawi's car. And the keys were still in the ignition.

It took him a long time to write his story; it was a process of paring away what he thought and leaving what he knew. First, there was the problem of whether to report the overthrow of the al-Saud dynasty. He abandoned that idea quickly; the situation was too fluid. Then he considered reporting the flight of King Khalil. He decided that this, too, would be speculative. He knew that six helicopters with the royal seal had flown from the palace and that shortly afterward the rebels had overrun it. He made that his lead. The implications would be clear enough.

Slowly, he filled in the details he had heard and observed since dawn that day. He paused again when he came to the execution of Marwan Sarawi.

Sarawi's death was a footnote to the story, but he wanted to write it. He tried to think of a way to do it. But each approach he considered foundered on the fact that to write about Sarawi, he would have to write about himself, and his own role. He could not imagine a piece with the word *I* in it and no byline.

No. He would save Sarawi's story for another day.

He closed the file and drove in the only direction that seemed to have no sites connected to the events of the day, northeast. It was a neighborhood of tenements and cement factories, vacant lots and warehouses. Judging by the people he saw in the streets, the revolt had entered a celebratory phase. They were singing something repetitive and rhythmic, like the songs soccer fans sang in Latin America.

He left the city behind and searched out a propitious spot in the desert. He found a ridge not far from the road, parked the car, and climbed it. His shoes slogged through the loose sand, and near the top he realized for the first time that day how tired he was. He wondered if it might possibly be safe to go back to the Inter-Continental to sleep. Then he laughed at himself. He would sleep in the car.

On the far side of the ridge, he opened the little transmitting dish, then used the compass to point it toward the Indian Ocean. The green Locator light flickered on. He plugged in the computer.

He heard the sound of brakes on the road, a couple of hundred yards behind him. He plugged the laptop into the phone.

Car doors slammed.

Pecking quickly at the keys, he dialed the number for the *Tribune*'s computer.

He heard voices behind him.

The disks inside the computer wheezed and honked, and it seemed to take forever for the electronics to do their work. Then a message blinked on the screen. UPLINK ESTABLISHED.

He pressed a button and began the transmission.

He looked around. Two men in turbans and a third man, in a standard Saudi *thobe*, were coming over the crest of the ridge. The men in turbans had rifles trained on him and the man in the suit was saying something to him.

He crouched where he was until the machine blinked and coughed up the message he wanted: TRANSMISSION COMPLETE.

Then he raised his hands and turned to face his captors.

CHAPTER 13

On the floor of the New York Mercantile Exchange, a young reporter named Chris Carruthers got set to do her opening stand-up for the markets segment of CNBC's financial news. Normally, her job was a superficial one, giving quick, thirty-second capsule reports and reading statistics. But at this moment she sensed for the first time that she had a piece of a historic story.

Behind her, in the trading pit for crude-oil futures, her cameraman recorded a scene of orgiastic capitalism. Men jumped. Men wagged fingers. Men roared and bellowed. In the air around them, postcard-size sales receipts drifted in a blizzard toward a net stretched over the central point at the bottom of the pit. A clerk in a plaid shirt and a yarmulke frantically clutched at them, shoved them into a machine that stamped the time on them, and handed them to another clerk, who raced off to an office to have them recorded.

"We're watching a scene of bedlam," Carruthers said, restating the obvious, raising her voice and pulling her mike closer to her mouth to make sure she could be heard over the din.

"Oil prices have skyrocketed this morning in response to news of a possible revolution in Saudi Arabia. Trading opened at twenty-three dollars a barrel and immediately soared to thirty-three. The exchange closed trading for ten minutes, but the delay only seemed to fuel the speculative frenzy. Trading closed again fifteen minutes ago with prices at forty-two dollars, but then it reopened again and prices immediately jumped toward fifty dollars. Right now oil is trading at—"

She turned her head around, toward a big electric scoreboard behind her. The camera followed.

"Fifty-one dollars—"

She never finished the sentence. A few feet from where she stood, a brawny clerk for a brokerage house named McGraw Brothers got a buy order at fifty-three dollars on one of the telephones mounted in banks on the floor of the exchange. He sprinted toward the pit, the phone still in his ear. On-screen, CNBC viewers got a glimpse of a mop of curly brown hair and a red St. John's T-shirt as he flashed in front of Carruthers. The cord caught around her neck and she pitched immediately to the floor like a bottle knocked off a fence post.

For a few seconds the CNBC cameraman stayed fixed on the chaotic scene in front of him. Then he panned down to the floor, where Carruthers lay, glassy-eyed and gasping for breath. She had, it seemed, worn gym shorts and sneakers to work that day underneath the white silk blouse that was the only thing she expected to be seen on camera.

CNBC cut to Raquel Desmond in the studio, whose eyes were wide and almost equally glassy.

"Well," she finally managed to say. "It's certainly turning out to be a big day on Wall Street. The buying frenzy in oil is matched by the dump-off at the New York Stock Exchange, where the Dow has lost four hundred and fifty points. For a live report, we go now . . ."

"Turn it off," Henry Hoffman said.

Brian Barrett reached over to a coffee table and found the remote. He clicked the set off.

Hoffman turned to Alicia Parkside-Burns, his economics expert.

"Get me a three-page paper on steps the president can take to hold the price of oil down. Everything from selling stock from our strategic reserve to declaring an emergency and shutting the exchange down for a few days. Like Roosevelt's bank holiday," he said.

Parkside-Burns rose from her seat on the couch in Hoffman's office, set under a painting of Benjamin Franklin presenting his credentials to King George III.

"When do you want it, Dr. Hoffman?"

Hoffman looked at his watch. "Ten minutes ago," he said. But he smiled as he said it, and he saw that Parkside-Burns's stride, as she left his office, conveyed the attitude he wanted—brisk, not hurried, and thoughtful, not harried.

It was important, Hoffman thought, to give everyone—his staff, the media, the president—the impression that this crisis was under control. Especially the president. If Peter Scott Detwiler could project a calm confidence, then the country, and the world, would follow his lead.

Hoffman did not find it pleasant to contemplate the consequences if the country panicked. In the short run, there would be hoarding and long lines at gas stations, sharp inflation. In the medium term—a recession, if not worse, at home, and instability abroad as fragile democratic regimes cracked under the burden of rising energy costs.

The medium term was as far as Hoffman thought. If this crisis metastasized, neither he nor Detwiler would be around to worry about the long term.

He was determined that it would not. Not on his watch.

Rather than nerves or anxiety, Hoffman felt a sense of detachment, strength, and awareness. Managing a situation of these proportions was what he had worked his adult life to be able to do. He reminded himself yet again to focus his mind on what he wanted to happen, not on what he was afraid might happen—to the country and to himself.

"Let's go see the president, Brian," he said to Barrett. "We're going to earn our pittances this week."

They walked down the internal West Wing corridor that linked Hoffman's office with the staircase that led to the White House basement. There were two more Secret Service agents than normal in the hallway, and Hoffman realized that the service had quietly ticked security up a notch around the White House, as it was supposed to do whenever a crisis erupted in a part of the world that had terrorist connections. On the roof of the building, he knew, behind blinds that were supposed to look like air-conditioning ducts, the army had posted sentinels with shoulder-fired Stinger antiaircraft weapons. And lightly armed marine helicopters were flying patrols over central Washington's airspace, patrols designed to look like civilian helicopters shuttling dignitaries to and from the Pentagon and Bethesda Naval Hospital.

Thaddeus Hirsch was walking toward the staircase from the White House's West Wing entrance as Barrett and Hoffman arrived. Hoffman stopped, Barrett behind him, in ostentatious deference to Hirsch's rank.

"Brian," Hirsch said coldly. "Henry."

He walked past without shaking hands.

Hoffman watched Hirsch's back for a second as the man descended toward the Situation Room. He wondered if Hirsch could cope.

No, he thought. Not Hirsch. They would have to work around him.

The Situation Room was small, made to seem even smaller by the dark wood paneling. It was not at all like the place the movies had conditioned Hoffman to expect when he first came to work at the White House. There were no cavernous ceilings, no glass display maps. There was a display screen for film for projections hidden behind a retractable panel on one wall. The place was heavily wired, both to help the people inside to communicate and to prevent people outside from hearing what they said. But like everything else in the White House, it felt cramped. It was a nineteenth-century room forced to serve the needs of a twenty-first-century National Security Council.

Secretary of Defense Alan Seifert and General Bruce Stewart, the chairman of the joint chiefs of staff, were already at the mahogany conference table when Hoffman and Barrett entered. A navy steward, a Filipino despite all the services' efforts to eradicate racial distinctions and categories, took Hoffman's order. The principals sat, awkwardly, sipping coffee, with Hirsch off to himself. Aides, like Barrett, took chairs along the wall and pulled out notepads.

"It was something the way that son-of-a-bitch left his troops fighting at the palace wall, wasn't it?" Seifert said to Stewart.

Seifert, who was from Oklahoma, had been chairman of the Senate Armed Services Committee, but he had never served in uniform. He was one of those national defense hawks who had managed to stay in graduate school all through the Vietnam War, and he always went out of his way to broadcast his allegiance to the military ethos.

"Yes, Mr. Secretary," Stewart replied. His voice was flat and neutral, betraying nothing of what he actually thought of Seifert.

Stewart rose as he said this and Hoffman turned to the door. Peter Scott Detwiler walked in, followed by Maynard Walters, Don Tobin, the chief of the White House staff, Bernard Nuñez, the White House photographer, and a retinue of others.

Detwiler took his coat off and sat down at the table in his shirtsleeves. Nuñez started inching and squeezing his way around the crowded room, taking pictures. Hoffman had long since gotten used to the intrusion at the beginning of any significant meeting. And he understood the need for a photographic record of the administration. But he sometimes found himself wishing silently that people would be more concerned with the substance of a meeting. It could have been worse. Walters had wanted to equip Nuñez with a video camera.

"Good morning," Detwiler said. "Thad, why don't you give us a rundown of what's going on over there. As the Sundance Kid said to Butch Cassidy, 'Who are these guys?' "

Hirsch cleared his throat, pulled out his eyeglasses, which had half lenses, and picked up a plain manila folder bordered in red.

"The core of the opposition seems to be a radical Islamic movement called the Ikhwan, but it is only the core," he said. "What we've seen in the past twenty-four hours is that opposition to the Saud-dynasty regime comes from nearly every segment of society. The army by and large declined to fight. The National Guard, which was supposed to be the elite force, was initially held back. Apparently, Prince Turki and the faction pushing Faisal for the throne thought that allowing the disturbances to continue for a while would embarrass Khalil, Ahmed, and the other Hussara brothers, and assure that none of them succeeded Khalil.

"But Turki evidently miscalculated. When he finally unleashed the National Guard to defend the palace, Khalil was already in a state of advanced panic. He took off, and that totally deflated the Guard's morale. It stopped fighting."

"What's the situation now?" Detwiler asked.

Hirsch ran an index finger down the second page of his briefing paper.

"The rebels control Riyadh. The Shiite population in Dhahran has begun rioting, but thus far present no direct threat to the oil fields. The Saudis, however, seem to be holding on in Jedda. The king, we've been told, is on his yacht in the Red Sea off Jedda, and there are rumors he either has abdicated or will abdicate to his brother Ahmed. But we haven't seen any signs that Ahmed is even in the country."

"How would you know?"

The speaker was Tobin, the chief of staff. Tobin, balding, redhaired, and forty-five, had worked for Detwiler since he was a congressman. He had one goal in his life: he protected the interests of his boss. Sometimes he did it by supplying the nastiness that Detwiler lacked. It was a role for which Tobin was well suited, and Henry Hoffman was looking forward to what he was going to do to Thaddeus Hirsch.

Hirsch began to flush at the neck.

"Well, Don, if you'd like a separate briefing on our assets and methods in Saudi Arabia, we can arrange that."

"Assets my ass," Tobin growled. "I don't think you could tell us the place is a desert without looking up back issues of *National Geographic*."

Hirsch's face went from red to pale. He looked to Detwiler, but Detwiler was scanning a briefing paper on his desk. At that moment, Hoffman could sense, Hirsch saw his situation clearly.

To his credit, Hirsch responded calmly.

"When this is over, I suggest we conduct a full review. It will show, contrary to the story that was leaked into the *Post* this morning, presumably from sources in this building who speak anonymously to the press, that the Agency has warned repeatedly over the last twenty years that Saudi Arabia was inherently unstable—"

"You warn repeatedly that all countries are unstable—" Tobin cut in, but this time Hirsch was not going to be intimidated.

"I'll finish what I have to say, if you don't mind," he said.

"We have warned repeatedly of the folly of allowing this country to remain addicted to cheap oil from Saudi Arabia. No administration, including this one, has paid any attention to those warnings.

"So, no, we didn't predict the hour and day. But we predicted that it could come."

Hoffman looked at the president. Detwiler squirmed in his seat. He quickly got his fill of this kind of friction at meetings. He preferred that people meekly accept Tobin's harangues.

Tobin's voice rose perilously close to a shout. "Are you suggesting—" he began.

It was time, Hoffman decided, to bring the meeting under control.

"Let's not suggest anything," he said quietly. "When the dust settles, if you'll excuse a pun, we can sort out who shot John. But in the meantime we'd better focus on our next steps. General Stewart, what capabilities do you have on the ground there?"

Stewart rose and pressed a button by his place. The panel in the wall opposite Detwiler slid back and a chart appeared, showing American military forces deployed in the Persian Gulf region.

Hoffman suppressed a smile. Stewart was from the Pentagon school that said never brief civilians without visual aids to make it easy for them.

"Our joint task force in the Gulf presently numbers twenty thousand men. We have, of course, overwhelming air and sea superiority. We have a brigade of marines based on ships in the Gulf. We have a SEALs unit based clandestinely at King Abdul-Aziz Air Base in Dhahran. The rest of our people are there on TDY, as advisers to the Saudi armed forces, and are not formed into units. But within forty-eight hours, we have the capability to put four divisions on the ground around the airfields. Their equipment is predeployed."

"But whom would we put them into action against, General?"

The speaker was Marcia Acton, the deputy secretary of state, filling in for her boss, who was in Japan.

"Good question, Ms. Acton," Stewart said. "I was getting to it. We have intelligence units operating now to ascertain the strength of the rebels and where their command post is. But we don't know yet."

"They seem," Hirsch said, "to be led by this Sheikh al-Jubail, the one who was on television yesterday. But there's obviously a structure of some kind, based in the mosques. We're expecting them to make an announcement shortly."

"And whom do we fight in favor of?" Acton asked.

"Well, it's not clear now. Whoever 'those who tie and untie' pick to succeed Khalil, I assume."

"Then I suggest it's a bit premature to be talking about military action. We don't know whom we'd be fighting against or for," Acton said. "For that matter, we don't even know that a new regime would be necessarily inimical to our interests."

"Oil is already fifty goddamn dollars a barrel, Ms. Acton," Tobin snapped. "How inimical do they have to be? We can't afford to risk another Khomeini."

"I know how much oil is selling f—" Acton began to reply, but Hoffman cut her off.

"Perhaps we can work best if we concentrate on tasking for the next twelve to twenty-four hours," Hoffman said as mildly, but firmly, as he could.

Acton and Tobin scowled and slid back in their chairs.

"By all means," Detwiler agreed.

"First, I think we can all agree that the intelligence community has got to put on a full-court press to identify the sources of this revolt and potential targets for action," Hoffman said. He looked directly at Acton. Cowed, she said nothing.

Alicia Parkside-Burns walked into the room, clutching some papers.

"Second, I suggest we ought to implement plans to begin controlled releases of oil from the Strategic Petroleum Reserves to help us get over any disruption in Saudi supplies. Alicia, how many days' worth is that?"

"We can pump two million barrels a day for forty-five days," she said. "That would replace the Saudi oil consumed in the United States."

"We could announce that right away," Walters said.

Detwiler nodded. "Might help soothe the markets," the president said.

"Third, we ought to begin urgent consultations with NATO, the Russians, the Egyptians, and the Israelis about potential steps they might be willing to support."

Acton nodded.

"Finally," Hoffman said, "there's the question of deploying troops. Should we start it, and when?"

Acton looked about to say something, but Barrett beat her to it.

"That would be a mistake," he said. "No government put into place by U.S. troops over there would ever have a shred of legitimacy."

"Well, let's hope we don't have to choose between oil and legitimacy," Hoffman replied.

In the Old Executive Office Building, Brian Barrett could sense an atmosphere of crisis. Even the secretaries and the guards looked grim and purposeful. He liked the way they looked at him. He was a player.

He shut the door behind him as he entered his office. Alone, he punched keys on his computer until his screen filled with the daily log of reporters' calls to the office of the NSC's spokeswoman, Marney Hutton. As he had anticipated, all of the major papers and networks had called to ask for background interviews on the Saudi situation. Marney was recommending that he set aside an hour and a half, beginning at 5:30, for calls to the *Times*, the *Tribune*, and the *Post*, plus two group briefings—ABC, CBS, NBC, and CNN in one, and *Time*, *Newsweek*, and *U.S. News* in the second.

He barely registered that information as he scrolled down the list of reporters. Apart from the favored few at the elite media outlets, they would hear from a National Security Council staffer of his rank only at public White House briefings. They were reporters for newspapers in cities like Chicago and Philadelphia, local television correspondents, wire-service people. Marney would handle their questions.

The foreign journalists on the list did not generally rate even Marney's time. A few of them—the writers from papers like the *Guardian* and *Le Monde*—were enterprising enough to cultivate contacts in the State Department, with diplomats who had served in England or France and still regarded those papers as important. The rest got what they were fed at the State Department briefings or by the USIA, which ran its own press room at the National Press Club. It didn't matter—they generally wrote what they were predisposed to write, anyway.

He found the name he was looking for toward the bottom of the list, sandwiched between the calls from *Mainichi Shimbun* and *Der Spiegel*: Mustafa Sadeq, correspondent of a newspaper whose name, in English, meant the *Beirut Star*.

Barrett had spent twenty disastrous minutes with Mustafa Sadeq a year ago, when the previous press secretary had made the mistake of scheduling a briefing for Lebanese and Syrian correspondents on the Israeli–Syrian negotiations. The *Beirut Star* had been included because it circulated widely among Islamic fundamentalists throughout the Middle East.

But Sadeq had turned the briefing into a farce, a harangue in which he expounded on his own worldview for nearly ten minutes. Sadeq was one of those journalists who explained everything that happened in his part of the world in terms of conspiracies between the CIA and perfidious local leaders in the CIA's pocket. Zionism, he said, was a CIA creation to divide and weaken the Arab nation. The CIA had even induced Saddam Hussein to invade Kuwait so that the United States could expand its military presence in the Persian Gulf. In the extant case, Sadeq had said in his peroration, the CIA was clearly paying the Israelis to let Hafez el-Assad back into the Golan Heights in order to break the links between Hezbollah in Lebanon and the regime in Iran.

But Sadeq, Barrett had learned, had one redeeming quality. He played by the rules of attribution. Though the briefing had been on background, some of the journalists present had written their stories in such a way that Barrett's identity was clear. A few had simply violated the rule and named him outright. But the piece in the *Beirut Star* had referred only to "administration sources." It had been a wildly tendentious and inaccurate piece in which Sadeq ignored what he had heard and amplified on his CIA conspiracy theory. But the attribution had been scrupulously correct.

Since then, Sadeq had frequently called Barrett's office for comment, and his calls were always ignored. Barrett had seen a couple of translated excerpts of Sadeq's stories in the *National Intelligence Daily*'s press digest. Apparently, he liked being able to write that Brian Barrett refused to return his phone calls, implying that Barrett was unable to rebut his magisterial theories.

He might be ideal, Barrett thought.

He hesitated for a barely perceptible moment. What he was about to do would violate the NSC's rules. But they were, he knew, rules that everyone in the White House violated anyway. What was important was not the rules, but stanching the leak in Saudi Arabia. He reached toward the phone pad more decisively.

He punched in Sadeq's number, which had a Virginia area code. He heard three rings; a woman answered. In the background, he could hear a television set and a baby crying—or perhaps a television show with a crying baby.

Barrett identified himself and asked for Mustafa Sadeq. In halting English, the woman asked him to wait. He heard her calling Sadeq's name.

"You called," Barrett said after the formalities. He was going to make Sadeq lead this conversation.

"Yes, Dr. Barrett," Sadeq said. He made the name sound like "Bahr-it." There was a moment of silence while, Barrett assumed, Sadeq recovered from his surprise at being called back and tried to remember the questions he wanted to ask.

"Well," Sadeq said, "everyone knows that the CIA employs many spies in the Saudi royal household and Abdulrahman Massoud was only one of them. Isn't it a fact that they allowed Prince Ahmed to catch this one to warn the king to stop subsidizing the Hezbollah in Lebanon?"

All right, Barrett thought. That's the conspiracy theory *du jour*. Sadeq was as predictable as mud slides in Los Angeles. This should not be hard.

"What are the ground rules?" Barrett asked.

"Background," Sadeq offered.

"No, it has to be off the record, because you're getting into intelligence matters," Barrett said.

"Yes. All right." Sadeq sounded pleased and excited.

"Now then," Barrett continued. "Your theory sounds plausible, but it's not true."

"But—" Sadeq started to respond.

"And I'll tell you why," Barrett continued. "If the United States wanted to warn King Khalil, there would be lots of ways to do it. We wouldn't have to give up an agent."

He let Sadeq ruminate on that for a second.

"Then the CIA has made a deal with Ahmed and Turki to displace the Hussara brothers," Sadeq said. He had taken the hook.

"Your conclusion, not mine," Barrett said, giving him more line to play with.

Sadeq thought for another moment.

"But for that plan to work, the CIA needed to publicize the trial," Sadeq said. "And the CIA is not supposed to use journalistic cover."

"Except in certain unusual cases," Barrett reminded him. It was true. The Agency had carefully preserved a loophole in the general prohibition against using journalistic cover.

"The *Tribune*!" Sadeq whispered excitedly. "The CIA is using the *Tribune*! Its correspondent!"

"Sorry," Barrett said. "Now you're getting into questions about sources and methods that I can't comment on. Even off the record."

Chapter 14

Burke awoke to the sounds of footsteps in a corridor beyond a wall. His eyes opened, and he saw a filigree of cracks in a roughly plastered ceiling above his head. The ceiling looked slanted, as if it were sagging.

He sat up. He was in a small room, furnished with one straw mattress that crunched and jabbed him when he moved. There was a window, but it was barred and screened by wooden shutters. The light that filtered through was dim.

He was surprised he had slept at all. He had been blindfolded and shoved into the backseat of a car the night before. His belongings had been taken. He remembered his blindfold coming off in a room in this building, men poring over his passport, his driver's license, his telephone and his computer, his credit cards. He had been unable to speak to them. They had pushed him, firmly but without injuring him, into this room and locked the door.

He remembered staring for what seemed like hours at the dark ceiling, images swirling in front of his mind's eye: Janet Kane and Abdulrahman Massoud, the bodies on the plaza in front of the television station, Desdemona McCoy, the execution of Marwan Sarawi, and the flight of the helicopters from the king's palace.

He had been frightened and he still was frightened. He had told himself that if his captors had wanted to kill him, they would have done so. And although he had believed this to be true, and told himself repeatedly that it was true, and that he had done nothing wrong, he could not repress the knowledge that he was in a violent, chaotic situation, where people of his nationality and his occupation were not liked.

He was, he realized, terribly thirsty. His mouth felt like sandpaper and his lips were dry and beginning to crack where the sun of the day before had burned them. He looked around again. There was nothing in the room to drink.

The footsteps in the corridor stopped, and he could hear the jingling of metal against metal and then the sound of a key in the lock in his door. He got to his feet, searching instinctively and vainly for someplace to hide in the bare room.

The door opened and three men entered. They were, he knew, soldiers of the Ikhwan. Two had automatic rifles slung over their shoulders. They wore turbans instead of the *ghotra* of the Saudi townspeople, and their beards were long and shaggy rather than the closely cropped goatees favored by the royal family. Their robes fell only to the middle of their calves, and underneath he could see worn sandals and grime.

One of them, pulling his rifle to a ready position, pointed it at Burke and prodded him under the shoulder blade. Burke turned and faced the wall. He was prodded again. He raised his hands and pressed the palms against the wall. A blindfold was slipped over his eyes and tightened.

Another silent poke from the barrel of the rifle and he began walking toward the door, letting the man behind him prod him to stay on course, putting one foot carefully in front of the other, shuffling.

The image of a firing squad leaped into his mind and he could not dismiss it. He thought of his son, and his ex-wife, and McCoy. He started to wonder how many people would show up at his funeral, then forced himself to tear his mind away. That would do him no good.

They made their way down a flight of stairs, and he could smell coffee laced with cardamom coming from a room to his right. He thought he should ask for some, not to slake his thirst, but to postpone whatever was going to happen to him. But he did not, of course, have the words.

He heard a door open and then they were outside, judging by the light slipping through the blindfold and by the sounds. He had heard street noises, the sounds of dozens of people chatting. He heard those people fall silent as he passed. The air was thick with dust. He could taste it on his tongue.

He almost tripped over a threshold, and the character of the light changed again, and he knew that they had entered a building, but this time there was no sound of a door closing, or at least he could not hear it over the din of voices. He felt slightly relieved. He did not think they would shoot him indoors, in front of people.

A hand on his collar jerked him to a halt, and he could feel fingers working on his shoes. He raised his feet, one at a time, and they came off. More fingers worked at the knot that held the blindfold. It fell away. He blinked.

He was in a mosque, a large one, the size of a gymnasium with a low ceiling. The walls were of pale, white stone inlaid with blue tiles that he assumed were lapis lazuli. There were columns holding up the ceiling, carved from the same white stone. Red, woven carpets, more than a hundred of them, covered the floors.

The mosque was full of milling males, like the parking lot of a football stadium before a game. It must not have been prayer time, for only a few of them were praying. They stood in clusters, talking and gesturing, their voices loud and passionate. Some wore the snowy, white *thobe* of the well-to-do Saudi. But most were in poorer clothes, *thobes* that came down barely past their knees and showed the wear and grime of long use. If Saudi Arabia had had a blue collar, he thought, it would be this short, dirty robe. Their heads were all covered, but in an assortment of knit caps and turbans as well as *ghotras*.

And they all seemed young to him. Some were boys, no more than ten years old. Others were teenagers with wispy mustaches, and many were young men, with rifles slung over their shoulders, cultivating an aura of danger and bravado. But there was no one he could see with even a streak of gray in his hair.

That, he guessed, was the reason that Boris Yeltsin had not suffered a revolt in the streets and the al-Saud had. Yeltsin made sure that the brunt of the sacrifice in Russia fell on the aged, whose pensions withered to nothing. All they could do about it was sit in their apartments and grumble. The al-Saud had made a key strategic mistake. They had allowed the *ulama*, the Muslim clergy, to make sure that no forms of contraception were permitted, that women were rarely educated and even less often permitted to work outside their homes. They had imported the best Western health-care systems they could buy.

Those two things had produced an exploding birth rate. There could not be enough jobs to go around for the young males that needed them. And unlike the elderly Russians, the young Saudi males could go into the streets to protest. They had.

It would make, he thought, an interesting analytical lead for his next piece. All he had to do was make sure he wrote a next piece.

They prodded him, using their hands this time, toward the side of the hall, in the shadows behind the pillars. The men in their way parted slowly, grudgingly. He saw in their flat, brown eyes a sheen of hatred. He sensed that they respected the authority of his captors and would not harm him as long as he was in their custody. But he would not have wanted to find out how they would have treated him had he wandered in off the streets, unescorted, looking for some quotes for a voice-of-the-people angle.

His captors paused before an oaken door and knocked. It opened from the inside.

He walked into a room that appeared to be a library or an office. The walls were lined with books and there were two desks. The carpets were soft and plush. In this room, the building's air-conditioning worked.

He was prodded to a chair next to the desk and he sat down. In a corner, just out of his arm's reach, he saw his satellite telephone, its case spread open. His wallet, passport, and the contents of his briefcase were on the desk. He picked them up.

A man in bare feet approached with a cup and a pot. He placed the cup on the desk and filled it with hot, amber coffee. Greedily, Burke picked up the cup and drained it in small sips, relishing the way the liquid felt as it passed over his dry lips.

When he had finished, the men with the rifles indicated by gesture that he might have more. He declined. One of them put a hand under his elbow. He got up, and they exited via a second door, which led to a staircase. This time, they walked up.

They entered a narrow corridor, at the end of which were posted three guards armed with automatic rifles. They passed on the word of Burke's escorts and entered another study. Sheikh al-Jubail, the mullah with one bad eye who had been on television the day before, sat at the room's lone desk, which was covered with papers. He had thick, pink lips under the graying hair of his beard and mustache and his nose had been flattened. A faint scar ran down the left side of his jaw. He wore a cloak of coarse brown cloth over a short robe.

Next to him was an Ikhwan guerrilla of perhaps forty—old enough, Burke thought, to be an officer.

A young Arab with a precisely trimmed beard strode from the side of the room and took a position at Burke's side. Another came and poured coffee into three cups.

"Please do not shake hands," the translator whispered into Burke's ear.

The sheikh's good eye focused on Burke and he had the sense he was being inspected. The sheikh said something brief and quiet, in a voice Burke had to strain to hear.

"What is your religion?" the man at Burke's side translated.

"Pardon me?" Burke replied. In all of his years as a journalist, no one had ever asked that question.

Upon hearing the translation, the sheikh's eyes narrowed and the thick, pink lips flickered upward briefly in a smile.

The guerrilla next to him, Burke noticed, had pulled out a string of beads and was fingering them.

"Your religion," the translator repeated.

In fact, he had no religion. His parents were deracinated easterners who had given up the Protestant churches of their youth when they moved to California.

Russia had strengthened Burke's atheism. He could not believe in a deity that would permit such suffering and evil as this century had visited upon the Russians.

But he knew enough of the Koran to know that Jews and Christians were regarded as People of the Book—infidels, but nevertheless a step above atheists.

"I'm a Catholic," he said.

The clicking of the guerrilla's worry beads was the only sound in the room for a few seconds.

The sheikh spoke again.

"How could God have a son if he had no consort?" the interpreter translated.

Burke hesitated as if actually reflecting on the question.

"I'm afraid my lack of learning leaves me unqualified to engage in such a discussion with Sheikh al-Jubail," he said.

The sheikh snorted quietly but triumphantly when he heard the translation. Then he replied.

"Any Arab boy, even one who cannot read, could answer this question. And yet you in the West tell us how to live," came the interpretation. "You proclaim that your education is superior."

As long as he was groveling, Burke thought, he might as well make a thorough job of it.

"Well, our schools do have many problems," he said.

The translation came back.

"Is it true that men and women attend classes together, and that infidels and homosexuals are permitted to teach them?"

Burke nodded.

The sheikh glowered. "This is the root of your problems," he said.

"With such wisdom, you could have a radio show in my country," Burke replied. "Millions of people would listen."

As soon as the words were out of his mouth, he regretted them.

He watched for a reaction. The sheikh, however, evinced only satisfaction as he heard the translation.

"You are the journalist who has been reporting for the newspaper in Washington?" the sheikh asked.

It would have been futile, he realized, to lie about it. They'd caught him transmitting. He nodded.

The sheikh leaned back in his chair and placed his hands in front of his chest in a prayerful position. "We have decided to grant you an interview, so that the West will know who we are and what we require of them."

Burke could not suppress a sigh of relief.

"Good," he said, trying to sound as if this was what he had expected. He took out some notepaper.

The guerrilla sitting next to the sheikh said something that the translator did not convey to Burke. He felt again the inadequacy of the journalistic parachute artist. In Russia, he had learned a lot from people who didn't know he spoke the language.

The sheikh spoke again. "I would like to present the commander of our military forces, Saad bin-Mansour bin-Turki bin-Abdul-Aziz."

Burke had a sense that the lineage was not being laid out for him casually.

"Bin-Abdul-Aziz?" Burke queried. "You're a member of the royal family?"

The guerrilla leader seemed to straighten up in his chair. He had a deep voice, verging on baritone, and the deep, lined tan of a man of the desert.

"I am a great-grandson of King Abdul-Aziz. My grandfather was his firstborn son, Turki. He died at the age of nineteen, and his son and his grandsons were shunted aside by Saud and his brothers. But our line lives."

"And what is your role in this"—Burke wondered whether to use the word, and decided he must—"revolution?"

Saad's lips curled slightly upward. "Be clear," he said. "There will be no more kings in Arabia. The Koran does not recognize kings. We will have an Islamic state, governed by the just, on the principle that all that the heavens and earth contain belong to God."

The sheikh broke in. "He is a colonel in the National Guard. He will continue to command our armed force."

Burke scribbled notes.

"I thought this already was an Islamic state," he said. He had said the same thing to Marwan Sarawi, but he needed an answer on the record from these men.

The sheikh scowled. "The al-Saud are not Muslims. They are drunkards. They are thieves. They mock Islam. They desecrate the holy places. They pray for the sake of ostentation. God has promised that such hypocrites shall be cast into the lowest depths of the fire, and there shall be none to help them."

"So I've heard," Burke said. He scribbled quickly, trying to get enough detail in his notes to be assured that his story would convey the sense of flat certitude with which al-Jubail pronounced his judgments.

"God commands believers to take neither Jews nor Christians for friends," the sheikh said. "But the al-Saud have invited them into our land. They deal secretly with Israel. Did you know that during the war, American Jewish women soldiers threw their used"—the translator hesitated, uncertain he had heard correctly, then went on—"their used menstrual rags at the Holy Ka'abah in Mecca?"

Burke wondered what a psychiatrist would make of the last sentence.

"No, I didn't know that," he replied. "Those army censors must have kept that story out of the newspapers."

The sheikh nodded. Burke saw Saad's eyes narrow, but the man said nothing.

The pairing of Saad and the sheikh fascinated him. Centuries ago, he knew, the Saud dynasty was founded in an alliance between a zealous, reforming Muslim cleric and the warrior chief of a desert village. Now the pattern was repeating itself, and he wanted to ask about it.

But the sheikh was only completing his peroration.

"An Islamic government cannot tolerate the presence of infidel soldiers and spies on Arabian soil," he said. "Our government will have correct relations with all countries. But there cannot be relations with countries that seek to keep soldiers on our land, that undermine us with spies."

"You make it sound like you've already created a government and are in control," Burke said.

"The king has fled," the sheikh replied. "The people give thanks to God."

"But are you in control?" Burke persisted.

"In most places," Saad answered. "Where we are not, we soon will be. The old regime has no support."

"You're an officer in the National Guard," Burke said, turning to Saad. "Men in National Guard uniforms fired at the crowd in front of the television station yesterday morning. They allowed themselves to be seen, to be filmed, they killed just enough people to inflame the situation, and then they left. Do you know who they were?"

Saad looked surprised as the interpretation unfolded, then glared at him.

"No, I do not know," he said. "And I would advise you to be careful not to speculate in your reporting."

He was lying. Burke knew it from his face. But he couldn't imagine a question that would get Saad to admit the truth. He could imagine a lot of questions that would get him in more trouble than he already had. So he pushed on. He would add the National Guard angle to the list of threads he would have to pursue later.

He turned to al-Jubail.

"You want all the U.S. troops removed?"

The sheikh nodded. "Within two weeks. And all the other infidels as well."

"And what exactly do you think the CIA is doing here that you want stopped?"

The sheikh's expression darkened.

"They are doing everything."

"Can you give me an example?"

"They murdered King Feisal because he tried to resist them."

Burke vaguely remembered Feisal's assassination, which occurred in 1975.

"I thought Feisal was murdered by a nephew."

The sheikh's face curled and he nearly spat in contempt.

"He studied in America. The CIA put him on drugs. He became their tool. Everyone knows this."

"Do you have any evidence?"

"Everyone knows!" The sheikh was getting agitated. "This is the nature of the CIA. Do you require proof that vultures eat carrion?"

Again, Burke thought, the risks of debating the man with follow-up questions could not be justified by the information he might gain. He would let readers judge the sheikh by his words.

"There will be no oil," the sheikh continued, "if the foreign presence is not removed in two weeks."

Burke wanted to make certain he had heard correctly.

"You will sell no oil? From eight million barrels a day down to zero?"

The sheikh nodded, evidently pleased by the way his threat had caught the Westerner's attention.

"But how will you replace the revenue?"

The sheikh shrugged. "For centuries God provided for our people without oil. We lived well. We can do so again."

"Aren't you worried about the Iraqis or the Iranians invading if you have no American troops?"

Saad leaped into the conversation. He pounded a fist on the table, and the tanned skin around his hatchet-shaped nose got mottled and white.

"This is a myth! They can threaten us only if the West supplies them with weapons. Now they have no weapons. The Americans are not needed. They are here only to protect the old regime. We drain our treasury to pay for them and buy your weapons."

Burke nodded, again seeing nothing to be gained by thrusting reality into the conversation.

He felt suddenly woozy, and he took time for a sip of coffee, savoring the smell of cardamom. Physically, he realized, he was running on fumes. As the coffee washed past the film on his teeth, he felt dirty and malodorous.

"And if the Americans do withdraw, what would your oil policy be?"

Saad answered the question.

"For years the old regime conspired with the West. They pumped too much oil. They broke OPEC. Prices were artificially low. In return, the West protected the regime. That deal is no more. We will pump less oil, and the price will be higher."

"How much less?"

"We will produce three, four million barrels a day."

"And what do you think the price will be?"

"We think fifty or sixty dollars a barrel would be a fair price."

There were arguments, he knew, that an economist would be able to make to Saad. Cutting Saudi production in half might well drive prices to fifty or sixty dollars. But oil at that level would cause ruinous inflation in the West and undermine the value of the dollars the Arabs received. It would cause a depression. It would make alternative fuels competitive. And all of those things would eventually reduce the demand for oil and undermine the Arabian economy. But he knew he had as much chance of explaining that to these men as he had of convincing them of Christ's divinity.

Before he could ask another question, the sheikh rose to his feet. "We have delivered our message," he said. "Now you will write our interview and send it to your newspaper."

"And then?"

Saad answered. "When it is published," he said, "you will be free to go."

His meal was rice, smelling strongly of cumin, a quartered raw onion, and a bony, blackened fish that looked as if it had been fried whole in crude oil. Had it not been a day since he had eaten, he could not have stomached it.

There were no utensils. He watched his guards, who had the same food. They squatted on the floor next to their plates, picking at the rice and fish with their right hands, scooping up morsels with pieces of onion.

He wished that they had left his translator with him. But the interpreter, whose name was Talal, had gone away once Burke had finished his article and transmitted it.

He was stuck, then, in the room on the first floor of the mosque he had passed through on his way to al-Jubail's headquarters. He could see nothing from the windows. They were covered with heavy curtains.

It had been difficult, typing with Talal peering unabashed over his shoulder, jotting an occasional note about what he was writing. He had played the story as straight as he could, leaving out his own opinions about al-Jubail and Saad, hoping that their words would portray them accurately enough.

It would have been an uncomfortable story to write without the observation and the fear. He had the feeling that language was only the first of the barriers that separated them. These men thought differently, perceived differently. An interview with them was like a conversation between the deaf and the blind.

But at least he could have asked Talal if there was anything else to eat or petitioned Talal for a chance to get outside and exercise. The men he was with had responded to his first questions with a grunt and a shaken head.

He was hungry, so he began breaking layers of the quartered onion and using them to scoop rice into his mouth. It tasted like leftover Tex-Mex takeout, aged overnight on the kitchen counter and consumed for breakfast the next morning.

"Might be a hell of a diet business here if you decide to stop selling oil," he said to the guard nearest him. "The Arabian weight-loss plan. Let us take you prisoner and we'll take off the weight."

The guard looked at Burke suspiciously but uncomprehendingly. His fingers drummed nervously on the stock of his rifle.

"I kind of wish you had worry beads instead of that gun," Burke said.

The man looked studiously at the wall to his right.

Burke opened the computer again and scanned the directories, hoping that some previous user from the *Tribune* staff had loaded some games. But there was nothing. He looked at his watch. He had about ten hours before the next edition hit the streets and whoever Saad and al-Jubail had working for them in Washington could relay word that the interview had been published.

The door at the other end of the room opened, and Talal stepped in, followed by three more men dressed in turbans and bandoliers.

Talal had a small, triumphant smile on his face.

"You are exposed, Mr. Burke," he said.

Burke looked at his zipper. It was closed. "What do you mean?"

Talal waved a piece of fax-machine paper at him.

"By this article in the *Beirut Star*. You are a CIA agent, Mr. Burke."

CHAPTER 15

A huge fly, glistening black and iridescent green, alighted on Burke's nose, twitched there for a few seconds, and prepared to feed. Slowly, Burke moved his hands up in front of his chest. When he was ready, he wrinkled his nose and shook his head. At the same time he clapped his hands, hard, six inches in front of his eyes.

He felt the stinging smack on his palms, saw the sweat fly off the back of his hands, and noted the squishy, liquid feel of the fly's carcass between them. He opened his palms and, with a flick of his wrist, tossed the insect's body into a nearby corner, where it joined a small pile of similar corpses.

"Ten," Burke murmured to himself. As if to mock him, two more flies, equally huge, landed on his arm. The air in his cell was thick with them.

A gust of hot air from the corridor outside carried the scent of feces more strongly to his nose, and he turned away from it, trying to control the urge to vomit.

His cell was a long, narrow concrete chamber, perhaps fifteen feet by forty feet. It held eight men. At one end, the opposite end, was a trench in the floor, supposedly connected to a sewage pipe under the prison. It was ringed with the droppings of men who had become sick from the prison food and failed to find the slit in time. The flies were particularly thick in that end.

The cell had no furniture. His fellow prisoners, for the most part, sat or squatted on grimy rugs. Burke had nothing, and he spent his time sitting on the floor, his back propped against the rough, concrete wall.

He heard a stick rattling the bars of the cells and a deep voice calling out something in Arabic. He looked at his watch. The sun must be setting. It was time again for prayer.

The *mutaween*, dressed in a rough brown cloak, passed by Burke's cell, banging the bars and repeating his rhythmic call. Burke watched as his fellow prisoners dutifully got off their rugs and down on their knees and prepared to pray.

He knew almost nothing about them. None of them had uttered a word in English. A few had stumps where their right hands had been, which suggested previous experience with the criminal justice system. But for the twenty-seven hours he had passed in this cell, they had left him alone.

The previous evening, when the *mutaween* had first come through at prayer time, he had considered joining the others. Maybe it would cause someone to take pity on him. But then he had remembered the sheikh's words about hypocrites, and thought better of it.

In a corner of his brain he was struggling to suppress panic. When they had first brought him to this cell, he had felt mostly contempt for his jailers and confidence that someone outside would somehow learn of his plight and set him free. The *Tribune* knew he was in Riyadh, and they would not want to piss off the *Tribune*. The United States government knew he was in Riyadh, and they would not want to piss off the U.S. government. Mentally, he began making notes for the vicious little story he would write about prison conditions.

But as the hours passed he began to dwell more and more on the thought that neither al-Jubail nor Saad nor their legions on the streets gave a damn about the *Tribune* or the U.S. government and would probably think it righteous to annoy them. And the little drop of fear welled to a trickle, and then a rivulet, and then threatened to wash over his mind and flood it with panic.

He sat and listened as the murmured prayers continued. He found the sound oddly soothing. If the previous evening was any gauge, the prayers would be followed by a meal of groats and slightly rotten vegetables, followed by another prayer session and then a night spent sweating on the hard floor, listening to the moans and whispers around him.

He resumed what he had been doing before the fly landed on his nose: compiling a mental list of all the vacations he had ever taken and attempting to rank them in order of pleasure. He had already been through women he had known and he suspected he would soon move on to movies or books.

He heard the sound of footsteps in the corridor outside and the babble of voices in Arabic, one of them deep, powerful, and louder than the rest.

The footsteps ended outside the cell door. Keys clinked together, the door opened, and a man stepped inside.

He was tall and well built, Burke could see, with close-cropped, thinning dark hair, a mustache, a goatee, and about two days' growth of dark beard on the rest of his face. He wore jeans, a plain white T-shirt, and some kind of hiking boots. He did not look like an Arab.

"Shukrun," the man said to the jailers as they closed the cell door again, and Burke could hear the irony in his voice.

The newcomer peered around the cell, saw Burke, and walked toward him. Burke got to his feet.

"You must be the other American spy," the man said, extending a hand. The forearm was sinewy and the grip strong. His accent suggested an origin somewhere in the Middle Atlantic states.

Burke felt foolishly glad to have company.

"So they tell me," he said. "Colin Burke."

"Strouder. Mac Strouder."

"What do you do when you're not being a Yankee spy?"

Strouder looked directly in Burke's eye. "I'm a consultant," he said.

"Well," Burke said, smiling faintly. "We have something in common."

He sat back down on the floor and Strouder sat beside him.

"You been interrogated yet?" Strouder asked.

"No," Burke said. "I've been looking forward to it."

"Well, the good news is that they don't ever cut someone's head off unless he confesses," Strouder said.

"What's the bad news?"

"The bad news is that they'll keep you here and torture you until you confess."

"Torture shouldn't be necessary," Burke said. "I figure I'll last maybe a week in this place. Then I'll tell 'em whatever they want. Without torture."

"Nah," Strouder said. "This place isn't so bad. I've seen worse. Jails where the rats'll climb up next to you at night, blow in your ear till your dick is hard, and then bite it off."

"That's a comforting thought," Burke said. He wondered what Strouder actually did. He spoke Arabic. He seemed to know something about the culture here.

Before he could ask, Strouder broke the silence.

"Do me a favor, will you? Go up to the cell door and start yelling that you're thirsty and need water."

"I don't think they speak English," Burke said.

"All the better. Do it," Strouder said.

"I was right in the middle of some urgent daydreaming, but I guess it can wait," Burke said.

He walked to the cell door, picking his way past the feet of the other prisoners.

"Guard!" he yelled. "Guard!"

He pounded with his open palm against the bars until it felt as if he had bruised something. In the corner of his eye, he could see that everyone in the cell was staring at him, except for Strouder. He appeared to be fidgeting with his belt buckle.

A guard appeared, carrying a thick wooden club. "I'm thirsty," Burke said. "Can you get me some water?"

With the club, the man gestured for Burke to back away. "Gotta have water," Burke said, remaining where he was.

The guard swung the club against the bars. Burke pulled his hand back an instant before the club struck, but it still caught him on the tip of his right index finger. The finger split open and gushed blood. Immediately, the guard pulled the club back and used it as a ram, jabbing it through the bars and into Burke's ribs. He doubled over in pain. He felt light-headed, and he sank to his knees.

Burke shook his head and looked up. The guard was still there, scowling. The men in the cell were watching quietly. And Strouder was grinning at his end of the cell.

Woozy, he got to his feet and staggered back to his place, where he sank down next to Strouder.

"Looks like you need to do some sit-ups," Strouder said. "Little soft down there in the abs."

"You're welcome," Burke said sourly.

He held his finger up to the fading light. The fingernail was getting black, and the tip throbbed. Gingerly, he pressed it against the palm of his left hand. He felt a lance of pain shoot up from his finger to his shoulder. Something bony inside moved. The finger was rapidly swelling.

"Nail'll fall off in a few days," Strouder said, leaning in for a closer look. "No big deal."

"It's a big deal to me," Burke replied. "This is one of my typing fingers."

"So you've got an excuse not to do your paperwork," Strouder said, expansively.

He could, Burke thought, easily develop an intense dislike for this man.

"What was the point?" Burke asked.

Strouder grinned. "Can't tell you," he said. "But don't worry. It'll be worth it."

He might, Burke thought, be one of the military consultants hired by the Saudis to train their troops. If he was, the performance of the troops did not speak highly of his abilities. But he had been out on the streets longer than Burke had been. He might know something useful.

"So what's been going on out there?" he asked.

"The fuckin' tangos are taking over," Strouder replied.

"Tangos?"

"Terrorists, man," Strouder responded disdainfully, as if Burke had revealed that he could not read. "As in, the guys who blew up the truck bomb at our air-force base in Dhahran. As in, the guys who set up the car bomb here in Riyadh outside Mitcorp's offices a few years ago. Terrorists. Latest rumor is they're declaring an Islamic government and moving the capital to Mecca."

"What happened to the army?"

"The army." Strouder spat. "The army here has never been worth a rat's ass. And besides, the dumb fucks didn't pay their salaries last month."

"Didn't pay the soldiers' salaries?"

"Nah. Temporary case of the shorts. You got four thousand princes in this country, man. By the time they all get through sucking at the public tit, it can get pretty wrung out."

"What about the National Guard? Did they get paid?"

"Oh, they always get paid. But they had a turncoat, from what I hear. He was in on this with the Ikhwan and took most of the troops with him."

"A traitor? Who was that?" Burke asked.

"Not sure."

Burke kept what he knew about Prince Saad to himself.

"So is anyone fighting for the Saudis?"

Strouder nodded, picking at his long, broad fingernails. "Yeah. Some troops. The ones with tribal affiliations to a particular branch of the family."

"And Khalil?"

Strouder snorted and smiled. His lips, Burke saw, were very thin.

"The fat man? Off on his boat in the Red Sea, playing Nintendo and porking twelve-year-olds. Probably trying to decide who to abdicate to."

"So what's going to happen?"

Strouder shrugged. "I know what could happen."

"What's that?"

"The right thousand men could come into this place right now, kick the shit out of the Ikhwan in about six hours, and find themselves sitting on ten trillion dollars' worth of oil, is what."

"A thousand men?"

Strouder nodded. "Fuckin'-a, man. Buy yourself some beer and ass with a piece of that now, couldn't you?"

"Fuckin'-a," Burke agreed. "Who're the right thousand men?"

Strouder looked suspiciously at him. "You ask a lot of questions."

"Passes the time," Burke said.

He did not think Strouder's suspicions were allayed.

Strouder got up. "Doesn't matter, anyway," he said. "The right thousand men never get the chance."

He clasped his hands together, raised them over his head, and stretched for ten seconds, loosening his broad shoulders. Then he dropped to the floor and started doing push-ups. Burke stopped counting after fifty. His finger throbbed and he vomited up what was left of his groats.

In his dream, he was with his wife, Barbara. It was about a year after Sam's birth, and they were hiking among the redwoods near Mt. Tamalpais. The boy was wriggling in a carrier on his back. Burke lost his balance somehow, and he had the sensation of falling backward for a long time, as if down a funnel, watching the sky and the redwood branches swirl above him. He landed on his back on a flat rock. Sam was beneath him. He was paralyzed. Barbara turned and started poking at him with the toe of her boot, trying to flip him over, but the cold, hard rock had somehow fastened itself to his back, and he was quite immovable.

He opened his eyes. Strouder was poking him in the shoulder. "Get up, man," he whispered in Burke's ear. "We gotta move."

Burke started completely awake. The cell was in darkness, and the inmates were dark figures stretched out on the floor. He looked at his watch and pressed the button that lit it up. He rediscovered that the tip of his index finger had been shattered. It was just after two in the morning.

"We gotta get over there," Strouder whispered, and Burke could hear an undercurrent of stress in his voice.

As quietly as he could, Burke got up and duck-waddled across the cell, following Strouder, to an empty spot against the wall.

"You don't want to be across from that door," Strouder whispered.

In the darkness, Burke heard faint sounds—a thud, some scraping of shoes on concrete. Then a short, sharp exhalation of breath from the corridor outside, as if someone had been punched. Then more faint scraping of shoes, this time directly outside the cell.

"They're being awfully damn noisy about it," Strouder whispered again. Now that his own eyes had adjusted somewhat to the darkness, Burke could see that Strouder's were glittering. A tooth glinted behind the thin lips.

Strouder half rose to a squat. "Get ready," he whispered to Burke.

There was a little more noise in the corridor now, and one of the prisoners stirred, groaned, and started to awaken. But Burke's curiosity about what was going on outside was restrained by Strouder's forearm, which effectively pinned him to the wall.

"Duck your head," Strouder said.

Burke did as he was told.

There were two popping sounds, like the bursting of paper bags filled with air. An acrid smell made Burke's eyes water briefly. Then he saw the cell door fall in. Before it hit the ground, two pairs of hands caught the bars and lowered them gently and quietly.

Now the rest of the prisoners were awake and getting up. Two men dressed entirely in black, their faces smeared with lampblack, burst into the room, brandished M-16s, and hissed a command in Arabic. One of the prisoners yelled. A quick jab with the stock of the rifle crumpled him back to the floor.

A third man in black entered, followed by a fourth. The fourth was holding a device slightly larger than a remote control. On its face, Burke could see a dial and a glowing orange arrow, big and bold, pointing directly at Strouder's belt buckle.

"Saved the family jewels, Colonel," the man said.

"About fuckin' time, Hound," Strouder whispered. The man he was talking to, Burke noticed, had big floppy ears and a goatee just like Strouder's.

He turned to Burke. "Now you see why getting popped on the finger was worth it. I needed a diversion so no one would see me turn this thing on."

"He with you?" the fourth man asked Strouder.

"Met him here. An American."

"Okay, let's move out."

The fourth man moved the barrel of the rifle in an arc that covered the entire cell. He said something terse in Arabic. All four of the soldiers who had sprung them, Burke noticed, had goatees.

In the hallway, the guard who had swung the club at Burke lay motionless, blood seeping from an arc that began at his left ear and extended under his jaw to the right ear. On his belt was a ring of keys.

Burke tapped Strouder on the shoulder. "How come they didn't just use the guy's keys?"

Strouder grinned. "More fun when you can blow something up," he said.

They stopped in the office at the entrance to the prison. Using a pistol with a silencer, Strouder shot open the closets and file cabinets and a closet until he came to the one holding prisoners' effects. He pulled out his own wallet. He pawed through the cabinet some more and pulled out a long, lethal-looking knife in a nylon scabbard.

"Sandvik 77," Strouder said to Burke, as if Burke would know brand names in commando knives. "Can't leave this baby."

"Oh, definitely," Burke said.

He looked in the open drawer, found his passport, and saw the aluminum case for the transmitter. He grabbed that, too.

On the street, two commercial vans with signs in Arabic and pictures of smiling maids dusting furniture were waiting with their engines running. Strouder and Burke got into the first of them.

They drove through the darkened streets of the city. It did not, Burke could see, look like there had been much more fighting in the two days he had been incarcerated. A few government office buildings had blackened windows. There were a few checkpoints, but the drivers of the vans seemed to know ways to skirt them, and they were never stopped. Riyadh did not look appreciably different from the city he had seen when he first arrived.

"Amazing how calm it is," he said to Strouder.

"Yeah, now that all the expats have been evacuated. The Saudis collapsed like a house of cards around here. The only fighting's out near the oil fields on the Gulf," Strouder said.

"All the foreigners evacuated?"

"Yeah. The tangos declared a twenty-four-hour humanitarian truce for non-Muslims to get out. Yesterday, the 747s were flying in and out of here like beetles on shit. Twenty-four thousand people left for Amman and Cairo."

The vans hit an expressway and soon left the city. Ten miles into the desert, they approached a big, walled enclosure. He could see barbed wire atop the walls and guard towers in the corners. Powerful lights inside cast a soft glow into the black sky. It might have been a factory complex. It might have been a prison. There were no signs to identify it.

After a few minutes of conversation between the first driver and a guard, the gates, which Burke could see were on heavy steel, swung open on a noiseless mechanism. Then he knew where he was.

It was an American military base. The trucks and Jeeps and armor were all painted in brown camouflage without insignia, but the cultural signs were all classic army, down to the neat rows of whitewashed stones that delineated "lawn" areas from pavement.

The van pulled up to a one-story building painted a dull beige and parked. Strouder escorted Burke into a conference room that contained a half-dozen maps, one of Riyadh, one of the entire Arabian peninsula, and others for cities he did not immediately recognize.

A clerk in brown fatigues with sergeant's stripes brought them coffee.

"Need some chow," Strouder said. He pulled out a yellow legal tablet and sat down across from Burke at the conference table.

"I figured," he went on, "that we ought to debrief you before we get you on your way."

"Well, I'm not sure I can tell you much," Burke said.

"Let's start with your name and coordinates."

Burke told him who he was and where he worked.

"You're a reporter?" Strouder demanded, consternation evident on his face. "You're not Christians in Action? You said you were a fuckin' consultant!"

Burke smiled thinly. "I said we had something in common. Which was that we were both telling people we were consultants."

Strouder was not amused.

"Shit," he said. "This is a secret installation. Do you know I could kill you where you sit if I thought it was necessary to safeguard the security of this base?"

"I'm not surprised," Burke said. "But come on. I'm sure a thousand Arabs give people directions to their farms out here by saying, 'Drive two miles past the secret American base and turn left.' "

"If there's one thing I dislike more than reporters," Strouder said, "it's wiseass reporters."

Burke decided not to tell the man what he thought of macho commandos.

Strouder looked around the room. "We gotta get you out of here," he said.

He called the sergeant who had brought the coffee. Together, they took Burke by the elbows and frog-walked him down a corridor to a small, windowless room that contained a desk and two chairs. It looked to Burke like an interrogation room.

But it didn't look too bad after the cell in the Saudi prison. He listened to the sound of the door locking from the outside. Exhausted, he stretched out on the desk, propped his feet on the back of the chair, and lay there, staring at the ceiling.

He did not know how much time had passed before he heard the sound of feet in the hallway again. The door opened and Desdemona McCoy walked in. She looked frazzled. She was wearing long slacks with a fading crease and a yellow blouse with long sleeves. Her hair had gone limp at the edges and her clothes were wrinkled in ways she normally would not allow.

He realized suddenly how attractive he must look: unshaven, bloody, reeking of his cell. He sat up, feet dangling over the desk.

She stepped into his arms as he got to his feet and squeezed him quickly, almost desperately. Then she kissed him. Just as he was starting to respond to the kiss, she broke away.

"Do you realize what a mess you've made?" she said.

Burke was hung up somewhere between wanting her and bristling at her. The smell of her and the taste of her still warmed him, but he would have liked a hint that she respected what he was doing, or at least acknowledged the craft that went into it. Her rejection seemed to encompass not just his work, but himself. He did not respond gracefully.

"Yeah, right," he snapped. "I write a piece in the *Tribune* and five million previously happy Arabs just up and decide to have a revolution. Get real, Des. This place was a sand castle."

"Me get real?" Her face was taut. "Do you ever think before you write something? About the real consequences?"

"Do you mean do I care if it helps your boss get reelected? No."

It was a cheap shot and an errant one. He knew she had no particular loyalty to Detwiler.

It inflamed Desdemona McCoy.

"You think that's what this is about?" The cords in her neck stood out in relief against her skin.

"Maybe not for you, but for Detwiler," he said, trying to placate her.

She was not placated.

"This is about people who are going to suffer," she said.

"Why? Because they'll have to take the bus to work instead of the car?"

"No. Because they'll lose their jobs. They won't have work to go to."

Maybe that was true, he thought. And it was certainly true that he hadn't thought about it before he published his stories. The truth, he guessed, was that he couldn't afford to think about all the consequences of what he wrote. If he did, nothing would ever get written. He could just make his way from one story to the next, like a hiker hacking away at the underbrush with a machete, too busy trying to find the path to wonder where it would eventually lead.

But that was not what he said to McCoy. He was too angry for that.

"Well, if the sensibilities of the Saudis are so important, maybe you should have thought about it before you started using the king's doctor as a source of information," he said.

If they had been conducting a high-school debate, he could see, she would have credited him with a point. But this was not a debate.

"Look," he said. "I don't want to argue with you about this. I don't want to argue with you about anything." He paused. "I like it much better when we're not arguing."

She sat ruefully on the edge of the desk, not close enough to touch him.

"Oh, Burke," she said. "What am I going to do about you?"

"You mean now or forever?"

She smiled. "Let's just try to get through now."

"For now you can help me get out of here."

She shook her head. "It's not that simple. I think the army is going to want you detained until this is over."

"You mean until the guys with the goatees have had a chance to kick some butt?"

Her eyes widened for just an instant, but it was long enough for him to realize that his question had been on target. He felt instantly ashamed that he had taken advantage of her that way.

"You seem to have a knack for making things harder, don't you?" she asked grimly.

"You inspire me," he said, and she flushed.

"Be serious."

"Okay."

"What you just said is very dangerous. If you give me or anyone else any reason to believe you'll write anything about what you've seen here, you make it very likely that you'll be detained here indefinitely," she said in clipped, formal tones.

"You don't have any charges," he replied. "If you made a mistake by bringing me here, the way to rectify it is to let me go."

It was an argument, he knew, that might work at the Supreme Court. This wasn't the Supreme Court.

"Wait," she said. "I'll see what I can do."

He watched her walk out the door. He felt as if he had awakened in a hospital somewhere, bandaged and immobile, unable to remember the accident or the chain of events that led up to it. He had never decided to do things to anger her. He had made decisions that he thought had no connection to her, that were connected only to his work. And yet there they were—they had gone from lovers to adversaries in a matter of days.

Worse, the farther apart they grew, the more he wanted her.

He paced the room, working the kinks out of his legs, wishing that someone had left something in it to distract him. He would have gladly leafed through the Riyadh telephone book. But the room was antiseptically clean and bare.

He tried the door. It was locked, and he banged on it. Almost instantly, a soldier in desert fatigues opened it. He had a black, oiled M-16 that he pointed at Burke.

"Gotta use the head," Burke said. "Gotta clean up."

Wordlessly, the soldier gestured across the hall, where there was a sign that said MEN.

Burke turned the water on until it ran hot, and looked in the mirror. The face that looked back was not attractive. He scrubbed as best he could until he had cleaned his hands and face, but he still had a splotchy, darkened complexion and a two-day stubble.

As he washed he thought about what McCoy had said. He wished he had a better response.

He had never been the type to sit around and ponder the role of the media. He had found that getting information and conveying it accurately were problems enough to worry about. He protected his sources if they asked for protection. He picked up his own checks. He left the pondering and pontificating to the professoriat and the pundits.

He knew, of course, that reporters did more than simply report what they saw. He had seen in Moscow how the old Soviet dissident class used the American press corps as both shield and megaphone in their effort to undermine the system. He had frequently been willing to be used.

The problem was that once journalists acknowledged that their choices of who and what to cover affected as well as reflected the outcome of events, they were knee-deep in a tar pit. What criteria should they use to choose? And since their choices affected society, shouldn't society, in the form of the government, be allowed to influence the choices? It was easier to maintain the fiction that journalists merely observed.

So Burke, like a lot of reporters, took refuge in a vague adherence to the principles of Jefferson and Wilson. He believed in the free market of ideas and in a foreign policy of open covenants openly arrived at. Except that he sometimes felt privately that for the American media of the 1990s to argue for the free market in ideas was a little like John D. Rockefeller arguing for the free market in oil in 1910. And he suspected that if Wilson and Jefferson had been in the room with him and McCoy, they would have taken her side.

He dried his face and wondered if he could talk someone into allowing him access to a shower and a razor. He glanced at the sentry in the hall, who had ostentatiously opened the door to keep an eye on Burke, as if he might otherwise dive into the sink and escape through the drain. It didn't seem likely.

"Done?" the guard asked curtly.

Burke nodded. The gun barrel pointed the way back to his interrogation room. As he walked across the hall he heard voices raised in an argument. One was McCoy's. He couldn't be sure, but he thought the other was Strouder's. The door shut behind him before he could make out any words.

McCoy came in two minutes later. She was starting to look haggard, and he imagined that it had been a long time since she'd slept. He wanted to hold her, to take her in his arms and rock her. But he didn't.

"You have two choices," she said abruptly. "And you're lucky to have them."

"Thanks," he said. "I've always been pro-choice."

She looked at him and he thought he saw that she was fighting not to smile.

"Burke, you're charming, but that's not going to help you out of here."

"Okay. What will?"

"There is a caravan of sorts leaving Riyadh that will pass about ten miles from here within the hour. It's headed for Jedda. From Jedda, the people in the caravan will be taking a *dhow* up the Red Sea to Aqaba, in Jordan. It should take about four days."

"Who are these people?"

McCoy paused. "Friends of ours. People who couldn't get out because they have Saudi passports."

"And who's running it?"

"A man named Jawar. He's half-Saudi, half-Lebanese. He's got a lot of experience."

"And you're certain they'll be able to get out?"

She shrugged. "Nothing's certain. But Jawar knows how to do it. I'd say the odds are very good."

"How'd he get this experience?"

"I can't tell you that."

Burke looked carefully at her. She seemed sincere.

"What's the other option?"

She cocked her head slightly.

"You could stay here incommunicado until Strouder decides to let you out."

"When would that be?"

She sighed. "I don't know."

"A few days? A week?"

"I can't speculate."

Oh, Jesus, Des, he thought, don't act like a press secretary. But then he realized she had to be careful what she said to him. She probably didn't know when Strouder would let him out because she didn't know if and when Strouder and his commandos would be going into action.

"Staying here sounds a bit safer," he said.

She shook her head. "Don't bet on it. Strouder is furious. He says you tricked him."

"I didn't."

"But you misled him. You got him to make a mistake."

"So?"

"These people are trained to erase their mistakes."

"Oh, come on. They wouldn't."

Her eyebrows arched suggestively.

"They wouldn't have to. They could just leave you someplace in harm's way and let the Ikhwan take care of you."

"You think so?"

"Don't test them. I'm going to be gone in half an hour. If you're not gone with me, you're in their hands."

"So I'm safer in the desert with some camel jockey named Jawar than I would be with the U.S. Army?"

She nodded. She put a hand on his forearm. "I think so."

He had always distrusted women who put their hands on his forearms. It was a gesture of false intimacy.

But he couldn't believe that McCoy would set him up.

"Damn," he said. "And here I'm a guy who's always rooted for Army in the Army–Navy game."

"There's just no loyalty anymore," she said.

Colonel Strouder did not see them out. A guard with a grim, taut face escorted them to the parking area in front of the administration building, where a blue Ford Explorer with Saudi license plates was waiting, lights on and motor running.

"I don't guess it would do much good to ask for my computer and transmitter back," Burke said.

"You'd be pressing your luck," she said.

They got into the backseat of the car, which was driven by a young man in a khaki suit, his tie neatly knotted. McCoy did not bother to introduce him.

"Let's get to the rendezvous point," McCoy said to him.

The man picked up what appeared to be a CB radio mike. "Gamecock, this is Cloverleaf. We're on our way," he said.

There was a burst of static. Burke thought he heard the word *affirmative*.

Then they were off. The Explorer jounced across a rutted track in the sand. Burke could see no lights ahead of them—nothing except the barren, rocky desert and some tire marks.

" 'Cloverleaf,' " he said. "Couldn't you have gotten a better secret code name than that, Ms. McCoy? It sounds like that interchange by the Pentagon where I always get lost when I go out to Virginia."

"Well, I asked for 007, but it was already taken," McCoy replied.

Ahead of them, he saw the lights of another car atop a low ridge. The lights canted downward, and he could tell that the other car was approaching. McCoy's driver stopped and flipped his beams to low, then back to high, then off. The approaching car drew up and went through the same procedure with its lights.

"It's your ride," McCoy said. They got out.

The air was bracingly cool at this time of night, perhaps an hour before dawn. The sky seemed black and infinitely deep, with stars layered thickly, galaxy after galaxy. A faint breeze blew from the west, kicking up small clouds of sand around their feet.

The car opposite them was a Land Rover, painted deep green. A lone man got out of it. He had to step down carefully, sliding his butt off the seat until his feet were down, because his legs were dwarfish.

When he stood up, Burke estimated that he was five feet tall. He wore a white *thobe* and a Stetson that hung low over his ears.

He stepped forward, hand outstretched.

"Hi," he greeted them cheerfully. "How y'all doing?"

He had the words down, but not the vowel sounds. His accent went with what he was saying as well as his hat matched the rest of his clothes.

The driver of their Ford made the introductions. "Jawar," he said. "This is Ms. McCoy. Mr. Burke."

Jawar shook hands. "You the passenger?" he said to Burke.

"I guess so," Burke said.

Jawar looked at McCoy with an undisguised leer. "Just my luck," he said. "I never get to take any pretty ones."

"It is too bad," McCoy said. "I've been looking all my life for a really short man in a big cowboy hat."

Jawar, for an instant, looked simultaneously lecherous and surprised. Then he realized she was needling him. He laughed.

"I'll give you a rain pass," he said.

"You mean a rain check," McCoy corrected him.

Jawar grinned. He turned to Burke. "American women." He shook his head. "Toughest in the world."

"You don't know the half of it," Burke replied.

The man in the suit looked at his watch. "Ms. McCoy," he said. "We're running late."

McCoy nodded. She turned to Burke. Her face looked soft and shadowed in the starlight.

She stuck out her hand.

He took it. It felt warm and strong.

"Good-bye, Mr. Burke. Good luck."

He tried to read her eyes, but in the dim light he couldn't see them. He clung to the hand as long as he could.

"Thanks for your help," he said. He let the hand go.

"Stay well," she said softly, then turned and got back into the car.

His arms and body felt empty and deprived as he watched the car turn ponderously around and head back toward the base.

He could not decide precisely what made her so attractive to him. Maybe it was complementarity. She was crisp and neat; he was rumpled. She was dark; he was pale. She kept secrets; he exposed them. He only knew that the farther she got from him, the more he wanted to be close to her. He inhaled, and thought he could still smell a faint trace of her in the air.

Then the taillights of the Explorer disappeared behind a brown, furrowed dune. He turned and realized that Jawar was watching him watch her disappear.

"American women," Jawar said, shaking his head.

"Toughest in the world," Burke murmured.

Chapter 16

The sun, a swollen orange orb, had dropped well below the top edge of the windscreen of Jawar's Land Rover when he pulled off the dirt track they had been following and announced that they were going to camp for the night.

Burke gratefully nodded. The preceding ten hours had overheated his body and shaken the pieces together until he felt as if his left hip was jammed up where his liver should have been and his head pulsed with a dull, throbbing ache. His tongue felt like a cinder block.

"I've got to call and order some gas," Jawar said.

He reached past Burke's knees and flipped open the glove box. He pulled out a small cellular phone, punched a number in, and waited about ten seconds. Then he spoke, tersely, in Arabic. The call lasted perhaps ten seconds. He flipped the phone off and stashed it in a slot in the console between their seats.

"Where are we?" Burke asked.

"About thirty-five miles east of Jedda, maybe fifteen miles north of Mecca," Jawar said.

"Mecca?"

"I'm using the infidel pronunciation for your benefit," Jawar said, grinning. "It's Makkah."

"We going through it?"

Jawar snorted. "That would be looking for trouble. Infidels aren't allowed in Mecca. It's *harram*. They've even got a special bypass road they have to take if they're going from Jedda to Taif."

Jawar opened the door and stepped out. Burke looked longingly at the open space and the opportunity to stretch his legs. But he hesitated.

"You can get out," Jawar said. "No one's going to notice you. I told you, you look just like a Pakistani laborer."

Burke looked dubiously at the clothes Jawar had ordered him to change into before the sun rose. He was wearing a shapeless brown tunic over a pair of tight polyester pants and black sandals. The tunic fell to his knees. On his head was a tight little knit pillbox cap, peakless, that came down over his forehead halfway to his eyebrows.

He craned his neck and looked in the rearview mirror. His face had become darker as his skin tanned. The dirt helped. His beard was almost grown in now. Maybe from a distance someone might mistake him for one of the millions of foreigners doing scut work in Saudi Arabia. But not from up close.

"I haven't worn so many costumes since I stopped dressing up for Halloween," he said.

"Relax," Jawar said. "The people here are like rich people anywhere. They don't really look at the people who scrub their floors and take out their garbage. Put a set of orange coveralls on you and they'd expect you to be sweeping streets."

Gratefully, Burke stepped out of the Land Rover. There was no breeze, and the air was still and hot—he guessed 105 degrees. He wondered why the Arabs couldn't have had their revolution in December.

Behind him, the other elements of the caravan were parking, forming a loose circle in the desert. Somewhat to Burke's disappointment, there were no camels. It was strictly an internal-combustion caravan, headed by Jawar's Land Rover and half a dozen Toyota pickups. There were two eighteen-wheelers, a Mercedes, and a Volvo, each garishly decorated. One was strung with extra running lights like a Christmas tree—red, green, and blue. The other had an enormous, crude painting of a tropical island, complete with palm trees, a lagoon, and a woman in a red sarong, running across the length of the van. A couple of jitneylike Chevy Suburbans completed the collection.

Like Jawar, the truckers left their engines running after they parked to give them a chance to cool slightly before shutting them off.

Jawar reached into the back of the Land Rover and pulled out a blue nylon duffel bag.

"Know how to set up a tent?" he asked Burke.

Burke stared at the bag, baffled.

"What were you expecting, poles and carpets? It's Swedish, man," Jawar said. "This ain't *Lawrence of Arabia*."

Burke accepted the bag, opened it up, and shook out the contents. He saw a vaguely familiar package of dull beige tent fabric and fiberglass poles.

His mind clicked back to a summer years ago, just before he and his ex-wife had split up. He'd bought a tent with similar components and suggested that they go hiking near Lake Tahoe. He remembered sweating and cursing, convinced that some key parts were missing, before finally getting the tent up. And then neither Barbara nor their son had been able to sleep, it had started to rain, and they had wound up in a cheap motel, wet and unhappy. That had been the last effort he had made at family camping. He'd successfully repressed the memory of the tent for all the years since.

He wondered what Barbara would say if she could see him now. And what she would think if she knew that he had finally gotten interested in trying marriage again.

She would probably tell him, he thought, that he wasn't really interested, and that was why he had picked an impossible woman to fall in love with.

Or maybe that was what he was telling himself.

He looked around. Women in black *abayas* had emerged from the jitneys and were busy getting the camp ready while the men, who had driven the cars, had begun to cluster in small groups, squatting in the shade of the trucks, talking softly.

He had been relegated, he realized, to women's work.

He watched some women at the other side of the caravan circle working on a similar tent, and the knowledge came back to him. Within five minutes he had it up. It was dome-shaped, with an entry and window of fine black mesh. It had a nylon partition running down the middle, making two elemental rooms.

As he staked it a figure in an *abaya* appeared with a heavy trunk on her back. Saying nothing to Burke, she laid it in the sand, opened it, and began to set up a kitchen. She had a Coleman stove with two burners and a plastic cooler full of water and food.

Just like Yellowstone Park, Burke thought.

Jawar approached him with two tall glass tumblers in his hands. He offered one to Burke and Burke took it. A couple of cubes of ice floated on the top of a brownish liquid, and he thought for a second he was being offered iced tea. Then he smelled it.

He looked upward at Jawar, unable to conceal his surprise.

"My stock-in-trade," Jawar said. "Jack Daniel's."

Burke gazed longingly at the glass for a few seconds, letting the sweet fumes drift upward. His mouth felt parched and raspy when he swallowed.

"Sorry," he said. "Can't. Quit."

Jawar shrugged amiably and took the tumbler back. He took a long swallow of his own and poured Burke's into the sand, which sucked it down instantly.

"I'll have Farida make you some coffee," he said. Then he turned to the woman who was working with the stove and said something to her in Arabic.

Jawar sipped again and smiled at Burke.

"Too bad you quit," he said. "This stuff really cuts the dust." He spat. "One of the things I learned in Texas."

Jawar had been reticent about himself during the day, either preferring to concentrate on his driving or simply unwilling to talk about himself. Now Burke exercised his curiosity.

"You went to college there?"

"Hook 'em Horns," Jawar replied.

"And, uh, how'd you get into the Jack Daniel's business?"

"My father set me up."

"Your father?"

Jawar squatted down in the shade next to the Land Rover and pulled from a pocket a bag of pistachio nuts. He offered them to Burke. They tasted salty and his thirst grew.

"My father," Jawar said, "is kind of a collateral member of the royal family. His cousin was married to one of Abdul-Aziz's grandsons."

He took another long pull on the product.

"Anyway, he was a student at AUB—the American University in Beirut—when he met my mother. They fell in love, but his family wouldn't let him marry her, because she's a Maronite. She wouldn't convert."

Jawar's voice seemed distant as he recounted this bit of family history, as if he were distancing himself from the unpleasant circumstances of his own birth.

"Anyway, my father has always looked out for me. He sent me to school, to UT. And then he got me the Jack Daniel's franchise and helped me get started."

"Franchise?"

"Someone's gotta run the stuff in here. Other guys have Tanqueray and Glenfiddich and Absolut. He used his connections to make sure I'd get Jack Daniel's. Every couple of months I load up those trucks with the stuff and bring it in over the desert from Jordan. I maintain the distribution network. Some of the people who work for me are the folks traveling with us."

Burke wondered what Jawar did for the CIA on the side. At the moment it didn't seem politic to ask.

The woman in the *abaya* came up with a tray containing a coffeepot and a cup. She poured for Burke. The coffee was freighted with cardamom and sugar. After a day in which the only thing to drink had been warm water in plastic bottles, it tasted good.

"So what's going to happen to the business now?"

"What do you mean?"

"Well, uh, aren't you afraid that if the Ikhwan takes over, they're not going to tolerate alcohol?"

Jawar snorted. "Neither do the Saudis. But people will still drink it. It'll just cost more. And besides, the Ikhwan aren't going to take over. We just need to lay under for a little while."

"You mean lay low."

"Yeah."

"Why do you think the Ikhwan won't take over? They're doing pretty well up to now."

"They're idiots," Jawar said. "They've set up their supposed capitol at the Grand Mosque in Mecca. That phony holy man Jubail is making speeches all day. How're they going to run a country like that? He's liable to make Khomeini look like Abraham Lincoln."

Burke took another sip of the coffee, drained the cup, and poured another for himself. Even though he had consumed a fair amount of water that day, his body craved fluids. He suspected it was an unconscious reaction to the environment.

"I suspect you may look at the situation a little more pragmatically than the Ikhwan does at the moment," he said.

"You got that straight," Jawar said.

"But why don't you think they can take over? They're no more fanatical than Abdul-Aziz was ninety years ago."

Jawar looked at him skeptically from under the brim of the cowboy hat.

"You're supposed to be a reporter? From Washington? And you can't figure it out?"

"You mean the U.S. is going to come in and remove them?"

Jawar shrugged. "Everybody knows they will. They wouldn't let Saddam have the oil in this place. Why should they let some wall-eyed crackpot like Jubail?"

Burke sighed. He had not admitted to himself how much he had been looking forward to being pushed out of Arabia. Now he had all the more reason to try to stay—the possibility of an American effort to oust the Ikhwan and restore the House of Saud.

"Well"—he nodded—"the soldiers on that base you picked me up near did seem to have strange shaving habits. Why?"

Jawar snorted. "Put 'em in National Guard uniforms, now, and who could tell where they come from?"

Burke understood. "So it wouldn't look like they'd been restored to power by the Americans?"

Jawar nodded. "As one of my UT professors used to say, you can get a C-plus just by restating the obvious."

A diesel horn blew in the near distance and Burke looked up. A gasoline truck was lumbering toward their campsite, trailing a cloud of dust. Burke watched it come.

Jawar stood up. "Got to do a little business, get some gas," he said. He walked away toward the truck; all of the men in the camp followed him.

Burke's eyes moved, almost involuntarily, to the door of Jawar's Land Rover—and his thoughts to the cell phone inside. He did not, at this point, have enough evidence to write that the United States was planning a military move against Jubail and the Ikhwan. But he certainly had heard and seen enough to alert the *Tribune* to start asking questions.

But it was more than that, he realized. He wanted desperately to hear a friendly, supportive voice. He wanted to tell someone where he was, to know that someone might start looking for him.

If he could grab Jawar's phone, he might be able to call the *Tribune*. It was possible the Ikhwan had cut the international phone connections, but he doubted it. Revolutions tended to be messy about such things. He remembered that the coup plotters in Moscow in 1991 had inexplicably left international lines open to the Russian White House, which Yeltsin's people had used to keep the world apprised of what they were doing.

He looked around. The men of the caravan were watching Jawar's negotiation with the driver of the gasoline truck. The women were intent on preparing food and shelter.

He began sidling toward the Land Rover, then reminded himself to look like he ought to be doing what he was about to do. He had left a few things in the Land Rover. He would look like he was merely retrieving one of them. He straightened up and walked briskly to the car. The light sweat on his forehead started to drip.

The phone was stashed in the console, as he remembered it. He grabbed it and slipped it into the pocket of his trousers. Then he reached into the backseat and found the polo shirt he'd taken off that morning. It was, he thought, dirty enough to look like it could be the property of a Pakistani laborer.

He left the car, the shirt displayed prominently over his left arm. Trying to be casual, he looked toward the gasoline truck. No one was watching. He looked toward the center of camp, where the women were working. They were intent on their cooking stoves.

The sun was descending rapidly toward the horizon, coloring the sky a pale mauve as it fell. Burke barely noticed it. He was trying to decide when and where it would be safe to try to call in.

Not now. Not here. The group at the gas truck was breaking up. Jawar gave orders to some of them to supervise the filling of the gas tanks. He ambled back toward Burke.

Burke looked at his watch. It would have to be later. For one thing, the time difference meant that the *Tribune*'s editors wouldn't be at their desks yet. For another, he would need a modicum of privacy. The time would be after dark, after dinner. The place would be as far away from the camp as he could sneak.

As he approached, Jawar leaned down over a scrubby green bush that was clinging stubbornly to the sand. He pulled a knife from his pocket and cut a couple of twigs. He whittled at them as he walked.

When he reached Burke, he handed him a twig that had been cut to the size of a large toothpick. He popped the other one in his mouth and started chewing on it.

"*Miswak,* it's called," he said. "Good to chew in the desert."

Dubiously, Burke put it in his mouth and chewed. It tasted bitter.

But he noticed that chewing it seemed to take the cotton from his mouth.

Jawar rummaged in the bottom of the woman's trunk as she continued to prepare the dinner. He could see rice and tomatoes and a smoked fish. He realized he was ravenous.

Jawar drew a few small dusty rugs from the trunk and handed one to Burke. "Time for prayer," he said.

Burke blinked. It seemed incongruous that the man who held the Jack Daniel's franchise for Saudi Arabia would be praying. But all around, he noticed, people were setting similar rugs in the sand and casting an eye toward the setting sun.

As the bottom of the orange disk sank into the earth, Jawar knelt down and prostrated himself toward it. It was a second before Burke realized that the sun was falling over Mecca, just over the horizon.

He threw his own rug on the ground and did his best to imitate Jawar's posture. Around him, he could hear the murmur of the prayers.

He wondered, for a second, whether he should say one for himself. He decided against it. A just God would no doubt deem a prayer from Colin Burke at this time as exceedingly hypocritical.

In a minute the prayer was over. Jawar took the rug and packed it away. The woman in the *abaya* took two plates and heaped nearly all the food on them. She handed them to Burke and Jawar.

He thought he saw a bit of her eyes behind the veil that covered her face, and he wondered about her. Was she Jawar's wife? His only wife? What did she look like? And what did she think of him?

There was no way to tell, no way to ask.

"Shukrun," he murmured, and she said something to him in Arabic that was punctuated by a brief but unmistakable giggle. Then she turned and disappeared into the tent. Apparently, she would not be dining with them.

He looked around for a fork or a spoon, then noticed that Jawar, squatting in the sand, was simply shoveling the food into his mouth with the fingers of his right hand.

The fish and rice were spiced with something hot that he could not identify. He only knew that in another place, at another time, he would have washed it down with beer.

In a moment the food was gone. He was thirsty, but his right hand was greasy, so he took the coffeepot in his left hand and offered it first to Jawar.

Jawar recoiled. "Not with that hand," he said. "Haven't you learned that?"

"No," Burke said. "Why not with the left hand?"

"Unclean," Jawar grimaced.

"Why?"

Jawar only smirked. "You'll find out," he said. "There's no toilet paper in this country."

Jawar stood up and walked over to the Land Rover. Burke watched him carefully, trying to decide what he would do if Jawar found that the phone was missing. Probably, he thought, tell the truth. He doubted that Jawar would be surprised. The phone suddenly felt big and bulky in his pocket and he cast his eyes involuntarily downward, reassuring himself that it did not bulge against the outline of his dirty tunic.

But instead of heading toward the passenger compartment, Jawar went to the back of the Land Rover and opened the hatch. He pulled out a small black box and carried it back toward Burke.

He set it on the ground and pulled an antenna up. It appeared to be a small, compact radio, but one with a microphone attached for transmitting as well as receiving.

"Your tax dollars at work." Jawar grinned at him. "Best desert radio in the world. Sends, receives, fixes your position by satellite."

He flipped on the power switch and Burke heard a whining sound, then bursts of static, then a voice.

"BBC Arabic service," Jawar murmured.

He listened for a moment, then let out a breath slowly. He pushed the cowboy hat back on his brow.

"The king has abdicated. To Prince Ahmed," he translated for Burke.

Burke could imagine, for a moment, the consternation in Washington.

"Where is Ahmed?" he asked Jawar.

"They don't say," Jawar muttered.

He listened further. "Sheikh Jubail is calling for a boycott of America by all Muslim countries until it withdraws all military personnel from Arabia and recognizes the Islamic government," he translated.

Not consternation in Washington, he thought. Panic.

"Any idea of how much of the country he controls?"

"Doesn't say," Jawar said, shaking his head. "But he's still in Mecca at the Grand Mosque. The king's off on his yacht, heading for Marbella. And Ahmed is nowhere in sight. What does that tell you?"

"Not all that much."

Jawar shrugged. "Radio says it's unclear who controls what except that the Ikhwan seems to have Riyadh and Mecca. And private planes are landing all over Europe, full of rich Saudis."

"How does this affect us?"

Jawar looked surprised.

"Why should it affect us?"

Burke had the feeling that he was constantly saying things that anyone with common sense about this country would never say, that he was the one uninformed character in a play where everyone else knew a secret.

"Oh, I don't know. It just seemed like the abdication of the king might be a major political event," he said.

"The border patrols and the coast guard aren't going to change," Jawar said, oblivious to Burke's sarcasm. "The price may go up for a while, but that's all."

"You could've been a reporter, Jawar," Burke said. "Your cynicism rivals my own."

Jawar spat. He pulled another *miswak* twig from a pocket and began picking his teeth.

Burke looked up at the sky. Night had fallen quickly. There was a low moon, a new, thin crescent, hanging in the sky.

"There's a sleeping bag in the back of the Land Rover," Jawar said. "Sorry I can't offer you tent space."

"I didn't expect it," Burke said.

"Better get to sleep soon," Jawar said. "We pull out at three A.M. Gotta get clear of Jedda before dawn."

Burke looked at his watch. He would get up early. Half-past one in the morning here would coincide with the hour when all his editors would be in place in Washington. He would call then.

He carried the sleeping bag about fifty feet out into the desert, until he was beyond the ring of pale light cast by the stoves and lanterns of the caravan. With his foot, he scuffled in the sand until he had cleared a spot relatively free of stones. He laid out the bag and slipped into it.

He set the alarm on his watch. He bunched the dirty polo shirt into a ball and laid his head down.

The stars were blazing now, and he marveled again at the purity of the night sky.

He thought for a while about the information he would be calling in to the *Tribune*, the various angles, the qualifiers he would have to use to make certain it was clear that he was reporting only what people said, not what he himself knew.

Then he thought about McCoy, and he could almost hear her asking him whether he ever thought before he published something.

Well, in this case he would. It was not as if the scant information he had—the presence of American commandos with beards, the opinion of Jawar—was conclusive. It would be up to the paper to get sources in Washington to confirm it if an attack was imminent.

But in her eyes, he thought, that would not relieve him of responsibility. She would see the operation as a matter of highest secrecy.

That was crap, he thought. If Jawar thought it was coming, the Ikhwan surely must. But it wasn't only the attack itself that was a secret. It was the identity of the attackers.

He rolled in his sleeping bag until his cheek hit the sand.

McCoy would say that just by phoning in, he would not only be jeopardizing the lives of the commandos. He would be helping to blow the propaganda cover for their mission. Even if they then succeeded, they would fail, because Prince Ahmed would have no legitimacy. No Arab set on his throne by the United States could have legitimacy.

Yes, he thought. But what about the Bay of Pigs? What about the Iranian hostage rescue mission? Those were both secrets that should have been blown. *The New York Times* had even known about the Bay of Pigs and had a story ready to go when Kennedy phoned the publisher and persuaded him not to run it. It was the biggest mistake Kennedy ever made.

The lights of the caravan flickered out one by one and the darkness enveloped him. The trucks and tents were vague black shadows in the starlight. He was almost asleep when he heard the sound of movement and the soft splashing of water to his right.

He looked, and perhaps twenty-five yards away he saw the outlines of two women, still wearing their *abayas*. As he watched, one of them shed her *abaya*. When she turned and raised her arms over her head, he could see that she was naked. Her breasts carved a ripe, silver-tinged shadow. The other woman, still veiled, slowly began to bathe her, using an old cloth. She rubbed slowly over the woman's neck, back, and hips, sloshing the soapy water, then forward over her breasts and belly. She was murmuring something as she worked, and her words carried over to Burke like rustling sands.

He heard a noise behind him, and as quietly as he could, he turned. He saw the shadow of a man in the dim light reflected off of one of the trucks.

He wondered at the social engineering of this situation. Was this man a prospective husband to the woman being bathed? Was this an arranged opportunity for him to inspect before buying? Or was he just a truck driver who had gotten lucky?

Or was this show for him?

Burke turned his eyes back toward the two women. The bather was being toweled off. She turned and arched her body to allow the woman serving her access to her back and what seemed to be a plump, firm rump.

Burke squinted, and he thought for a second that he could see the woman's eyes and a bit of starlight glinting off her teeth. Was she looking at him? Was she smiling at him?

He turned his head away, bemused by the eroticism of the event. When he looked back, the woman was dressed, the water had been tossed back into the sands, and the bather and her servant were again black lumps, scuttling across the desert toward their tent.

Burke rolled halfway over and felt the phone in his hip pocket. He took it out and placed it in the bag next to his shoulder.

With the memory of the bathing beauty flitting across his brain, he fell asleep.

The sound of an engine awoke him. It was the trucks, throaty and powerful, coughing to life. Startled, Burke opened his eyes. The night sky looked just as it had when he fell asleep. He looked at his watch. It was ten after one.

He jerked fully awake and twisted around. All the tents had been struck. Every vehicle in the caravan had its engines running. The Chevy Suburbans were a hundred yards down the dirt track toward Jedda.

Burke clawed at the sleeping bag's zipper. It jammed in the thin nylon fabric. Angrily, he reached down with both hands and tried to tear the sleeping bag open. The jammed zipper held fast.

As he worked at it the Toyota pickup trucks fell in behind the Suburbans, and the lead truck, its gaudy lights off, started to roll.

Burke skinned the sleeping bag down to his waist and squirmed out, filling the back of his tunic with sand in the process.

He didn't care. He sprinted across the sand to the Land Rover, which was falling in at the rear of the procession and picking up speed. He could see Jawar's profile inside it, his hat pulled low over his head, face lit by the pale dashboard controls.

The Land Rover was going as fast as he was by the time Burke reached it. Trying to lengthen his stride, he lost a sandal. He managed to reach out and pound with his right hand against the left rear fender of the car. Jawar accelerated, pulling ten, fifty, then a hundred yards ahead.

Burke ran on for a few seconds, then stopped, realizing the futility of it. Panting, he stood in the tracks of the caravan, coughing as its dust entered his lungs.

Then the Land Rover's brake lights came on, and he thought for a second that Jawar was going to put the car in reverse and come back, laughing about the joke they'd all played on the infidel.

He did not. But the window of the car came down and the cowboy hat emerged.

"Wait!" Burke yelled. He started to run again.

"Sorry, pardner," Jawar yelled back. "But the orders changed."

With that, he drew his head in and punched down on the accelerator, spewing sand to the rear as he caught up with his caravan. Burke stopped running before hitting the Land Rover's dust.

He flipped his middle finger toward the departing cars and then turned forlornly back toward the campsite and his sleeping bag.

He looked around. The site appeared to have been picked clean. There was nothing left—not a drop of water.

Orders changed. What did that mean?

Jawar could be lying. He could simply have decided that it was too risky to take Burke out through Jedda.

But someone could have told Jawar to dump him. He thought about McCoy. Then he put the thought out of his mind.

He considered his options. He had the phone—he doubted Jawar would come back for it once he discovered it was missing. But who could he call for help? Maybe the *Tribune* could find a foreign consulate in Jedda that would help him. It didn't seem likely.

But his first problem was going to be finding water. He was already thirsty. He did not think he could make it thirty-five miles to Jedda without something to drink. It would be tough enough doing fifteen miles to Mecca—and then he would face the possibility of getting into deeper trouble for being inside a city closed to nonbelievers.

He would have to worry about that later.

He pulled the sandal that he had dropped back onto his foot and tightened it. Then he looked at the sky, found the Big Dipper, and used it to locate Polaris. He turned his back to it and started walking.

He wondered what the temperature would be after the sun rose.

Chapter 17

"One hundred and two," Delores Hoffman said. She was holding a strip of heat-sensitive plastic to the light coming from his bedroom reading lamp, assessing it professionally, like the nurse she had once been.

"That's not so bad," her husband replied.

His voice sounded like gravel scraping against sandpaper. He coughed to clear his throat. Then he swept the sheets off the bed and stood. He felt dizzy, but he spread his legs like a sailor keeping his balance on the pitching deck of a ship. The dizziness passed.

This feat did not impress Delores Hoffman.

"Henry, please," she said. "You have the flu. You need to stay in bed."

He put a hand on her shoulder, partly to steady himself and partly to nudge her out of the way.

"Thanks, but I can't today. This Saudi thing. I'll take a shower and I'll feel better."

She would not, he thought, argue with him.

"Henry," she said, proving him wrong, "you're going to ruin your health doing this job and then what'll I be left with?"

He hated it when she started to whine. And the intimation of mortality, the suggestion that he might burn himself out and die, perturbed him. He was only forty-six. He thought of himself as being in the prime of his life.

"Sorry," he said, "but this is when I earn that salary that supports us."

He lowered his head and shuffled past her, signaling that the discussion was over.

Under the shower, he let the hot water run over his back until it seemed that his joints fit together. He wondered whether he should have made another effort at explaining the White House culture to her. Playing hurt was part of the job, just as it was with the Redskins. If someone wanted to be a player, he had to make sure he was always on the field during a crisis. She should understand that.

When he stepped from the shower his dizziness was behind him. His head throbbed steadily, but a few aspirin would take care of that.

The bedroom was empty, and he could hear her downstairs, preparing breakfast. With effort, he could smell bacon.

Of course, he couldn't bear the thought of eating this morning. It would all just come back up. Roddy would have it all when he awakened. Roddy's seventh-grade classes didn't start till half-past eight, and he was still asleep, the heavy, almost drugged sleep of a boy in the early stages of puberty. For that, at least, Hoffman envied him.

He stopped before his closet, thinking about the suit he ought to wear. It was the sort of day when Detwiler's photographer would be all over the West Wing, sensing that the most important pages of the administration's foreign-policy record were being written. And so they would be.

He was tempted to go with something new and somber, a blue pinstripe in very light wool. But, no. Everyone else in the White House would have pinstripes on. He would wear khaki, a poplin he had picked up from a tailor in Hong Kong during the Far East trip last March. And the bow tie—a Black Watch plaid. That was the Hoffman signature—a little mordant humor.

Outside, a band of gray was beginning to tinge the night sky in the east, over Washington. He frowned. He would not have time for the Universal gym in the basement. Not that he felt up to it, in any case. But he was a person who made lists of things to accomplish each day and liked to check them off.

Delores had breakfast laid out in the dining nook off the kitchen—eggs, bacon, coffee, juice.

"Don't have time, Dee," he said. He grabbed the glass of juice and drained it.

"All right, dear," she said stonily, and he realized she was angry for some reason, an anger he felt patently unfair.

He sighed, blew her a kiss, and walked out the door.

The Chrysler was idling in the driveway, Reynaldo behind the wheel.

Hoffman smiled as he shut the front door behind him. Reynaldo never took a day off, either.

Reynaldo stepped out of the car and held the door open for him.

The usual reading material was laid out on the seat, under the lamp: four morning papers, the White House press office's summary of international reporting, and a thin red envelope that contained his numbered copy of the *National Intelligence Daily*.

As the car pulled out of Exeter Drive and onto Glebe Road, heading toward the river, Hoffman pulled the front section of the *Washington Tribune* from the pile of newspapers and scanned it quickly. There was nothing from within Saudi Arabia, and he felt pleased. The lead story was headlined WHITE HOUSE MULLS ARABIAN OPTIONS. They had finally gotten control of the spin on this story.

But the rest of the front page was devoted to something the White House did not control—the reappearance of lines at gasoline stations for the first time in America since the Arab oil embargo of 1973. An argument at a Chevron station in Los Angeles had escalated into near warfare. Three people had died when drivers started shooting each other over the rights to the last fill-up available. People were reportedly hoarding gasoline all over the country.

The president, Hoffman knew, would be focused on the lines at the gasoline stations to the exclusion of almost everything today. A revolution by Islamic militants in Saudi Arabia was an abstraction to him. But the people waiting in line at gas stations were voters.

Normally, Henry Hoffman took a very cynical view of the effect of public opinion on foreign policy. If there were any American policies shaped by popular emotions and ethnic loyalties that were not stupid and ineffective, he was not aware of them. But in this case, he thought, the public's anger was welcome. It would help Peter Scott Detwiler make the right choice and do the right thing.

"Maybe," the president said, "we should just tell the people that we've been guzzling Saudi oil for too long and we've got to cut back."

Detwiler, his National Security Council, and assorted aides were gathered in the Cabinet Room. Henry Hoffman looked at the Sully portrait of Jefferson that hung on the cream-colored wall, just behind Detwiler's chair in the middle of the table. Jefferson, he thought, could afford to look serene. He didn't have to deal with Saudi Arabia.

"I think that a gasoline tax might not be a bad idea," said John Riding, the secretary of state. Hoffman wished Riding were still on the road. "If we raised the price by a dollar a gallon, we still wouldn't be close to the price the Europeans and the Japanese pay."

"John, it's easy to say if you've never run for election," Maynard Walters broke in. "But we have to. Next year."

"I know that, Maynard," Riding snapped. His face was starting to flush, and Hoffman knew he was outraged by the notion that Walters, a press secretary, would dare to contradict the secretary of state. In Riding's old law firm, that would be like a stenographer arguing with the senior partner.

Riding pushed a slender left hand out in front of him, palm up. He had a slightly frayed cuff, Hoffman noticed. Back in prep school, he had probably been the kind of kid who never wore his shirts until the maid back home had laundered them enough to make sure that the collar was fashionably threadbare.

Riding started ticking off all the profligate steps the government had taken as the American memory of the 1973 embargo grew dimmer and the memory of what had happened to the Shah of Iran in 1978, the King of Libya in 1967, and the King of Iraq in 1956 faded completely.

"You're correct, Mr. President, that we've been guzzling Saudi oil. We repealed the fifty-five-mile-an-hour speed limit. We gave in to Detroit on mileage standards. We gave in to Detroit on electric cars—"

"That's all in the past, John," Detwiler cut him off. "The question is what we do now."

He turned to the secretary of defense.

"Alan, have you got any sharper numbers than you had yesterday?"

Seifert reached back without looking to a military aide sitting behind him. The aide, a two-star general, reached into a briefcase that had been chained to his wrist when he entered the White House. He produced a manila envelope and handed it to Seifert.

"Yes, Mr. President," Seifert said, clearing his throat, "we could, in response to a request from the Saudi government, send a task force composed primarily of army and marine units to assist in restoring order in the country. This force, we estimate, would require four hundred thousand men. It would take six weeks to assemble. We estimate that casualties as it entered the country would be light, but not insubstantial. Perhaps in the neighborhood of a thousand dead and five times that many wounded.

"But we have to assume that in the six weeks before we could intervene, the Ikhwan"—he pronounced it "ick-one"—"would be arming itself, probably with help from Iran. We have to assume that at least some elements of the Ikhwan would be zealots, and that they would go to ground and fight as long as there were American troops on the ground and bullets to shoot them with."

"Somalia writ large," Riding said.

Seifert nodded slightly. "We estimate that we would sustain perhaps three hundred casualties a month for as long as our force was in Saudi Arabia. And we think it might have to be there . . ."

Seifert paused. Clearly, this was the part of the estimate that he found to be the purest guesswork.

"Anywhere from one to four years," he finished.

Detwiler's posture sagged just enough to be visible to Hoffman. He rubbed his eyes with his hands. Detwiler did not need to enunciate what Seifert's timetable meant: American troops would be on the ground, taking casualties, during his reelection campaign.

Hoffman decided it was time to prod the discussion.

"What about Option B, Alan?"

"Option B," Seifert said with a slight note of reluctance in his voice.

The two-star handed him another envelope with another sheaf of papers inside.

But that was mostly for backup. Seifert already knew the pertinent numbers.

"As you know, we have in Saudi Arabia a mixed detachment of about twelve hundred special forces troops, mostly army Delta units with a few navy SEALs thrown in. They're there largely as an antiterrorist element, but also as a spearhead in the event of a sudden conflict with, say, Iraq."

He paused. There were nods around the table.

"Now, it appears that the leadership of the rebels, the Ikhwan, has set itself up in the Grand Mosque in Mecca. Whatever the religious symbolism involved, this has one practical effect."

"No good Muslim boy's going to go in there and shoot," Thaddeus Hirsch chimed in.

Seifert nodded.

"The reliability of the forces defending the royal family is questionable. But there's no likelihood they'd obey orders to go into that mosque and root those people out."

There was a pause while a steward walked in and circled the table, refilling the glasses of mineral water and cups of coffee. Hoffman thought for a second that in other days, in other crises, the steward might also have emptied the ashtrays of the cigarette and cigar smokers. But here there was no smoke.

"Which is where the SEALs and the Deltas come in," Hirsch said.

Hoffman looked at him more fondly than he ever had. Hirsch was a fool, but he would back this mission.

Seifert spoke carefully, knowing, no doubt, that what he said might someday be picked over by congressional committees and historians.

"They have been trained to do what amounts to an undercover operation, using Saudi uniforms. A number of them are fluent in Arabic—"

Detwiler interrupted. "Can twelve hundred be enough to do the job?"

"Not on their own, Mr. President. The planning for this mission has envisioned a Saudi component, essentially protecting the rear of our men."

Hirsch broke on. "We estimate that there are two thousand men, lightly armed and poorly trained, inside the mosque. The SEALs and Delta units can take care of them. But once the fight begins, we have to protect them against Ikhwan reinforcements coming into the city. That's where the Saudis come in."

Detwiler looked skeptical.

"Can the Saudis do this job?"

Hirsch replied.

"We believe they can, Mr. President. In fact, we know it. Ahmed and Qabos tell us that they have two divisions of loyal National Guard troops, highly mobile and highly motivated, ready to deploy."

"Why didn't they use them in Riyadh?"

"These men weren't stationed in Riyadh, sir. They were in Dhahran, protecting the oil fields."

"Why is he so sure they'll be loyal?"

"It's a tribal thing, Mr. President," Hirsch replied. "These troops are all related by blood to the royal family. If the royal family goes, they're up shit's creek. They'll fight."

Detwiler slowly tapped a pencil against the blank notepad on the table in front of him. That, Hoffman knew, was not a good sign. It generally meant that he was displeased with the options he had before him and didn't want to make a decision.

"Alan," Hoffman said, "what's your evaluation? Could Option B work?"

Seifert hesitated, then committed himself. "Our troops have a great deal of confidence. They know they can get the job done. They've also assisted in the training and participated in some joint exercises of the Saudi National Guard troops. They have confidence in them."

Hoffman prodded.

"So what's your assessment?"

Seifert nodded. "There's a high probability it would be successful—maybe ninety-five percent."

"But not a certainty," Riding broke in.

"Nothing's certain, John," Hirsch replied.

"I can certainly predict one thing," Riding said. "This operation can't stay secret. It'll get out."

"Not if we move fast," Hirsch rejoined.

"I don't mean the fact of the operation," Riding replied. "But the fact of our participation. Someone will talk about it."

Hirsch shrugged. "At some point. But there are no journalists in Saudi Arabia right now—"

"What about the guy from the *Tribune*?" Riding interrupted.

"Out of the picture. On a slow boat to Aqaba," Hirsch said. "You notice he's not filing anymore."

Riding had only begun to argue.

"It doesn't matter. In a few weeks, a few months, someone will talk, if not sooner. It'll get out."

Brian Barrett, sitting in a row of chairs along the wall, broke in.

"By then, Ahmed will have consolidated his position. He'll deny it. We'll deny it. It won't matter. The Ikhwan will be squelched."

Technically, Barrett was out of line. Cabinet secretaries were supposed to have independent opinions. NSC staffers were supposed to clear anything they wanted to say at a meeting like this with the national security adviser. But Hoffman believed in letting experts have their say. And right now the task at hand was to position Option B as the middle option. Barrett was being helpful.

"So what do you suggest, John?" he asked Riding.

"Sit tight and let this situation sort itself out," Riding said. "Let's not make the mistake of assuming Jubail will be another Khomeini. Let's not condemn him before we find out whether we can work with him. No matter who comes to power, they're still going to be a small country sitting on a big pot of oil. They're going to have to protect it, and they're going to have to sell it."

"Well then, why not let Saddam walk in and take over?" Hirsch said, and Riding glared at him.

"General Stewart?" Hoffman broke in before they could launch a full-scale argument.

Bruce Stewart, chairman of the joint chiefs, turned his buzz-cut head from Riding toward the president. Stewart had been a tackle at West Point and still had the neck of a lineman. He'd been an armored man in his field days. Hoffman had no doubt what he'd say.

"I can't speak to Secretary Riding's suggestion," Stewart began, his voice a low bass. "That kind of thing is above my pay grade. But between the two military options, we favor the full-force deployment. If we're going to do the job, we need to do it right. We need adequate men and matériel."

It was a predictable position. Officers of Stewart's generation had been shaped by Vietnam and the Persian Gulf War. It gave them a heavy bias toward overwhelming force, applied with few restraints. Moreover, Stewart knew that the full-force option would never go operational without a congressional authorization. His generation of officers was loath to do anything without complete public support. The fact that the full-force option was not politically convenient for Peter Scott Detwiler bothered him not a whit. It probably made it more attractive.

Detwiler was squirming in his chair. He had clearly heard enough. He had, Hoffman knew, a short attention span for unpleasant material.

"All right ladies and gentlemen," he said. "Thanks very much. Mr. President, shall we reconvene at, say, four o'clock?"

Detwiler nodded. "Fine," he said.

Hoffman noticed that his heart was pounding. He decided it must be due to his fever.

"You kept your counsel in there, Henry," the president said. They were in the corridor between the Cabinet Room and the Oval Office. A silent Secret Service agent trailed behind them.

"Bit of a sore throat, Mr. President," Hoffman said.

Detwiler laughed. Then his expression grew solicitous. "You do look a bit under the weather," he said. "Well, cough and tell me."

Hoffman coughed, and the effort started a genuine spasm in his chest. For a few seconds he hacked and rasped, until his face was red and his eyes watery.

"You seen the doctor?" Detwiler asked.

"No, sir. Don't want to."

"I know," Detwiler said softly. "I appreciate it, Henry."

Hoffman regained his breath. "I think, sir, that you might want more input on this." He swallowed. "It's important enough to get every scrap of information you can."

"I agree," Detwiler said. He would, Hoffman knew, agree with almost anything that would enable him honorably to postpone this decision for a few hours. Detwiler was, by nature, a temporizer.

"I'll try to round up an old hand or two," Hoffman said. "I think a few wise men are in town."

Gabor Szentmihaly and John Rogers Clark, Hoffman knew, were the perfect choices. Clark, the elder of the two, was tall, stooped, and snowy-haired, and he needed a cane to get around now. But that only emphasized his long experience with the Saudis. As a young aide to Cordell Hull, Clark had witnessed the first meeting between an American and a Saudi prince, when FDR met King Abdul-Aziz on a ship in the Red Sea on his way back from Yalta. As secretary of state, Clark had initialed the first accords on stationing American forces on Saudi soil.

Gabor Szentmihaly, shorter, rounder, and florid, had occupied Hoffman's own office when the Shah of Iran fell. Hoffman knew exactly whom and what Szentmihaly blamed for that.

He deferred to both of them as they entered the Oval Office. Szentmihaly, ever the climber, strode forward in front of Clark and shook hands first. But Hoffman could tell from Detwiler's body language that it was Clark he wanted to hear from. The president all but took his arm as he guided Clark to the wing chair next to the fireplace and opposite the president's own, the chair that was normally reserved for visiting heads of state. Hoffman and Szentmihaly perched on the sofa.

"So, when you introduced Roosevelt to old Abdul-Aziz, did you ever think it would come to this?" Detwiler asked Clark after the small talk had ended.

"Well, Mr. President," Clark began. His voice was wispy, and Detwiler leaned closer to hear him, "Back in those days, we knew the Saudis had oil. But no one knew how much. St. John Philby—his son was Kim Philby—only persuaded Abdul-Aziz to grant some exploration concessions in 1931. And then it was all suspended because of the war. Back in those days, the rumor was that Abdul-Aziz carried the entire national treasury with him on two camels. So, no, we didn't."

"Two camels?" Detwiler laughed.

Clark nodded. "But it was already clear that the British were not going to be able to hold on in the Middle East after the war. Churchill said as much to FDR. And Mr. Roosevelt accepted the responsibility."

"As has everyone in this office since," Detwiler said.

"Of course, it's not the oil that's important here," Szentmihaly chimed in. He pronounced the words "de awl," with the accent of his native Hungary. "It's something that is less tangible but more important."

"Our resolve," Detwiler said, like a good student in a graduate seminar.

"Precisely." Szentmihaly nodded. "As the last and only superpower, the United States must be perceived to have the capacity and the will to act and act decisively. Otherwise, your problems will multiply. This was the mistake we made with the shah, Mr. President. That was, unfortunately, the defining moment of Mr. Carter's presidency. He chose to listen to those who counseled inaction."

Szentmihaly did not have to mention that he was not among those who advised Carter to cut the shah loose. He had already made the point in his memoirs.

"And you think this will be the defining moment of my presidency?" Detwiler asked.

Szentmihaly shrugged. "Times change and circumstances change. I would not be so arrogant as to presume that, Mr. President."

Detwiler nodded.

Hoffman simply watched, content to let Clark and Szentmihaly do the work. Neither one of them, he thought, had lost a step.

He lingered in the office as the president showed the two men out. Detwiler put a helping hand on Clark's elbow as he turned them over to a military aide. They would be escorted to the South Gate, where the press was not allowed. But if Hoffman knew Szentmihaly, the gist of the conversation, spun to make Szentmihaly look good, would be in *The New York Times* within a day or two.

Detwiler returned and closed the door behind him.

"So, Henry, what do you think?"

Hoffman bowed his head very slightly. "Well, Mr. President, I'm sure you have a pretty good idea from the fact that I picked Clark and Szentmihaly to come and talk to you."

Detwiler grinned. Part of the trick of being influential, Hoffman had learned, was allowing those in power to feel that they knew they were being manipulated. Presidents, in his experience, wanted to be guided to the right choice. They just wanted some assurance that they were still in control of the process. Detwiler only got recalcitrant when he felt that he was being influenced by forces he did not know or understand.

Moreover, Hoffman was telling the truth, which he found generally worked wonders in Washington. He saw the situation much as Gabor Szentmihaly did. The United States had to act decisively. It had to protect its interests. It had to remind the world that it would do both.

"Is there anything the Pentagon or the Agency came up with that falls somewhere between massive force and Option B?" Detwiler asked.

"No, sir. I wish there were," Hoffman said, again truthfully.

Detwiler picked up a paper clip from his desk and bent it until it was straight. In films, Hoffman knew, the president always gazed out the window toward the Washington Monument when he faced a lonely moment of decision. In real life, presidents cracked their knuckles, gnawed at their fingernails, or bent paper clips like everyone else.

"I want to lance this fucking boil," Detwiler finally said.

So did Hoffman.

"Well, sir, Option B is the only one that offers that possibility."

Detwiler nodded. "All right," he said. "The last thing I want is Hill hearings. If this works, we might not have any. If it doesn't work, we can still fall back on Option A. Get together with the Pentagon and work up the PDM." PDM was a presidential decision memorandum. "Make sure all the *i*'s are dotted and the findings found."

Hoffman nodded. The law required the president to make certain formal "findings" before he could order covert military action.

"Have it ready for the four o'clock meeting," Detwiler said. "There's no sense dillydallying."

Hoffman felt his head break out in a profuse sweat. He thought for a second it was nervous tension. Then he thought it might be the heat, that the air conditioning had faltered. But he realized it was neither of these. His fever had broken. He felt much better.

CHAPTER 18

Desdemona McCoy believed in her instincts. Her instincts, at the moment, were telling her to turn and flee. She did not feel this way often.

She remembered once, in high school, when she'd been invited to join a white girls' sorority, the Chi Deltas. Against her mother's advice, and against her instincts, she had accepted just to show that she could. That had lasted three unhappy months.

Then there had been the time a man she loved had offered to set her up in an apartment in Firenze while she did graduate work in art history at the Uffizi. She had bucked her instincts and accepted. He'd proven to be a man who didn't know the difference between a mistress and a whore.

His Royal Highness Prince Qabos bin-Abdul-Aziz gave her a similar feeling, a feeling that she was about to embark on something misguided and ill-fated.

Maybe, she thought, it was just a reaction to the man's crude display of his wealth. She had nothing against gold—in necklaces and earrings. She didn't think it was particularly appropriate for coffee tables. Yet the table in front of her was clearly a large, oblong chunk of solid gold, mounted on a thick, black marble pedestal. She could see nicks and scratches in the surface that suggested its softness. She could only guess how many ounces it contained. Sixteen hundred? Three thousand? Who knew how much a slab of gold that was four feet long, two feet wide, and six inches thick would weigh?

And this was only his Jedda residence. The one in Riyadh, she assumed, was even more opulent.

Or perhaps it was the color of the servant pouring their coffee—a deep, Nubian, purplish black—and the fact that the servant wore no shoes. She had heard that slavery, thinly veneered, persisted in Saudi Arabia.

Or maybe it was the man sitting next to her, Mac Strouder. Strouder seemed like the sort of man who would admire and envy a solid gold coffee table. It suggested to her a certain deficiency in judgment that had been on display when he rashly drove Burke into the base south of Riyadh. She was afraid his poor judgment spilled over into military matters. And yet Strouder was supposed to be the field commander of this operation.

Strouder made her miss Burke, she realized. She would have enjoyed his reaction to this place and these people. He would have made her laugh.

She wondered where he was—in a *dhow* by now most likely, heading for Aqaba. She said a small, quick prayer for a fair, safe wind. And she wondered why her instincts didn't seem to know how to guide her with him.

She sipped the coffee that the servant had poured, conscious of the smell of spice and sugar.

Across the table, Prince Qabos was pondering, his lips pursed delicately, his legs splayed out inside the khaki trousers he was wearing as part of his Saudi National Guard uniform.

"I believe they are all loyal, except for a few traitorous officers," he said at last.

Strouder's face reddened and his eyes bulged. McCoy could see that he was making an effort to control his reaction. She intervened.

"Well, Your Highness, perhaps we should ask how many men do you have under the command of officers whose loyalty is beyond question?"

Qabos blinked, his eyes closing down like a snake's in his jowly face, and McCoy could see that he was also making an effort to control his reaction. He was clearly not accustomed to having American colonels—to say nothing of black American women—question the loyalty of his troops.

"Obviously," McCoy said, trying to be deferential, "we start with the loyal men guarding this compound. How many are there?"

The prince nodded. "A thousand," he said. "But they are not to be included in this operation."

Of course not, McCoy thought. Otherwise, who would protect your precious royal hide?

"Your Majesty," Strouder said, confusing Qabos's title with the king's, "we can save your bacon, but only if you provide us with three thousand absolutely loyal, well-trained men."

Qabos's nose wrinkled at the mention of "bacon," but Strouder either didn't notice or ignored him.

"I don't care where you get them, but this mission has to have the absolute highest priority," Strouder went on. "Otherwise, we can forget about it right now."

The prince nodded and murmured something McCoy didn't quite catch.

"Let me explain again why we need them," Strouder said. "One, we need our rear covered and we don't have enough of our men to do it. We're going to be too busy working inside the mosque. Two, we need people to believe this is your operation. The troops everyone will see are the ones protecting our rear. They have to be your men, Saudi men."

Qabos nodded.

"Three thousand is not a problem," he said.

"We want the attack to begin tomorrow morning, just before dawn," Strouder said. "We'll need to designate a staging area outside of Mecca where we can land twenty helos. We need a rendezvous time. We'll need maps and interior plans of the Grand Mosque."

Qabos's face tightened, and McCoy sensed his humiliation at the thought of handing over plans for the Grand Mosque to a foreigner, to an unbeliever.

But as quickly as the notion of sympathy for this man entered her mind, she dismissed it. The House of Saud had made this bed for itself. This was a man of enormous wealth and enormous corruption. Were it not for the oil at stake, she would be inclined to let the Saudis fend for themselves.

Even with the oil, she realized, she would be inclined that way. And that was probably why her instincts were in revolt.

Well, there was nothing she could do about it. Decisions had been made. Her job was to carry them out. Bad as the Saudis were, the Ikhwan would no doubt be worse.

"I think we should also have someone you trust, perhaps a member of your family, designated to act as liaison," she said.

Qabos thought about it for a moment. "There is my nephew Hamad. He is a graduate of your army's school at Fort Leavenworth. He is a brigadier general."

"He'll do," Strouder said. "Where is he?"

McCoy hoped Qabos would reply that Hamad was out in the field, fighting the Ikhwan.

"He is in this house," Qabos said.

It could have been worse, she thought. He could have been off on a boat somewhere, hiding like half the rest of the royal family.

Qabos got up and, without asking that they follow, walked over to a corner of the room and picked up a telephone. She watched him punch a number into a machine, using his left hand. She had been told that his right arm was nearly useless, the result of a high-speed collision on the corniche above Cannes years ago. She imagined the enduring humiliation that must have meant for him in this society. Qabos began a muttered conversation in Arabic.

"Can you hear?" she whispered to Strouder.

He shook his head.

She looked about the room. It was roughly the size of the gymnasium at Columbia, with pillars of marble supporting the ceiling, rich carpets on the floor, and a few suites of furniture, looking tiny and out of place, scattered at random. His *majlis* room, she guessed, the place where in better days he had received supplicants.

Strouder could not sit still. He got up and paced around the sofa, like a tiger in a cage.

A door opened at the far end of the room and the tallest Saudi McCoy had ever seen entered the room. He was wearing brown fatigues with the sleeves rolled up to reveal well-sinewed forearms. Instead of a *ghotra*, he wore a red beret. He was six feet six and he had a pale, jagged scar running along the jawbone on the left side of his face. He had a pistol strapped to his waist and he looked like a warrior. A junior officer walked ten paces behind him, carrying a sheaf of maps under his arm.

"Hamad," the tall man said, shaking hands first with McCoy, then with Strouder.

"I've heard a lot about you, Colonel," he said to Strouder.

Strouder straightened slightly. "Yeah, well, believe nothing of what you hear and half of what you see," he said. "Lot of false rumors going around."

"I hope not all false." Hamad smiled. "It's going to be an honor working with you."

His accent was nearly flawless. If she had closed her eyes, McCoy might have thought she was listening to an Iowa farmer.

"I will leave you now," Qabos said. "I believe you two have professional matters to discuss."

Hamad bowed slightly toward his uncle. They watched in silence as the older man walked slowly toward a door at the far end of the room.

"Right, then," Hamad said, taking the maps and moving toward a large table. "We have some butt-kicking to discuss."

Strouder smiled for the first time since they had entered Qabos's compound.

He winked at McCoy. "Piece of cake," he whispered as he fell into step behind Hamad.

CHAPTER 19

Burke stayed until dark in the shadow of a crevice worn by the wind in a sandstone mesa that seemed to rise from the desert floor like a billiard table, monolithic and imposing.

He had lasted on foot until ten in the morning, following a path parallel to a power transmission line. He had become an expert in the variety of the desert floor. Some of it was hard-packed dirt strewn with rocks the size of fists that twisted his ankles and strained his hips. Some of it was soft and powdery, and his feet kicked up little clouds of dust in front of him as he walked. Some of it was bare reefs of rock, blown nearly clean by the winds. None of it was pleasant.

He had had no water, no moisture at all, save for the bits he scraped from the leaves of stunted little juniper bushes. There was not enough in them to drink, but they moistened his hands, and for that he was grateful.

At first he had been certain he was going in the proper direction to make Mecca, judging by the position of Polaris and then of the rising sun. But by sunrise, he knew he was only guessing.

There was one thing he did not have to guess about. He needed water. By mid-morning, the sun had become so hot that his head felt swollen and his tongue seemed dusty and he did not think he could survive another hour in the sun. So the rational course had seemed to him to take shelter, to get out of the sun, and to wait until dark before traveling again. It was a choice, he knew, that he could make only once, unless he found water. He would have to find water by the end of this night, even if it meant turning himself in to the Ikhwan to get it.

So in the heat of the day he had slept in the shade of the crevice, seeking sleep as a way to rid his mind of the question of McCoy, a question that, like the sun overhead, seemed to want to beat on his head until it exploded.

Orders changed, Jawar had said.

Maybe Jawar had been lying. Or maybe someone else had changed the orders. But his mind kept coming back to her. The hotter it got and the more his head throbbed, the more likely it seemed to him that she had betrayed him.

Now, feeling slightly cooler, he was only confused. What was the American chain of command in Saudi Arabia and what was her place in it? Who gave orders to Jawar? He didn't know.

He thought he knew her, and it was inconceivable to him that she could do this. She might be ready to dump him—but not in the desert.

On the other hand, he had thought there was a good chance she would marry him. He'd been wrong about that.

He could remember a time in his life when he took pride in not giving a woman the benefit of any doubt. If a woman so much as broke a date, he smiled and said good-bye.

When had he become so needy? It must have happened during the years in Moscow, or maybe the months in Washington. He had started to sense his own aging, to feel his solitude as a burden rather than an opportunity. And she had come into his life at that time.

"I shall wear the bottom of my trousers rolled," he said to himself.

He shook his head. It would do him no good to keep thinking about it. He needed to find water.

The sun was striping the western horizon in bands of orange and lavender. A breeze, slightly cooler, wafted in from the north. He looked at the closest two pylons in the electricity transmission line. Judging by the setting sun, they were following a line that went northeast to southwest—toward Mecca, or where he presumed Mecca to be.

He got to his feet and started to walk. For a moment his head swirled, but he took a deliberate breath and started setting one foot in front of the other, keeping the far pylon directly in front of him.

A pale sliver of moon rose above the low hills before him and the first stars appeared as the sky grew purplish and then black.

He started to consider exactly what he would do when he reached Mecca. There would be, he guessed, some kind of well or communal spigot. There would have to be. He started thinking about how he would approach it. Would he turn it on and try to push his head under the water, mouth open, and let it gush down his throat? Or would he turn it on, let it grow cool, then kneel down with his hands cupped in front of him, slip the hands under the stream of water and let the water pool in his palms, then bring it quickly to his mouth to drink?

His shuffling feet stubbed against a low, sharp rock wedged in the tan powder. He cursed as pain shot up from his right big toe. He bent down to examine it.

As he did he heard the low rumble of an engine from over the horizon behind him. He looked back. In the distance, to the east, he saw the silhouette of a helicopter, flying very low, perhaps a hundred feet off the ground. It seemed to swerve around the mesa that had sheltered him.

With surprising speed it bore down upon him, flying parallel to the line of power pylons, then roared past. It was huge, bulbous—the size of a truck. And entirely black. Even the windows looked opaque. He could see no lights inside or outside. He wondered how the pilot could see.

Within seconds another, identical helicopter appeared over the eastern horizon, following roughly the same path, and passed him. Then a third, and a fourth, spectral figures, like bats flying from a cave at dusk. Hunched in the sand, he did the reflexive thing. He counted them.

He had reached twelve when the sound of an oncoming engine distinguished itself from those that had preceded it. It was not the low, powerful hum of the first twelve engines. He could hear this engine missing, coughing in the night air.

He looked back and saw the helicopter start to yaw to the left, then lose its line, sinking lower and to the left, like a kite that hits a crosswind. Burke, half a mile away, could see what was going to happen three seconds before it happened, and he wondered whether the pilot knew what was going to befall him.

The forward rotor of the helicopter clipped the side of the mesa. He could hear the high-pitched, scraping sound of metal against rock, then a tearing noise. The helicopter jerked clumsily in the air, pirouetted like a drunk trying to turn a cartwheel, and them tumbled precipitously to earth. He heard a thud, and the sound of sheet metal tearing apart.

Burke froze, waiting for the sound of an explosion. He heard nothing. Quickly but carefully, half jogging and half walking, he began moving toward the scene of the crash.

Yet another helicopter appeared in the sky to the east, and then a second and a third, making a total of sixteen. He expected at least one of them to slow down, hover, and descend to the crash site. But none of them did. They followed the same route that the first twelve had done, disappearing over a low sand ridge in the west.

He heard voices before he got to the wreck. He clambered up a small hill, crouching low, and flattened himself in the sand, peering down below.

The pilot had managed to land the helicopter on its side rather than nose down. The tip of one rotor was stuck in the sand at an acute angle, like a pitchfork left in the ground by a gardener. He was struck again by the size of the machine. On the ground, it looked massive, heavy.

Men were crawling from the hatch on the high side of the wreck. He could hear moans from within it, presumably from the injured. Two men were clinging to the fuselage, extending their hands into the hatch and helping their comrades out. A dozen men were on their feet around the wreck, some walking in small, dazed circles. They wore camouflage fatigues and their faces were blackened. Burke strained to hear the language they were speaking.

"My fucking leg is broken," someone screeched from within the wreck.

Burke winced, aware of the pain in the man's voice. They were Americans, he decided. He was about to stand up, call out a greeting, and walk toward them when he hesitated, remembering again what Jawar had done to him.

Over his shoulder, from the west, he heard the sound of another helicopter, and he glanced back. This one appeared to be coming from the direction in which the first ones had flown, to be coming back for the machine that had gone down.

The big black machine roared over him and the wash from the rotors kicked sand into the air, stinging his eyes.

Burke lay still in the sand, watching as it banked, hovered, and then settled to the sand twenty yards from the wreck.

A dozen men were leaping from the helicopter before its rotor stopped turning. Half of them carried stretchers. They began quickly and deftly extricating the men still inside the wreck.

Two men separated themselves from the group and walked over toward the hillside where Burke lay. When the engine from the second helicopter cut off, Burke could hear them, and he immediately recognized one of the voices. It was Strouder. He could see the broad shoulders and, faintly, the bristle of the mustache and goatee.

"How many injured?" Strouder was asking.

"I count six, Colonel," said the second man, shorter and more slender.

"They absolutely can't go?"

"Fractures, I think," the shorter man said.

"The rest?"

"A few sprains, a lot of bruises, some cuts."

"Well, we've got eight hours to patch 'em up," Strouder said. "We hit the mosque at 0530."

"They'll be ready, sir," the shorter man promised.

Burke stiffened. He was not surprised. Nor would anyone be who knew what was going on in Arabia. Burke was afraid, afraid of the responsibility this information gave him. He was afraid of what might happen if Strouder saw him.

"Blow the avionics," Strouder ordered.

Inside the downed helicopter, someone threw a switch and a puff of acrid smoke emerged from the hatch.

Burke squirmed slightly in the sand and felt the telephone he had stolen from Jawar, still in his pocket.

As he watched, the men from the first helicopter transferred into the second. Some limped. Six, true to the shorter man's count, were carried on stretchers. He heard the thump as the hatch closed and then the whine as the engine started and then accelerated. The rotors kicked sand down the back of his neck and he thought, for an instant, of how good it would feel to take a shower. Then the helicopter rose into the night sky, now black and dotted with an infinite number of stars. In less than a minute it was gone.

He still needed water.

He walked down the short slope to the wrecked helicopter, feeling the sand and small pebbles slide between his feet and the soles of his sandals.

Feeling ghoulish, he got a foot onto a strut in the landing gear and pulled himself up to the hatch. He could barely see inside at first, but then his eyes adjusted a little and he could make out benches, dangling ropes—and something checked on the floor underneath a bench.

This was the back of the helicopter where the soldiers sat as it lifted them into battle, and the checked thing he had seen was fabric. He picked it up. It was a *ghotra*, just like the ones worn by troops of the Saudi National Guard.

The significance of the *ghotra* registered in the back of his mind, but he did not think about it. His attention remained focused on one thing only: water.

He moved forward toward the cockpit of the helicopter. His nostrils filled with the smell of the scuttled avionics in the instrument panel; it reminded him vaguely of the New Jersey Turnpike. His eyes flickering quickly, almost feverishly about the small enclosure. He barely noticed the enormous array of dials and screens on the instrument panel. They were all blank and lifeless. He saw what he was looking for on the deck, wedged under the copilot's seat: a canteen.

It was covered in camouflage cloth and looked to contain about a pint. Straining, he squatted down and extended his arm until he could grasp it. Then he smiled. It felt heavy.

Quickly, he brought it into his chest and unscrewed the cap. He raised it to his lips. The water was warm and tasted of the metal that lined the canteen, but he finished half of it off before he realized what he was doing. He tore his mouth away from the neck of the canteen and slowly sloshed the water in his mouth from side to side, letting it wash the dry crust off his tongue and the roof of his mouth.

Burke understood in a physical way why the Koran described Paradise as a place of gardens and flowing water.

He told himself that he must save the remaining water and he started to screw the cap back on the canteen. Then he decided to allow himself one last, small swig and he drained half the remaining water before he managed to stop drinking and screw the cap on tight.

With his thirst checked, if not slaked, his thoughts went back to the information he might obtain in this ship.

And then he thought of McCoy and her question to him—did he ever think about what he reported?

Reflexively, he searched. There was virtually nothing to note except the *ghotra*. The inside walls had some signs about the distribution of cargo weight. But the men who had left it had taken almost everything with them. He stuffed the *ghotra* inside the pocket of his laborer's smock, and as he did he felt again the cellular phone.

Carefully, he stepped down through the hatch and out over the landing gear. He fell gracelessly the last three feet to the ground.

He looked at his watch in the dim light from the stars and the crescent moon. He always kept the digital readout on Washington time, and it said 16:00. It was a good time to catch his editors, between lunch and the afternoon story conference.

His thoughts whirled. He wanted to tell them about the things he had seen in the desert. He wanted to ask for help in getting out. More than anything else, he just wanted to talk to someone who appreciated him.

He punched in what he hoped was the code for an international call to the United States, followed by the number of the foreign desk at the *Tribune*. He listened. There was a long silence, followed by a burst of unintelligible, recorded Arabic.

He sighed. He tried to recall how Jawar had dialed, but he couldn't. Jawar hadn't been calling the United States, in any case.

He flipped the phone over. Jawar or someone had written some Arabic letters and four-digit numbers on a piece of paper and attached it to the back of the phone. He thought perhaps that the letters were cities and the numbers were roaming access codes.

He had picked up enough Arabic to know the digits. Zero was a dot, eight was an upside down V, and five looked like an inverted heart. The first number was 8055.

He tried punching that into the phone. Nothing happened. He tried the next one, 7126. As he listened the dial tone changed character from a high-pitched sound to a deeper buzz.

He tried to dial the *Tribune* again. He heard the sound of twinkling satellite beams, and then a ringing. Someone picked up the phone.

"Graves," the voice said.

"I will never again question the beneficence of technology." Burke sighed. His voice startled him. It sounded harsh and guttural, as if the words were scraping as they came out of his mouth.

"Who's this?" Graves sounded annoyed.

"It's Burke," he rasped. "Sorry I haven't checked in."

"Burke! Where the hell are you? We figured you must've shacked up in a harem," Graves shouted.

"Not quite," Burke said.

"Seriously, it's good to hear from you. We were starting to get worried. Lyle Nelson himself went over to the State Department this morning to demand that they help us find you. We've had guys on the phones to the Pentagon, the White House, the CIA. Not a word. So what happened?"

"Well," Burke began, trying to figure out what was best left unsaid.

"Some Beirut paper printed a story that I was a spy. I got arrested. I got out, and, uh, I sort of hitched a ride that was supposed to take me to Jedda. I was going to catch a boat to Aqaba there. But I got dumped. I'm somewhere in the desert."

"Jesus," Graves said. "Where?"

"I'm not sure," Burke said. "And even if I knew, I'm not sure I'd tell you on an open line. Don't know who's listening. But I'm going to try to get to Jedda. Is there any way you can get some help to me there?"

"We'll do our best," Graves said.

Burke thanked him.

"So," Graves said. "The town is full of rumors about American intervention over there. It's going to be our lead story tomorrow, for sure. You know anything we can add?"

Burke looked back at the wreckage of the helicopter. He felt the *ghotra* in his pocket. He remembered what he had overheard Strouder say to the junior officer half an hour ago.

Then he thought about McCoy, and what she had said. If ever there was a time to think about the repercussions of what he knew before he published it, this was it. He could dictate a story to Graves that would appear a couple of hours before the operation against the Grand Mosque in Mecca was supposed to begin. He could expose the deception involved, the attempt to pass American commandos off as Saudis.

He could force them to scuttle the operation.

He thought again of *The New York Times* in 1961, censoring its own story on the imminent invasion of Cuba at the Bay of Pigs. If the *Times* had gone ahead and published everything it had known, it might have prevented that fiasco, doing the nation a service.

That lore about the *Times*'s mistake was part of the bedrock of his beliefs about journalism. He had always believed in disclosing the facts and letting the public and the politicians sort them out. He had believed in it so strongly that it was like faith to the Pope—something he had long since ceased to question.

But now McCoy was making him question it.

He could argue with her about whether his reporting had precipitated a revolt in Saudi Arabia that would otherwise not have happened. He could maintain that it would have happened sooner or later. He could say, as indeed he had, that if the CIA hadn't wanted to destabilize the House of Saud, it should not have enlisted the Saudis' physician as a source of information.

But in the back of his mind, as he said those things, he would be thinking that McCoy was at least partly right. And he would be hoping that he would not lose her.

And that reminded him of something else. If he broke this story and the attack was aborted, there would be an inquiry. It would encounter the simple syllogism that he knew and McCoy knew about the operation, and she must, therefore, have been its source.

"Burke!" Graves sounded as if he were squawking. "You there? Burke!"

"Yeah, I'm here, Ken," Burke said.

"Well? Have you got anything?"

"No, Ken," Burke said. "I've been completely out of touch."

CHAPTER 20

It was two A.M. when Burke finally saw the lights of Mecca.

He was shuffling up a ridge of rough, gritty sand and sharp, cutting stones. His thirst had returned. The canteen had long since been emptied. He came to the top of the ridge.

Everything about his body hurt. His feet were rubbed raw where pebbles had lodged in his sandals. His right ankle was swollen.

The city surprised him with its smallness. It was no more than a tenth the size of Riyadh, and he could see clearly to its eastern outskirts, perhaps three miles distant.

Mecca was quiet, its residential buildings uniformly dark. Powerful street lamps illuminated the main roads and cast a hazy glow into the sky. A few trucks and an occasional car rumbled along the roads, but the stillness was such that he could hear their engines receding into the distance after the road had curved away and he could no longer see them.

It was not, he suspected, a great town for nightlife.

In the center of it, brightly lit, he saw what could only be the Grand Mosque. It appeared to be the size of a stadium, but with seven minarets, each slender and graceful, each illuminated against the night sky. He could imagine, for a moment, the thoughts of pilgrims who had come for the *hajj* and stopped, as he was stopping, to take in this sight for the first time. This was where the Prophet had been born, and Islam. It was the site of the ancient stone, the Ka'abah, that had been an object of veneration for centuries before the Prophet.

The thought of the stone reminded him that Mecca was forbidden to nonbelievers. Even if he were not an American, even if he were not a journalist, he could be arrested and punished merely for setting foot in the city.

The wind shifted slightly, blowing from the south, and brought with it a foul odor. He turned toward the source and saw a series of long, low sheds. They smelled like slaughterhouses, like spilled blood and feces.

This must, he thought, be Mina, the place to the east of Mecca where pilgrims came to cast stones at three pillars in the desert, the places where the devil appeared to Abraham and had to be cast out. After fulfilling the ritual, the pilgrim slaughtered a sheep. Those slaughterhouses must be where they did it, or where it was done for them.

Burke sat down in the sand and pondered what to do next.

Thirst and a guilty conscience had driven him this far. Every step of the way he had castigated himself for lying to Graves, for suppressing what he knew. He could think of only one way to atone for his transgression. He had to see the attack Strouder and his men were preparing. He had to report on it.

He reminded himself that in every revolution he had covered, guns and vigilantes had both abounded. The Ikhwan would have heard the same rumors he and Jawar had heard. They would have checkpoints around the city and sentinels at its edges. He had to figure out a way to avoid them until the attack started.

And he had to find water.

The first thing to do was avoid main roads. He peered carefully down a north–south road that lay between him and the Grand Mosque. Far away, in the north, he thought he could see a couple of military trucks parked by the side of the road. If so, that would be one checkpoint.

The ground ahead of him was barren and gritty, with only a few planted cypress trees trying to anchor the thin soil against the wind. Keeping his head down, he scuttled forward to the closest tree. He peered around again. Nothing was stirring.

He struck out on a heading he calculated was northwest, judging by the position of Polaris. He kept himself parallel to a road that carried, by his count, about two trucks or cars every three minutes.

Ahead of him lay two choices. There was a complex of lesser mosques and what appeared to be a hospital or hotel to his left. And to his right was a dark, crowded neighborhood of baked mud houses jammed close together—a slum. He chose the slum.

Slowly, he approached the road. Fifty yards away, he heard the sound of an engine, and he froze. It sounded like a truck, coming closer. He saw a rock about two feet high, ten yards to his right. He dove behind it. A stone as sharp as an ax blade dug into his hip, and he winced.

The truck rolled past, and he could see, vaguely, soldiers in red-and-white checked *ghotras* like the one he had stuffed in his pocket from the downed helicopter. He saw the glint of metal from an oiled rifle barrel. The truck rolled past. He waited until the sound of the engine had completely died away. They were, he assumed, from a unit that had gone over to the rebel side.

He crossed the pavement, aware of the sound his sandals made as his feet hit the concrete. He heard another engine approaching, but this time he did not hide. Fifty yards away he saw what appeared to be an alley. He sprinted toward it, and by the time the approaching truck rolled by, he was sheltered in its shadows.

Burke looked around. It was indeed a slum, as mean as anything he had seen in Asia or Africa. The street itself was a mixture of sand and rock. In the faded yellow glow of a street lamp a couple of blocks away, he looked for a spigot. He saw one, jutting out from the mud-brick wall of the biggest house on the block. Quickly, furtively, he scurried to it and filled his canteen.

He was happy he did not have to see what the water looked like, because he knew he would drink it even if it were brown.

Surely, he consoled himself, if there were one place where the House of Saud would have made certain of decent drinking water, it was this city. He put the canteen to his lips and drank. It tasted of chlorine. He found that reassuring.

His thirst again slaked, he suddenly felt hungry. It had been more than a day since he had eaten and in a while that problem would become as acute as his thirst. He had only a few hundred rials left in his wallet.

He did not imagine that many restaurants in Mecca accepted American Express.

But the more immediate problem was getting to the vicinity of the Grand Mosque before dawn without being stopped and asked to produce identification.

He had an idea as to how he might do that, and he walked slowly along the dirty street, peering into every alley and garage, until he found what he was looking for.

It was a trash cart, dented by years of use, mounted on a couple of old automobile tires. Three brooms and a flat shovel protruded, handles first, from a compartment that adjoined the trash bin. And folded neatly over the handle was a pair of orange coveralls. Burke assumed that whoever worked with this cart lived in one of the hovels nearby.

He did not like to think of himself as a thief, so he rationalized: the man would probably be a lot safer if he took the day off.

Slowly, he pulled the cart from its parking space in a narrow alley that smelled of urine and old food. It rattled loudly; the lid on the trash bin was battered, bent, and coming loose at the hinges. Burke froze. He waited for a sound from one of the surrounding huts, or the explosion of light as someone awakened. Nothing happened.

As quietly as he could, he backed into the street, pulling the cart along. The left wheel bumped up against a rock protruding from the dirt. The cart stopped. Gently, he tried to extricate it. Tin rattled against tin and he thought that certainly he would wake the neighbors. The wheel slid over its hump and he set off in the direction of the Grand Mosque, opting for speed over stealth.

But speed was hard to achieve. One of the wheels needed grease, and the cart constantly pulled to the right. Wheeling it through the dirt and over the rocks was only slightly easier than carrying a refrigerator; inside of a minute, his arms and shoulders started to feel tired. He wondered at the poverty in Yemen, or Pakistan, or wherever this trash collector came from, wondered what it would take to prompt a man to leave his home and live in a Mecca hovel, pushing this cart under the Arabian sun for a Saudi pittance.

When he had covered a few hundred yards, he stopped and tried to pull the coveralls on. The man must have been a Yemeni, only a few inches more than five feet tall. The coveralls rode up his shins and forearms and jammed against his crotch. They were flimsy, made of cotton, and he took them off. With his hands, he ripped at the cuffs on both the sleeves and the legs, tearing them open. The coverall fit a little better with that done, and he did not think looking more ragged would hurt him.

He looked at his watch. It was a few minutes after three A.M. If he took Strouder at his word, he needed to hole up somewhere for an hour and a half, so as to arrive in the center of the city just before the attack on the mosque. He saw a small, vest-pocket square with a dry fountain, a few palm trees, and a couple of benches. He pushed the cart toward it, grunting as it rose up over a curb. He parked it by a bench and stretched out underneath it, watching the stars through the warped wooden slats. He dozed.

The sound of footsteps moving through the streets awakened him. He looked at his watch. He had been asleep for an hour.

Burke rolled out from under the bench and looked toward the sound of the footsteps. He saw men and women shrouded in white walking slowly and silently toward the Grand Mosque. The men wore two pieces of white cloth, one wrapped around their waists like a towel and the second draped over their torsos, leaving the right shoulder bare. The women looked almost like nuns from Africa, in white gowns that dragged along the street and veils that covered their hair but not their faces. After days in which he had seen women only in black *abayas*, he found himself staring curiously at them.

He forced himself to turn his face away. It would not do for a street sweeper to be staring like a tourist. He remembered reading that pilgrims to the Grand Mosque wore white.

He pushed the cart into the street and began making his way in the same direction as the pilgrims. The street merged with another, broader one and the procession of pilgrims swelled.

Up ahead, he saw a checkpoint. The people in white were forming two lines and passing under the gaze of a half-dozen Arabs dressed in an assortment of fatigues and *ghotras*, each with an M-16 cradled loosely in his hands.

It was his last chance to turn back. Burke pulled a broom from the cart and started to sweep, pushing dust into piles and then onto his flat shovel, then emptying the shovel into the bin. He stuck close to the curb, kept his eyes in the gutter, and moved forward.

Very slowly, he made his way to the checkpoint, keeping clear of the flow of pilgrims. He did not know whether he would be expected to get in line with them; he trusted he would not. Sweeping and shuffling, he advanced, telling himself to act as if he had been doing this every day for years.

He felt, rather than saw, the eyes of one of the Ikhwan guerrillas. He kept sweeping, waiting for the sharp, challenging sound of the guerrilla's voice. His empty stomach turned over. But he heard nothing, and in five minutes he had put the checkpoint behind him.

The sun was starting to color the horizon behind him a pale gray, and the ranks of the pilgrims continued to swell when he rounded a corner and caught sight again of the Grand Mosque.

People in white were making their way toward it. Pairs and trios were becoming clusters and clusters were becoming crowds as the time for dawn prayers approached.

Burke drew close enough to the doors of the mosque to see people taking off their shoes and sandals and depositing them in boxes, then proceeding inward on bare feet. Through a portal, he glimpsed a corner of the Ka'abah, covered in a black cloth embroidered with gold. The pilgrims had grouped themselves in great circles around it and were moving, almost dancing, holding hands. He could faintly hear their shouted, ecstatic prayers and exclamations.

The mosque glowed with a greenish light. Burke scanned the plaza around it, looking for a site from which he could safely observe whatever was going to happen. What appeared to be a hotel and a bus parking area occupied the east end of the plaza, and there were some hedges around the hotel that might help give him cover. He trundled his cart and brooms in that direction, looking cautiously around him. People were moving in various directions, but no one met his eye.

Jawar had been right about at least one thing, he thought. No one noticed the people who picked up the trash.

CHAPTER 21

Desdemona McCoy closed her eyes and searched for a calm spot within herself as her helicopter, plain and unmarked, completed its descent and settled into the garden of a large, walled compound in Mecca. The property belonged to a cousin of Prince Qabos, a devout and elderly man who had died six months ago. It would be McCoy's operations center. She reminded herself that the only way she would succeed in this task was to be calm, to focus on one thing at a time, and not to surrender to the fearful fragments of information that seemed to be attacking her from every direction.

As soon as the pilot unlocked the hatch, she bounded out, followed by two technicians bearing trunks full of communications equipment.

She watched as a second, identical helicopter hovered and descended, barely missing a date-palm tree before coming to rest on the ground beside her own. She looked around.

This was, by any normal measure, a wealthy man's home. The walls enclosed about three acres of land, and the garden, a trifle weedy now, still smelled of oleander and roses. There were three smaller houses in addition to the main building. But it was modest in comparison to the palaces of men like Qabos. The two helicopters all but filled the open space in the garden.

She looked around the perimeter. Three dozen of Qabos's loyal troops had arrived in cars ahead of them, dressed like Ikhwan fighters. They now carried their M-16s and machine guns openly as they stood guard.

"You satisfied with the security?" she asked a man who was stepping from the second helicopter. His name was Chris Gallegos and he was deputy chief of station in Riyadh. He was, in her judgment, one of the few people in the station who had maintained anything close to objective distance from the royal family.

"Adequate for the time being," Gallegos said. "But let's keep our engines warm."

She nodded. "You see all the pilgrims heading for the mosque?"

Gallegos nodded. His mouth tightened. "Hard to miss them."

"How many, do you think?"

"A thousand. Number's probably going to grow."

"I guesstimated two thousand," McCoy said.

Gallegos shrugged.

"God," McCoy said, exasperated. "You're sure there were no pilgrims there yesterday?"

They walked toward the house.

"None," Gallegos said. "The Ikhwan had closed the area off. But overnight, they put the word out that it was open for pilgrims who wanted to make the *umrah*."

"The *umrah*?"

"The short version of the *hajj*. It can happen any time of year. It's basically just the circumambulation of the Ka'abah."

"They're using these people as a shield," McCoy said.

Gallegos nodded.

She wanted to demand that he tell her why he and his men had failed to predict this. It was just what Saddam had done in Iraq, what Arafat had done in his days under siege in Beirut.

She should, she realized, have foreseen it herself.

But there was nothing to be gained now from recriminations. They walked through a delicately carved wooden door and into the *majlis* of the house. It was, McCoy noted quickly, an austere and simple room, furnished with good carpets and unadorned with gold, marble, or any of the other extravagances favored by the wealthier members of the Saud clan. The technicians had already gotten one computer up and running. They were working on a second.

She rubbed her face with her hands. "I don't suppose there's some way to warn those people, get them out of there."

"You'd have to ask Strouder," Gallegos said. "But I doubt it."

McCoy scowled. She walked over to the computer and called up the agency's Saudi file. It was being updated hourly now, she saw, from all the sources reporting in to Langley. The digest at the top read like a litany of disaster.

STRIKE HALTS OIL PRODUCTION

Striking oil-field workers halted production yesterday at all major fields in Dhahran area, according to eyewitness, source accounts, verification probability 98 percent.

Strikers predominantly Shiites, strike incited by mullahs known to have close ties with Hezbollah in Iran, sources, verification probability 70 percent.

Ikhwan consolidates control in Riyadh, eyewitnesses, verification probability 98 percent. Ikhwan controls Mecca, Taif, Medina, Bukayriyah, sources, verification probability 60 percent. . . .

Gallegos, looking over her shoulder, whistled softly.

"What does that leave the government in control of?" she asked.

"Jedda," he said. "A few military bases."

She had the feeling, not for the first time, that all of their efforts were going to be too late, that the House of Saud was beyond salvation and that their efforts to resuscitate it would be like giving a heart transplant to a patient whose liver and kidneys had ceased to function. But she kept those thoughts to herself.

She stepped over toward the next monitor. She saw a grainy picture of people moving, people dressed in white.

"The Grand Mosque?" she asked.

"That's right," Gallegos said, a touch of pride in his voice. "Microcams mounted on lampposts. They're the size of thimbles, so small no one notices them. Have a range of about two miles. This one's pointed at the west entrance. We'll have a good look at what happens."

"There must be five thousand pilgrims by now, judging by the density," McCoy said. "Any sensors in the mosque itself?"

"Uh, no," Gallegos said. "We didn't think we could get anyone in there."

"So how do we know where Sheikh Jubail is?"

"Well, we will know as soon as the attack starts. Their communications will give them away. We'll get all their radio and telephone transmissions."

"But you don't know now if he's even still in there?"

Gallegos nodded.

McCoy was appalled. "I thought they said they had a fix on him!"

"We did," Gallegos said, slightly abashed. "Until about midnight. Then he went silent. Probably asleep."

"Or else he realized what was happening and decided not to make it easy for us," McCoy said. "He could be anywhere!"

"Well," Gallegos said, "we're pretty sure he's in the mosque."

"Pretty sure?"

"We have all the exits covered," Gallegos protested. "We would have seen him if he'd left."

"Who's we?"

"Well, the Saudis. Their agents."

"So we're trusting the Saudis that he's still in the mosque?"

Gallegos flushed.

"The Saudis have a highly professional intelligence service—" he began.

"I'm sure the station here trained them," McCoy said.

"Of course."

McCoy shook her head. "That's reassuring," she snapped, not bothering to hide the sarcasm in her voice.

She strode to a window and looked out, trying to decide what to do. Something caught her eye.

"How many guards are we supposed to have out there?" she said to Gallegos.

"Two platoons," he responded. "We thought any larger number would attract too much attention."

McCoy counted carefully. "Well, you may have the opposite problem. I only count about eighteen out there."

Gallegos joined her at the window and peered out. He coughed nervously.

"I'll go out and see what's going on," he said. "They're probably just on patrol in the neighborhood."

Right, she thought. And the Russian soldiers who deserted the Romanovs just stepped out for vodka.

It was time, she knew, to make a decision. The helicopters were in the air. They would be landing in ten minutes in the plaza in front of the mosque.

She turned from the window and walked over to the communications table. "Get me the NSC," she said. "And patch Strouder in."

The tech, a short, stocky man whose name was Martin, nodded emphatically. In ten seconds she was holding the receiver and talking to Henry Hoffman.

She could imagine him, Walters, Barrett, and the president sitting around the chestnut table in the Situation Room, their faces pallid underneath the bright lights mounted in the ceiling. She could see the clusters of aides sitting unobtrusively against the dark, paneled walls, proud simply to be in the room at a moment of crisis, functionally anonymous.

The thought flashed through McCoy's mind that that was where she belonged, back against that paneled wall. She didn't want to be here, taking responsibilities that no one should have to shoulder, making decisions that would affect, perhaps terminate, the lives and well-being of millions of people she didn't even know.

But that's the job you wanted. That's the job you pushed for, she reminded herself. She just wished that once in her life something would not evoke ambivalence in her.

She took a deep breath.

"Mr. President, Dr. Hoffman, I hate to be the one to tell you this, but I think we ought to call this operation off while there's still time," she said.

There was a long silence on the other end. Then came a burst of static, and Strouder responded. "That's the most chickenshit idea I ever heard," he sputtered, speaking from the staging area somewhere east of Mecca.

The silence from the Situation Room continued for another five seconds.

"What makes you want to abort, Des?" Hoffman said.

His voice sounded strained. McCoy could imagine him sitting at the table in shirtsleeves, his bow tie still tight against his collar, breaking paper clips in his fingers under the table.

McCoy marshaled her thoughts. If she were to pull this off, it would have to be with a brief, cogent argument.

"First, the mosque is filling up with pilgrims. If we go ahead, we're going to kill a lot of them."

"We've always known there would be collateral casualties," Strouder rebutted her.

"Not on this scale," McCoy said. "Second, we haven't monitored any communications from Sheikh Jubail for five hours."

"But he's still in the mosque," Hoffman said.

"We only assume that," McCoy said. "I'd say there's at least a twenty percent chance we could find that he's gotten out somehow. And third, I don't like the trend in the reports we're seeing. Support for Prince Ahmed is disappearing in Dhahran, in Riyadh, all over. I'm frankly not sure we can count on Qabos's men to cover the operation."

"They're warming up their helos right behind us," Strouder shouted. "Jesus! This woman doesn't know what she's talking about! She doesn't know operations, she doesn't know Arabs. She doesn't know shit!"

There was another minute of silence from the White House. McCoy realized how welcome her counsel was. No one wanted to hear a Cassandra on the verge of a commando operation.

If she was wrong, she realized, if the operation succeeded, her tenure at the White House would be over, her judgment exposed as weak and pusillanimous. And if she was right, if the operation failed, no one would want her around, either. She would only serve as a reminder that disaster could have been averted.

Detwiler spoke for the first time. "Colonel, I realize you're in a stressful situation. But don't resort to *ad hominem* attacks and watch your language."

Strouder was not abashed. "Sorry, Mr. President, but we've been through this before. This operation isn't going to be difficult. We're going up against amateurs. Qabos's men have every reason to fight. They know what's in store for them and their tribes if the Ikhwan takes over. Respectfully, sir, I request that you allow us to do what you've trained us to do."

She imagined that she could hear the sound of rotors beating, and she wondered if Strouder had given the order to take off. Once in the air, she knew, they were only three minutes from the touchdown point in the plaza south of the mosque.

Detwiler sighed heavily, a sound that clearly conveyed doubts over six thousand miles. McCoy did not envy him. She could imagine the calculus of interests: gasoline lines in the United States, depression of the economy, his own reelection chances on one side; and the fate of some Muslim pilgrims on the other. That was assuming Strouder's operation worked.

And if it didn't work? The consequences still would be gas lines in the United States, a possible depression, and a failed bid for reelection.

And if he called it off? The same.

She knew, looking at it that way, what he would choose.

"Well, I think the potential gains outweigh the risks, ladies and gentlemen. If we wait, the situation could deteriorate further. So it's a go," Detwiler said.

McCoy wanted to argue. She stifled it. She had done what she was paid to do. She had assessed the situation and given her advice. Now it was up to Detwiler.

"Good luck to you all," she said, and hung up the phone.

She moved to the window and looked out. The number of men in her Saudi guard, if she counted correctly, had dwindled to five.

CHAPTER 22

Peering into the black metal well by the copilot's right knee, at the screen that displayed the helicopter's projected aerial map, Strouder could see the four northwestern minarets of the Grand Mosque. The helicopter banked and he grabbed a shelf in the bank of the avionics equipment the air force people called the pizza rack. Otherwise, he might have pitched into the pilot's lap.

"Okay," he said, peering at the screen. "That's the landing area. Twenty-five meters inside the right-hand pair of minarets." Strouder still found it hard to trust the navigational displays on the screens in the cockpit. They were, in the end, just the product of computers and filmstrips. But the visibility through the cockpit windows was still very low. It was just before dawn.

"Have you over it in ninety seconds, Colonel," the pilot replied. His face was a pale green in the glow of the instrument panel, and his cheeks were drawn. Strouder could see his jaws clenching and relaxing.

But Strouder wasn't worried about the pilot. He knew his business. He could set this machine down on a palm tree in a hurricane if he had to. He would get them where they needed to be.

He was worried about the other part of the operation, his own team's part. Keeping his feet spread wide for balance, he sidestepped back into the cabin of the helicopter and surveyed his men. The sixteen commandos of Team D peered back at him. On the upper arms of their desert camouflage fatigues they wore the red insignia of the Saudi National Guard; underneath it, they were laden with body armor and a red-and-white checked *ghotra*, which they would don as they pulled out when the mission was completed. On their faces he could see the inevitable tension of men about to be launched into battle.

They were the backdoor team. The other teams would be landing in the plaza in front of the mosque and making their assault frontally. Team D, the most skilled unit of mixed navy and army commandos that CENTCOM had, would be striking where the Ikhwan did not expect to be hit, from the roof.

"Eddie, you ready?" he asked quietly.

Sergeant Eddie Fortelli nodded. He was the demolitions expert. "All checked out, sir."

He patted Fortelli on the shoulder. "You'll be the first out after me," he said.

"Just give me twenty-five seconds," Fortelli said. The operation plan allocated thirty.

"Good man," Strouder said.

Strouder raised his voice. "Everybody got their Walkmans on? Channel two?"

In unison, the men nodded. They were not, of course, Walkmans. They were minitransceivers that clipped onto a webbed belt and were connected, by means of a wire that ran up a man's back, to a pair of earplugs and a tiny microphone. That way, they could listen to and respond to Strouder without raising their voices in the labyrinth of rooms and corridors under the mosque's roof.

Strouder's own communications equipment was three pounds heavier, because it was designed to link him to the EC-130 reconnaissance plane that had, ten minutes ago, flown into position five thousand feet over Mecca, training its electronic surveillance equipment on the mosque. The EC-130 could hear someone hiccup into a phone. It could pinpoint the source of every call, every radio transmission from within the mosque. It would be like having a spy inside Jubail's command center, and Strouder did not begrudge the extra weight he would have to carry to gain the benefit of that intelligence. He had seen how useful it was.

The Grand Mosque was a two-story rectangle enclosing a courtyard 154 meters long and 72 meters wide; this they knew from KH-12 photos taken from space. To the north ran a long, covered corridor called the M'asa, the running place, where pilgrims reenacted the wanderings of Hagar, searching for water between the hills of Safa and Marwah.

The ground floor was the public space, areas for prayer. It was on the second floor that the Ikhwan had set up its headquarters, in space formerly used for an Islamic school. It was a warren of offices and classrooms and dormitory space. Somewhere within it they would find Sheikh Jubail.

That was what worried Strouder. The intelligence for this operation was soft. He had had to bargain and wheedle with Qabos for everything: floor plans and diagrams; permission to send scouts into Mecca to eyeball the scene; and particularly for permission to blow a hole in the roof. And every time it had been made clear that it was only with the greatest of distaste that Qabos contemplated allowing infidels to desecrate the Grand Mosque.

Strouder could live with that. But they had never managed to agree on a practical plan for getting someone inside the mosque in advance, and Strouder hated to conduct an operation in a building that had not been eyeballed thoroughly by someone he trusted. Floor plans were fine, but who knew how accurate they were?

His radio headset crackled to life with a message from the EC-130. "A, B, C, and E are down, entering the target. The rest are right behind them," the tech above them reported.

Strouder glanced at his watch. Right on schedule. "Okay," he whispered into his own mike. "Let's go."

The first rays of dawn, streaming from the east, momentarily stunned him as the rear ramp opened. The helicopter was precisely where it was supposed to be, ten meters over the flat roof of the mosque. Strouder grabbed the top rung of the rope ladder, descended hand over hand for about half its length, and jumped. He felt his boots land with a satisfying thump. Fortelli followed a second later.

Strouder could hear the shots and explosions below as the main body of the assault force attacked the mosque from the southwest portal. He could see parts of the city stretched out below him, a warren of four- and five-story apartment blocks, dun-colored in the light of the rising sun. The streets were empty, except for the pilgrims that McCoy had mentioned. Evidently, they had achieved surprise.

Fortelli had already sprinted to the inside edge of the roof and begun laying out his specialty, a circle of plastic ribbon explosive contained in an inverted V of steel casing. He called it Eddie's Spaghetti.

Strouder used hand signals to direct the remaining fourteen men on the team to form a perimeter defense around Fortelli. He didn't have to. They knew their jobs and were already doing them.

Fortelli leaped up and ran to Strouder's side. When he was in the clear, he turned and aimed a remote detonator at Eddie's Spaghetti. As he pressed the button Strouder closed his eyes.

The blast was curiously muted. Fortelli's handiwork directed nearly all of the explosive power downward. When the dust cleared, there was a circular hole in the roof about ten feet wide.

"Okay, after me," Strouder said. He ran to the edge of the hole and peered inside. There was one Ikhwan guerrilla lying sprawled below him. To make sure he was dead, Strouder aimed his H&K MP5 down the hole and squeezed the trigger. The weapon burped, the body twitched.

Score one for the visitors, he thought. But he knew the body meant that there might be other guerrillas, armed and irritated, waiting for them below.

So did Dirty Dicky Murphy, his second-in-command. Dicky tossed a flash-bang into the hole. Precisely five-tenths of a second later, it went off. It would stun and disorient anyone within fifty feet, and by the time their eyes started working again, Strouder would be on their level, his H&K wide open.

The mixed, acrid odors of Eddie's Spaghetti and the flash-bang filled his nostrils, a sensory signal that it was time to move. He jumped.

The landing was a surprise, on soft carpet. He did not get the expected bone-jarring when his feet hit the floor, but his boot sole caught in a wrinkle in the carpet and twisted his ankle. He could feel something tear inside the joint, and pain lanced up his leg.

He didn't mind too much. Pain was always part of close-quarters battle. It reminded him to pay attention.

Murphy was right beside him. Without speaking, they started establishing their fields of fire, Strouder to the left and Murphy to the right. The remaining men dropped in behind them, forming lines.

Immediately, the first intelligence failure presented itself to Strouder. According to the floor plan from Qabos, they were supposed to be in a large, bare room, a room of prayer within the Islamic school. But it had clearly been subdivided and turned into sleeping quarters. The floor was strewn with bedding and the room was perhaps a third the size they had expected.

Operationally, it did not matter. The timing of their plan was supposed to lure the bulk of the Ikhwan's fighters down to the ground floor, where the main assault was taking place, leaving only a remnant guarding Jubail for Team D to deal with. But the discrepancy between reality and the floor plan bothered Strouder. He did not like surprises, even though there were always going to be a few in even the best-planned operations. He felt his bowels tighten up.

"Okay, Dicky," he said to Murphy. "You know the plan. Room to room."

"Insh-fucking-allah," Murphy replied, and the line of commandos behind him split off to the right. Strouder led his team to the left, in the direction the EC-130 reports had suggested Jubail would be found.

They entered a corridor thirty meters long, lined with doors. It was what they had expected, but that was scant comfort. Room-to-room neutralization of an area like this was one of the nastiest jobs he knew of.

He moved to the first door and kicked it in. The hinges tore easily from the wood; it was old construction. As the door hit the floor Casper Kowalchuk, the whitest man in the platoon, his hair matted from a bad black dye job, tossed a flash-bang inside.

Strouder stepped inside, the H&K up in firing position, scanned the room in a split second, saw nothing, and inserted a frieze of bullet holes into the room's walls, crotch-high. Then he peered through the smoke. Empty, except for a few prayer rugs and tea glasses.

He decided, for the sake of speed, that it was worth risking splitting the team up into groups of three, each taking a different side of the corridor—one to kick the doors in, one to toss the flash-bang, and one to cover.

They worked their way down the corridor, spraying four empty rooms. The team had established a rhythm and was taking only about fifteen seconds per room. But Strouder was worried. There should have been some resistance by now.

Like an automaton, he kicked in the fifth door and waited, counting, one, two, three. This time Willie Duhon, the lanky Cajun sniper on his team, tossed in the flash-bang. Kowalchuk laid down the fire. He heard two sharp, piercing cries.

Strouder peered through the smoke. Two old men, white beards, unarmed. They'd been shot in the back; evidently they had been lying prone when he kicked the door down. Just to be certain, he rolled them over. Their eyes, wide open and pupils dilated, were normal. He was looking for a wall eye. He didn't see one. And he suspected that when he found it, it would be surrounded by bodyguards.

Kowalchuk was right behind him.

"Old dudes," he said. "Well, if they didn't want trouble, they shouldn'a been in this fucking place."

"Discriminate fire," Strouder reminded Kowalchuk. "You've got a half second to look. Use it."

Commandos were trained constantly to look before shooting, to make instant judgments, to discriminate among potential targets. But Strouder knew it was one thing to do that in a training exercise. It was another thing to do it in real close-quarters combat, where the other people were not shooting paint capsules.

He turned and looked out the window toward the courtyard below. He saw a scene of bedlam. The units entering through the southwest portal were meeting resistance, exchanging fire with Ikhwan guerrillas hiding in the pillared arcades that lined the courtyard. Some of the Americans were clustered around the Ka'abah, using it for cover. And all over the courtyard he saw the prostrate figures of pilgrims, their white garments stained red. The screams of the survivors rose through the air and into the window.

"Let's get moving," Strouder said.

The unit moved out, working its way down the corridor, cleaning four more empty rooms. They came to a junction.

He flipped to Murphy's channel.

"How's it going, Dicky?"

"No problems," Murphy replied. "Couple of tangos nailed. No resistance."

"Keep going right," Strouder said.

He flipped to the EC-130.

"Any sign of Jubail?"

"No, sir, we're not picking anything up yet."

Strouder felt a brief, tickling sensation of fear, a different fear than the sort he normally felt upon entering combat. In combat, he operated on the faith that he could minimize, even control the risks by superior preparation and planning. This was fear of a situation out of control.

"Listen harder," he said, realizing that he was nearly shouting and that his demand was irrational.

"Yes, sir, will do, sir," said the voice from the plane.

"It's fucked up, isn't it sir?" Kowalchuk asked.

"Not unless you start thinking it is," Strouder said. "Let's go."

The next corridor they swept yielded nothing, not even any old men. Murphy reported the same results, except that he had found an empty broadcasting studio, equipped for both television and radio.

"Keep looking," Strouder ordered.

They turned a corner and the walls fell away as they entered an enormous room covered in carpets, with pillars of marble and blue tiles on the walls. Strouder had spent some time in the *souks* of half a dozen Middle East cities, buying rugs. The one under his feet was of a quality he had never seen before. The reds were as bright as fresh blood, the blacks as dark as the desert sky on a moonless night.

It seemed to be a room used for prayer or instruction. He had seen once, in Cairo, a less opulent room of this size used as a place for religious seminars, with half a dozen groups of students clustered around different teachers in various corners.

It was the sort of room, he thought, that a man like Jubail would use. And against one wall, on low tables arranged in a U, he saw a few accoutrements of modern management—three computers, a couple of fax machines, a half-dozen telephones.

Staying low, he jogged to the tables and found that they were strewn with papers. His Arabic was almost entirely verbal because that was the sort of communication he needed to be capable of. But he could read enough to see that these were official documents of some sort, and he thought he recognized Jubail's name at the bottom of several of them. He scooped them up, folded them, and began to stuff them into a pouch in the right leg of his fatigues.

"Dicky, I think we may have found Jubail's command post," he said softly into his microphone.

"No sign of him?" Murphy asked.

"Not yet."

"Nor—"

The sound of machine-gun fire cut off Murphy's response. For ten seconds Strouder listened to the sound of a hail of bullets. He could hear the soft, muffled sound of Murphy's H&K. But he could hear other sounds as well. Murphy must have stumbled onto a major group of Ikhwan.

"I'm hit, Mac," Murphy groaned. "So's Rodriguez."

"Hang on, Dicky," Strouder whispered. He switched to his link with the plane overhead and demanded a reading on Murphy's position.

"About a hundred and fifty meters from you in corridor C," said the tech, referring to the mosque diagram that the entire operation was using.

Strouder pointed out the direction to his men. But before they could leave the headquarters room, a burst of fire from the opposite end cut Kowalchuk down.

Strouder instinctively hit the floor, rolled, and came up firing. He heard a moan and the clatter of a rifle hitting the floor. He took a position behind one of the computer tables Jubail had been using and peered out.

A fusillade pinned him back against the wall. Across the room, he could see Duhon pinned in a similar position. They had reached a temporary stalemate. The Ikhwan couldn't get them without coming into their field of fire. But neither could they move.

There was a window up against his ear, and he cast a quick glance downward. What he saw caused him to teeter for a second on the edge of panic.

The units in the courtyard around the Ka'abah had changed their positions. Some were still firing into the building, at the Ikhwan. Others, though, had turned around and were directing their fire out of the mosque, toward the plaza from which they had entered.

"We're pinned," he said to the EC-130. "And what the hell's going on on the ground? Where are the Saudis securing the fucking perimeter?"

"Not sure I can tell you, D leader," the tech said. "They seem to have disappeared."

CHAPTER 23

Burke squatted in the crevice between a *miswak* bush and the cement foundation of an apartment building across the plaza from the Grand Mosque, trying to see without being seen. The air around him was hazy with acrid smoke and still vibrating with the shrieks, the cries, and the curses of pilgrims. Though most had fled, some of them lingered on the edges of the plaza, shouting at the backs of the troops attacking the mosque. Several times, Burke had seen unarmed men run madly toward the commandos, leaping on their backs and flailing away with fists until the butt of a rifle had cracked them across the forehead, leaving them stunned on the dusty pavement until friends had arrived to help them get up and limp away. Once he had seen two women make this kind of suicidal charge. He did not envy the soldiers carrying out this mission.

Inside the mosque, he could hear the sound of constant gunfire, like the contrapuntal strings of a symphony, varying occasionally in pitch and intensity but always there. He had become almost inured to it. He was engaged in smaller things, like counting the bodies of pilgrims being carried from the mosque, massaging the cramping muscle in his right thigh that caused him periodically to extend his leg from behind the bush, and composing, in his mind, the story he would file.

He looked at his watch. Twenty minutes had passed since the assault began, and he had about an hour until the next edition of the *Tribune* closed.

He was no expert in military matters, but he would have thought that the assault would be over by this time. It was clearly intended to work quickly, using surprise.

For the first time he heard shots coming from behind the plaza, and he craned his neck to see. A squad of six guerrillas, dressed in the mixed assortment of *ghotras*, turbans, and fatigues he had seen on the rebel fighters in Riyadh, made its way out of a side street and began sprinting across the plaza, zigzagging, firing wildly at the portals in the southwest corner of the mosque. The leader of the six men reached the entrance, ducking to one side as he inserted a fresh clip into what looked like an AK-47. Then he bounded into the center of the portal and fired a long burst in the direction of the Ka'abah within. An instant later a round of fire from inside cut him down. But his comrades had reached the portal area behind him, taking shelter in the western wall.

One of them, he saw, had lugged a box of grenades and a launcher with him, and he was setting it up. A few seconds later he aimed the launcher inside the mosque and fired it. Then he was cut down by the answering fire from within.

Burke hunched lower behind the bush. Until this time all the fire had been going in one direction. Now, clearly, it was a two-way fight, and more Ikhwan guerrillas were sprinting into the plaza. Whatever had been holding the perimeter secure for the American commandos had evidently collapsed. Soon enough, he realized, bullets would be flying in all directions.

He spotted a pair of buses parked at the side of the plaza, buses that had evidently brought aging pilgrims to the mosque that morning. They would block his view in one direction, but they might serve as better shelter. He rose to a half squat and scurried toward them, trying to stay in the shadows of the building.

He sniffed the air and smelled something different. His eyes started to water. Tear gas, he thought. That must have been what was in the grenade that the Ikhwan had launched into the mosque. He imagined that the Ikhwan was still taking its weapons where it could find them. He pulled the red-and-white *ghotra* he had found in the helicopter in the desert from his pocket. He tied it around his head to cover his mouth and nose.

There were at least a hundred Ikhwan men in the plaza now, and he could hear, over the sound of rifle fire, their shouted affirmation that Allah was great. He could imagine that, to them, no martyrdom could be more glorious than death met in an effort to free the Grand Mosque.

Overhead, he heard the beating rotors of a helicopter, then a second pair. He guessed that the commandos inside the mosque had called for help, and he flattened himself against the ground.

He could see two of the black choppers homing in on the plaza, flying no more than one hundred feet over the rooftops of the city, one from the east and one from the north. When they were a few hundred yards from the plaza, he saw the guns mounted underneath their fusilages start to fire. Little puffs of dust and shards of rock began to rise from the stones in the plaza as the bullets hit.

The helicopters evidently knew exactly where to direct their fire, because they all but pirouetted when they were over the plaza, turning their cockpits toward the southwest portal, where the guerrillas had clustered, trying to fight their way into the mosque. They hovered there like great avenging birds, and he could see the bodies of some of the rebels literally torn in two by the heavy barrage of bullets they laid down.

Suddenly one of the helicopters exploded.

Burke had seen, he thought, a brief flicker of flame rising rapidly toward the helicopter, just before it burst into an orange fireball and disintegrated. Pieces fell to the square.

A Stinger, he thought—the surface-to-air missile that the CIA had supplied to the *mujahedeen* in Afghanistan to turn around their war against the Soviets. Now it was being employed against the United States by the *mujahedeen*'s allies, the Ikhwan.

As if to confirm this, he saw the second helicopter drop a series of flares as it rose rapidly from the plaza. Another rising missile took the bait and veered away from the helicopter, chasing a flare.

But the damage was done. Burke could hear triumphal screams from the guerrillas filtering into the plaza. A figure, his back on fire, emerged from the largest piece of wreckage, the cockpit, lurching blindly. He was shot as soon as his feet touched the ground. Guerrillas gathered around the flaming wreckage, firing into it. Burke saw one of them cut down by bullets from his own side.

It reminded him of the danger stray bullets were beginning to pose. He flattened himself against the ground, watching the battle as best he could from underneath the bus. He was, he noticed, starting to sweat. The dust from the street mingled with the tear gas in the air and he coughed. His chest heaved and spasmed with coughing until he was out of breath and tears were running down his cheeks.

Then he heard yet another helicopter overhead. He looked up. The gap between the bus and the buildings lining the plaza gave him a clear view of the east wing of the mosque, and he could see the chopper edging down toward the roof, dropping flares. A Stinger rose from the ground, chased a flare, and disappeared. Rifles fired from the alleys near the mosque, sounding like boxes of firecrackers going off on the Fourth of July. Another Stinger rose from the ground and barely missed the helicopter, swerving at the last instant to chase a flare.

Now he could see figures on the rooftop, waiting for the chopper to land. One of them ran to the edge of the roof, dropped to one knee, and began firing at the guerrillas on the ground. Burke squinted through the smoke.

It was Strouder, trying to cover the helicopter's approach.

Slowly, the helicopter eased toward the roof. It was big and an easy target. Burke heard two hollow *thunks* from the alleys to the east, and then something tore into the chopper's tail section. He did not know weaponry, but he suspected this must have been some kind of rocket-propelled grenade that did not have a heat-seeking warhead. At this range, it was more effective than the Stinger.

The helicopter, its tail rotor stopping like a windmill on a calm day, lurched to the right and crashed into the facade of a building across the street from the mosque. Then it fell heavily to the ground.

Burke felt the ground shake with the impact. He closed his eyes and shuddered.

All around him, he saw signs that this assault had become a fiasco. The Ikhwan guerrillas now seemed securely entrenched around the southwest portal of the mosque, but they were advancing no farther. Clearly, the plan to evacuate at least some of the attackers from the roof had failed. It looked like a bloody and calamitous stalemate that, in time, could only tilt toward the rebels.

Burke looked at his watch. There were only thirty minutes left before the city edition closed. He would have to go with what he had.

He felt the phone in his pocket and began crawling away from the plaza. Once clear of the sheltering shadow of the bus, he got down on his belly and started to squirm. Ahead of him, two guerrillas carried the body of a third toward a building that he had taken for an apartment. He looked to the right and saw that he had been wrong. It was a hotel, and the plaque by the door, in several languages, identified it as the Zahrat Mecca. He rose again to his hands and knees and crawled past it.

Next to it was another large hotel, and in between them was an alley. Burke waited for a moment when he heard no bullets whining, straightened up, and sprinted for it. The *ghotra* fell from his head, leaving only his knit cap. He did not go after it.

He felt as if he had entered a maze. The alley, only about forty yards long, led to another alley, paved in cobblestones. There seemed to be no streets. The buildings around him were all three or four stories high and jammed so close together that they kept the alley shaded and almost cool. To his right, a group of six or eight guerrillas had taken shelter behind a delivery truck and were scanning the sky, looking for more helicopters.

His body was trembling, his hands shaking, and he thought that the guerrillas would surely notice this and realize that he was not supposed to be there. But they were preoccupied with the larger game to be had in the skies, and did not even look at him.

He felt relieved, foolishly glad just to be out of the plaza and away from the bullets, and he reminded himself that he was still in an extremely unfriendly neighborhood.

The building to his left and across the alley seemed to contain some sort of pharmacy, with living quarters occupying the upper floors; it had a picture of a mortar and pestle in blue plastic on a white field over the small, shuttered window. Next to it was a gated entrance. He tried the gate. It was unlocked.

He stepped inside and slowly closed the gate behind him. He looked at the upper stories of the buildings around him. Their windows were shuttered and he saw no signs of life within, save for an air conditioner mounted in a wall that was still humming and some towels hung on a line to dry. The inhabitants, he guessed, were either out on the streets or under their beds.

Burke hunkered down in the shadow of the closed gate, pulled out the phone, and dialed the *Tribune*. On the first try, he got through to Graves.

"Burke! You make it to Jedda?"

"I wish," he said. "I'm in Mecca."

"Mecca! How the fuck did you get there?"

"I thought I might as well make the goddamn *hajj* while I was in the neighborhood, Ken," Burke hissed. "I don't have much time and I've got a story to dictate."

"What's it about?"

"American commandos tried to storm the Grand Mosque this morning. Right now the attack has bogged down and it looks like they're stuck in there," he summarized.

"Holy shit," Graves said. It was the highest compliment he paid.

"I better dictate."

"Can you speak up?"

"No."

"But there's a racket in the background."

"Those are guns, Ken."

"Oh. Okay. You can whisper. Dateline Mecca?"

"Yeah."

He thought for a few seconds about something grandiloquent for the lead on this story, something about the smoke and the torn metal, the red blood on white garments and the minarets. He decided against it. This story would supply its own grandiloquence. It demanded a factual telling, unadorned, like the pyramidal stories *The Oakland Tribune* had taught him to write about bank robberies and school-board meetings.

"American commandos attacked the Grand Mosque, holiest site in Islam and seat of Saudi Arabia's—no, make that Arabia's, delete Saudi—rebel government this morning. But after two hours they were trapped inside the mosque by a counterattack," Burke began.

He described the initial helicopter landings, the dead pilgrims being carried from the area around the Ka'abah, and the subsequent Stinger and RPG hits on the choppers.

"Wait a minute," Graves said. "You saw all this?"

"Yeah."

"How'd you know they were Americans? The Pentagon's saying they're not doing anything."

It was a key point, and it would need all the evidence he could muster. He told Graves about his encounter with Strouder in jail, the helicopter crash in the desert, and seeing Strouder again on the rooftop.

When he spoke of the crash, he swallowed hard. He hoped Graves wouldn't ask him what time the crash occurred and then ask him why he hadn't said anything about it in their last conversation.

But Graves did.

"You saw that chopper crash? When?"

Burke gave him the time. He couldn't fudge it. It would come out eventually.

"And we talked after that and you told me you hadn't seen anything."

He thought about McCoy and feeling alone and how that would sound to Graves on the other end.

"Sorry, Ken. I just couldn't take the responsibility for blowing their plans."

Now Graves was enraged.

"Shit, Colin! That's not your call to make! We might've sat on it, too. Probably would have. But that's our judgment. And if you'd reported it and we'd published it, the folks in the White House might not have gotten their dicks caught in this crack!"

"I know," Burke said. "I'm sorry."

"You had a Pulitzer in your hands," Graves said. "And you blew it. Lyle's not going to like this."

"Well, screw him," Burke snapped. His patience evaporated. He felt very tired. He noticed that his voice had risen.

"Let him come out to the desert and wander around and make that judgment and we'll see how smart he looks."

"Calm down," Graves said. He sounded sympathetic.

Burke simmered, but his anger was spent. So was just about everything else.

"That's about all I can give you, Ken."

"What kind of shape are you in? Can you call with an update? We'll have the printers stay late and replate the final. And this time can we use your byline?"

"Why not?" Burke said. "It's not going to help anyone find me. And I'll try to call and update the piece."

He heard the squeal of brakes as a vehicle of some kind stopped in the alley. He heard doors open and shut.

"Only if it's not risky," Graves continued.

The gate Burke was using for cover burst open, and four rifle barrels pointed at his head. Four Ikhwan guerrillas were aiming them.

And behind them, Burke could see a white van with a rotating antenna on the roof. It was a truck designed to pinpoint the source of cellular-phone transmissions. He wondered which American contractor had sold it to the Saudis and how it had fallen into Ikhwan hands.

"Uh, Ken," Burke said. "I think you can let the printers go home."

CHAPTER 24

At least, Burke thought, he was not yet in a cell.

The room was a small, bare adjunct to what appeared to be an ad hoc military command post half a mile from the Grand Mosque. A dusty, worn carpet covered the floor. It showed signs of wear from a desk and chair, but those had been removed. There was an empty file cabinet and a few pale rectangles, framed by grime, on the beige walls. Portraits of the Saudi kings must have hung there, he figured. It seemed to be the former office of a petty bureaucrat—a police lieutenant, maybe, or a captain in the local detachment of the National Guard. But the door was stout and securely locked. The window was tightly shuttered. A ceiling fan turned lazily overhead. In the distance, he could still hear the sound of battle, though the firing had grown more sporadic over the past hour.

He felt filthy. His captors had taken his clothing, his phone, his wallet, his passport, even his shoes, and given him a pair of trousers and an old smock that was, if anything, even grimier than the ones he had been wearing. They had, however, allowed him to scribble a note to Sheikh Jubail, requesting another interview. He had little hope that Jubail would get it, but there was nothing else he could think of to do. He thought that while they considered it they might forgo punishing him. He did not know what the punishment would be, but he told himself he did not feel afraid of it.

There had been times, he thought, when he might have felt afraid of it, times when he might have worried about how it would have affected his ability to support his family or secure the next job. But he no longer cared, or had to care, about much. He thought he feared only two things now, physical torture and his own censure. He did not think they would torture a foreigner, even an infidel caught in Mecca. They could put him in a cell, but he had gotten resigned to being alone with his thoughts. He found them decent company.

He had done one thing worthy of his own censure, failing to report what he knew after seeing the helicopter crash in the desert. It would not be pleasant to meditate on what might have happened if he had reported what he had known, on his responsibility for what was happening on the streets outside. But he had acted with good intentions, and he believed in the centrality of intentions. If they locked him away for a while, he could live with himself. It would be no worse than going back to Washington to be chewed out by Lyle Nelson and excoriated in the *Columbia Journalism Review*. It was like a choice between vacationing in Siberia and vacationing in Mongolia.

He heard footsteps in the corridor outside; they stopped at his door, and a key was inserted into the lock. He thought they had come for him and his stomach turned over. He smiled involuntarily at his persistent capacity for self-deception. Everything he had told himself was true, more or less, except for one thing. He was afraid.

The door opened, and Desdemona McCoy stepped inside.

She did so unwillingly. Two Ikhwan fighters, almost leering at their close proximity to an unveiled woman, pushed her by the elbows. She caught sight of him, and he could see the surprise and consternation spread across her face. The door closed behind her, and the lock clicked shut.

He stared at her for a moment. Her makeup was gone and her clothes were dirty. She still looked good. He got up, and for a second they faced one another, unable to find words.

"You're supposed to be in Aqaba," she finally said.

It was what he wanted to hear her say.

"Must've taken a wrong turn somewhere," he replied lamely.

They stepped toward each other. She felt warm in his arms. Her hands came up over his shoulder blades and she squeezed.

"Oh, Lord," she said, "I shouldn't say this, but it is good to see you."

"I can't think of anyone I'd rather share a cell with," Burke said. He inhaled her, the sweet scent of her hair and skin.

She pulled back far enough so she could see his face. Her eyes were wide and brown. "How did you get here?"

"Same as you, apparently. Under guard," he said.

She smiled, almost involuntarily. "That's not what I meant. I mean to Mecca."

He scowled. "Your friend dumped me in the desert. Said the orders had changed. I had to try to find water. Mecca had the closest spigot."

"What?" She seemed dumbfounded.

He repeated the story.

"Strouder," she said. "He's the only one who could have done it. Those guys have their own intelligence networks. Jawar must be part of his."

He believed her. He didn't really care whether she was telling the truth. He wanted to believe her.

Without speaking of it, they sat down next to each other on the floor, their backs propped against the wall.

"What happened to you?" he asked.

He could almost watch her brain working, calculating how much she could tell him.

"Let's just say I was here and I miscalculated someone's ability to provide security."

"Like Strouder and the guys in the Grand Mosque," he said, for no reason other than to let her know that he knew.

Her eyes widened.

"I was out there," he said. "I saw them."

"And if and when you get out of here, you're going to file a story about it," she said.

But there was something in her voice that had changed. He could sense that she didn't care anymore whether he broke their secrecy, maybe even wanted him to.

"I already did," he said.

She nodded and smiled. "You're good at what you do, you know that?"

"Not good enough," he said. "I could have done something about it a day and a half ago, but I didn't."

He told her how he had first learned of the Americans' involvement in the mosque attack, and that he had decided not to report it. He left out the role she had played in his calculations.

Ruefully, she shook her head. "I wish you'd reported it," she said.

"Now you tell me," he said.

"But your intentions were good."

"So I keep telling myself," he said. "I get paid for being right, not for intentions."

He put an arm around her shoulders and she leaned closer to him. He let her stay there for a moment, then he pulled away.

"What's the matter?" she said.

"You mean besides the fact that we're being held captive by a revolutionary Islamic government?"

She smiled and nodded. "Besides that."

"Well," he said, "I was just thinking that it's too damned bad you were right about our lives being incompatible."

His words surprised him. He was hoping, he realized, that she would say no, he was wrong. He disliked being oblique. But the direct approach had gotten him nowhere. What surprised him was how persistent his desire for her was.

But she was not open to that kind of manipulation.

"Right now," she said, "I'm not sure how relevant that is. We're in serious trouble, Colin."

Hurt, he fell back on sarcasm.

"I know. I'm afraid they might cut off my typing fingers."

She moved away from him and sat straight up, staring at the floor beyond her feet.

"Colin, I love the way you make me laugh, but stop joking about this."

"If I didn't joke about it, I might have to cry," he told her.

She nodded sorrowfully. "We've got to have a plan," she said.

"What do you have in mind?" he replied. "I'm afraid the cavalry is already busy."

"There must be some way."

They heard footsteps in the corridor again. Then a key turned in the lock and the door opened.

It was the same pair of guerrillas who had prodded McCoy into the cell. But behind them was a short young Arab with a neatly trimmed beard whom Burke recognized. It was Talal, Jubail's translator.

"If I'm not mistaken, the sheikh has decided to talk to one of us," he said to McCoy.

One of the guerrillas grabbed Burke by the shoulder and nearly pulled his dirty smock off as he forced him to his feet.

"Looks like it's me," Burke said to McCoy.

Her face, he saw, had frozen into the same neutral mask she had

had on when she entered the room, the only face she would show to her captors.

"Lyublyu tebya," she whispered to him.

It was Russian. It meant that she loved him. He realized she was saying it that way because she did not want the Ikhwan to know of their relationship, because she thought that she, as a spy, was going to fare worse than he, as a journalist.

He wanted desperately to say something back, but he could see Talal straining forward to hear as the guards turned him around and led him out.

"Hello, Mr. Burke," Talal greeted him in the hall. "What was that she just said?"

"Oh, it was about a fellow named Lou who was trying to pass the bar examination, but he blew it," he said. He willed himself not to look backward at McCoy. He heard the door shut again.

Talal looked suspiciously at him.

"A mutual acquaintance?"

"Yes. Someone on the White House press staff."

Talal seemed to accept it. He opened a door on the right and gestured for Burke to enter. The two guards followed him as he did.

It was a locker room, presumably for the policemen who worked from this building. There were two sinks at the far end.

"You may wish to clean yourself," Talal said.

"Almost as much as I wish to be out of here," Burke said. In fact, he did not. He was still remembering her last words to him.

He turned the water on and let it run over his hands for a moment, then his arms. He cupped his palms and started splashing water on his face, then rubbing it in. He could see the grime from his body cloud the water as it bubbled over the drain before disappearing.

A couple of thin towels were draped over a rack on the side of the sink and he grabbed one. It felt stiff and starched against his skin, but he was grateful for it. He rubbed until his skin felt chafed.

"You still working for the sheikh?" he asked Talal when he was finished.

"I am privileged to translate for the Enlightened One," Talal replied.

The sheikh's new title suggested to Burke that he was consolidating his control over the revolution.

"And he wants to talk to me?"

"He has decided to publish another interview."

Burke reflexively started to correct the man, to tell him that the newspapers published interviews. Politicans gave them. But he let it pass.

Talal opened a locker. An old khaki poplin suit, a shirt and tie, and some shoes and socks were inside.

"You will put these on, please," he said to Burke.

Burke was startled, but not unhappy to comply.

"You'll burn these, I hope," he said to Talal as he tossed his clothes into a corner of the room.

The suit did not fit properly; the shirtsleeves stopped about halfway between his elbows and his wrists. The shoes were loose. He looked at himself in the mirror.

"Well, I guess Ralph Lauren hasn't opened a store in Mecca yet," he said. "It'll have to do."

They left the locker room and turned right, out a back door and across an alley. Then they were in a school, what the Arabs called a *madrasseh*, a seminary. In the rooms to his left and right, he could see occasional clusters of young scholars gathered around older men, listening.

But as they progressed he began to see more soldiers, and the knots of people in the hallway thickened. They all seemed to be engaged in animated conversations, and they interrupted them to stare at him curiously.

"It looks like the Enlightened One's entourage is growing," he said to Talal.

"Oh, yes, everyone wants to be near him."

"I'm not surprised," Burke said.

Talal opened half of a high, double door and motioned for Burke to step inside.

It was a small audience room. A single gilded chair, in the nature of a throne, had been placed on a platform about two feet high. Two smaller chairs had been placed before it, with a pen, a notebook, and a tape recorder resting on the seat of one of them. The occupants of those chairs would be in the deferential position, looking up at the occupant of the gilded chair. Burke had no doubt who that would be.

In the back of the room, an Arab was setting up a television camera on a tripod. Two studio lights were already burning. Burke understood why he had been asked to change clothes. He was going to be playing a role in a staged event, and he had to be properly costumed. He was to play the infidel, sitting at the feet of the Enlightened One, hearing the new terms on which Arabia would deal with the world.

"If I had known you were going to televise this, I would have asked to see a tailor," he said to Talal. The Arab did not smile.

"Please, be seated," he said. He gestured at the chair.

Talal sat next to him. "Please refrain from trying to shake hands with him when he enters," he whispered.

A side door opened, and three armed guards entered. They wore fatigues, *ghotras,* and they carried, in addition to rifles, curved scimitars hanging from their belts.

"Why not shake hands?" Burke said.

"You are unclean," Talal whispered.

Burke looked at his hands. They were not that bad.

"In the religious sense?" he asked Talal.

Talal nodded.

Burke thought again, suddenly, of McCoy. There had to be something he could say to the sheikh that would help her. He could not think of what it might be.

He kept his eye on the open side door and saw shadows playing on the wall in the corridor outside. There was a bustle of footsteps. Four more security guards entered the room, followed by a couple of wizened men with gray beards. Only when these acolytes had taken their places did Jubail enter.

He looked just as he had the last time Burke had seen him. The rough cloth of his robe, the wrinkles in his face, and the jaundiced tinge of his wall eye, though, had begun to seem more ascetic against the backdrop of power and influence that was growing around him. He would, Burke suspected, project himself well over television in this culture.

Talal rose and bowed stiffly from the waist. Burke rose, but did not bow.

Jubail moved slowly to the gilded chair above them; he wore an odd pair of shoes with pointed toes and no heels. Burke imagined they were easier to slip off when entering a mosque.

Jubail did not seem to notice Burke, but sat down with an abstracted look. He began to speak. Burke punched the record button on the tape machine he had been provided.

"In the name of God, the almighty and the merciful," Talal began.

"You are trespassing in a city that is forbidden to you," was the next phrase Burke heard. He swallowed.

"So are the soldiers of your government, shedding the blood of pilgrims and desecrating the Grand Mosque."

Now Jubail was looking over his head, as if Shrouder and the commandos were also before him. The good eye was focused on the distance and the wall eye peered obliquely at Burke.

"They wear the uniforms of the former corrupt regime as if to fool us," Jubail continued. "But God cannot be fooled."

Slowly, Jubail turned his head so that the good eye was staring into Burke's face. Burke had the sensation of being sized up by a cyclops. He spoke in a tone that was slightly less stilted, more personal.

"I have been told you are a CIA agent," Talal translated. "Yet the interview with me that you published was truthful. The report you dictated to your newspaper this morning said that American soldiers were involved in the attack. Why did you say this?"

Burke realized that everything he had said to Graves must have been recorded. He wondered what the right answer was to this question.

"I am not a CIA agent," he said. "I reported what I did because it was accurate."

After hearing the translation, Jubail appeared to consider it for a moment. Then he responded. Burke thought he detected a note of uncertainty in the man's voice.

"The media in your country are opposed to the government?"

"Some are. Some are for it. Most try to be independent."

"But your newspaper is in a conspiracy against President Detwiler."

It was a statement, not a question. No doubt it reflected what Jubail had been told for years. Burke realized that he had a slight advantage due to the fact that he had accurately portrayed Jubail's interview. He did not want to squander it by arguing with the man, but he did not want to lose it by compromising himself, either.

"I don't know of any conspiracies," he said.

Jubail became angry. The skin on his face flushed and reddened, the thin lips turned downward, and his tone became grating.

"You are wrong. Your newspapers and television are in conspiracy against Islam, always smearing Islam, always in favor of the Jews."

Burke felt as if he were standing on a frozen pond, listening to the ice crack underneath him.

"I don't know of any conspiracies," he repeated. "Perhaps if you stopped arresting reporters you might see more positive stories."

As Talal translated this answer Burke could see Jubail's entourage frowning and whispering among themselves. He did not think they were expressing admiration for the erudition of his answer.

Before Talal finished, he started again.

"But I'm sure there are many practices of the old government here that you wish to change. Perhaps we could begin the interview by letting me ask you about them."

Jubail had opened his mouth, but stopped and let Talal translate. Then he spoke.

"No. I wish to speak of the unprovoked, sacrilegious attack by your army against the Grand Mosque."

At least they were no longer discussing media conspiracies.

"Would you please tell me your reaction to the attack," Burke said.

For ten minutes Jubail spoke in an angry monotone, pausing occasionally to allow Talal to translate. Burke realized the old man was performing for the television camera in the back of the room rather than answering, and he stopped taking notes, letting the tape recorder absorb it all.

"Arrogant . . . imperialist . . . evil . . ." The words washed over him. But he heard nothing to match the rhetorical excesses of the Iranian revolution, no calls for the downfall of the United States, nor any references to Satan.

Jubail, he realized, was in a curiously ambivalent position. On the one hand, he was working from a position of strength. He had escaped his own demise and cornered a detachment of American commandos. He could, if he chose, close the ring on them and kill at least some of them. Most of the world would cheer the Arabs on. Certainly the Islamic world would.

But he was dealing from inherent weakness, too. Crushing the American force in the mosque would invite a massive American rescue effort, one that the Arabs had no means to resist. Even if the United States did not directly intervene, it would usher in an era of hostility, of American boycotts and embargoes. If he had a tough, resilient people, he might hope to lead them through such a time. But he didn't. The Saudis had seen to that.

That explained the interview, he decided. Jubail wanted a deal. But Burke was the only American he could afford to be seen talking with.

He waited until the old man's wrath had ebbed, and interjected a question:

"What do you propose to do about the situation at the mosque?"

"God would allow us to kill them all, all the infidels," the sheikh said slowly.

"But what do you propose to do?"

"We would let them leave with their lives if"—Jubail reached for a sheet of paper in an inside pocket—". . . if the United States apologizes for the attack, withdraws all its forces from the Middle East, withdraws all its personnel from Arabia, stops arming the Zionists, and recognizes a Palestinian state."

Burke blinked. It was an opening bid. He wondered how much Jubail would insist upon at the end.

"And what will your oil policy be?"

"We have told you. We will cut production in half."

Burke wrote that down.

"For how long?"

"Until we decide to change it."

"And are you prepared to fight on if the United States rejects your terms?"

"The word of God is 'Fight for the sake of God those that fight against you, but do not attack them first. God does not love the aggressors,' " Jubail said.

"Do you—" Burke began another question. But Jubail cut him off.

"This is all we have to say. Publish it as we have said it," he instructed Burke. He turned and began walking slowly to the side door.

"One more thing," Burke insisted loudly. Jubail frowned and looked on as Talal translated.

"You know that there is someone here with whom you could negotiate directly."

Jubail looked puzzled.

"The American woman your men have taken captive. She works for the White House."

Jubail listened to the translation and said something in Arabic to the armed man who appeared to head his security detachment. The guard whispered and nodded.

"You mean the black woman?"

Burke nodded.

Jubail looked skeptical. "What is her position in the White House?"

"She's an adviser to the president on foreign policy," Burke said, lying only a little.

Jubail looked as if Burke had told him the president wore black lace panties underneath his suits.

"It's the way things are done in Washington," he said, trying to seem empathetic.

Jubail said something to the chief of the guard.

"He has sent for her," Talal whispered. Behind them, the television lights went off. Apparently, Jubail had ordered that as well.

Jubail returned to his chair. Burke's mind moved to the story he would write. This was a man people would be curious about.

"This was your school, your *madrasseh*?" he asked.

Jubail nodded.

"When did you start?"

"When I was ten years old."

"And you have studied and taught here ever since?"

Jubail nodded again. "For forty-five years."

"Have you ever been abroad?"

"Of course. I have taught in Bahrain and Yemen."

"And I had heard that your headquarters were in the Grand Mosque. How did you manage to get out of there?"

Jubail's face softened slightly and the suggestion of a smile flitted around his mouth.

"Nothing happens in this land that is not known to us," he said.

"So you were warned," Burke pressed him.

Jubail did not answer. A commotion outside the door interrupted the interview.

"I will not wear that!" a woman said. It was McCoy.

The door opened and she strode in, face set in angry lines. One of Jubail's security men trailed behind her, holding an *abaya*, still attempting to throw it over her head and shoulders.

"You might want to try it, Des," Burke said. "Surprisingly comfortable."

She glared at him. Then her face softened.

"So that was how . . . ?"

He nodded.

A trace of a smile flickered at her lips. "I'd have liked to see that."

"Play your cards right and I might oblige you," he said. "Sheikh Jubail was telling me about his terms for ending the siege at the mosque. I told him he didn't need to wait for the *Tribune* to publish them. He could negotiate right now with someone from the White House staff."

He turned to Jubail, whose face was frozen in disapproval. Someone needed to perform introductions.

"Sheikh Jubail, I have the pleasure to present Ms. McCoy," Burke said. "She works on President Detwiler's National Security Council staff at the White House."

He noticed the guard, still hovering close by with the *abaya*.

"Um, as you can see, she has a religious conviction against wearing the *abaya*. I hope you'll excuse her."

McCoy's face went through three distinct stages: a fleeting instant of shock at seeing Jubail; a second's dismay at the possible repercussions of the small scene she had created; and then an impassive, diplomatic face like the one she had worn while dealing with Ambassador Thorne and the Massouds.

She kept her hand extended backward, fending off the *abaya*.

"Your Excellency," she said, "as the apparent new leader of a member of the United Nations, I'm sure you are aware that diplomatic protocol requires tolerance of other nations' national dress."

That was a crock, as far as Burke knew. Diplomats in the Court of St. James had to wear what the Queen expected them to wear.

But it had the effect McCoy intended on Jubail, whose posture grew slightly more erect when he heard her refer to him as a leader of a UN member state. He waved the security guard away and sat down.

"He has terms for ending the situation at the mosque," Burke prompted. McCoy asked to hear them.

With the cameras off, Jubail cut the tirade from ten minutes to five. McCoy listened patiently. Then, without reference to his written list, he ticked off the conditions for allowing the commandos to leave.

"And we will cut oil production by fifty percent, to four million barrels," Talal finished translating.

Burke blinked. The oil production question had been a separate issue when he first heard it.

But McCoy seized on it.

"I am not acknowledging that American forces are involved in any attack on the mosque," she said. "But my government might be of service in separating the forces that are there and preventing further bloodshed. If the fighting continues, I cannot guarantee that there would not be massive intervention—" She paused to let the words be translated and sink in.

"—by outside forces," she continued, leaving the threat vague. "We might be able to help by supplying airplanes to evacuate those forces who wish to withdraw plus any other Americans. Your other proposals on Middle East policy are simply unacceptable, no business of yours," she said. "And there will be no apology. Moreover, we cannot endorse a cut to four million barrels a day. We insist on seven million."

Jubail took the bait.

"It must be four million," he said.

"Six million," McCoy countered.

"We will make oil policy for our country now," Jubail growled. "Four million."

McCoy shook her head. "Five million."

Now Jubail was fixed on the oil production question.

"Four million."

McCoy's body sagged. "All right. I will call my superiors and recommend that they accept four million and the other terms we've outlined."

Jubail's scowl deepened, but Burke could see that the advisers and security people in the room were happy. A couple of them smiled openly.

McCoy continued. "I'm sure you will want time to consult with your"—again she paused—"colleagues," she finished.

Jubail's lip curled. "No consultations are necessary," he said.

"Then I think we have an agreement," McCoy said, and stuck out her hand.

Jubail looked dubiously at it, as if she were a leper.

He turned and left the room. Burke had the impression that he knew exactly what he had done, that he knew that he had extracted from McCoy something that seemed to his entourage to be a concession but in fact was not. The Arabs would set their oil production to satisfy themselves. The Saudis had. So would the Ikhwan. But Jubail, he judged, had been more anxious for a deal than McCoy.

"I will get you a telephone," Talal said, and he shuffled off.

Burke and McCoy were alone—except for the guards that still surrounded them.

She looked drained. The skin around her eyes seemed almost gray and he realized how long she must have gone with little or no sleep.

He leaned closer to her.

"If I'm ever elected president, you're going to be my secretary of state," he whispered.

Her face brightened slightly. "Fat chance. But you think it was a good deal?"

"Not bad," he said. "I think he was afraid that he might be looking at Desert Storm Two if he didn't agree with you."

She nodded.

"I'm just disappointed," Burke finished, "that you couldn't get him to shake hands. Then he would have had to undergo a ritual cleansing. I'd pay to see that."

CHAPTER 25

Not even the interns, the college kids doing the grunt work, would look Burke in the eye.

He had stepped into indifferent newsrooms before. He remembered his first interview at the *Berkeley Barb*, feeling as if everyone in the room had urgent work to do except him. Newsrooms cultivated that atmosphere; they were like clubs, intimidating to nonmembers.

But he had never had the feeling that he had made everyone in a newsroom uncomfortable just by stepping into it.

The receptionist outside the elevator doors looked up from her gray metal desk long enough to identify him. Her eyes widened slightly, she nodded, and then she bent industriously over the crossword puzzle.

He faced the long, narrow room and all the desks and cubicles in it, lit harshly by a seemingly endless row of fluorescent fixtures in the ceiling.

All hands on the city desk, from the editor down, found something fascinating to read on their computer monitors as he walked by. The same thing happened on the national desk as he passed it, and then on the obit desk. The room started to feel like a gauntlet.

He had not expected the slaying of the fatted calf, but a few hellos would have been nice. He got none, not even from Graves, who sighed heavily as he saw Burke. But at least Graves looked at him.

"I should've brought back a case of leprosy, Ken," Burke said. "People would be happier to see me."

Graves was in shirtsleeves, his tie pulled down. He shook the last two pieces from a package of nicotine gum, popped them into his mouth, crumpled the package, and missed the wastebasket with it.

"You didn't see *Nightline* last night, I take it," he said.

"I was at the airport in Amman," Burke replied. "Trying to get a flight back here. I came here straight from Dulles."

"You look it," Graves said. "Where'd you get those clothes?"

Burke was wearing a gray pinstriped jacket and black stovepipe pants. The sleeves of the jacket fell to his knuckles and the pants stopped short of his ankles.

"In the *souk* in Amman. Best I could find in a few minutes," he said.

He sat down. "What was on *Nightline*?"

"Lyle Nelson," Graves replied. "Getting crucified over why the *Tribune* covered up what it knew about the attack on the mosque."

"Sorry," Burke said.

"That's not going to appease Lyle," Graves said. "It's bad enough you flout his authority and make your own decision on withholding that information. But then he gets humiliated about it on television. That fucking Koppel was so sanctimonious. And then they had some pissant journalism professor on saying he agreed with the *Tribune* reporter who withheld the information! If there's one thing Nelson can't stand, it's journalism professors."

Burke could imagine Nelson's anger. And he was not one to forget a slight. "I guess I better go face the music," he said.

"Not now," Graves said. "He had to fly to New York to meet with the suits. He'll be back tomorrow."

Graves shook his head. "Jesus, Colin. You were a hero. You had the Pulitzer bagged. Why'd you do it?"

Burke took off the cheap coat and sat down at his desk. Mail had piled up in the ten days he'd been gone.

"It seemed like the right thing to do at the time."

"Well, if I were you I'd claim you were suffering from heatstroke or something out on the desert," Graves advised. He paused. "Wouldn't have anything to do with Desdemona McCoy, would it?"

Burke blinked and tried, unsuccessfully he thought, to control a blush. He did not want to lie to Graves, but he did not want to admit anything, either. So he hedged.

"Why do you ask?"

Graves grimaced and chomped on his gum. "Been a lot of gossip, Colin."

"Why?" Burke was determined to wrest as much information from Graves as he could before he acknowledged anything.

"Well, you know, you obviously know her from that time in Russia, and then she shows up in this Saudi business. Her ass is in a sling, by the way."

"What do you mean?"

"You didn't get a chance to read the *Post* this morning." Graves tossed a copy of the paper across Burke's desk. It fluttered down and split into half a dozen pieces. "Check out the Big Crock o' Shit column."

Burke opened the paper and found it, top left, the most prominent position on the op-ed page:

BIGGS & CROCKETT

POINTING FINGERS IN THE MECCA FIASCO

A previously obscure National Security Council staffer bears the blame for last week's disaster in Saudi Arabia, according to White House and Pentagon insiders.

The staffer, Desdemona McCoy, is likely to be fired as soon as the White House completes its internal investigation. She may then face a congressional inquiry.

The mess in Mecca is the worst scandal to hit the National Security Council since the Iran-Contra affair more than a decade ago.

The repercussions, of course, have been enormous. The stock market nosedive of last week is only the beginning of the economic troubles sparked by the abrupt doubling of gasoline prices.

McCoy was the handpicked troubleshooter of President Peter Scott Detwiler in the Saudi crisis. But "she panicked under pressure," according to our sources.

McCoy, who was the senior American official on the scene in Mecca, "painted an overwhelmingly bleak picture of the military situation and failed to give the American forces there a chance to win," the sources said.

She is also suspected of being the source who leaked word to the *Washington Tribune* of the trial of an American intelligence asset. The report on that trial sparked the Arabian revolt. . . .

"Biggs and Crockett earned their nickname with that one," Burke said. He tossed the paper down on the desk.

"Maybe," Graves said. "But it's ass-covering time and someone is going to get screwed. McCoy looks like she's been nominated."

"It's not fair," Burke said. He could feel the anger in his voice and sense his face getting warm. "She got the best deal possible out of the situation. Those commandos were stuck. Now some bozo back in the White House second-guesses it and says they should've kept on fighting. But if they had they'd have all gotten killed. And so would a lot of people sent in after them. It's so easy to feed bullshit to some columnists—"

"Maybe you're not the most objective judge of that," Graves cut him off.

Burke ran a hand through his hair, distracted. He wondered where McCoy was at the moment, what she was thinking of the Biggs & Crockett column, but mostly how the damage to her career would affect his chances with her.

God, he thought, he was selfish.

"What do you mean?" he asked Graves.

"Oh, come on, Colin. Talk about bullshit!"

"All right," he said. "I've had a, um, relationship with her ever since St. Petersburg. But we had an understanding that we never talked about her work. She didn't tell me squat about the Massoud trial."

"What did she tell you about reporting on the crashed helicopters?"

"Nothing," he said. It was, technically, true.

Graves stared at him. Burke stared back, afraid to flinch.

"Look, Ken," he said. "I met her. I fell in love. I won't apologize for it. But she didn't tell me what to write. Ever."

Graves put his head in his left hand and shook it in mild disgust.

"Do me a favor," he said.

"Okay."

"When Nelson comes back tomorrow, don't tell him that you love this woman. Just say you were having an affair. It'll sound better."

There were, Burke thought, at least three people who had the information he needed to save his own job and maybe Desdemona McCoy's—Stokes Burnham, Candace Ross, and Prince Mishaal, the Saudi ambassador. He could not imagine any of them talking to him, let alone divulging anything. They might, under pressure, confirm with a word or a gesture something he had already learned. But he would have to learn it first.

Pondering, he went to the elevator, no longer conscious of the way people averted their eyes as he passed. He punched the button for the second floor, got out, and went to a bank of vending machines. He bought himself a diet Coke. He seemed to be constantly thirsty and the canned mix of water and chemicals was soothing. On the plane back from Amman, he'd drunk a dozen.

He walked across the hall to a door marked INFORMATION RESOURCES CENTER. When he'd started at the newspaper, this room had been called the morgue, and it was full of iron-gray filing cabinets; the cabinets were full of files; and the files were full of clippings. Now the files were stored somewhere in a basement, and the room he was entering looked like a data-processing center for an insurance company.

He approached a central desk and a plump black woman who was typing on a computer keyboard. She wore horn-rim glasses, jeans, and a T-shirt that celebrated the last Redskins' Super Bowl. A small plaque on her desk identified her as Constance Johnson. Burke gave her his name and she got up, slowly, from behind the desk.

"You can use this monitor and the same log-on password you use upstairs," she said, escorting him to another monitor at a desk fifteen feet away.

A display on the monitor said, *To start, press the screen*. He poked it with an index finger.

A menu appeared on the screen. He pressed *Log On*. When the machine asked for his password, he entered it: *Sam*. And when it asked for the subject of his search, he typed, *Ross, Candace*.

In a few seconds the machine replied that there was one recorded reference to Candace Ross in the *Tribune* files, a picture caption dated May 3, 1996. He called it up.

It was a picture from the Living section, showing a charity event at the Kennedy Center, a breast-cancer benefit. Candace Ross was seated between two men, Stokes Burnham and Prince Mishaal. She wore a black cocktail dress with a square neckline that stopped just short of revealing cleavage, accented by what looked to be a slender chain of diamonds around her neck. She was fashionably bony, with prominent cheekbones, and she wore her blond hair swept back from her forehead and down over her shoulders. She looked lacquered, and she could have been anywhere from twenty-eight to forty-eight. He would have bet she was from Texas, from one of those places where women wore their hair big and spent a lot of time on their nails. She was smiling. It was hard to tell, given the grain of the photo, but he would have bet she had perfect teeth. Burke didn't find the picture very attractive, but he could imagine that it was a matter of taste. Other men might. One, at least, apparently had.

He printed out a copy and took the elevator back upstairs to his desk. There, he pulled out his phone books: one for Washington, one for the Virginia suburbs, one for the Maryland suburbs. There were several columns of Rosses, but none of them had a Candace Ross. There were five Rosses identified by the initial *C*, two in the District, one in Arlington, one in McLean, and one in Silver Spring. Assuming she was single, the odds favored her living in the District rather than the suburbs. One of the District's C. Rosses lived on Buchanan Street NE. If it was Candace, she would be the only white person in the neighborhood, and she didn't look like the type. The other was listed at 2937 O Street NW, in Georgetown. He copied that address in his notebook. Then he walked across the newsroom to the city desk's territory and found their big, yellow reverse directory. He looked up 2937 O Street NW. *Ross, Candace,* it said.

He was impressed. Georgetown houses were not cheap.

He went outside. It had begun to sprinkle. The first fat drops of water were hitting the pavement, evaporating instantly. But there was a dark line of clouds rolling in from the west, and a thunderstorm was coming. Burke turned his face upward and let the rain splash on his nose.

He groaned when he rounded the corner. A pink parking ticket was clipped to the windshield of the Grand Marquis. He looked at the sign along the curb. NO STANDING, 3:00 P.M. TO 6:30 P.M., it said. He looked at his watch. It was 3:05. The District, he thought, would be a much more livable place if they put the parking enforcement people to work in city hall and put the city hall workers out on the streets to write tickets.

He stuffed the ticket in the glove compartment and pulled out into traffic, turning on M Street and heading for Georgetown. The scale of the buildings gradually diminished until he crossed the bridge over Rock Creek Park and entered Georgetown, where nothing was more than three stories high and the architecture was studiously Federal. He turned up Twenty-ninth Street and then left on O. Number 2937 was a small, flat-faced town house, its brick facade painted white and its shutters and front door black. Burke slowed down and looked around. The curbs on both sides were lined tight with cars. Two women pushed strollers along the sidewalk and a couple of kids wearing backpacks were chatting in front of the house across the street. There was a small deli on the corner. It was a busy block, and senior government officials were driven around the city in big, black Chryslers. Detwiler rode in a limo with a Secret Service escort. If anyone thought to dally with Candace Ross in this house, he would no doubt worry about being seen or about his car being seen.

Burke pulled around the corner and found the alley entrance behind O street. He drove through it. Neighbors on both sides could overlook Candace Ross's tiny backyard. She had no garage.

It didn't look to Burke like a good place for an assignation. Neither did anyplace in the neighborhood occupied by Burnham, Maxwell & Curran, which was on Pennsylvania Avenue between the Capitol and the White House. It would be hard to pick a place with more traffic. There was always the possibility, he thought, that the affair had taken place in a White House bedroom. In that case, he would be trying to get evidence on Detwiler himself. It would be hard to come by, though there might be Secret Service visitor logs. He didn't imagine Maynard Walters would part with them easily.

He pointed the car east and drove downtown, to Fourteenth Street, rain pouring down now, and parked in a garage. An office building of cream-colored stone and tinted glass occupied the corner of New York Avenue, a corner that once housed a strip club where the mayor had scored cocaine. As he checked the tenant list in the lobby, he saw that the building was full of lawyers and lobbyists. He was not sure it was an improvement.

The office he was seeking, the Foreign Agents' Registration Office, was on the ninth floor, behind glass doors that bore the seal of the Department of Justice. He walked in, presented his press card, and was seated at a small desk and a computer very similar to the one at the *Tribune*.

Enter search key word(s), the machine prompted him.

Burnham, Maxwell & Curran, he typed in.

No records, the machine replied.

Burke scratched his head.

Saudi Arabia, he typed in.

This time, the machine replied. Saudi Arabia's lobbyist was Burnham & Associates, located on the sixth floor of the Watergate office building on Virginia Avenue.

Burke wrote the address in his notebook. It made sense in several ways. The Watergate was right across the street from the large old life-insurance building that the Saudis had bought, gutted, lined with marble, and reopened as their embassy's chancery. For Stokes Burnham, having a separate entity handle Saudi lobbying probably kept his law partners from taking a big slice of the fees. And it insulated the law firm from criticism that might be involved in the Saudi account.

And there was a hotel in the Watergate complex.

Burnham & Associates, he typed in. A report came up on the screen.

Burnham & Associates conducts educational activities on behalf of the Saudi-American Research Fund, the report began. *Its purpose is to familiarize American government officials and media with Saudi Arabian history, culture, and issues of the day.*

There was nothing about winning congressional approval for the sale of F-15s, but he guessed that came under "issues of the day."

The report listed four people as active on the Saudi account: Stokes Burnham, Joseph Treen, Mollie Conti, and Candace Ross.

He pressed the button for the next screen. A list of activities Burnham & Associates had conducted for the Saudis came up.

It was all standard lobbying stuff. Burnham & Associates had helped keep the profit margins up at the Greenbrier Hotel and the Williamsburg Inn, entertaining congressmen at "seminars." They had organized press conferences at the Saudi embassy. They had helped Prince Mishaal host a series of dinners at Jean-Pierre, the French restaurant in the Watergate. And they had organized a concert by the Guarneri String Quartet at the Kennedy Center for the benefit of breast-cancer research, the one that had been pictured in the Living section. A nice way, Burke thought, to help keep the American feminists from complaining about American aid to a medieval patriarchy.

There was nothing specific about Candace Ross. Burke had not expected an entry noting that she had done her bit by screwing Secretary X of Department Y. But it would have been nice.

All that he had was a faint geographic pattern. All of the in-town activities revolved around the Watergate and the contiguous Saudi embassy and Kennedy Center.

He pressed the Print Screen button and waited for the information to reproduce itself on paper. He stuffed it in his notebook.

The rain had ended, leaving the air steamy. He drove home, turned on the air-conditioning, took a quick shower, and changed into a suit and tie. Then he drove down to the Mall, turned right on Constitution Avenue and right again on Virginia Avenue. The early-shift deskhands from the Interior Department and the Federal Reserve were headed home to Virginia and traffic was heavy.

Burke turned the radio to an all-news station. President Detwiler had abandoned consideration of a fifty-cent increase in the federal gasoline tax, a move that some advisers recommended as a way to dampen and cut back on panic buying and lines at filling stations. The newscast cut to an actuality.

"I'm glad the White House has come to its senses," Senator Higgins said. "There's been enough bungling of this situation already."

Meanwhile White House sources were saying that NSC staff member Desdemona McCoy would soon be relieved of her duties. That might be another way to find out who'd slept with Ross, he thought. Whoever was the leaker trying to make McCoy the scapegoat would have a good motive.

Burke drummed his fingers on the steering wheel and blew his horn at a Federal Express truck stopped in the right-hand lane opposite the Red Cross. The driver waved as he entered the building. He didn't move the truck. It was nearly four o'clock when Burke reached the Watergate.

The building had not aged well in the decades since it became famous as the site of the burglary that brought down the Nixon administration. Its pebbly, curved facade, made of precast concrete with exposed aggregate, had gone from beige to dingy. The fountains had poorly patched cracks. It was the architectural equivalent of the leisure suit.

But people still lived there, worked there, and, he hoped, trysted there.

He drove the Grand Marquis in through a break in the Watergate's facade, a tunnel dividing the hotel portion of the complex from the office portion. Half a dozen flags hung limp in the tepid, late-afternoon air. Flowers grew in a bed bordering a small, carefully clipped and tended lawn. A couple of black limousines stood, engines running, in the circular drive that fronted the hotel's white awning.

It was, Burke thought, the sort of place he would have chosen for an assignation if he were a government official and the assignee was a lobbyist with an expense account. The office building housed a few embassies. The hotel hosted its share of conferences and seminars and its entrance was off the street in any case. The restaurant attracted some of the town's gourmands. His presence here would attract no special attention. Neither would Candace Ross's.

He drove once around the drive, looking for anything that resembled a staff entrance. He saw nothing. He turned the car over to an attendant at the hotel garage, ignoring the fleeting look of disdain it elicited. Parking-garage attendants, he had discovered, were, like most Washingtonians, avid elitists.

Burke walked out past Saks-Jandel and down the street to the banks of the Potomac. No staff entrance.

He retraced his steps until he came to a bus stop and waited. An H-3 bus pulled up and two stocky women with black hair, black eyes, and coppery skin got out, each carrying a bulging shopping bag, chatting in Spanish. He watched as they walked through the tunnel and turned left, into the garage.

Burke waited thirty seconds and followed. "Gotta get something from my car," he said to the attendant, who looked up only long enough to recognize Burke and wave a finger vaguely toward the bowels of the garage.

He found the staff door and took up a position outside it, standing behind a pillar that he hoped would screen him from the garage attendant. The garage was dark and full of echoes from odd bits of sound; he could hear car doors slamming next to the porte cochere of the hotel, truck brakes squealing out on Virginia Avenue, and a few snatches of words coming from unseen mouths.

He felt uncomfortable with what he was doing, not because he had any moral qualms about exposing someone's secret affair, but because of the ignominy involved in slipping into a garage trying to prise information out of chambermaids and doormen. He was glad he didn't work for the *National Enquirer*. Of course, at the rate his career was deteriorating, that small pleasure might soon be denied him. The prospect, combined with the gloom in the garage, threw him into a minor depression and he thought about going home to Capitol Hill, turning the telephone off, and waiting for someone else to take the initiative. He stifled the thought, but not easily.

Then he heard footsteps coming down the corridor from the interior of the building, and he came to attention. His hand moved to the pocket of his jacket, and he pulled out the photocopy of Candace Ross's picture he had made from the computer archive.

The door opened, and to his disappointment, two men walked out. He had figured that women would be more talkative.

The men were a disparate pair. One looked like he came from the Asian subcontinent, perhaps Bangladesh. He had straight black hair and a translucent sheen to his skin. The other, tall and knock-kneed, seemed to Burke to be from western Africa. He had skin that was so dark it was almost purple, and the English he was speaking seemed to emanate from one of the old British colonies.

He stepped in front of them.

"Hi," he said, extending a hand. "I'm Colin Burke from the *Washington Tribune*. I know you guys have been working hard all day and you've got lots of things to do, but I wonder if I could ask you to help with a story we're working on?"

He was being as ingratiating as he could, but he could sense that he was about as welcome as Pat Boone on MTV. The men looked dubiously at him and his outstretched hand. They shrank back an inch and did not take it.

"What kind of story?" the Bangladeshi asked.

"It's a story about this revolution in Saudi Arabia," Burke said, trying to suck them in. "A little piece of the story might have taken place here in the hotel, and I'm trying to get confirmation. Where do you guys work?"

"I'm a waiter," the Bangladeshi said.

"I work in the kitchen," the African replied.

Burke focused on the Bangladeshi. "Ever deliver room service?"

The man nodded.

"Would you like to go somewhere for a drink or a cup of coffee?"

The man's eyes tightened and Burke could see the muscles in his jaws start to grind.

"I think you better go," he said. "Do you have permission to be here asking us questions?"

Burke stayed where he was and showed the man Candace Ross's picture. "Ever see this woman?"

The Bangladeshi turned to the African. "I think you had better go get security," he said. The African turned away and went back inside.

The Bangladeshi turned to Burke. "I would not answer you if I were allowed to," he said, in his precisely clipped consonants. "I don't like the media."

"It's all right," Burke said. "There are times when I don't, either."

He didn't know whether or when the African would return with a hotel detective, but he saw no purpose in hanging around to find out.

He stuffed the picture back in his pocket and retreated to the car. The garage attendant carefully gave him five singles and a couple of quarters in exchange for the ten-dollar bill Burke proffered to pay the one-hour parking fee. Burke put it all into his pocket and drove away.

He turned the corner between the Saudi embassy and the Watergate and drove into the underground lot at the Kennedy Center, trying to think of an alternative path to the information he wanted. The woman tending the tollbooth wanted five dollars in advance. Burke gave her the change from the Watergate garage.

He walked to the bank of pay phones in the stairwell leading from the garage to the foyer level. One of the phones had an intact directory. It must, he thought, be the only place in D.C. where the phone books were not instantly removed by the homeless to fuel their winter warming fires.

He ran a finger over the listings for *Watergate*. There was a Watergate Liquors, a Watergate Opticians, and a Watergate Pastry. And there was a Watergate Salon. He called it.

"Uh, hi," he said to the woman who picked up the phone. "I'm a friend of Candace Ross's and in town for a few meetings and I need to get my hair, um . . ." He paused, trying to decide on the right word. Did they say "cut" in a salon, or "done"?

". . . taken care of, and Candace suggested that I go to the person who does her hair, but the name has dropped out of my mind, I think it starts with—"

"Anthony," the woman on the phone said. "Starts with A. Anthony."

"That's it," Burke said, trying to mask the exultation he felt at finally getting lucky. "Anthony. She recommended him highly. Could I get him to take care of me?"

"Are you close by?" the woman asked. She was evidently British.

"In the neighborhood."

"Very good, sir. Anthony will squeeze you in if you can get here right away."

He walked over from the Kennedy Center. The early-evening joggers were pounding the pavement along the Potomac and an eight-oared shell was plying its way toward Memorial Bridge. Burke envied them. He entered the Watergate complex from the east, keeping his distance from the hotel garage.

Leather handbags by an Italian named Lorenzo hung in the window of the Watergate Salon like chickens and rabbits in the window of a French butcher. He stepped inside, inhaling a mixture of hair spray and perfume.

The woman with the British accent stood behind a small desk. She wore large round eyeglasses of battleship-gray plastic, and her fingernails were painted to match.

Pretend, Burke told himself, that you have your hair cut all the time in places like this.

"I'm the one who called for Anthony," he said.

She looked dubiously at him for an instant, but her face resumed its professional pleasantness when he handed over his credit card for an imprint.

"This way, Mr. Burke," she said.

He hung his coat in the closet, glad to be out of it, and sat where she told him to, in front of an enormous poster of a model with artfully clipped brown hair and a suit with gold buttons, gazing coldly into a camera lens. A black woman approached and lathered up his hair.

"Where have you been?" she said. He could feel the sand scratching under her fingers.

"At the beach," he answered.

The woman in the gray eyeglasses walked past and asked him whether he would like coffee or tea. He chose coffee. The black woman finished rinsing his hair and led him out into the main room of the salon. He sat in a chair.

Mirrors dominated the room, mirrors in front of him and to each side, bordered in a white wallpaper that suggested silk. He could see all of the stations in the salon, and he was the only male customer. Behind him, a woman sat with cotton balls stuffed between her fingers, getting a manicure. To his left, a stylist was smearing what appeared to be mud over the hairline of an elderly woman.

For the first time Burke started feeling ambivalent about the *abaya*.

In the mirror he could see walking toward him a tall, thin man with curly gray hair combed in a pompadour, a two-day beard, and tortoiseshell glasses. He was wearing a double-breasted gray blazer, checked pants, and a flowered tie. He looked like he spent a lot more on clothes than Burke did.

The man extended his hand and Burke shook it. He picked up a scissors.

"So how is Candace?" he asked, fingering the wet hair over Burke's ear. "And how would you like this cut?"

"She's a little stressed-out these days," Burke said. "But she told me I should just let you cut it the way you want. She said you're the best."

Anthony warmed up a little bit at the compliment. He looked at Burke's head from several angles and then started snipping behind his neck.

"Stressed-out?" he said. "Why?"

"Well, professionally, you know, this is not the easiest time to be a lobbyist for the Saudis," Burke said.

Anthony moved up to the hair behind Burke's ear. Burke was tempted to tell him that he didn't want any hair falling over the ear, but he stifled it.

"And personally?" Anthony asked.

Burke kept his mouth shut long enough, he hoped, to give Anthony the impression that he was a reluctant gossip.

"Something bothering Candace?" Anthony persisted.

"Well," Burke said, "she's been having relationship problems. Broken off with someone."

Anthony sighed. He moved around to Burke's forehead. "I knew that wasn't a smart thing for her to do. But she was impressed by the power. Women are, even if it's just the power of serving the president," he said.

Burke stiffened so much that Anthony stopped snipping for a moment. He reached for his coffee and sipped it, trying to think of the next thing to say. Detwiler was ruled out. It was someone close to him, someone either in the Cabinet or the NSC, someone with access to intelligence reports.

"I don't know the man personally," he ventured. "Is he married?"

"Of course," Anthony said, and moved to the left ear. "Aren't they all?"

"Seems very indiscreet," Burke said, "but at this White House . . ."

"They think they can get away with anything," Anthony finished.

Burke sat silent for a moment, trying to collect his thoughts as Anthony started trimming his sideburns. The man was in the White House, not a Cabinet department. He thought of Brian Barrett. Barrett was a leaker of the worst kind. He only talked when he had something he wanted to plant anonymously, usually something damaging to a rival. He could always find someone at *Time* or *Newsweek* to print it. He reminded himself not to let his dislike for the man prod him toward the wrong conclusion. It could still be almost anyone on the White House staff with access to intelligence reports.

"I never could understand what Candace saw in him," he said. "Maybe she likes short guys."

"Short guys?" Anthony sounded perplexed.

Scratch Barrett, Burke thought. He needed to say something fast before Anthony realized Burke was fishing.

"Either that or bow ties," he said.

Anthony stopped shearing and chuckled. "Oh, heavens no," he said. "She hated those ties. She asked me once where I bought mine. Said she wanted to give him a regular tie and get him out of those bow ties."

Burke swallowed hard. He was on the brink, but he had to be certain.

"Did you ever cut Hoffman's hair?" he said, trying to sound as casual as he could.

Anthony smiled. "Oh, no. When he came over here to see her, I gather they had better things to do with their time."

Burke raised a hand and grabbed Anthony's wrist just as he was about to begin the final snipping.

"Thanks, Anthony. You've done a great job. But I'll have to run now. Got an appointment."

Anthony stepped back, startled. "But I haven't dried it or combed it out."

"Next time," Burke said.

He parked the Grand Marquis on O Street as the long summer dusk set in, gliding through a puddle left by the thunderstorm to claim an illegal space in front of a hydrant. The lights in Number 2937 were still out. He wondered if she was out of town.

He settled in to wait. Someone in a Volvo, a man in a gray suit, pulled into the driveway across the street, punched a button, and opened the garage door. The man got out and helped a girl of about ten carry her saddle into the house.

He thought for a long time about Henry Hoffman. He had met Delores Hoffman once, at a dinner at the State Department. She had seemed like a nice woman. He remembered bits and pieces of conversations with Hoffman, snatches of interviews. He could not recall Hoffman ever lying to him. He would have tabbed Hoffman as the most upright man in Detwiler's White House.

Sex makes fools of us all, he decided.

He thought about Janet Kane. He had called her in Amman. She and her family were safe in Marbella, trying to arrange a visa to return to England.

He thought about what she said about building trust, and about McCoy, and his mind drifted for a long time, and he tried not to linger on the question of whether sex was making a fool out of him.

At around 7:30, a D.C. cab, black and orange, pulled up in front of Number 2937. Its brakes squealed. A woman got out, and he could recognize the angular face in the light cast by the street lamp. It was Candace Ross.

She wore a tailored suit, dark stockings, and black pumps. She carried a black, alligator-leather briefcase. Her hair was swept back and fell over her shoulders just as it had in her picture. She looked very carefully put together.

He got out of the Grand Marquis as she was paying her fare. He stopped about ten feet away from her and waited until she noticed him.

"Ms. Ross, I'm Colin Burke from the *Washington Tribune*," he said. "I'd like to ask you a couple of questions."

She stiffened, and even in the pale light from the street lamp, her face looked older as her thin, red lips froze into a straight line.

"I have nothing to say to the press," she said, and she turned and started up the three brick steps that led to her front door.

"It's about your affair with Henry Hoffman," he said softly as she tried, with a shaking hand, to put her key in the lock.

She turned around to him abruptly, making the golden hair swirl against her blue collar. "That's over," she said vehemently. "That's—" and then she stopped talking, realized what she had said, and her mouth curled downward and Burke thought she might lose her composure.

"No," he said. "It's not quite over."

CHAPTER 26

Burke pulled the Grand Marquis over to the side of L Street just before it crossed Connecticut Avenue, in front of a bookstore. It was the corner where Mikhail Gorbachev had impulsively stopped his car, gotten out, and shaken the hands of average Americans for the first time, during the summit of 1987. If he let his eyes lose their focus, he could still see the bald head with its purple birthmark, bobbing in the midst of Secret Service agents frantically scanning the hands of people pushing to get closer, to touch him. He remembered that the scene had genuinely moved him, as he suspected it had moved Gorbachev. It seemed, in retrospect, to be one of the last moments of clear, pure hope he could remember witnessing and writing about.

Now everything was muddier, including the decision he had to make. Straight ahead, six blocks to the east, was the *Tribune* newsroom. To the right, three blocks down and glowing in its floodlights, was the White House. He turned right, stopping the car at a bus stop on Connecticut Avenue, opposite a pay phone. He got out, inserted a quarter, dialed the White House press office, and identified himself. A secretary said that Maynard Walters was in a meeting and asked for a number.

"Tell him it's urgent," Burke said. "Tell him it's about the Saudi story. And tell him I'm at a pay phone and can't leave a number."

In a minute Maynard Walters got on the phone. "Burke of Arabia," he said. "You've been causing me a few stressful mornings."

In a sense, Burke liked Walters. Walters did not make a pretense of being fond of the reporters he worked with. Nor did he, in more than a formal sense, try to hide the fact that his job, most of the time, was to deceive and manipulate them. Burke admired the bluntness of Walters's cynicism.

"Nice to talk to you, too, Maynard," he said. "But I'm afraid I've got one more story that may cause you some stress."

"What's that?" Walters said. His tone was guarded, but Burke thought he detected what he had wanted to hear, a low note of fear.

"It's about the real spark that set off the revolt in Saudi Arabia," he said.

"And what would that be?"

"It came from within the administration," Burke said.

"I've got to have more than that if you want a reaction quote," Walters said.

"I want the reaction from Detwiler," Burke said. "And I want to get it personally."

"You and a thousand other people," Walters said. "You know it doesn't work that way."

Burke was prepared for that answer.

"Look, Maynard, let me put it to you this way," he said. "You can handle it the way you usually do, and give me a two-sentence nondenial denial that I'll stick in paragraph six. Do that and I promise you your briefing tomorrow morning will make the last few seem like a week at the beach. Or you can get me in to see Detwiler tonight and have a chance to substantially alter the way the story is played."

"What've you got?" Walters asked.

"I've told you as much as I'm going to tell you," Burke replied. "I want to tell the rest to Detwiler."

"He doesn't react well to being pressured," Walters said. "You know that. And from what I hear about the way Lyle Nelson feels, you're not in a great position to put pressure on anyone."

"Maynard, I'm not trying to pressure him," Burke lied. "I'm trying to do him a favor. I'm at a pay phone. The number is 462-9989. I'll wait here ten minutes. If you don't call back, I'll go into the newsroom, let the editors know what I have, write my story, and call you for your one-paragraph canned reaction."

"What was the number again?" Walters said.

Burke gave it to him and hung up.

He looked down the street toward the Mayflower Hotel. Someone was holding an event there, a dance or a banquet. Cars pulled up to the portico and men emerged in black tie, women in long dresses. That meant it was a charity of some kind. For political fund-raisers, Washington's other form of mass evening gathering, men and women wore business clothes, which was, he guessed, appropriate. He watched as a gray Lincoln pulled up and a woman emerged from the right side, dressed in a light, flowery gown that left her shoulders bare. She waited for her escort to join her, put a hand lightly through his crooked arm, and laughed at something he said. For some reason, the noise of the traffic diminished at just that moment, and Burke could hear the laughter. It sounded warm and relaxed and very attractive.

He looked at his watch. Eight minutes had passed, and for the first time he doubted that Walters was going to call back. Maybe it had been a bad idea, on several counts. It would not be the first bad idea he had had in the past week. And maybe Walters would be doing him a favor if he didn't call back.

The phone rang. He picked it up. It was Walters.

"Come to the Pennsylvania Avenue gate in ten minutes," he said. Burke agreed.

He left the car where it was and walked, slipping past the homeless men in Farragut Square, past the small, permanent coterie of protesters camped under polyethylene sheets and cardboard boxes in Lafayette Park, past the antiterrorist barriers, concrete pilings that stood where traffic had once flowed on Pennsylvania Avenue. It was a warm night, and he was beginning to sweat when he reached the White House.

The guard inside the gatehouse looked curiously at him as he approached. Burke slid his press pass under the glass, got it back, and waited for the sound that meant the turnstile had opened.

"Mr. Walters is expecting you. Use the West Wing door," the guard said.

The enormous elms on the North Lawn looked black and full against the bright facade of the West Wing and the North Portico. He could vaguely make out the bare spots in the grass where the network correspondents habitually stood to deliver their reports. It was now empty and quiet.

Another White House policeman opened the swinging glass doors to the West Wing lobby, and a young woman stood up from the sofa under the portrait of Andrew Jackson. He recognized her. It was the girl from Mississippi whose father owned all the chickens. She led him down a narrow corridor, carpeted in thick, beige pile, to Walters's office.

The press secretary looked rumpled and cranky. His tie was pulled down and skewed to the left, his cuffs were rolled up, and the bags under his eyes were big enough for a week's groceries.

"Burke," he said, leaning back in his chair slightly. "This better be good. I was hoping to tuck my kids in tonight for the first time in a week."

Walters's kids, Burke vaguely remembered, were students at St. Albans and Holton-Arms, ready to apply for college. But he took the comment in the spirit in which it was offered, as a ploy to make him uncomfortable.

"Maynard," he said, "I can't tell you how comforting it is to me, as a citizen, to have such a pillar of family values at the president's side."

Walters grimaced and he leaned forward over the desk. "Okay, let's be serious, shall we?"

"By all means."

"What've you got?"

Burke was slightly annoyed that Walters would be wasting time like this.

"I've told you what I'm going to tell you, Maynard."

"Do you want to see the president or don't you?"

He wanted, Burke knew, a chance to whisper quickly in Detwiler's ear whatever it was that Burke was going to unload, to help him prepare a considered response. That was precisely what Burke didn't want.

"Sorry, Maynard, I'd like to help you. But I wouldn't have gotten inside the gate if Detwiler wasn't going to see me."

Walters sighed, and for a moment Burke almost felt sorry for him.

"Wait here," Walters said. He got up, adjusted his tie, and left the room.

Burke chewed a fingernail and looked around the room. It was remarkably anonymous. There were a couple of landscapes from the Hudson River School, on loan from the National Gallery of Art. The rest of the room could have belonged to anyone. Walters didn't even have the requisite photos, framed and signed, of himself at work with the powerful. He must, Burke thought, keep them at home. There weren't even many papers on his desk. When the time came for him to give up this job, he could be gone in ten minutes, with a single box under his arm.

Burke was wrestling with the dilemma of whether to try to read the papers Walters did have on his desk when the man returned.

"Okay," he said. "Follow me."

They walked a few steps toward the briefing room, then turned right and out a door. They were in the colonnade between the Rose Garden and the Oval Office, walking toward the South Lawn. A sliver of moon was rising in the east, and he could see the stubby shadows of the rosebushes outlining the patch of lawn where, only eight days previously, he had watched Detwiler joke with the Southern Cal women's basketball team. It seemed as if more time had passed.

They left the colonnade and walked over the grass, through a path cut in some hedges, and he could hear the swish and click of a golf club meeting a golf ball.

They emerged in a clearing, bounded by high hedges on three sides and a low hedge on the south side. It was all illuminated by floodlights. Peter Scott Detwiler was standing on a level patch of closely mown grass, a metal-headed golf club in his hand, a pile of golf balls near his feet. He wore casual khaki trousers and a blue golf shirt. He was sweating. Two Secret Service bodyguards flanked him, scanning the roofs of nearby buildings. Behind one of the agents, arms folded over his chest, a scowl on his face, stood Henry Hoffman.

As Burke and Walters emerged, Detwiler pulled the club back, rotated, and swung. Burke did not know golf, but he knew balance and rhythm, and Detwiler's swing lacked both. The ball took off over the hedge toward the Washington Monument, then seemed to slow in midair, curved sharply to the right, and dropped to the ground about a hundred and twenty yards away, well inside the south fence. A Secret Service agent with a shag bag trotted toward it and picked it up. Detwiler watched it for a moment, then turned to face Walters and Burke.

"They're Cayman Island balls," he said, though neither man had commented on the distance the ball had flown. "Jack Nicklaus designed them for the practice range on a course he built in the islands where there wasn't enough room for a full-sized range. Go about half the distance a regular ball goes. Not the same satisfaction, but it's still therapeutic."

He stepped forward and extended his hand. One of the Secret Service agents took the golf club.

Burke swallowed and barely managed to avoid stumbling as he stepped forward to return the handshake. His muscles felt stiff and spastic. His mouth, suddenly, was dry. From a distance, covering the White House's media events, he had developed a disdain bordering on contempt for Detwiler. But he was still the president, even in a sweat and even with an outside-in golf swing. He realized that in some corner of his mind, he wanted the President of the United States to like him. Burke mumbled something unintelligible even to himself as their hands met. Detwiler's grip felt practiced, strong, and confident.

"I've been wanting to ask you," Detwiler said. "How the hell did you cover that trial? It was a nifty piece of reporting."

For a fleeting second Burke blushed with pleasure. Then he reminded himself of the dozens of Rose Garden ceremonies where he had heard Detwiler make similarly flattering remarks.

"It was kind of an undercover operation, Mr. President," he said.

"I'll bet," Detwiler said. "Too bad we don't have people with skills like that working for us, eh, Henry?"

Hoffman reacted to his inclusion in the conversation by dropping his arms and stepping quickly to Detwiler's right side.

"We do, Mr. President," he said. "We try to keep them on a tight leash."

His eyes, staring at Burke, were cold—but then they shifted down toward the ground.

He knows, Burke thought. Or at least he suspects.

Walters joined them, and Burke felt surrounded. There was a moment of strained silence. The party started walking slowly toward the Rose Garden and the West Wing

"So," Detwiler said, "Maynard tells me you have another big story."

"I think so," Burke replied.

He had not expected that Hoffman would be present at this moment, and his presence was inhibiting. Burke had broken stories that he knew would make the subjects angry or uncomfortable or even ruin them. He had never done it to the subject's face, and he was suddenly grateful for the insulation that the newsroom and the newspaper provided.

But at that moment Detwiler glanced at his wristwatch, and Burke plunged ahead.

"There was a witness at the Massoud trial I didn't write about at the time," he began. He laid out what Burnham had testified.

They reached the colonnade outside the Oval Office. Detwiler stopped and so did everyone else.

"When I got back to town today, I pursued that," Burke continued. "I found Candace Ross and spoke to her."

He glanced past Detwiler at Hoffman. Hoffman had the look of a man being walked toward an execution chamber. His features were frozen in stiff relief against the backdrop of a white column. Burke felt sorry for him.

"And she confirmed that the person who leaked the information to her was you, Dr. Hoffman," he said softly.

Detwiler turned toward Hoffman, his eyebrows raised.

"That's a serious accusation, Henry," he said.

Hoffman's face twisted slowly into an expression of pain so intense that the skin on his nose furrowed. Burke could not look at him. He cast his eyes toward the ground.

"The press is full of biased liberals," he said, but he was mumbling, and Burke could hear the defeat in his voice. "And they hate me because I don't leak to them.

"And you," Hoffman continued, his voice rising, "you're more arrogant and biased than any of them.

Burke blinked. He did not need to argue. Hoffman was a dead man. You didn't debate the dead.

But he couldn't help it. "It used to be that patriotism was the last refuge of the scoundrel," he said. "Now it's complaining about the bias of the press."

Detwiler looked at Hoffman with undisguised anger. His lips were a tight, thin line. "Henry, why don't you wait in your office," he said.

Hoffman managed to look outraged. "But it's bias!" he muttered.

He walked away, head high, and disappeared into the West Wing through the door Burke and Walters had used to enter the Rose Garden.

Detwiler turned to Burke. He looked shaken, Burke thought, too shaken even to be charming.

"If you want my comment on this," he began dully, "there will be a full and uncompromising investigation."

Walters intervened. "You said there was something that might substantially alter the way the story is played," he said to Burke.

Burke nodded.

"What is it?" Walters prodded him.

"It's about Desdemona McCoy," he said.

"Shit," Walters said. "Even with what Henry did, she's still partly responsible for the mess over there."

Burke's temper flared. "McCoy did her job. She did it well. The responsibility lies with all the people who decided we could rely on Saudi Arabia for an endless supply of oil."

Detwiler sighed. "You're right, of course. The responsibility goes back to Roosevelt. It includes me."

"The fact remains," Walters argued, "that our standard of living is going to nosedive because of the deal she cut. People can't afford two-fifty or three dollars for a gallon of gasoline. People are going to be thrown out of work."

"So they'll walk to work, or they'll take the bus, or work at home," Burke said. "Or they'll use electric cars. They'll adjust. And eventually the Arabs will see again that it's in their interests to keep oil plentiful and relatively cheap. They'll raise their production back."

"Perhaps," Detwiler said.

"McCoy did as well as anyone could with the situation she was given. Those commandos were dead if she didn't. And I promise you, she did not leak anything to me. The only thing she did was chew me out for irresponsibility and try to get me out of the country."

"Did she?"

"She served you well, Mr. President." Burke nodded.

"So what do you want?" Walters said.

Burke took a deep breath.

"If you reinstate her and issue a statement commending her service over there," he said, "I'll hold off on this story for a day. That would give you a chance to deal with Hoffman on your own, announce it in your own way. Take the credit for cleaning house."

"You'd lose the exclusive," Walters said.

"I know," Burke replied.

"What's your relationship to her?" Walters demanded.

"To borrow one of your dodges, Maynard, I don't comment on personal matters," Burke said.

"That speaks volumes," Walters said to Detwiler.

Detwiler nodded. "Whatever your relationship with her is," he said, "I have your word that she leaked nothing to you?"

Burke nodded. “You do.”

Detwiler smiled. It was not the campaign smile, not the intimate, charming smile. It was a smile of bemusement more than anything else.

He extended his hand to Burke. “Then I think we have an understanding,” he said.

“A deal,” Burke said. He was finicky about words.

CHAPTER 27

He finished editing the last piece for the World News section, a report from Rwanda about renewed ethnic slaughter. It was one of those stories whose play suffered from the newspaper's unwritten index of human-life value. The news value assigned to lost life depended on the number of losers; whether they were white, black, or yellow; rich or poor; American, European, or foreign; famous or unknown. Put another way, the deaths of five thousand Rwandans counted roughly the same as the death of a couple of reasonably wealthy white lawyers murdered in their beds in McLean. And there was a severe discount for ennui. Rwandans had been killing themselves for a couple of years now and there seemed to be little prospect that they would stop in the near future. Even before his trip to Arabia, Burke had learned to pick his battles against this system carefully, limiting himself to about one per week; given his present low standing with Lyle Nelson, it would probably be months before he felt safe enough to pick one again. It might be a year before he got sprung from the desk and got to do any reporting.

So he consigned the story to page A-32, put on his coat, and got ready to go home.

"Night, Mr. Burke," the clerk on the foreign desk said.

His name was Phil and he had just graduated from Columbia Journalism. Burke took it as a good sign that kids like Phil, who had preternaturally sharp instincts for the flow of power and favor in the newsroom, felt it was safe to say hello and good-bye to him again. If and when Phil resumed using his first name, Burke would take it as a sign that Nelson had finally decided to forgive, if not to forget. It had still been just a week. He would have to give it time.

Burke walked outside and felt the night air wash across his face like steam. The worst of the summer was setting in, and it would be months before he would be able to walk down the streets without sweating. The National Weather Service had predicted an unusually hot August, causing more pressure on energy supplies, and the price of oil had jumped another five dollars per barrel on the commodities market in New York. That, along with Senator Higgins's call for gasoline rationing, had led the paper. Burke loosened his tie and pulled his jacket off, carrying it over his shoulder.

He walked past the garage where, in palmier days, he had parked the Grand Marquis. The car sat outside his house on G Street now, semipermanently idled by the rising price of gasoline. If he had a job that required him to drive, he would have to sell it and buy something else. But the market for dented old cars that got fifteen miles to the gallon no longer existed; the Grand Marquis was technically worthless. His economically rational choice was to keep and use it only on rare occasions. He had taken to walking the three miles to work, no matter how sticky it got. He saw it as a form of penance, the sweat as a form of purging.

Except for a few cabs and limos, the streets seemed almost quiet. A couple of bicyclists rode by, out in the traffic lanes, clips protecting their pants from the oil on their chains. The gasoline crisis had done that, forcing people into car pools and subway trains and onto bikes, restoring traffic in Washington to a pace and freedom unseen since the fifties. Not many people seemed grateful.

He strode past the White House and down along the Mall, past the Smithsonian buildings and the Capitol, down along Pennsylvania Avenue to a bar called the Tune Inn, a few blocks from his house, where he had taken to having dinner. His shirt was soaked through when he walked in. The air-conditioning felt frigid.

It was a dark place, a relic of the days when Capitol Hill was a blue-collar neighborhood and people brought the stuffed deer heads and Potomac rockfish they had caught to hang on the walls as if it were a rod-and-gun club. Those people were mostly gone. Those that were left had been forced to cede the place, during the daytime and early evening, to the tweedy types who worked on the Hill and found the Tune Inn stylishly grungy for their lunches and happy hours. But by this time of night the Hill workers had gone home and the old regulars sat in a line at the bar, drinking Miller beer and watching the Orioles game on television.

Burke sat at a booth just beyond the bar, his back to the television, and ordered a shot of Jack Daniel's on the rocks, a bacon cheeseburger with french fries, and a Miller. He had permitted himself to resume drinking again, experimentally, and thus far he had managed to confine himself to two or three, only in the evening, only after work, only at a bar, never at home.

He sipped the whiskey when it came, sloshing it over his tongue, savoring the chill sweetness of it, trying to get it to wash the tension out of his body. This was one of the worst things about being an editor, he thought. When he had worked as a correspondent, he had always been able to fill his evenings, arranging interviews, trolling for information at receptions, even saving string for a story about the post-communist Russian theater. He hadn't figured out what an editor did with his evenings, but he was beginning to understand why Graves spent so many hours at the office.

The food came and he salted it, took a bite from the burger, and discovered it was overcooked. Probably left over from the evening rush. He considered calling the waitress over and sending it back.

A brown paper bag descended slowly from behind his back, landing on the table next to his cheeseburger, connected to a slender, brown hand with carefully polished nails. The bag contained about a pound and a half of shrimp, some pasta, and a bottle of Pouilly-Fumé. The bottle was just out of some store's refrigerator. It was sweating.

"Meat, cheese, bacon," she said. "That stuff is bad for you. And besides, you still owe me a shrimp dinner."

He turned and almost fell over trying to get up. When he was standing and facing her, Desdemona McCoy smiled, a little tentatively. She wore jeans and a polo shirt with the top two buttons open and a perfume that he remembered with great fondness.

"If you're still willing to have me for dinner," she said. For almost the first time he could remember, she sounded uncertain about him.

"You're sure you want to do this?" he asked her.

She reached into her purse, pulled out a twenty, and flipped it onto the scarred brown table.

"I'm sure," she said. "Your check's paid. Let's get out of here."

"What about your employers?" he asked.

"I have a new job," she said.

He felt a little giddy.

"Tell me."

"Well, after I was reinstated, I thought about it for a couple of days. Went out of town, in fact. I thought about the Agency. I thought about you. And I quit."

For the first time in a week he smiled.

"Just like that?"

She smiled, a sort of ironic smile. "Of course not just like that. I lined something else up first."

They left the bar. He set the bag of groceries in his left arm and took her hand with his right. They walked past a deli. Its lights blinked out. A bus trundled by on Pennsylvania Avenue. Burke noticed very little of it.

"What did you line up?"

"Off the record?"

"Of course."

"As of September first, I'm a visiting scholar at the school of foreign service at Georgetown. But they want to announce it."

Ahead of them, the Capitol dome glowed like alabaster in a gathering fog.

"I tried to call you," he said.

"I'm sorry. I had to disconnect the phone and get an unlisted number. Your brethren in the media had me under siege for a few days."

"You could have called."

"I know," she said. "And I'm sorry. But I wanted to sort things out first."

He nodded.

She stopped and turned so she was looking at him, looking directly at him.

"I know what you did with the president," she said. "Maynard Walters told me. I want you to know I'm grateful." She smiled. "It's the sort of thing that makes a man very lovable," she went on. She reached out and touched his cheek. "And attractive."

"Be still, my heart," he responded.

She turned, gave him her hand again, and they walked down Sixth Street toward his house.

"Why'd you do it?"

"Do what?"

"You know what. Cut that deal with Detwiler. I mean, if you wanted me out of the Agency, all you had to do was nothing. I'd've been out."

"Would you believe it's because I'm an inherently nice guy?" he asked.

"No."

"Would you believe it's because wearing an *abaya* made me more sensitive to the problems of women?"

"No."

"Well, it did," he protested.

She laughed. "Okay, Burke. You're a feminist now. But I still can't believe that's why you did it."

"I was afraid you wouldn't. Well, since you ask—I thought I knew you well enough to know that you wouldn't be available unless you felt secure. You weren't going to be with me if that meant being dependent, and if your career was messed up, you'd see it as being dependent."

She swung around then, wordlessly, and kissed him, on the corner of Sixth and F streets, kissed him with her mouth open and her arms tight around his neck. She tasted sweet, like honeysuckle on a summer evening. She broke it off only when they heard whistling and applause from a couple of men hanging out on the opposite corner.

"Why do I get the feeling we're still not going to have that shrimp dinner?" she asked.

"We'll put 'em in the fridge. They'll keep for an hour," he said. He began to smile.

"Or two," she replied.

Burke put his arm around her shoulders and steered her toward home.

ABOUT THE AUTHOR

ROBERT CULLEN, a reporter abroad and in Washington, DC, for two decades, won an Overseas Press Club award for foreign reporting while he was *Newsweek*'s Moscow correspondent. His novels include *Dispatch from a Cold Country*, *Cover Story*, and *Soviet Sources*, a *New York Times* Notable Book of the Year. He is also the author of *The Killer Department*, which was made into an HBO original movie called *Citizen X*. Cullen makes his home in Chevy Chase, Maryland. He can be reached online at 71370.1620@compuserve.com.